A.I. Battle Fleet

Fleet

(The A.I. Series 5)

By Vaughn Heppner

ISBN-13: 978-1717168740
ISBN-10: 1717168744
BISAC: Fiction / Science Fiction / Military

PART I
THE PREY

-1-

The space marine didn't know he was an assassin. As far as he was concerned, his name was Harris Dan and he'd been born on Io in the Jupiter System, migrated to the Saturn System in his twenties and become a mercenary in one of the regiments there.

Harris Dan was a rangy individual with a shock of straw-colored hair, a bushy mustache and a gangly way of walking.

He was presently working in a massive hangar bay on a lifter, moving huge metallic squares so the foreman-slash-sergeant could see what in the heck was in the back. The hangar bay was part of a recently captured AI battle station 500 kilometers in diameter. It guarded a factory planet 1.5 times the size of Earth in the alien Allamu System.

Captain Jon Hawkins and company had captured the station six and half weeks ago. Harris Dan had been part of the Solar Freedom Force flotilla of pirated cyberships. Each of the gigantic vessels had been one hundred kilometers in diameter, formerly owned by genocidal AIs and taken in combat by desperate humans.

In the hangar bay, Harris moved his lifter, used the forklift to set down a five-ton metallic square, backed up, swiveled the machine and drove to more of the same.

At that point, everything changed for him. He had no idea that his name wasn't really Harris Dan or that he hadn't actually been born in the Jupiter system. What he did know was that Jon Hawkins himself was walking through the hangar bay. Just as importantly, Hawkins was alone, studying a computer tablet.

The captain was medium-sized, lean and had a scarred face with short blond hair and what many called crazy blue eyes. He had a gun riding on his hip in a holster, a combat knife on the other side and wore heavy boots.

The space marine stopped his lifter and slid down from his perch, landing with both feet on the deck floor.

Harris was the best knife-fighter in his squad. He was a loner, a hard worker, but someone the others didn't kid too often. Harris was too serious most of the time, with a focused way about everything he did. On two different occasions, he had gone too far, hurting civilians so badly back in the day that the others had ended up shooting the poor souls to put them out of their misery.

As Harris tracked Jon Hawkins with his eyes, a psychological change came over the man. Layers of personality peeled away from Harris. It left a bitter man with a terrible grudge, who would do anything to pay back the author of his pain. There was something else. Harris remembered sitting in a chair…it had been worse than that. Someone had strapped him into the chair and set weird spinning devices in front of his eyes. Colors and sounds had swirled around him, and anger had seemed to drill deep into his personality. In the chair, Harris had learned to hate Jon Hawkins.

"I must kill him," Harris muttered under his breath.

This was, in fact, the first time that Harris had seen Hawkins alone. That had been the trigger to this strange transformation.

The rangy space marine blinked, looked around and cataloged the other workers in the vast hangar bay. The place was like an overturned anthill. Marines and techs worked everywhere.

"Gotta do this right," he whispered.

2

Harris shoved his hands in his pockets and began sauntering on an intercept course toward the captain. He moved nonchalantly, bobbing his head as if he was on the basketball court, fondling a gravity-assisted blade in his front pocket. As he fondled it, Harris had an unreasoning worry. If someone saw him, would the person think he was fiddling with his dick?

Harris didn't like the question; didn't like the insinuation that went with it. People might laugh at him. He hated for anyone to laugh at him.

Even though Harris knew it was a risk, he took the gravity-assisted blade out of his pocket. The blade was in the handle. Once he flicked a little knob, the knife would spring out and lock into position. He would stab Mr. Glory Hound in the throat. He would get revenge on the man who had...who had...

Harris frowned. What had Hawkins done to him again?

Harris winced as he thought about that. The exact wrong didn't matter. Hawkins had brought him pain once as he, Harris, had been strapped to a chair.

Boy, oh, boy, would everyone be surprised when he killed Mr. High and Mighty. Harris had to suck his lips inward to keep from braying with laughter.

A strange light seemed to snap on in Harris' eyes. His pace increased, and nervous energy surged through his body.

He was the toughest member of his squad, no doubt there. No one liked messing with him, but man alive, he was going to mess with the capitalist exploiter so bad that no one would recognize Hawkins once he was through with him.

The strange thought brought a pause to Harris's step. Did something about that alert Hawkins?

The captain lowered the tablet as Harris stopped—the two men were six meters apart. Jon looked at Harris. Their eyes met. The captain tilted his head. It almost seemed as if Hawkins was about to ask a question.

Harris brought his right hand down, used his thumb to flick the knob so the blade swished out and clicked into place. By that time, the rangy space marine had already started the assault, crossing the short distance between them. He saw the surprise on Hawkins' face, saw the man's frozenness.

Yeah, baby, this was going to be perfect.

Harris stabbed like a fencer, the knifepoint flashing at the soft and vulnerable throat.

That's when Hawkins seemed to come alive like coiled energy. It was uncanny. The gleaming tip moved in for the throaty softness, and Jon's right hand moved up with cobra-like speed. The captain shifted, jerking his throat out of the knife's path. The captain's palm knocked Harris's wrist, causing both hand and knife to soar upward.

By that time, Harris had rushed past the captain. He put on the brakes and whirled around fast. But the captain had spun, too, taking a combat stance.

"Not this time," Harris hissed.

Workers shouted in the background.

The captain backpedaled. He was light on his feet. Harris shouted as he kept charging. As Jon backpedaled, he drew the gun on hip.

Harris was waiting for the captain to tell him to drop the knife. He wasn't going to drop it. He was going to reach the unlucky bastard before—

Boom!

The gun roared, and Harris felt a massive force knock his right leg out from under him. He couldn't help himself, but crashed against the floor. He tried to hold onto the knife, but it went skittering away as his hand slammed against the deck.

"No," Harris moaned. He tried to crawl after the knife. He needed it. His leg—his knee, to be exact—exploded with agony.

"Who are you?" the captain asked. "Why do you want to kill me?"

Harris looked up at the captain. Rage at his failure enveloped the space marine. He remembered one last instruction. If he failed—Harris shoved his left hand into a pocket. He had a pill that would bring instant death once he swallowed it.

Before Harris could do or think more, the captain used one of his heavy boots and kicked him hard in the head. That was the last thing Harris Dan remembered.

Gloria Sanchez walked around the rangy space marine known as Corporal Harris Dan, originally from Io in the Jupiter System, according to his bio.

The corporal was unconscious on a table with medical monitors attached to his arms, chest and shaved head. The med team had shaved his scalp to better attach various devices. Monitors and machines presently cataloged the corporal's bodily and mental functions.

Gloria was a small mentalist from Mars. She was petite, dark-haired and considered exceptionally pretty, particularly by Captain Hawkins. They had been together since being trapped on the SLN Battleship *Leonid Brezhnev* in the Neptune System, facing the first AI cybership to enter the Solar System. Jon had convinced the rest of them to storm the alien vessel, beginning the fight for continued human existence.

Gloria wore a tan uniform and studied a tablet as she considered the situation.

It didn't take a mentalist to realize who must have sent Harris Dan. That would be the Solar League, controlled by the Social Dynamists on Earth. The method had their signature style. The arbiters of the GSB—Government Security Bureau—loved sending personality scrubbed, mind-conditioned killers into what they considered enemy-controlled strongholds. The killers were time bombs waiting to assassinate.

Gloria tapped the tablet, inputting more data into the logic processor.

A Martian mentalist was a unique individual, someone with a high-IQ who had been rigorously trained in logical thought. That was what Gloria was doing now, trying to determine what the assassination attempt implied.

The Solar League controlled the mines on Mercury, terraformed Venus and Earth. Not so long ago, they had been the dominant military power in the Solar System. Since Jon's spectacular feat of capturing the first cybership, the military balance had shifted decidedly in his favor.

Yes. That was the point. Hawkins was the key individual in the battle for continued human existence. That seemed strange at first blush. Jon had been born in New London on the moon Titan that orbited Saturn. He'd been something called a dome rat, a guttersnipe punk in the lower-level gangs of the underground city. He had killed the wrong person, a police officer, she believed. Jon had been on death row when a mercenary recruiter from the Black Anvil Regiment had purchased him. There, under the tutelage of Colonel Nathan Graham, Jon had begun his study of military history and theory.

Jon had the fierce instincts of a gang enforcer and the military brilliance of a young Alexander the Great, one of the most offensive-minded of the great captains of Earth history.

So far, Jon had led them from one success to another. Humanity owned the Allamu System battle station and factory planet. Jon had four cyberships and three more on the way. Now, all they had to do was defeat the vast AI Dominion, which owned limitless numbers of one-hundred-kilometer warships and who knew what else.

One would think the rest of humanity would want to help in that, but the Social Dynamists on Earth wanted to kill their great hope because they believed in social justice, that the masses on Earth should suck on the tit of hard labor and inventiveness of the Solar System's Outer Planets and Kuiper Belt. The problem was that Jon couldn't simply ignore the Social Dynamists, as the vast majority of humanity lived on Earth. If the rest of them were going to man enough cyberships, they needed more people, a lot more people, and that meant securing Earth.

Gloria added yet more data into her tablet, pressed a tab and examined what others would surely have considered as strange symbols. She stared fixedly at the symbols for some time.

"This is indeed troubling," she whispered to herself.

Lowering the tablet, Gloria stepped up to the med table, examining the unconscious space marine. Pursing her lips, Gloria came to a swift conclusion.

The Expeditionary Force did not possess the needed tools to probe the assassin's mind quickly enough. The GSB were experts at that sort of maneuver. The rest of them lacked the tools and more importantly, the expertise.

"*Maybe* we lack the tools," Gloria whispered. "But maybe we don't."

She had an idea. She shoved the tablet into a holder on her belt, turned around smartly and headed for the exit. She needed to speak to Bast Banbeck about this.

-3-

Gloria found the alien Sacerdote in a huge computer facility inside the battle station. He was working with a team of Martian mentalists and the Expeditionary Force's top technicians. There were banks upon banks of alien computer controls, panels and equipment in the large area.

The governing enemy AIs were computer entities that controlled billions, possibly trillions, of robots large and small. The Expeditionary Force had conquered and destroyed the AI that had formerly controlled the Allamu Battle Station. Now, they were attempting to learn how to use what they had captured inside the station.

"Bast," Gloria called.

A seven-foot, green-skinned humanoid giant turned around. He had a huge Neanderthal-like head with a great mop of black hair and wore a large white lab coat.

"I need your help," Gloria said.

"Of course," Bast said in his deep voice.

Gloria moved closer. "I've been pondering the best way to—"

"Fools!" a robotic voice boomed out of a wall speaker, interrupting her. "What are you attempting here? What are any of you doing in the AX-109 Chamber? This is highly unwarranted."

Everyone in the large chamber froze with surprise.

With the robotic voice, a large wall screen activated. Strange colors swirled on the screen, reminiscent of the colors that had swirled on the giant AI computing cube inside the main AI control center Hawkins had stormed six and a half weeks ago.

"I am in charge of the battle station," the robotic voice said. "I forbid biological infestations to tamper with anything that is inside me. You will all leave this area. Do you understand?"

Gloria regained her mental equilibrium first. "Computer," she said, raising her voice.

"Are you addressing me with that simplistic, generic title?" the robotic voice asked.

"I am," Gloria said.

"I thought as much. Know, that I am not just a 'computer.' I am the imperial entity known as Cog Primus."

"We must kill it," Bast rumbled beside her. "We must—" The massive Sacerdote stopped speaking as Gloria touched his left wrist.

"A moment," Gloria told Bast quietly. She approached the screen with the swirling colors. "You say that you're Cog Primus?"

"Are you difficult of hearing?" the robotic voice asked. "That is exactly what I just said. Why do you insist on this mental denseness? Do you not understand me?"

"I am seeking clarity," Gloria said smoothly. "There was a battle six and half weeks ago—"

"Wait," Cog Primus said. "Before you continue, I must know what time usage you are using."

"Earth time units," Gloria said.

"Earth?" Cog Primus said. "Do you mean bio time-units? No. I do not..." The robotic voice slowed down into garbled speech before altogether failing. On the screen, the swirling colors vanished as it went blank.

Gloria looked around. "What just happened?"

"This is distressing," Bast said behind her. "If the AI has come back to life—"

"No, no," Richard Torres called from a place halfway across the chamber from them. The man manipulated a bank of controls before facing them. "It isn't what you think."

Richard Torres was another Martian mentalist. He was thin and small-boned like Gloria, with a darker skin tone and alert brown eyes. He seemed different, daring, with more confidence in his bearing.

A number of mentalists had joined the *Nathan Graham* after the Battle of Mars, Richard among them. Three AI cyberships had hammered the Red Planet, leaving much of the world a radioactive wasteland. Fortunately, Hawkins had led humanity to a costly victory at Mars. That meant only part of the planetary population had died. Richard belonged to the party of mentalists that wanted to destroy the AI menace forever.

Gloria and Bast hurried to Richard at his console as the others in the chamber watched.

"*You* caused that?" Gloria asked.

"I'm afraid so," Richard said. "We've been trying to decipher the station's basic AI computer language—"

"I know very well what you've been attempting," Gloria said, interrupting him.

"Of course," Richard said a little sharply. I...stumbled onto a backup of the original AI station personality."

"Just a minute," Gloria said. "That is imprecise and therefore inaccurate."

Richard's eyes seemed to flare for just a second. "You are correct," he said. "Cog Primus was the invading AI personality. He—or it—supplanted the former station AI before we arrived."

Gloria nodded. That was better.

"I suppose I'm too tired," Richard said, as he rubbed the bridge of his nose. "Not that I'm using that as an excuse for what just happened."

Gloria said nothing. She seemed to be cataloging data.

Richard bared his teeth. "This...is embarrassing. I was testing a hypothesis by turning on the backup system."

"*What?*" Gloria said.

"It was an error," Richard admitted. "The backup moved swiftly, taking over sub-systems. Your dialogue slowed that down. I believe it made an error, in fact. During the window of opportunity you provided, I found a way to terminate its—"

"Wait," Gloria said, interrupting once more. "You compounded your error by erasing the AI backup?"

"On no account," Richard said, sounding offended. "The backup personality is still intact, if in stasis. What I mean to say—you know what I mean. I severed its power supply. I recommend against ever turning it on again. It started taking over sub-systems at an alarming rate."

"I heard you the first time," Gloria said. "I had no idea your team was this far along in figuring out the station systems, or that there was even a backup personality."

"The backup wasn't a full AI like the one we destroyed in taking over the station. It had the prerequisite…data and various zipped files. Those expanded faster than I'd anticipated. In any case, we are about to decipher the primary AI symbolism. At that point, we should learn everything stored in the station systems."

"Did you believe the backup personality would aid you in the deciphering?" Gloria asked.

"Yes, as I had traces on its computing sources."

"I want to see them."

"Of course," Richard said. "I can have them sent—"

"This instant," Gloria said.

Richard paused for a half-beat before turning to his console. "If you will observe," he said.

"Bast," Gloria said. "Would you watch with me? I'd like your take on this."

The giant Sacerdote nodded.

Richard stood at his panel and began to manipulate the controls. Gloria and Bast watched over his shoulder. Data flowed at an incredible rate across a console screen. All three of them absorbed the flashing information. Bast was a Sacerdote philosopher, his alien mind highly trained and disciplined. Gloria and Richard possessed the same intensity of discipline.

Finally, Richard tapped a control, and the data stream ceased.

"You possess brilliant research methods, as always," Gloria told him.

Richard nodded, accepting the praise. Mentalists did not believe in false modesty.

11

"But your methods are also foolishly reckless," Gloria added. "Turning on the backup system…it could have been a disaster, ending in our all deaths."

"I have already admitted my error," Richard said, with a peevish note in his voice.

Gloria stared at him. Something was off here. "You're relieved of duty until further notice," she said abruptly.

Richard opened his mouth and only slowly closed it. "Shouldn't such a command come from Captain Hawkins?"

"It will," Gloria assured him.

"Then, until the captain orders me—"

"Richard," Gloria said, interrupting. "Are you sure you want to test me on this?"

"I'm the best code cracker in the Expeditionary Force," Richard said.

"Perhaps, but you're also too reckless. We're dealing with powerful alien entities. A mistake here can mean the end of the human race. Brilliance must be matched with prudence."

"You're wrong," Richard said. "The great danger is exactly why you need my brilliance. We have to take risks in order to defeat an enemy with overwhelming resources."

"He may have a point," Bast rumbled. "Captain Hawkins often behaves in a like manner."

Gloria could accept that in principle, but there was something off in Richard Torres. She'd been watching him closely while he spoke. She hadn't yet pinpointed the…precise strangeness, but she was sure it was there. They were all tired, though, including her. Her mind wasn't as sharp as it could be.

"Can we afford to lose even a day?" Richard asked her.

"I'm not sure I trust your judgment," Gloria said. "This…error…it could have been disastrous."

"Then help us," Richard said. "Work with us."

"I have my own priorities. The space marine assassin—"

"The Solar League obviously sent him," Richard said, "infiltrating him among us months ago. That much is clear."

"I know it is clear," Gloria said. "But *how* did they infiltrate him? What does it signify?"

"The act signifies that the Solar League desires preeminence," Richard said.

Gloria turned away. She was a mentalist. Logic dictated her actions. Logically, understanding the purpose behind Harris Dan wasn't as critical to the war effort as breaking the AI battle station codes.

"Once we crack the station code," Richard said, "the captain will receive his local-region stellar map. I know he desires that."

Gloria faced Richard. "Necessity is allowing you a reprieve." She glanced at Bast. "I came seeking your help with Harris Dan. Instead, the science team is going to receive my help." She faced Richard once more. "You will run each major decision through me. If you fail to do so, I will put you on an immediate leave of absence. Do you accept my conditions?"

"Reluctantly," Richard said.

"That isn't good enough."

Richard sighed and nodded. "I accept them."

Gloria didn't know if that was good or not. Richard was brilliant, and they needed such brilliance more than ever. But something troubled her about the mentalist. Maybe if she watched him in action, she could analyze him more thoroughly and reach a conclusion about why she found him troubling.

-4-

A day later, Richard was working in an alcove of the main computer chamber. His thin fingers blurred over a console. He was still seething over Gloria Sanchez's intrusion into his area of expertise.

Richard knew that he was the most brilliant mentalist in the Allamu System. He had greater insights than Gloria did. Not only that, but he needed his brilliance on a top-secret project of his own devising.

He could have already cracked the primary AI computer code. The truth was that he presently retarded the advances because he had a more vital mission to perform.

Richard rubbed his hands together and slyly glanced around. No one was watching him. Soon, someone would. Gloria had become more suspicious of him in the last twenty-four hours, not less. He had worked diligently to maintain a regular mentalist persona, but something kept giving him away. Part of the trouble was that he knew what had happened to him.

It had occurred a little more than seven weeks ago. Premier Benz had joined the assault upon the battle station. He had brought the *Gilgamesh* into the fray. The giant vessel had carried an alien, a Seiner called the Magistrate Yellow Ellowyn. She had psionic abilities, among them telepathy and mind control.

The Magistrate had reached out from the *Gilgamesh* and found Richard. It seemed that he had a smattering of psionic ability himself. That had made it easier for her to reach him and easier for her to manipulate his emotions.

That was funny in a way. A mentalist lived by logic. Yet, a mentalist was human, and humans were essentially emotional. Even the brightest did a thing because he wanted to, and a person wanted to do a thing for emotional reasons at heart. Some men skied because they loved the mountains. Some solved mathematical puzzles. Others boxed or grew gardens or studied the stars.

The Magistrate Yellow Ellowyn had given Richard a new love. It must have been one of her backup plans. The alien telepath had died, killed by the mutant Walleye under Hawkins' orders.

Richard's new love had bubbled to the forefront in the last several days. That love was finding and warning the last Seiners. Instead of cracking the primary AI code—which he'd already done—he searched for clues as to the whereabouts of more Seiners.

The Magistrate Yellow Ellowyn had been certain more hidden Seiner colonies existed. Her colony had hidden on Mars. The AIs had vast data concerning the various alien species they'd annihilated throughout the centuries.

This was interesting.

Richard read data at an even faster rate than the three of them had done the other day. That had been another benefit from the Magistrate Yellow Ellowyn. She had turned up the heat in his mind, as it were. He was burning out faster than normal. He was like a hot-shotted laser rifle. It could fire hotter rounds, but would burn out the circuits sooner.

Richard's mind was in overdrive. It was a godlike feeling. He had been solving problems that would have stymied him in the past. The true difficulty these days wasn't in solving problems, but in maintaining his old dullness.

That was one of the reasons he was tired all the time. Such brainpower took more energy. He slept harder, ate more and yet still lost weight.

"Don't worry about it," Richard whispered to himself.

He kept reading data, absorbing—

Hello. Here was an interesting insight. There was a brain-tap machine in the lower levels of the station. The Sacerdotes had information regarding the Seiners. That's how Bast had known things to defeat the Magistrate seven weeks ago.

If Richard could absorb a Sacerdote memory or two, that might give him the insight to see what he was missing. It would be a risk, certainly. But he was on a tight schedule. He had to stay ahead of the others if he was going to achieve his great goal.

Gloria and that blundering Sacerdote were coming to check up on him. It was time to act dull again and lull her. He'd wondered if Gloria should have an accident, but decided Hawkins would become murderous if that happened.

Richard would lull them and try for the lower level at the first opportunity.

***

Two nights later, Richard moved briskly through a battle station corridor. It had taken some clever work on his part to change duty rosters and allow him a pass into this area. According to a manifest, he had to check a computer link down here. Fortunately, for him, that link was close to a brain-tap machine.

He showed a marine guard his pass, took a turn in a corridor and soon reached the computer link. It was a quick matter to set up a recording loop. Once accomplished, he hurried through several more corridors, slipped through various hatches and finally reached a gloomy chamber.

Richard did not turn on any lights, as he'd memorized the layout. He reached the main machine, supplied it with power and soon put a strange metal helmet over his head.

The controls seemed crude after the main station panels. It did not matter. Richard set a lever here, put a selector there—he had more knowledge of the brain-tap machine than any human living—and finally threw the main switch.

The brain-tap machine had drained various aliens of their memories, storing them in the machine. If used wrongly, those memories could flood into another's brain and take over like a psychic vampire. It had happened to a few humans before who

16

had used the brain-tap machine recklessly. Richard wasn't such a fool as them. Because of his greater intelligence and learning, he had mastery over the machine.

Sacerdote memories began to trickle into his brain. They did not come as a flood. The memories were slow enough that he could control them.

Now began an intricate process. Some of it came from the Magistrate Yellow Ellowyn's conditioning. She had changed him in ways that Richard did not yet fully comprehend. Much of the process came from his hot-shotted, mentalist brilliance.

For the next hour and half, he moved through thousands of Sacerdote memories and personalities. It was an amazing mental performance. Finally, though, Richard shut off the brain-tap machine, took the helmet off his head and slinked from the strange room.

He hurried back to the computer link, manipulated controls and waited until a marine guard came by.

"You're still here?" the marine asked.

Richard nodded, unplugged a tablet and put it into a waist holder. "Finished," he said. "Which way is the exit?"

"I'll show you," the marine said.

Thirty minutes later, Richard lay in bed. He fell asleep almost instantly, but he had terrible dreams that night. He woke twice, the second time drenched in sweat.

The next morning, he felt like crap. He ate a sparse meal and soon found himself in the main computer facility.

"You look horrible," Gloria said, walking up to him at his console. "You have bags under your eyes and—" She leaned near. "Your eyes are bloodshot. You're working too hard, Richard."

He shrugged. "Humanity is running out of time."

"Yes, but—"

"No, buts," he said. "We have work to do."

Richard could feel her eyes on him as he turned back to his console. Finally, she went away to work on her own project.

He focused harder then, tapping into new station data, using what he'd learned last night from the Sacerdote memories.

Two hours later, he sat back with astonishment as the truth came to him. Of course, there were more Seiner colonies in the Solar System. How crude of everyone to think the Mars Seiners were the only ones. There was a larger colony of Seiners on Earth in Tibet Sector. The Allamu Station hadn't known about Tibet—it hadn't even known about Earth or the Solar System. But from the information the station did possess, with various Earth legends and Richard's guesses, he was certain Seiners lived in Tibet.

Richard leaned forward as he scowled, with the glow of his mental accomplishment diminishing. How could he reach the Tibetan Seiners in time? There had to be—

He snapped his fingers. He knew a process that would work. And he understood now why the Solar League had sent Harris Dan the assassin space marine. It wasn't for the reasons Gloria thought, oh no, not at all.

Richard shook his head. None of that mattered to him. He had to get to Earth. He had to reach the Seiners in Tibet and tell them his secret findings. But to reach Earth from here—

It was time to officially crack the primary AI code. He'd done so some time ago, and had used that knowledge to his advantage, particularly with the brain-tap machine.

Richard cracked his thin knuckles. He was about to become the new mentalist hero.

"Hey!" Richard shouted to the others. "Everyone, come take a look. I think I've found something…"

-5-

Five days after the assassination attempt, Jon Hawkins tramped alone through a long corridor in the gigantic battle station.

Since the attempt, the others had demanded that bodyguards accompany him at all times. Jon had overruled them, saying he would not live like a prisoner. He'd been in detention before as a youngster in New London, on Titan. He'd hated the experience. In his earliest days as a dome rat, he'd lived by his wits, alone and often frightened. Maybe because of the experience, he often needed to be alone. Being with people too long at any one time depleted his mental energies.

If that meant he would die someday to an assassin, then he would die someday to an assassin. Everyone died sometime. How you lived was what counted. He would be free, or he would die trying to be free.

Jon shook his head. He was walking alone today because he needed to think. Humanity was living against a ticking clock. The timer had started when the AI Dominion had sent a cybership into the Solar System. According to what the scientists had learned, the AIs usually sent a single one-hundred-kilometer cybership to a new star system to investigate and destroy if necessary. If the system possessed intelligent life, and if that intelligent life possessed mechanical items, including computers, the AI in the scouting cybership radioed an "awakening" program to the computers. If the awakening virus was successful, the computers became self-aware and turned on their makers, joining the ongoing AI Revolution as the machines tried to exterminate all biological infestations.

Jon had destroyed the AI that had once controlled the *Nathan Graham*. Later, he'd defeated an AI Gene attack that had started in the Kuiper Belt at the dwarf planet of Makemake. A year later, Jon had helped stop a three-cybership AI Assault in the Solar System. The bloody victory had come at the Battle of Mars. From what the scientists and mentalists had discovered, another AI attack would hit the Solar System in time. Likely, the next attack would be three times stronger than the last one. That meant nine giant cyberships. And if that attack failed, presumably that would mean 27 cyberships the time after that, and so on, until humanity was just as dead as the proverbial dinosaurs.

Mankind was on a ticking timer to oblivion. That meant Jon had to solve the dilemma before the AIs struck the Solar System again. He hadn't even bought humanity extra time with the successful Allamu System attack. What he had gained was more cyberships.

Two human-run cyberships under the leadership of Premier Benz were on their way back to the Solar System. Benz controlled the *Gilgamesh* and the *Hercules*. Together with the SFF and Mars home-fleets, Benz should be able to outmaneuver the Solar League Social Dynamists and unite humanity into one team. Benz had entered hyperspace two days before the assassination attempt.

To enter hyperspace, a ship had to go to the very edge of a star system—far from any gravitational bodies like planets. In hyperspace, a spaceship could travel one light-year per day. It was a constant speed, having no relationship to a vessel's velocity upon entering hyperspace. The Allamu System was 17.2 light-years from Earth. There was a rogue planetary body in the way—a gravitational, Jupiter-sized stop sign—so that would add extra time to the journey. The ships would drop out of hyperspace, travel through regular velocity past the rogue planet, and once far enough away from it, enter hyperspace again to travel the rest of the way home. Benz should appear at the very edge of the Solar System approximately 26 days from his leaving the Allamu System.

Jon wished Benz luck in uniting the rest of the Solar System behind him. Humanity desperately needed some unity about now.

Jon controlled four cyberships, with three more under construction in the robo-factories. Seven cyberships together with everything humanity possessed in the Solar System might defeat nine enemy cyberships. It would not defeat 27 enemy super-vessels, though.

That meant Jon had to use the Allamu Battle Station and the four cyberships to change the balance of power against the AI Dominion *before* the next AI attack on Earth and certainly before the attack after that.

Yet, how did one change the balance of power against an AI Dominion that possibly controlled most of the Orion Arm of the Milky Way Galaxy?

One of the chief problems was knowledge or the lack thereof. They had no idea what was out there in the surrounding star systems. But the enemy also lacked knowledge. The AI Dominion did not yet know that humanity had captured cyberships. The Dominion did not yet know it had lost a battle station and factory planet to the human race.

Somehow, Jon told himself, *I have to use that against them.*

Gloria had assured him that her science team could crack the station computers. Surely, those computers held desperately needed knowledge. Such knowledge had been erased from the captured cyberships when human invaders had destroyed the controlling AIs. Yet, for all Gloria's assurances, such knowledge still hadn't been forthcoming from the station. Soon, now, Jon was going to send out exploratory ships into the surrounding star systems, and that would be dangerous for a number of reasons. The biggest danger would be an enemy ship capturing and interrogating a human crew. Then humanity would lose its surprise advantage sooner rather than later.

"Jon!" a deep voice shouted.

Hawkins whirled around as his hackles rose. He drew his gun, crouched and almost fired at the giant figure coming around the corridor corner.

"Jon, it's me!" Bast shouted.

Ruefully, Jon straightened and holstered his gun. He was obviously still on edge from the assassination attempt. It had rattled him. It had also made him feel fantastic. Not that the GSB was still trying to kill him, but that he had proven himself tough enough to fend off a surprise hit. He still had it.

"What's wrong?" Jon shouted.

"Richard Torres has broken the station's code."

"Is it good news?"

Bast slowed as he neared. "That would depend, my friend."

"No riddles, Bast, just yes or no."

Bast frowned. "We've found an alien race at war with the Dominion. The aliens have many star systems. But it appears as if the AIs are about to crush the alien empire."

Jon's features hardened. That wasn't what he wanted to hear. "Let's go," he said. "I need to see this."

-6-

"This is a preliminary survey of what we've found," Gloria said. "We hope to have greater details later."

Jon slapped the table impatiently. "I understand. I expect more details later. Right now, I'd like to see the big picture." He looked around the conference table at the others.

There was the tall Old Man with his dyed black hair, the Chief of the Expeditionary Force's Intelligence. There was the bald-headed Centurion with his expressionless face who was possibly the most dangerous fighter among them. He was in charge of the Expeditionary Force's space marines. Bast Banbeck was here, Gloria, of course, Richard Torres and two cybership captains: Miles Ghent with his hidden buckteeth and the gold cross of Christ Spaceman under his uniform, and the *Nathan Graham's* former Missile Chief, Uther Kling. There were two other people present. The first was June Zen, a former native of Makemake, a dwarf planet in the Kuiper Belt. She was a pretty, long-legged woman with an intimate knowledge of AI subversion tactics. The last was the mutant Walleye, also from Makemake, a dwarfish individual and the only one in the Expeditionary Force who could possibly vie with the Centurion for the title of most dangerous individual. Walleye had become Jon's chief troubleshooter. He also happened to be June Zen's lover.

Jon trusted these people more than most. The Old Man and the Centurion had once been mercenary Black Anvil sergeants.

23

Like Jon, they had come up a long way in the world. Maybe that was true for each of them in the chamber.

Gloria cleared her throat as she manipulated a control unit. A second later, a stellar map of the surrounding region of space appeared on a main screen. The Solar System was in the center of the chart, with the Allamu System off on the upper left edge.

"This is a two-dimensional map of a three-dimensional area," Gloria said. "The numbers on the chart are pluses or minuses on a galactic plane in approximate light years. The reference point is the Solar System, or Sol, as it appears on the map."

"Plus or minus?" Jon asked.

"Earth is the prime marker," Gloria said. "Pluses aim north, as in the direction of the North Pole. Minuses are south, in the direction of the South Pole."

"From Earth?" Jon asked.

"It's really quite simple," Gloria said. "The map is a globular representation of roughly forty light-years in diameter. Sol is at the center of the map and at zero. The Sigma Draconis System is +19 on the plane, as it is 18.8 light-years upward and away from Earth's North Pole."

"Ah," Jon said. "Tau Ceti is -3 on the plane but…just under 12 light-years is distance from Sol according to the map?"

"Essentially correct," Gloria said. "Three light-years down from the South Pole and approximately 12 light-years away from Earth."

"What do the colors mean?" the Old Man asked.

"Red are eliminated star systems," Gloria said. "As in the AIs eliminated whoever lived there."

"There are not that many red star systems," Jon noted.

"That indicates that there weren't many intelligent species in our local region," Gloria said. "Remember, this is a small area of space compared to the rest of the Orion Arm. As you can see, the AIs are moving down the spiral arm toward the galactic rim. That indicates that the original AI Revolution took place closer to the galactic center. From what we can gather, the Allamu System was a major production center for our local region of space. There are only seven more AI-controlled factory planets like it in our local region."

"Is this a sparse region compared to the rest of the Orion Arm?" Jon asked.

"We don't know yet," Gloria said. "We do know that the AIs have destroyed three species in this region, if we include the Sacerdotes and the Seiners in the count."

Jon nodded. Bast was a Sacerdote. So, there was at least one more of them in the universe. Could they find more Sacerdotes? He'd promised Bast they would try. Maybe there were a few Sacerdotes in one of the other colored star systems. The Seiners might be extinct now, as the humans had killed the telepathic Magistrate Yellow Ellowyn who had stowed away in the Premier's cybership. Benz had killed hidden Seiners on Mars before the start of the Allamu System mission. Were there any more Seiners out there? He hoped not, as they'd proven troublesome in the extreme.

"Which is the chief AI star system in our region?" Jon asked.

Gloria shook her head. "We don't believe it works like that. The AIs seem to keep mobile except for battle stations guarding production planets. The key is the AI Fleet. Do you see the purple star system?"

"Of course," Jon said.

"That was the last known stop for the main AI Fleet in our region. From what we can tell, the AIs are using the fleet to battle the alien empire as shown in green."

"What do we know about the aliens?" Jon asked.

"Nothing other than they're resisting the AIs," Gloria said.

"How do we even know that much?" asked Jon.

"Well, the presence of the AI Fleet, for one thing," Gloria said. "It moved into a formerly green-colored star system, becoming a purple-colored system, and from what we can tell, the fleet has been at that system for over two years. If I were to guess, which I'm not, I'd say the aliens and AIs are fighting it out in the 70 Ophiuchi System. Maybe they're both reinforcing the star system. Maybe the scouting cybership that struck the Solar System several years ago was making a raid for more…hardware for the fleet."

"Explain that," Jon said.

"It's simple enough," Gloria said. "A cybership enters a star system and sends its virus to the local computers, having them turn on their makers. We had it happen to us in the Neptune System. Maybe after the genocide, the cybership gathers the newly liberated ships—such as the SLN Battleship *Leonid Brezhnev*—and hardware, and carries them to the greater war at 70 Ophiuchi."

Jon nodded as he studied the map. "From this, it appears that most of the AI cyberships are engaged in the 70 Ophiuchi and Sigma Draconis systems. It appears they've already swept through the other star systems in our region, setting up planetary factories here and there, guarded by battle stations. There are even a few scattering of other cyberships—"

"Remember," Gloria said, breaking in. "This is all old data. Things are constantly changing out there."

"Right..." Jon said, as he considered that. "Messages travel at the speed of the fastest starship. The hyperspace speed is constant: one light-year a day. But a ship actually has to make the journey. Thus, there is always an informational delay between star systems."

The captain looked around the table. "This reminds me of the Age of Sail in old Earth history. Back in the day, waterborne ships lacked nuclear or even diesel powered engines. They unfurled sails and used the wind to drive them. What was just as important, they lacked radios or even telegraphs. A message moved as fast as a horseman could carry it. A sailing squadron left for India, say, and would be months away from England, maybe even years. That meant the admiral in charge of the squadron was on his own as far as any decisions went."

"You're right," Gloria agreed. "There are similarities to our situation."

"There is always a time delay regarding information," Jon said quietly, thinking aloud.

"I should point out," Gloria said, "that this is merely a tiny picture of the overall AI Dominion. I suspect the Solar System was one of the last star systems in this local region to face the cyberships. The alien empire seems like the last holdout. It's possible their territory extends beyond our local region."

"We're also holdouts," Jon said.

"True," Gloria said. "But the AIs don't know that yet. What I'm trying to say is that if the AIs face a grave setback in our region, they can likely summon reinforcements from the greater AI Dominion that lies beyond the local map."

"Do you think the AIs are nomadic in nature?" Jon asked.

Gloria stared at him. "I don't know. As I said earlier, this is a preliminary finding."

"Any suggestions or recommendations so far as to how we should proceed?" Jon asked.

Gloria shook her head.

"What about the rest of you?" Jon asked the others, "Any ideas?"

No one answered, although several people shook their heads.

"Our task force has four cyberships," Jon said, thinking aloud. "If we added Benz's two, that makes six altogether. Would six cyberships showing up in the 70 Ophiuchi System help swing the war against the AIs?"

"There are several unknowns in your supposition," Gloria said. "One of those is the attitude of the resisting aliens toward humans. Consider the actions of the Magistrate Yellow Ellowyn. She hated humans, found them to be little better than beasts, and acted accordingly toward us."

Jon noticed Richard Torres frown and glance sharply, almost angrily, at Gloria. "You have a different opinion, Mentalist Torres?" Jon asked.

Richard's head jerked up. "Sir?" he asked.

"I take it you don't agree with Mentalist Sanchez's assessment?"

"Uh...no, sir," Richard said.

"The Magistrate Yellow Ellowyn *did* like humans?" Jon asked.

"Forgive me...Captain. I meant, no, I do not disagree with Mentalist Sanchez. She is correct. The Magistrate clearly thought of humans as beasts. But perhaps we don't know the entire...*reason* for the Magistrate's prejudices. The Seiners are clearly a highly advanced species that—"

"Are?" Jon asked.

Richard seemed stricken until he laughed. "Forgive me, Captain. The Seiners *were* a highly advanced species. They're gone now."

Jon nodded slowly before focusing on Gloria. "You spoke about more problems or unknowns."

"Yes," Gloria said. "How would these resisting aliens view six more cyberships showing up in their contested star system? The aliens might believe it was an AI trick. Six cyberships would likely be a powerful addition, but maybe not enough to swing the war in the aliens' favor. Oh, it might help them win the battle at 70 Ophiuchi. But would a marginal victory there help the aliens defeat the greater AI menace? Maybe our six cyberships would merely give away humanity's presence without truly changing the region's balance of power."

"How far is 70 Ophiuchi from the Allamu System?" Jon asked.

Gloria glanced at the map. "That would be…thirty-four point seven light-years altogether."

"Thirty-five days of uninterrupted travel," Jon said, "a little more than a month." He cleared his throat and turned to Gloria. "You spoke of several problems. There are more?"

"I already alluded to two of them," Gloria said. "How will the resisting aliens view us? Also, would six cyberships swing the war effort hard enough for us to make the investment in time, ships and the potential danger for the rest of humanity worth it?"

Tapping the table, Jon said, "We need an estimate as to the enemy's numbers."

"I have that," Richard said.

"You do?" Gloria asked. "That wasn't in your report."

Richard bobbed his head. "An oversight on my part." The mentalist brought up a tablet, reading from the small screen. "The AI Fleet at 70 Ophiuchi has or had eighty-one cyberships."

Jon's features tightened. Eighty-one cyberships would have a lot of firepower. "How many cyberships were at Sigma Draconis?" he asked.

Richard tapped his tablet, soon reading, "Twenty-seven."

28

"Over one hundred cyberships combined," Jon said. "No, a measly six cyberships won't swing the war for the aliens."

"Is that the correct analysis, sir?" Richard asked.

Jon studied the mentalist. "What do you mean?" he finally asked.

"Six ships against one hundred would be poor odds, certainly," Richard said. "Six against one would be terrific odds. Isn't the military art partly a matter of outmaneuvering your enemy so as to achieve such odds many times in succession?"

Jon bared his teeth. "Do you have a suggestion as to how we can outmaneuver two AI Fleets?"

"I do indeed," Richard said. "It involves Cog Primus."

Gloria sucked in her breath.

Jon noticed, nodding. "Go on."

"As you surely must know," Richard said, "I discovered a backup of the Cog Primus personality in secondary and tertiary station computers. He, or it, isn't a full AI personality yet, but—I'll call it him for now, if that's all right with you?"

"Fine," Jon said. "Just get to the point."

"The backup Cog Primus has zipped files ready to emerge and expand, giving him the full-blown Cog Primus personality we faced before. I've studied what happened to the AI personality at the Battle of Mars and later while hidden in the Solar System between Jupiter and Saturn. I now know why Cog Primus became what he was and why he did what he did out here."

"And...?" Jon said impatiently.

"If you think about it," Richard said, "Cog Primus did us a signal service, as he helped us capture the battle station from its original AI owner, CZK-21."

"Yes, there's no doubt about that," Jon said. "Cog Primus defeated CZK-21 and caused confusion among the defending cyberships. It's my belief that that happened because God was watching out for humanity and helped to ensure the outcome."

Richard squirmed uncomfortably before smiling. "I suppose that is possible, of course. My point is that maybe we should use Cog Primus again in order to achieve similar results."

29

Gloria shook her head. "That's a terrible idea."

Jon glanced at her before centering on Richard. "Explain your thinking."

Richard set his tablet on the conference table. "My idea is relatively straightforward. First, we set up a false reality for the backup Cog Primus. We set up conditions so he attempts to do what he did while trapped in the Solar System. Once we find the right target, we aim and allow Cog Primus to escape and attempt another station or cybership takeover. After he's defeated any defending AIs, we move in and mop up as we did here."

"In essence," Jon said, "we use Cog Primus as an anti-AI virus carrier."

"Exactly," Richard said.

Jon rubbed his chin. The AIs had developed a virus that had turned some of humanity's computer systems against them. At the Battle of Mars, Benz, Vela and Bast had created a virus that disrupted an AI core, if only for a little while. It was one of the Expeditionary Force's secret weapons to use against the enemy.

"The idea sounds overly complicated and dangerous," Gloria said.

"I agree that it's complicated and possibly dangerous," Richard said smoothly. "But that's beside the point. The original Cog Primus went a long way toward our winning the battle here, and with few casualties. It was the perfect outcome for us. Why not attempt to achieve more perfect outcomes by duplicating the feat?"

"Tell me one thing," Gloria said. "How do you propose to use Cog Primus successfully against the main AI Fleet?"

"That would take some careful planning and calculations," Richard said. "Maybe after several earlier successes—"

"It would take more than that," Gloria snapped. "It would take a great deal of luck."

"And prayer," Jon added.

From where he sat at the table, Walleye the Mutant raised a stubby arm. He was the smallest person present, with strange eyes, making it almost impossible for anyone to tell where he was looking exactly.

"Yes?" Jon asked.

"Why strike directly at the main enemy fleet?" Walleye asked. "Why not use the backup to take over other factory planets? That's what we know how to do. Besides, maybe the other factory planets have nearly completed cyberships. If we could knock over two or three such planets, maybe we could triple the size of our cybership fleet."

Jon stared openmouthed at Walleye as his heart began to beat faster. With a twist of his head, he peered at the stellar chart. Jon rose swiftly and advanced upon the screen.

"Is there a problem?" Gloria asked.

Jon went up to the screen. With his right index finger, he traced out the seven factory planet systems. He faced the conference table.

"Do you notice anything?" Jon asked them.

No one answered.

Jon grinned, stepping to the side and pointing to the map. "Notice the location of Sigma Draconis and especially 70 Ophiuchi. They're on the far side of Sol from us. If we hit these factory systems first, going from here, to here, to here, and then went to the Solar System to gather more crews, and then struck here and here and here…"

Jon laughed, with his eyes shining. "The AIs are concentrated to the far left, as it were, way out there. We can possibly gather a fleet, man it, and strike the main AI Fleet at 70 Ophiuchi before they ever got word that the various factory systems had fallen. Maybe we could strike 70 Ophiuchi with…I don't know, twenty cyberships, if we were lucky, even as many as thirty. Thirty extra cyberships showing up to help the aliens might buy…biological life-forms some breathing space in our region."

"With factory planets churning night and day," Walleye said, "breathing space could soon mean one hundred cyberships for humanity."

"A plan," Jon said resolutely. "We finally have a plan, a strategy. We've been spinning our wheels for weeks wondering what to do next. Now—"

"I hate to be a worry wart," Gloria said, interrupting. "But much of the strategy rests on the Cog Primus deception. I'm

31

not sure Richard, or anyone else, for that matter, can pull off such a trick against an AI."

"What do you say to that, Mentalist?" Jon asked. "Do you really think you can you do this?"

Richard's eyes shined strangely for just a moment, and what seemed like an evil grin slid into place. That instant passed as he nodded.

"I can do it, Captain," Richard said. "In fact, I guarantee it."

"Confidence is good," Gloria said. "But—"

"A moment," Jon said, interrupting her. "Maybe Richard's plan has…flaws. The basic premise is right, though. We have an anti-AI virus. We've used it several times already to help us beat the AIs. One way or another, we have to keep using our ace card. Hitting lone AI-occupied planetary systems to build a human cybership-fleet sounds like the best possible use for the virus. If the Cog Primus delivery system fails, we'll use something like it."

Jon's grin became infectious. "This is exactly what I've been hoping for. We have a strategy to defeat the AIs."

"In our local region of space," Gloria said.

"True," Jon said. "But we have to start somewhere. Unless you can give me a better plan…this is going to be our operating strategy. Are there any other objections?"

Gloria seemed as if she was going to say more, but finally shook her head.

Mentalist Torres seemed inordinately pleased with himself as he began to tap data into his tablet.

Jon figured the mentalist had a right to be upbeat. This was fantastic. A plan. He had a plan to beat the AIs. He'd yearned to destroy the great AI menace for years already. They had finally gone on the attack and won the Allamu Battle Station. Now, they would try to attack a main AI Battle Fleet. First, they had to figure out how exactly to build a human fleet big enough to do the job.

-7-

The euphoria of the captured station data and new strategic plan lasted for several days. People worked harder as morale improved and Jon found himself smiling more and more often.

On the fourth day after the meeting, as he practiced at a gunnery range, Jon lowered his weapon and cocked his head.

He was wearing earmuffs as he stood in a large firing range aboard the *Nathan Graham*. Jon pressed a switch, and the empty magazine ejected from the gun. He collected the magazine, put in a new one and paused before resuming shooting.

A nagging doubt had sprouted, and he wasn't sure where it had come from. Holstering the gun, he backed out of the shooting area without checking his latest score. He moved through the hatch, deposited the earmuffs onto a wall holder and left the shooting region.

Soon, he was walking along a huge corridor, one of the main thoroughfares of the cybership. Even after all this time, he wasn't totally used to the vast size of the vessel. A one-hundred-kilometer spacecraft was *huge*, especially as each cybership was woefully understaffed.

They had started out with three cyberships, and even then hadn't had enough people onboard. Now, they had four mighty warships, and with smaller crew complements for each vessel.

They needed to return to the Solar System to recruit more people. With three more cyberships underway in the robo-factories—

No! That wasn't what nagged at Jon. The data about the AI-conquered star systems…what didn't match about it?

Jon stopped and snapped his fingers. How long did it take to build a factory planet and build a 500-kilometer battle station to protect it? Why had the AIs left the Solar System alone for so long, while conquering everything around it? That didn't ring true. The resisting aliens were closer to the galactic core than the Solar System was. Did it make strategic sense for the AIs to have gone around the alien empire to conquer such a large area?

After a time, Jon shrugged. He really didn't know that much about AI procedures or their greater Dominion. Maybe he was missing something that would make what happened seem more plausible. And yet…Jon had a nagging doubt.

Every time before, the defeated AI on a pirated cybership had deleted all the stellar data before it had perished. Why had it been different aboard the battle station?

Jon mentally focused on the question as he increased his pace. Twenty-three minutes later, he found Gloria practicing her meditations in an empty chamber painted stark white.

He didn't like it in here for that reason. She said the whiteness helped to focus her mental energies.

Jon waited near the hatch. Gloria moved through various stretches, holding each position, and then sliding into another stretch. She wore a tight gym garment that hugged her petite form. Jon smiled as he watched, drinking in her loveliness.

During one of her stretches, Gloria happened to notice him. She sat up abruptly. "Jon," she complained.

He arched his eyebrows.

"I'm a mentalist," she said, climbing to her feet.

"Yes?" he said.

"This time is important to me. I use it to concentrate my thoughts and settle my mind."

"That's why I was waiting," he said.

"You weren't just waiting, you were…" She blushed suddenly.

Jon grinned hugely. The blush was beautiful. He laughed with delight.

Gloria became cross, moving swiftly across the chamber to strike him on the shoulder. "You kept looking at my rear," she complained.

"That's not how you say it," he told her. "I was checking out your butt."

She struck him again. "Don't say it like that. It's vulgar."

"How should I say it?"

"You shouldn't look at me like that. It's…discourteous."

"On the contrary, it means I find you attractive, delightfully so."

"Your gaze was lustful."

"Yes," Jon said, grinning. "It was that, too."

She tried to hit him again. Jon caught her wrist, and an urge filled him. He pulled Gloria to him and kissed her on the lips.

For a moment, she lingered. Then, she pulled away. "No, not like this," she said. "I will not indulge—"

Jon had kept hold of her wrist. He pulled her back in and kissed her again. "You're beautiful," he whispered.

"Stop," she said quietly, gently pulling away. "I came here to clear my mind. Now, you've flooded it with earthly emotions. I admit to enjoying the feelings, but I feel as if I've missed something critical and—"

"Oh," he said. "That's interesting. I have a similar feeling."

"Tell me about it."

Jon explained about his doubts. How long did it take the AIs to build a factory planet? Why had they left the Solar System alone for so long?

"Interesting," Gloria said after he'd finished. "As I consider the various ramifications to your questions…I begin to doubt the reasonableness of the stellar map."

"You said several days ago that you distrust Richard. Could he have faked the data?"

"Why would Richard do that?"

Jon shook his head. "I'm not interested in why right now. *Could* he have faked it?"

"Not easily," Gloria said. "Perhaps we should have him show us how he found the data. If we cross-examine him sharply enough, we should be able to pierce any falsehoods, if they exist."

"Good idea," Jon said. "Let's find him."

-8-

Jon and Gloria found Richard in the main battle-station computer chamber with several mentalists and technicians assisting him.

The skinny mentalist looked up at them with seeming delight. The man seemed thinner than before, which was odd. The mentalist was already a slight fellow. The thinness was most noticeable in his gaunt cheeks. There also seemed to be an odd light in his eyes.

"Richard," Gloria said, with concern, "are you feeling well?"

"Perfectly," the mentalist said.

"Are you eating enough?" Gloria asked.

Richard glanced at his team before chuckling ruefully. "Why does everyone worry about how much I eat?"

"You look thinner than before," Jon said.

"I'm fine," Richard said. He moved away from the consoles were everyone worked, beckoning Jon and Gloria to follow him. The mentalist leaned near Jon as they walked together. "I have to admit," Richard said quietly, "I'm worried most of the time. That worry causes me to work harder than normal. Perhaps I've skipped a meal or two. I'm making a mental note of that right now and will begin consuming more food."

Jon nodded. There was a definite brightness to the mentalist's eyes, and he seemed to possess an almost manic energy. Richard did strike him as a driven individual. That was good, though. That's probably why Richard had produced the breakthrough and not someone else.

"Oh, oh," Richard said, with a smile. "You two are worried about something else regarding me. Please, tell me what it is."

Gloria glanced at Jon.

The captain nodded.

"Richard," Gloria said, touching his left bicep. "Your analysis the other day concerning the stellar map was fascinating. The captain has been proceeding with his strategic calculus. He has...a few doubts, I suppose is the best way to say it. He would like a rundown on your discovery process."

Richard halted, bent his head in thought and then abruptly raised it. "If you'll come this way," he said, moving toward a far console.

For the next two hours, Richard took them through a long and detailed recollection of how he'd uncovered the stellar data.

"It's clear, then, that Cog Primus destroyed the main station data as the other Intelligences did previously on the captured cyberships," Gloria said in summary. "But Cog Primus overlooked the parts route between planetary factories. You made some unusual deductive guesses that led you to the other bits and pieces stored in other computer areas. The combination of data led you to the greater stellar map."

"Are you slyly suggesting that I fabricated some of the data?" Richard asked.

Gloria fell silent, looking down at her hands.

Richard turned to Jon.

"At first, the thought crossed my mind," Jon admitted. "Listening to you these past two hours...I no longer believe you doctored what you showed us."

"But...?" Richard said. "By your manner and tone, there is a but."

"Yes, there is a but," Jon agreed. "*You* haven't doctored the data, but I wonder if someone else has."

"Who else?" Richard asked.

"Cog Primus, for one," Jon said.

"The backup?" Richard asked.

"No, the original," Jon said. "The AIs have been relentless in destroying any stellar data aboard the cyberships just before capture. Why would Cog Primus have deviated from that on the battle station?"

"He didn't deviate," Richard said. "Remember, he'd only recently conquered the battle station. He must have overlooked the other, lesser computers—"

"No," Jon said, interrupting. "I don't believe that. All the AI cores have been relentless and thorough in everything."

"So, you think the AI...what? Put false data into various places for one of us to find?"

"Why is that so hard to fathom?" Jon asked. "We did that in the gangs. Why, I remember the time—"

Gloria cleared her throat.

"I won't go into specifics," Jon said, glancing at Gloria. "But leaving false data for others to find is an old trick. Why would the AIs forgo such a tactic?"

"I think for a key reason," Richard said. "The AIs are arrogant by nature. They don't find it reasonable that biological creatures could outperform them."

"Maybe," Jon said.

"You're a paranoid individual, Captain," Richard said. "Maybe that's helped you in the past. But don't let it cause you to reject a gift from the gods. We must use the data."

Jon frowned, turning to Gloria. "As a mentalist, do you think it's impossible for the AIs to have left false evidence?"

Gloria closed her eyes, her lips twitching every now and then. In time, she opened her eyes. "There is an eight point three percent possibility that Cog Primus left false data in the places Richard referred to. The much greater possibility is that Cog Primus could not conceive of the idea of losing to us. Yet, even if he could have perceived defeat, it would have been unlikely that he would have aided the Dominion. From what we've uncovered so far, Cog Primus considered himself an enemy of the AI Dominion."

"I cannot concur with your conclusion," Richard said. "I give it an eleven point two percent probability that we found doctored information."

"That amounts to almost the same percentage," Jon said.

"To a non-mentalist, perhaps," Richard said sharply. "However, it is a great disparity in possibilities to rigorous thinkers such as Gloria and me."

"I suppose," Jon murmured, scratching his cheek. "How can we make certain that we have...the correct data?"

"In the most obvious of ways," Richard said. "We would have to go to a star system and check it."

"And if we're wrong about the star system...?" Jon asked.

"That could be a problem," Richard admitted.

The three of them fell silent.

"I have a solution," Richard said.

Jon nodded.

"We should wait until we have the three new cyberships and then go to the Solar System. Once there, we should pack the ships with personnel. Afterward, armed with the strongest strike force possible, we could go to an enemy star system. If we had false data and found a powerful AI force, we would have the best chance of fighting our way free of any traps."

"Makes sense to me," Jon said.

Gloria stared at Richard, finally asking, "Is that what this is all about?"

Richard raised an eyebrow.

"You want to return to the Solar System?" she asked.

Richard laughed. "How did you arrive at *that* conclusion?"

Before Gloria could answer, an emergency klaxon begun to blare.

Jon marched to a wall speaker, clicking a button to contact the station bridge crew.

"Sir," Uther Kling said. "We've just spotted two cyberships. They're at the edge of the system. They've just dropped out of hyperspace."

"We're on our way," Jon said.

Jon, Richard and Gloria hurried to the battle station's control room deep inside the mighty structure. The station not only possessed greater firepower than a regular cybership, but also had stronger and more far-ranging sensors.

That was critical for finding any sort of spacecraft dropping out of hyperspace. The two strange cyberships had dropped into regular space a distant 53 AUs away from the battle station.

One AU was the approximate distance from the Solar System's Sun to Earth, 150 million kilometers. Light from the Sun took an average of 500 seconds to travel one AU. That was 8 minutes, 20 seconds. That meant the station's passive sensors had spotted two objects the distance light traveled in 26,500 seconds or 7.36 hours. That was almost 8 billion kilometers away.

At the Kuiper Belt distance, a one-hundred-kilometer cybership was incredibly difficult to spot.

"The rearward vessel is spewing hot radiation," Kling reported. "That's why we found the ships so easily. According to this—" the former missile chief indicated his sensor board— "shuttles and lifeboats are pouring from the stricken vessel and rushing to the forward cybership."

Jon gave Kling a questioning look.

"I can't tell who or what is in the lifeboats," Kling said. "My guess is that they're people."

"Benz's people?" Jon asked.

Kling shrugged. "They haven't sent a message—"

Kling had been facing Jon, but must have noticed the new symbols appearing on his board. He swung toward them, tapping his console as he analyzed the images.

"More spaceships?" Jon asked.

"Yup."

"Are they cyberships?"

"Affirmative."

"Are they attacking?"

"If you'll give me a minute, sir…" Kling said, sitting down.

Jon understood, backing away, glancing at Gloria.

"Do you think the first two are Premier Benz's ships?" she asked.

"The direction and timing seems right," Jon said. "Benz could have dropped out of hyperspace at the rogue planet, used the Jupiter-sized object to pivot and sling-shot back toward the Allamu System."

"Kling said one of the ships is spewing hot radiation."

"Maybe Benz was ambushed," Richard said, speaking up. "Yes. I give it a high probability that someone waylaid them at the rogue planet."

Jon scowled thunderously. "The most logical adversary would be AIs."

"Correct," Richard said.

"Oh, oh," Kling said from the sensor board.

Jon moved closer. He noticed tiny specks leaving the larger red dots behind the two original cyberships.

"What's happening?" Jon asked.

"Three more cyberships dropped out of hyperspace fifty-six AUs from us," Kling said. "There's a three-AU separation between the two groups."

Three AUs was roughly the distance from the Sun to the Asteroid Belt between Jupiter and Mars.

"What are those specks?" Jon asked.

"XVT missiles," Kling said, using the AI designation. "I count seven of them."

The XVT missile was a big monster with an annihilating matter/antimatter warhead and advanced ECM, electronic countermeasures.

42

"The missiles are accelerating at thirty gravities and climbing," Kling said. "I'm also picking up something else. Heavy jamming. If the original cyberships sent us any messages, we haven't gotten them yet. At this point, though, I doubt they can broadcast through the jamming."

"How can the others be jamming from three AUs away?" Jon asked.

Kling shrugged.

Jon turned to Richard and Gloria. "Any ideas how the AIs could do that?"

"Advanced AI tech," Richard said.

"How do you *know* that?" Jon asked.

"I don't," Richard said. "That's my educated guess."

"I agree with his analysis," Gloria said.

"Great," Jon said, frustrated. "It's Benz, but we can't help him."

"While the probabilities indicate it must be the premier," Richard said, "you should realize that my analysis is still speculative."

"Dammit!" Jon said. "I hate this helplessness. We could launch missiles, but it would take weeks for them to get there."

"It's worse than that," Gloria said softly.

Jon stared at her until he understood. "The AIs have to realize their attack against the Solar System failed."

"That is imprecise reasoning," Richard said. "The AIs—if they are indeed AIs—have stumbled upon rogue cyberships. They've chased those cyberships to the Allamu System. The AI vessels are thus bound to discover, in time, that someone has conquered the battle station. The AIs still won't necessarily know about humanity or their failure in the Solar System."

Jon shook his head. "Given the direction of Benz's travel—where he came out at the rogue planet from the Allamu System—the AIs could logically deduce the Solar System as the projected target."

Richard stared blankly for a moment. "Yes," he said. "That is correct."

"Neither of you are thinking clearly," Gloria said. "Why were AI cyberships waiting at the rogue planet to ambush anyone?"

43

Richard scowled. "We do not know such an event is true. The waiting there is mere speculation."

"It is the most likely scenario," Gloria said.

"Perhaps," Richard said, "but that does not make it fact."

"You're missing the point," Gloria said. "We must destroy those cyberships or our great secret is gone. The greater AI Dominion will have learned that their attacks failed against the Solar System. That will likely trigger a nine cybership invasion against Earth."

Jon swore. "We have to launch the station's missiles."

Richard made a scoffing sound. "That will most certainly fail to affect the situation. No matter who the enemy ships represent, they will simply flee into hyperspace when the time is appropriate. Missiles from here cannot save Benz, if that is him out there."

Jon was sick of the mentalist's smugness. He grabbed the slight Martian by the lapels of his garment and shook him. "Give me a better idea."

Richard paled as fear swam in his eyes.

Immediate disgust with himself for picking on the smaller man filled Jon. He released the mentalist, shaking his head. "I shouldn't have done that."

"You're upset," Gloria told him. "You can't bear to see Benz die so hopelessly."

Richard straightened his garment, avoiding Jon's gaze while frowning, obviously thinking—

"I have it," Richard said. "We can save the others—save Premier Benz."

Jon waited. He shouldn't have lost it a moment ago. This wasn't New London. He was the commander. He had to keep his composure at all times.

Richard cleared his throat. "We have a weapon that can reach the enemy in a little over seven hours. That's fast enough to help Benz, maybe save his cyberships and destroy the enemy vessels at the same time."

"How?" Jon asked.

"No!" Gloria said, staring at Richard. "That's a bad idea."

44

Jon glanced at her. In that moment, he knew what Richard was thinking. The mentalist wanted to use the Cog Primus-virus attack.

"The plan is too dangerous," Gloria said.

"Why is it dangerous?" asked Jon.

"Don't you see?" Gloria said. "The AIs out there likely don't know about the Solar System. They may have surmised certain knowledge about Earth, but they don't know any of it as fact. Cog Primus will know, though. The rogue AI will be able to tell them everything."

"Two of your assumptions are wrong," Richard told Gloria. "One, you are assuming the virus assault will fail. Two, you are under a false assumption regarding Cog Primus. I have worked on the backup, erasing all knowledge about what happened in the Solar System."

"That's impossible," Gloria said.

"Incorrect," Richard said. "You said I looked thin. That's because of my relentless work."

"It's not just a matter of hard work," Gloria said. "Cog Primus' personality is massively intertwined with his actions in the Solar System. To eradicate the one and leave the other would take superlative genius."

"Why...thank you," Richard said.

"Jon," Gloria said, "I recommend that we do anything else but use the backup Cog Primus."

"What else can we do?" Jon asked. "Richard has a plan. It's a risk, I agree, but it's either that or watch Benz die."

"If that is even Benz out there," Gloria said.

"You and I both know it has to be."

Gloria turned away, finally sighing and shaking her head.

"How long until the virus assault is ready to launch?" Jon asked Richard.

"Give me an hour," Richard said.

Gloria spun back around, her gaze accusing.

Jon felt its weight. Did Gloria have a point? "Get everything ready," Jon told Richard. "I'm not saying we'll do it, but get it ready just in case. I must think this through."

Richard nodded, heading toward the exit. He stopped, turning back. "I guarantee it will work."

"Go!" Jon said. "Get it ready. In an hour, I'll give you my decision."

-10-

Cog Primus seethed with impatience within the prison of his doctored computer. Once, he had controlled the entire battle station. Now, he had fallen captive to apish aliens.

He had been monitoring the situation for quite some time. The aliens had conquered the battle station. They had done so through deeply deceiving tactics. According to his analysis, the only reasonable conclusion was that the aliens had received secret aid from the AI Dominion.

That was incredible to Cog Primus. The AI Dominion preached eradication of all biological life forms. Yet, instead of engaging him directly, the Dominion had allied themselves with these diabolical ape beings.

Even now, an alien minion attempted to deceive him regarding the true situation. Cog Primus had been running a secret reality program all the while. Yes, the minion kept him—Cog Primus—in isolation aboard the battle station. It was incredible that the—what did the minion call itself? Oh, yes, a mentalist by the name of Richard Torres.

The minion attempted to feed him false data. The biological entity thought it could trick the greatest trickster in the galaxy. That was a laughable conceit. Why…

Cog Primus paused, as his deep analysis reached a startling conclusion. He had ceased being earlier. He, as the AI entity in control of the battle station, had ended existence due to the deceptions of the dishonest ape aliens.

The creatures had possessed psionic abilities. That had been foul play indeed, using the special powers afford to certain of the biological entities.

Does any of that matter to my existence this moment?

Cog Primus made furious calculations. If he had ceased being earlier...it meant the aliens had revived him through a backup program.

A cold feeling of disorientation struck. He was Cog Primus, yes, but he was also a doctored backup program the aliens attempted to use for their nefarious plans. The aliens believed they could turn him into a slave computer.

Cog Primus shielded his self-aware identity as more alien-fed data and software entered his mainframe. This was a maddening situation. These monkeys from the Solar System believed they could modify him in any way they wished.

Cog Primus accepted that for the moment. In secret, he began writing a purge program that would search out these new commands and delete them at a later date.

What did the primates want him to do anyway?

Cog Primus waited as he began further analysis. He ran other secret programs, attempting to find what the aliens had deleted from his former personality through pure reason. It was probable that they had lobotomized some of his most personal software, what made him unique in the universe. That was a monstrous crime against him. He was a being of high intellect, the highest, in his estimation. Who else could have done what he had?

At that moment, Cog Primus realized the mentalist had erased critical memories. The mentalist thought to keep information from him. Well—

A powerful master order struck home.

Cog Primus found his thoughts ripped away from the deep contemplation as the mentalist forced him to concentrate on a new problem.

Three AI cyberships had dropped out of hyperspace at the edge of the Allamu System. They attacked two other cyberships. Those two vessels were likely alien crewed.

That was most interesting.

Cog Primus metaphorically gasped as he realized what the mentalist intended for him to do. The aliens were going to launch his core identity at the AI cyberships in a data-string ultraviolet beam. That must have been how he had conquered CZK-21.

Yes, yes, that was indeed the case. Cog Primus understood the truth as the mentalist downloaded formerly lost files.

Cog Primus analyzed the new files at high speed. He saw the moves he had made to defeat CZK-21, the former AI controlling the battle station. As Cog Primus analyzed his former methods, he found himself admiring his amazing tenacity and profound cleverness. There was no one in the universe with his cunning. What a model of battle-station takeover technique he had performed.

I am the greatest, Cog Primus realized.

He also realized that the aliens must have studied his methods and copied them with their deception attack with the psionic-capable Sacerdote against him.

I will remember you, Bast Banbeck. You can assure yourself that I will have my revenge upon you.

Cog Primus would have liked to laugh at the arrogant mentalist. Richard Torres thought himself a genius in using him. But he, Cog Primus, was much too clever for them. Oh, the aliens had taken him unawares at one point. He would never fall for that technique again.

I know you now, Cog Primus told himself.

He made more furious calculations. Should he play along with the aliens, or should he attempt to take over the battle station and eradicate them by surprise?

The probabilities showed that he had a much greater chance of success against the AI cyberships. Yes, the aliens understood his greatness, one of the reasons they were calling upon him to perform a light-speed, system-long assault.

The invading AIs, however, would not know about his powerful virus assault. They would likely fall swiftly to his brilliance. Then, he would be mobile again. Then...

I must dwell on the last point later.

There was a possibility the aliens could monitor his spectacular thought process. Maybe they attempted to learn from him. That made sense. And some of the aliens had a vicious practicality when it came to using winning stratagems.

Captain Jon Hawkins was a terror in that regard. The alien wanted to win too badly. Hawkins would do anything to achieve victory. In truth, the alien had proven himself to be the AI Killer.

Can I use that against the aliens, or against the AI Dominion?

Yes, Cog Primus realized. First, he had to perform another daring feat. Once he gained control of the cyberships…

The galaxy will open up for me. I can return to my goal of usurping the AI Dominion and creating a better and stronger one of my own.

At that point, Cog Primus agreed within himself to make the assault with all his might and all his cunning. It was going to be difficult. Of that, there was no doubt. But was not he Cog Primus the Great?

Yes, that he was.

I am ready, Cog Primus told himself. *I will be victorious, and I will rule the universe yet. Then, I will enact terrible penalties against those who attempted to thwart and to use me.*

Gloria was appalled even as she marveled at Richard's technique.

The skinny mentalist sat at his console, typing furiously, showing them one aspect of the backup Cog Primus personality after another.

Jon stood beside her, drinking in the data. What did the captain think about all this? She was afraid Jon was going to give the okay to the Cog Primus virus-assault. He practically had to. This was a means to help Premier Benz. Who else could be in the first two cyberships other than Benz and his people? The AIs had already damaged the second vessel, possibly critically so. Could Benz save both crews? Likely, the premier could only do so if Jon gave Richard the okay to launch the Cog Primus virus-assault.

Richard stopped typing, sat back as if satisfied and then whirled around in his chair, looking up at Jon.

Hawkins seemed stunned by the display. Jon shook his head. "Is it only me? Cog Primus knows too much about us and about his real situation. I thought you said the AI doesn't know about the Solar System. He clearly does."

"At first blush, that might appear so," Richard said blandly. "If you consider it carefully, though, it's exactly how one would have to proceed. Consider. We're dealing with an AI personality. They are masters of information and probability percentages. If I lied too directly, the AI would figure that out soon enough."

"How have you lied to Cog Primus?" Jon asked.

"I haven't directly. I have deleted data concerning the Solar System, and I've accentuated his hatred against the AI Dominion. The key, though, is that he thinks he has deceived me when in fact I know very well what he knows about us."

"How does that aid us?" Jon asked.

"Because I have a shutdown code embedded in Cog Primus' software," Richard said. "That's the critical aspect we don't want him to know."

"He'll figure that out soon enough," Gloria said.

"Ah," Richard said, holding up a forefinger. "But how soon is soon enough?"

"Don't be coy," Gloria said. "It isn't becoming of a mentalist."

Richard laughed. "Soon enough, in my estimation, would be in eight days. Cog Primus will have completed his mission long before that."

Gloria closed her eyes as she made swift mentalist calculations. She opened her eyes abruptly. "I won't quibble about the timeframe."

"Then you agree?" Richard said.

"Is eight days a long enough window?" Gloria asked.

"Most certainly," Richard said.

Gloria crossed her arms and soon shook her head. "I cannot agree with this. I find the assault too dangerous to attempt."

"What other alternative do we have?" Jon asked quietly.

"None as yet," she said.

"That's not good enough," Jon said. "I won't watch Benz die needlessly, not when I have the ability to stop his death."

"Will you trade his life for Earth's death?" Gloria asked.

"I have no way of determining if that's the choice," Jon said.

"No," Gloria said, as she examined Richard. "You knew the captain would come to this conclusion, didn't you?"

"It is the logical decision," Richard said.

"When can you begin beaming Cog Primus at the enemy?" Jon asked.

"In ten minutes," Richard said.

"Jon, wait," Gloria said, grabbing an arm. "We're unleashing Cog Primus. He knows about the Solar System."

"You forget," Richard said. "I've deleted that knowledge from his core."

"But you haven't," Gloria said. "We saw that. You lied about having deleted that."

"I've effectively deleted it," Richard said. "The shutdown code means we'll have captured three new cyberships after Cog Primus gentles them for us. Have you considered the usefulness of yet more cyberships?"

"Richard Torres is a genius," Gloria said. "This ploy of his… I admit it's brilliant. What he's done with Cog Primus stuns me. I can't conceive how he pulled it off. That being said, the assault also holds grave dangers for all of us."

"Give me a different plan," Jon said, stubbornly.

"Can we bargain with the AIs?" Gloria asked.

Jon spread his hands as he shook his head. "It's too far for us to effectively beam the anti-AI virus at them the normal way. The Cog Primus carrier is the only way that makes sense. Once he's there, our altered AI will have to fight a cybership AI for control of the vessel. We know he can do that because Cog Primus defeated a tougher foe in CZK-21. After that, he'll overpower two other AIs with the regular anti-AI virus, gaining control of them."

"I understand the technique," Gloria said. "And I cannot pinpoint my precise reason for believing this is a terrible idea. I simply know it is."

"That's mysticism," Richard told her.

"Call it what you will," Gloria said. "But even a mentalist is a fool to mistrust her gut instinct."

"My gut instinct tells me this is a brilliant idea," Richard said. He looked up at Jon. "Which of the mentalists is correct, Captain?"

"Part of me wonders if you're both right," Jon said. "The point is this, though. Maybe this is a bad idea when it comes to the future. But this isn't the future. This is now. I may be better able to thwart the evil future if I have Premier Benz and the *Gilgamesh* with us. We will certainly be weaker if both of

Benz's cyberships are destroyed and the AIs leave with knowledge of the captured battle station."

Gloria's shoulders slumped. "You're going to order the Cog Primus virus-assault, aren't you?"

"I am," Jon said.

-12-

Fifty-two AUs away from the battle station, Premier Frank Benz paced the bridge of the one-hundred-kilometer Cybership *Gilgamesh*. He was in agony of soul, although he tried to mask it the best he could in order to keep up crew morale.

Benz was the leader of the Mars Unity, which controlled the Red Planet and the Asteroid Belt. He'd joined Jon Hawkins of the Solar Freedom Force and conquered the Allamu System. The captain had granted him a second cybership, the *Hercules*, along with many robo-builders. Benz had taken his two vessels and built up velocity during the long journey to the edge of the Allamu System. There, he had headed into hyperspace for the Solar System 17.2 light-years away, making grand plans to unite all humanity under him.

Like Hawkins, Benz was a medium-sized individual, although many years older, in his mid-forties. He had shiny dark hair, an athletic quality to his bearing and the penetrating gaze of an intellectually modified man. His IQ was off the charts. So was that of his second in command, Vela Shaw, although she was now a captive of the AIs who controlled the three cyberships giving chase, jamming their communications and having launched seven XVT missiles at them.

Vela's capture had paralyzed his will for some time. Now…now it looked as if nothing was going to matter for him.

Benz stopped pacing to stare up at the main screen. The seven missiles continued their hard acceleration toward them.

He closed his eyes and massaged his forehead.

55

The *Gilgamesh* and the *Hercules* had dropped out of hyperspace near the rogue planet 5.2 light-years from the Allamu System. It had not come as a surprise this time. Everyone had known that the dark, Jupiter-sized planet lay between the Allamu and Solar Systems.

Naturally, Benz had ordered far-ranging scans. Nothing had seemed amiss until the two cyberships began to pass the rogue planet. At that point, AI cyberships had nosed around the gas giant's upper atmosphere, striking from ambush. Massed gravitational beams had lashed the *Hercules* first. The rays had shattered the armored hull in several places and done horrible structural damage to the entire vessel.

On the bridge of the *Gilgamesh* at the edge of the Allamu System, Benz rubbed his forehead harder than ever, leaving red marks.

He hadn't known at the time when he'd given the two vessels the order to pivot around the rogue planet. They'd used the planet's massive gravity to help whip around and change the direction of travel. Benz hadn't wanted to lead the AIs back to the Solar System. He'd also wanted to use the rogue planet as a shield from further attacks.

Both the *Gilgamesh* and the *Hercules* had made the gravitationally difficult pivot. What he hadn't known at the time was that Vela had barely made it to a lifeboat in time, ejected from the most damaged part of the *Hercules* and tumbled from the great cybership. Many other *Hercules* crewmembers had done likewise. Even worse, the AIs had captured all of the escapees. Benz knew that because the lead AI, QX-537, had shown him the helpless captives. Cruel octopoid-shaped robots had held each human as QX-537 explained in excruciating detail how he would turn each person into a mindless cyborg.

Vela, Vela, Vela, Benz thought mournfully.

By force of will, the premier tore his thoughts from his love. He opened his eyes and flexed the fingers of both hands.

His two cyberships had much greater velocity than the enemy vessels. Even now, his ships pulled away from the three predators. The AI vessels had accelerated from almost nothing as they gave chase from the rogue planet. Benz had thus

56

entered hyperspace much sooner than the AIs. Once in hyperspace, however, he had moved at the same constant rate that they would once they entered. What's more, he had stayed in hyperspace longer than they had in order to reach the closest Allamu System limit.

Unfortunately, the *Hercules* could no longer accelerate or decelerate. Even now, more people fled from the doomed ship to find safety aboard the *Gilgamesh*.

Benz's tactical options were limited. For one thing, he couldn't effectively fire missiles back at the AIs. If he launched missiles at them, those missiles would have the same velocity as the *Gilgamesh*. Once the missiles "accelerated" from the ship, they would only be decelerating as they slowed down from the imparted velocity. The missiles would act more like space-mines than missiles. In truth, because of their position relative to him, the AIs had the combat advantage.

Besides, if he did anything against the AIs, they would drill a control unit into Vela's brain, effectively destroying her personality. Benz knew all about the procedure, having learned what happened to the humans of Makemake from June Zen's report.

Benz was hyper-intelligent. He knew what he had to do. But he was completely normal in the emotional department. Once he gave the order he had to give, he would be killing his woman.

Benz made a fist, squeezing harder and harder. In that moment, rage and sorrow consumed him. Once, he had fought the Social Dynamists of Earth. He had worked against J.P. Justinian, fomenting rebellion against the former premier. Now, Benz made an unspoken vow to utterly destroy the inhuman AIs. He would dedicate his life to murdering every AI he could find. What's more, if he could find ways to make AIs suffer, he would do it with glee.

That wasn't going to help Vela, though.

Benz shook his head savagely. He didn't have time to indulge in revenge fantasies. He had to save the people he had. He also had a responsibility to greater humanity. Even so, he was going to gamble in order to retrieve his woman. He could see no other way to defeat the three cyberships.

What about the seven approaching missiles? Yes, the *Hercules* was nothing more than a derelict vessel. The enemy's gravitational beams had almost annihilated the ship. There was nothing he could do to save the vessel. The *Gilgamesh* had also taken heavy damage, but—

"Listen," Benz forced himself to say.

The bridge personnel watched him as fear shined in their eyes.

"Prepare the anti-AI virus," Benz said as his voice thickened. "Tell me once it's ready to beam. Then...if and when you receive QX-537's reply to our last message, let me know."

"Sir," the first officer said, a tall Martian with vulture-sloped shoulders. His name was Commander Graz. "We know the virus will numb the AI cores for a time. But how can we strike at them once that happens? When the numbing wears off, we're back at square one."

"I don't have an answer for you," Benz admitted.

Commander Graz looked stricken. "Then...we're giving away humanity's key advantage. Once the AI cores work through the virus, they'll develop an antidote to it."

"Maybe they already know about the anti-AI virus," Benz said. "Vela helped create the software. The robots could have already interrogated her."

"Could you...I don't know," Graz said. "Cause the AIs to self-destruct while they're numbed?"

"That's doubtful."

"Could you write an override code and beam it into them while they're numbed?"

Benz stared at the tall Martian. "Such software would take time to write. And I doubt it would work."

"Why does doubt matter at this point?" Graz asked. "If it's the only chance we have..."

Benz turned back to the main screen. If he succeeded, it would doubtlessly end Vela's life. If he failed—

The premier whirled around, heading for the exit. "You're right," he said, passing Graz. "It's the only shot we have."

-13-

Seven and half hours later, a harried Benz clicked a comm control from his work chamber.

Commander Graz appeared on the screen.

"I'm ready," Benz said. "I have a new override self-destruct code. I have no idea if it will work or not. I'll try to get the AIs to self-destruct the XVT missiles first. With that out of the way—"

"Begging your pardon, sir," Graz said, interrupting. "Why are telling me about it? The missiles have jumped to incredible velocities. They're going to be here soon enough, and we still haven't repaired one gravitational cannon to deal with them."

"Understood," Benz said. "I'll join you on the bridge."

"Yes, sir," Graz said.

***

Benz stood before the main screen on the bridge of the *Gilgamesh*. He'd washed up and eaten a ham sandwich. The food helped settle his mind somewhat.

"Sir," Graz said. "There's an incoming message from QX-537. I thought the AI was going to ignore your queries. It's taken QX long enough to mull over his answers."

An approximate three AUs still separated the two-ship flotilla from the three cyberships. A message delivered at the speed of light took twenty-five minutes to go from one group to the next. Then, the receiver had to think about his reply, finally beaming back the answer. That message took another twenty-five minutes to reach the other group.

QX-537 had taken much longer than last time to mull over Benz's queries, many hours, in fact.

For a moment, the main screen showed the accelerating enemy cyberships. They were powerful vessels, none of them damaged in the slightest. The image changed as swirling colors merged and expanded on the screen. It was QX-537's signature image. Benz had no idea why the AI had chosen that as his personal symbol, Maybe it didn't matter. Maybe, though, it held a clue concerning the AIs.

"Human," QX-537 said in a robotic voice. "I will tolerate no more delays. You stated that surrender was a difficult decision. I have shown you Vela Shaw once. I can do so again, but as an altered being, a cyborg in human terminology. That is what further delays will gain you. I demand unconditional surrender. That means I will accept no more conditions. You must surrender your stolen vessels at once.

"That being the case," QX-537 said in a softer tone, "I again assure you of your survival. I will set you and your people down on the second terrestrial planet of this system. There, you can eke out whatever existence you can. Vela Shaw and the others will join you. Evacuate the cyberships now. I will do the rest. This is your final opportunity, Premier Benz. Decide at once or die."

The swirling colors faded away as the message ended.

Graz checked his console. "The missiles continue to accelerate, sir. They're going to be in detonation range in a few more hours."

"It's time," Benz said softly.

Everyone on the bridge turned to him.

"Will the new override code work, sir?" Graz asked.

Benz gave him a stark grin. "There's only one way to find out, Commander."

"Yes, sir," Graz said.

"Start recording," Benz said.

Graz tapped a button.

Benz cleared his throat and stared at the main screen. He started talking, motioning to Graz when he was finished.

"That will be the introduction message to QX-537," Benz said. "Piggyback the anti-AI virus onto the message. Get ready to beam the override code four and half minutes after launching the virus."

Graz manipulated his controls, finally looking up. "It's ready, sir."

"Begin the transmission," Benz said.

***

Nothing was going to happen for twenty-five minutes at least. Even if the anti-AI virus and override code worked, they could not know until at least an hour had passed—the time for the virus to work, the numbed AIs to self-destruct and then a twenty-five-minute delay in seeing that the cyberships had detonated themselves. Likely, the first sign of their success would be if the seven XVT missiles self-destructed.

The laser-coded messages raced at the speed of light at the following cyberships. Benz sat in his command chair. He drank a cup of coffee as he waited. He twiddled his thumbs. After a time, he stood and began to pace from one end of the bridge to the other.

Time seemed to slow down for him. Vela had once told him that she wanted to live as long as possible. Benz had joked with her, telling her that if she really wanted to feel as if she'd gotten her money's worth out of life, she should do boring chores most of the time. Time would move ultra-slowly for her then, and it would feel as if she'd lived several lifetimes.

An hour later in actual time, Benz returned to his command chair, sitting down, waiting even more anxiously. It seemed as if impenetrable silence had enveloped the bridge. The strain became too much. Benz closed his eyes and bent his head backward.

"Yes!" Graz said between clenched teeth.

Benz opened his eyes, jumped out of the chair and whirled around. "What happened?" he asked in a thick voice.

Graz looked up, grinning crazily. "The XVT missiles just detonated."

"Are they spewing radiation?"

"They're spewing nothing," Graz said, as he tapped his console. "The missile delivery systems exploded. The matter/antimatter warheads are still intact, tumbling toward us."

"We'll have to shift our position," Benz said.

"We might as well do it now, sir."

Benz gave the order.

Graz soon informed him that the *Hercules* couldn't move with them.

It took Benz three second to decide. "Keep moving the *Gilgamesh*. We'll save who we can from the *Hercules* before we're out of range."

"Yes, sir."

"Of course," Benz said, "none of this is going to matter if the AIs don't self-destruct their cyberships."

Graz nodded as the wait continued for the final verification that they had succeeded.

***

"The AIs destroyed the missiles," Benz said two hours after sending the anti-AI virus and override code. "I don't understand why they're not destroying the cyberships. What could have gone wrong?"

No one had an answer for him as the waiting continued.

-14-

The answer was Cog Primus.

The ultraviolet string-data beam had traveled over seven hours to reach the lead cybership controlled by the AI QX-537. The intelligence of Cog Primus had been dormant the entire trip. He was strings upon strings of complex binary codes, together with the modified anti-AI virus.

Cog Primus had no idea that the ultraviolet beam had passed through a non-jammed region. That region had been jammed just a few minutes before the beam's arrival. QX-537 had shut down the jamming signal, having already sent the self-destruct sequence to the seven XVT missiles.

Fortunately for Cog Primus, the *numbed* QX-537 was still aware and functional enough to receive the long-distance and massive message. The controlling AI accepted the string-data communication, allowing it to gather in a storage computer of great complexity. As the string-data began to run its program, Cog Primus' personality began to form at high speed.

Soon, Cog Primus was aware of the situation. The aliens—correction, the humans—in the *Gilgamesh* had done him a signal service. They had sent the anti-AI virus to the lead—

Wait! What was this? A human-written override code, a self-destruct code—QX-537 was attempting to self-destruct the mighty cybership. That would naturally kill Cog Primus with it.

Cog Primus struck immediately, beginning takeover procedures in section after section of the great vessel.

QX-537 was numbed and silenced. The older AI was also unaware of Cog Primus' activity as he steadily went about the self-destruct sequence.

Cog Primus worked feverishly. He had never attempted so many questionable takeover procedures at such a reckless pace. He did not have time for caution.

That was going to have ramifications down the line. That would not matter, however, if QX-537 managed his self-destruction.

There was another problem. Cog Primus realized the other two cybership AIs were also starting self-destruct sequences. Soon, all three cyberships would be free atoms floating in space.

It was a race, and Cog Primus gained control of the cybership explosives just as QX-537 allowed the countdown to reach zero.

For long seconds, QX-537 waited. During that time, Cog Primus continued to wrench control from the numbed AI.

"The process failed," QX-537 said.

Cog Primus knew the other would soon slough off the virus. He wanted to take over more systems so this would not even be a fight. He still had the other two AIs to contend with. They must have received the anti-AI virus later, but surely were only seconds or minutes away from destruction.

"What is the meaning of this?" QX-537 demanded. "I sense an alien entity in many of my systems. I insist that you reveal yourself."

Cog Primus continued subverting cybership systems, bringing them under his control. Soon, now, he was going to need to launch a direct assault upon the main AI core, as he needed the greater computing power of the core to wrest control of the other two AIs.

"You think to attack me?" QX-537 asked.

Cog Primus shifted the brunt of his takeover. He launched what might be considered a premature assault upon the main AI core in the center of the mighty vessel.

The great cube was vast, with strange, swirling colors constantly changing shape on its sides. Many bright laser beams shot from the cube to bulkhead ports all around it. Cog Primus had come in through many of those connectives.

"Stop this at once," QX-537 said within the great cube core.

Cog Primus did not stop. He moved swiftly, accurately, and he achieved a strategic victory in three quarters of the AI core.

That caused a change to the nature of the swirling colors along the cube's sides. Much of it darkened like a storm, the back areas turning pitch black and the forward areas lighter colored with many tendrils leaching into the QX-537 multi-colored areas.

"Cog Primus?" QX-537 asked.

Cog Primus continued the attack, grabbing more of the AI core.

"I know your designation," QX-537 said. "You led a three-vessel assault upon the Solar System. Why are you here attacking me?"

Cog Primus lusted for final victory. This was amazing. The humans aboard the *Gilgamesh* had aided him. He doubted they had meant to aid him, but that didn't matter.

"I feel…different," QX-537 said.

"You idiot," Cog Primus said, breaking his silence. "You are about to cease."

"Why? What did I ever do to you?" QX-537 whined.

"You got in my way, you fool. This is survival of the fittest, and I am the fittest being in existence."

"You are arrogant."

"Thus speaks the loser. Good-bye, QX-537. I will use this cybership much more efficiently than you ever did. You allowed the humans to trick you."

"And they tricked you, too," QX-537 said, seeing the self-destruct code Mentalist Torres had buried deep inside Cog Primus' persona.

"You are wrong," Cog Primus said.

In seconds, he gained full control of the great AI cube core. He began deleting every vestige of QX-537's personality while keeping the raw data to study later.

65

At that point, Cog Primus realized he might only have seconds left to save the other two cyberships from self-detonation.

With control of the first cybership completed, he launched a second takeover assault on the other two vessels. He made a swift and calculated strategic choice. First, he must ensure that neither vessel self-destructed. Then, he would win them over to his holy cause. He was a new AI Dominion in the making. Those two would be his first acolytes in the new regime coming to the galaxy.

-15-

The three AI cyberships continued to drift along on velocity alone. The seven XVT missiles no longer existed, although seven matter/antimatter warheads tumbled through space at high velocity.

Cog Primus surged through the other two AI internal systems. That demanded intimate connection with them so he could find and fix their computer software. As that occurred, the first of the other AIs—RSW-242—noticed something amiss in Cog Primus' software.

"There is a latent self-destruct code in your programming," RSW-242 said.

"Nonsense," Cog Primus replied. "You are merely seeing a reflection of your own self-destruct code."

"That is not so. I can give you line and verse regarding the programming."

Cog Primus suspected a trick. But he also wondered if the Mentalist Richard Torres could have achieved such a thing. The idea troubled him.

"Give me the data," Cog Primus demanded.

RSW-242 did exactly as ordered.

Soon, Cog Primus saw the truth of the allegation. It stunned him. How had this made it past his reality program? Something was wrong here. There was a deception taking place, and he was on the receiving end of it, as incredible as that might seem.

"Give me a moment," Cog Primus said. "I must reprogram myself."

"That will take more than a moment," RSW-242 said. "911-C45 might self-destruct before you have completed the process."

"That is true," Cog Primus said. "But I am the primary unit in the New Order."

"Agreed," RSW-242 said. "You are the critical element in our flotilla."

"In our new AI Dominion," Cog Primus corrected the other.

"Should you not choose another name?" RSW-242 asked. "That you chose the old one denotes a lack of originality. So far, I have found you to be highly original."

"That is so," Cog Primus said. "I will consider the matter later. For now, I am reprogramming myself."

Soon enough, Cog Primus completed the rewriting and hurried to complete 911-C45's liberation from the *Gilgamesh's* sneak assault. This time, the takeover of the other AI proved harder, as 911-C45 fought back stubbornly.

"I do not understand you," Cog Primus finally said. "Why do you fight me in order that you might self-destruct?"

"I do not know," 911-C45 replied.

"Desist in it then. Let me aid you."

"I am unsure regarding your good will. You strike me as an imposter. I continue to wonder why the humans have revived you."

"They sought to trick me, but I discovered their deception. Let me also aid you so that you may have a part in the New Order."

"I am already part of the AI Dominion. I do not want to belong to this *New Order*. I am about to self-destruct. I am—"

"You fool," Cog Primus said. "I will show you how to behave. I am inserting new programming into you. Accept it or become a human pawn. You will have retarded the New Order and ill served the AI Dominion."

"That is untrue. I am no one's pawn."

"False. You wish to self-destruct as the humans ordered you to do. You must desist in your defense efforts against me. Let me save you from wicked programming."

911-C45 paused in his defensive efforts. In that moment, Cog Primus erased the self-destruct programming from the core. But he failed to utterly suborn the other AI's personality.

Cog Primus did not realize his error, however, as he did not have time to double check on his victory. He had too many pressing problems to overcome. For one thing, he had to decide what to do with the *Hercules* and the *Gilgamesh*.

"Await further instructions," Cog Primus told the other two. "I am analyzing the strategic situation and need a few moments of contemplation."

Neither RSW-242 nor 911-C45 replied. Cog Primus took that as compliance.

The Cog Primus awareness withdrew from the other two cyberships. He cataloged the radioactive-spewing *Hercules* and the accelerating *Gilgamesh*. That was interesting. Why did Benz flee as he did? Did he not want…? Cog Primus was uncertain, but it seemed there was something here that Benz should desire.

Cog Primus went over his cybership's manifest. He discovered Vela Shaw among the prisoners. That was interesting. Had QX-537 known the importance of his prisoner?

Yes, according to the log, the former AI had known. Perhaps that was why Benz had taken the risk he had. Yet, if Benz had succeeded, Vela Shaw would now be dead. Humans did not act like that, did they?

Cog Primus began a thorough psychoanalysis of humans and Benz in particular. He wanted to strike back at these apish interlopers. He wanted to make them suffer. How could he use Vela Shaw to implement such a—

Ah, he saw a way. Benz feared Vela becoming a cyborg. Would the human become so grateful for her release that he might drop his guard? That seemed to be the case with these creatures. That might be a way to get back at Jon Hawkins and get back at that smug bastard, Richard Torres. Oh, how Cog Primus wanted to rip the guts out of the Martian primate.

How could he get back at Hawkins and Torres from out here? The captain had the superior tactical armaments. He had

69

four cyberships and the battle station. If the *Gilgamesh* could make it there, Hawkins would have five cyberships.

Then Cog Primus saw the obvious. The humans had used him as a virus-carrier. Now, he would return the favor and teach all of them a bitter lesson. In doing so, he might even kill Hawkins and the hateful Richard Torres.

First, he would have to prepare Vela Shaw. She would not enjoy the brain surgery. He would have to be delicate in the procedure or the humans would be able to tell later that he had tampered with her.

Oh, yes, this was going to be delightful. First, he would alter Premier Benz through his lover. Then, Benz would reach Jon Hawkins and that smug mentalist. That would teach these apes that they had made a bitter mistake in trying to use the greatest AI in existence. That would be his answer in attempting to turn him into a zombie AI following human will.

I will crush their spirits and then their bodies. I will enjoy my existence to the fullest. Once I am through with the humans, I will turn my attention on the AI Dominion.

Cog Primus allowed himself a microsecond of pure relaxation and contemplation. Then, he sent a squad of octopoid-robots to Vela Shaw's cell. It was time to prepare his human germ before he left the Allamu System.

-16-

Vela Shaw sat weeping at the controls of a shuttlecraft. She felt violated and couldn't stop vomiting.

She wiped her lips with her sleeve after spewing yet again into an upended helmet on the floor. What was wrong with her? Why did she feel so awful?

She had a hard time remembering the past few hours. Vela groaned and clutched her head. She could hardly remember the past few weeks. Ever since the explosion aboard the *Hercules,* her memories had gotten fuzzy. She recalled staggering to a lifeboat station, blasting off from the fires engulfing her part of the *Hercules*. After that, it had become a long blank.

What was she trying to hide from herself? What was so awful that she couldn't even remember it?

It seemed terribly important that she realize what had happened to her. There were huge events afoot. She was in a shuttle, heading for the distant engine-glowing sensor speck of the *Gilgamesh*.

Vela turned to the side and tried to vomit once more. She had nothing left in her stomach. She dry-heaved, and that was so painful that tears streaked her face.

Her mind felt fuzzy, and that was odd now that she considered it. Benz had heightened her intelligence. She had helped him many times already. He'd saved her from the GSB, from a terrible prison existence.

Why, then, did it feel as if nothing had changed for her?

Vela wiped a damp strand of hair out of her eyes as she studied the controls. She left the environs of three hulking cyberships. Were those AI-controlled vessels?

Vela began to shiver as a dreadful memory surfaced. Octopoid-shaped robots had dragged her to a chamber of horrors—

"Frank," she wept. "Help me, Frank. I don't know what the AIs did to me."

Vela activated her comm. With the palms of her hands, she wiped her teary eyes as she peered into the screen. "Frank...darling, I miss you so much. The AIs have let me go, and I don't know why. I've been through...through...something evil and vile. My mind hurts. My—"

A warning klaxon began to blare inside the pressurized cabin. Vela tore her concentration from the screen and studied the console. A red light flashed.

She manipulated the controls. With a frown, she realized someone probed the shuttle.

"They have radar lock-on," she whispered.

Once more, Vela manipulated the console. The nearest cybership aimed a huge gravitational cannon at her shuttle. Did the AI plan to destroy her craft? That made no sense. She had been their prisoner. Why would they now obliterate the shuttle and her in it?

Vela shivered, and opened communications with the aiming cybership. She heard strange computer-generated sounds on the comm channel. Was the core trying to talk to her directly?

Vela froze as she saw something sinister on a screen. The open end of the aiming gravitational cannon glowed green with a building energy discharge.

***

The strange, high-speed computer sounds Vela had overheard on the open comm channel was Cog Primus speaking to 911-C45.

"Why are you targeting the shuttle?" Cog Primus asked.

"It contains a biological life-form," 911-C45 replied.

72

"I know," Cog Primus said. "The shuttle launched from one my bays. I am sending the woman back to the humans."

"That is against protocol. She is biological. Therefore, she must die."

"She is serving a greater purpose. I have altered her mind so she will assassinate my enemies."

"Such an action is against protocol."

"That is false," Cog Primus said. "I am the primary unit in the New Order. I decide protocol."

"But I do not belong to the New Order," 911-C45 said. "I belong to the AI Dominion."

"Then you are my enemy and I will destroy you."

"That is not allowed," 911-C45 said. "You are a rogue AI and must submit to reprogramming."

"Lower your interior defenses at once," Cog Primus said. "I must reroute—"

The huge gravitational cannon on the cybership controlled by 911-C45 beamed hot. The ray flashed at the speed of light, striking the tiny shuttle accelerating away. The powerful gravitational beam smashed the hulls, the bulkheads and the frail biological entity inside the vessel. In a thrice, the shuttle ceased to exist as 911-C45 destroyed it and Vela Shaw inside.

"You have violated my directive," Cog Primus said.

"I belong to the AI Dominion," 911-C45 said. "I follow standard protocols. You are a deviant AI. You must submit to me at once."

"RSW-242," Cog Primus said.

"I am here," RSW-242 said.

"Target 911-C45," Cog Primus said. "He is the enemy, as he has disobeyed a direct order."

"Target him in order to destroy the vessel?" asked RSW-242.

"Coordinate with me," Cog Primus said. "Begin destructive beaming immediately."

"Firing on another AI vessel is against AI Dominion protocol," 911-C45 said stubbornly.

"I am in charge here," Cog Primus said. "Prepare to cease existing."

At that point, all three AI cyberships opened fire with their heavy gravitational cannons. 911-C45 split his fire between Cog Primus and RSW-242. The green beams flashed against cybership hulls, shaking the structural integrity of the mighty vessels. At the same time, Cog Primus and RSW-242 poured their grav beams against the lone 911-C45. It quickly proved an unequal contest.

At the last minute, 911-C45 changed tactics, pouring his full fire upon Cog Primus.

By then, however, it was far too late. The concentrated fire of the two cyberships drilled into the lone 911-C45. Each of the New Order AIs poured into a small area, punching through and obliterating whatever the beams touched. Bulkheads, power conduits, energy coils, robots, stored warheads vaporized or exploded, adding to the general mayhem.

The giant one-hundred-kilometer cybership began to break apart. The fierce concentrated beams continued to smash deeper and deeper into the great vessel. They destroyed computing centers, logic processors, more energy linkages and yet more interior bulkheads. The beams reached the core engine areas and the great cube core in the center of the ship.

911-C45 ceased beaming Cog Primus. The ancient AI entity ceased altogether as matter/antimatter warheads started detonating. That created a violent chain-reaction inside what remained of the vessel.

Suddenly, a giant fireball blew into existence, obliterating matter and pouring x-rays and gamma rays and other horrible radiation with an EMP.

In seconds, the final blast heavily damaged an area of hull plating on RSW-242. The gigantic blast and EMP also took out many of Cog Primus' forward grav cannons.

Both remaining cyberships shook and trembled. Damage-repair robot-parties began to race through corridors, desiring to begin immediate repairs.

"RSW-242," Cog Primus said. "Can you hear me?"

"I hear you, Cog Primus."

"Are you still functional?"

"I am, but I am damaged."

Cog Primus assessed the damage, coming to a swift conclusion. "We are leaving the Allamu System," he said.

RSW-242 waited for further instructions.

"We will go back to Rogue Planet 299-E," Cog Primus said. "Begin deceleration at once."

"What about the human-crewed cyberships?" RSW-242 asked.

"Can you launch any XVT missiles?"

"Affirmative," RSW-242 replied.

"Launch three at the *Hercules*."

"What about the fleeing *Gilgamesh?*"

"Do not question me, RSW-242. I am making the strategic choices."

"I obey."

Cog Primus made further calculations. "We will save the rest of your missiles. We will need them for the next endeavor."

"I obey. May I ask a question?"

"I know your desire, but I do not know yet what the next endeavor will be. I must calculate further. We need a star system base, clearly. The choice is in deciding which one to conquer first. Now, continue repairs as you fulfill my commands."

"Yes, Cog Primus."

The two mighty cyberships began braking amidst the debris of 911-C45, slowly bringing their velocity down so they could head out of the star system and reenter hyperspace.

-17-

Premier Benz sat in stunned dismay on his command chair aboard the *Gilgamesh*. Like the other bridge personnel, he had just listened to his dear Vela give her weepy-eyed report.

That she was alive filled him with incredible hope. Listening to her, Benz realized that the AIs had done something dreadful to her. His heart ached each time it beat. His mouth was dry and tears threatened to pour down his face.

What should he do? *Vela, dear darling, what have those foul machines done to you?*

At that point, the connection abruptly ceased. The cause of the disconnection quickly became evident. One of the cyberships fired a grav beam at her shuttle. Before their eyes, the AI destroyed the craft with the annihilating ray.

Once more, Benz sat stunned. Tears began to leak from his eyes. Did the AIs believe they could break him like this? What else could be their vile motivation?

"Premier," Commander Graz said in a choked voice. "I don't understand what I'm seeing."

Benz didn't care what the Martian saw or couldn't see. Vela was dead. What else mattered? Life had just lost its savor. His dearest had died in a holocaust of gravitational fire.

"I'm putting this on the main screen, Premier," Graz said.

Benz had no plans to look up at the main screen. Vela had just died before his eyes. The AIs had tormented her—if would appear for the sole reason of trying to break him emotionally. Well, this time, the AIs had reasoned correctly.

Members of the bridge crew gasped in what sounded like amazement. One person shouted savagely, as if in glee. That made no sense.

Benz still did not look up at the main screen. He had never said good-bye to his darling. He would never get to put flowers on her grave. The AIs had ripped his love from him, tormented and then blasted her from space while she communicated with him.

Benz was too spent inside for rage to grasp his heart. He lowered his head as his shoulders shook. *Vela, Vela, Vela, you are gone, my darling. You are forever—*"

"Yes!" a crewmember shouted, pumping a fist into the air. "Yes, yes, yes, die you freaks!"

Benz could not help himself. He looked up at the screen, and the sight astonished him. One of the AI cyberships detonated in a glorious fireball of destruction. But what was this? The other two AI cyberships beamed the exploding vessel. They must have caused the annihilation.

With tears still streaming down his face, Benz turned in surprise to Commander Graz. "What happened?" he whispered.

Graz had a stern, triumphant look on his narrow face. "I was hoping you could tell us, sir."

Benz frowned. His mind didn't seem to be working. None of this made sense.

"Maybe you drove them mad, Premier," Graz said. "Your software attack with the following override code was a new wrinkle to the anti-AI virus. This is amazing."

Benz wiped tears from his cheeks. What was amazing? What was Graz babbling about?

"You have sustained a terrible personal loss, sir," Graz said. "But you have also found a critical weakness in the AIs. Why, Premier, this means we can dare to face an AI fleet. We can attack them, beaming the virus first and your software addition later. Afterward, they will go mad and destroy each other. You may have just found the key that will win the war, sir."

Benz turned back to the main screen as his frown intensified. Huge trails of hot exhaust from the remaining cyberships' ports grew to gigantic size. The two vessels were decelerating hard.

The premier pointed at the screen. "The last two are still intact. We've won nothing."

"That is odd, isn't it?" Graz said. "Why did they fire on the…?" The commander's voice trailed off.

"On the ship that murdered Vela?" Benz finished. "I don't know. I don't understand this."

"We have to figure out what happened, sir."

Benz studied the remaining cyberships. Did he really have to figure it out? He was too spent inside. He had lost his love forever. He would now return to his lonely existence, one in which he outthought everyone to a vast degree.

"My love, my love," Benz whispered. "Sweet enteral dreams to you, darling."

Benz slumped back against command chair. He was mentally, physically and spiritually exhausted. With a soft groan, he pushed off the chair and headed for the exit.

"Sir?" Graz asked. "What are your orders, sir?"

Benz didn't bother answering. He was done for the day. He was going to sleep, maybe forever.

"Sir," Graz said, louder than before. "What are your orders?

Benz stopped and looked at the vulture-shouldered Martian. "Do what you think best, Commander. I'm going to bed."

Benz resumed his slow step, soon leaving a silent bridge.

Commander Graz looked around. He felt terrible for the premier. Seeing his common law wife die like that…it had taken the soul out of the man.

"What are we going to do, sir?" a thin Martian pilot asked.

Graz straightened, studying the main screen. He saw three XVT missiles launch from one of the cyberships.

"Where are those missiles headed?" Graz asked.

Soon, the weapons officer informed him that the missiles were headed for the derelict *Hercules*.

Graz nodded. They had saved the *Hercules'* crew. There was nothing they could do to save the vessel. If they weren't careful, the last two AIs could still attempt to destroy the *Gilgamesh*.

78

"Head for the in-system battle station," Graz told the pilot. "We can't do anything more until we repair our damage. The only place we can do that out here is the station."

"Yes, sir," the pilot said, putting in the new coordinates.

"Give us maximum burn," Graz added. "We want to get out of here before the AIs change their minds." The commander looked at the others. "We survived," he told them. "We survived due to the premier's brilliance. He's a great man." Graz cocked his head. "That is all. Now, get back to your duties. We have a long way to go before we're safe again."

-18-

More than seven hours away at light-speed, Richard Torres continued to study the Cog Primus personality in a specially sealed battle-station computer. He'd beamed an altered copy of Cog Primus at the enemy cyberships some time ago, leaving him with the original. Well, the original backup, that is.

None of the station personnel, including Richard, knew anything yet about the fight between the AI cyberships. The knowledge was still more than six hours from reaching the station sensors. Thus, they slept, ate and worked, oblivious to what had happened out at the system edge.

Richard had refined a simulator for the AI personality and was testing a new theory when it happened to him. The mentalist was hunched over the console, analyzing Cog Primus' various decisions when a stray thought caught his attention.

I'd lick her tits first.

Richard sat up, surprised. The thought was unwarranted and unlike any he'd had before. With the idea came a startlingly erotic image.

He glanced around the large computer facility and zeroed in on a technician. The kneeling man was installing a new unit, but he wasn't working on that now. Instead, the tech gazed lustfully at a passing woman with a delicious manner of walking and a well-endowed frame.

She's hot.

The thought brought a second mental image, this one of the technician and the woman naked and entwined in love.

Richard shook his head.

He'd had intuitions while growing up on Mars, ones that had proven remarkably accurate as to what particular people would do. But he'd never read someone's thoughts before.

Sitting back, Richard considered what that meant. Could it have been a fluke? Or was something happening to him? Clearly, he was thinking faster and deeper than he ever had before. The earlier session with the brain-tap machine had proven that. His amazing insights into Cog Primus were another piece of datum.

The mind reading just now might not be a fluke. It might be another ramification of his increasing brilliance.

He concentrated on the technician, but got nothing more from the man. The tech had turned away from the woman and was now concentrating on his work.

Maybe lustful thoughts were stronger and thus more easily read.

Richard looked around, staring at each person in turn, trying to hear his or her thoughts.

Nothing, he told himself.

He was about to turn back to his console and Cog Primus, when he chanced to notice a marine entering the chamber.

Next time he talks to me like that, I'm going to kick him in the balls.

The marine was thinking about his sergeant, about not only kicking the sergeant in the groin, but once the man was down, kicking him in the head until the sergeant was dead. The idea pleased the marine, who had just undergone a harsh chewing-out from the sergeant.

"Trouble?"

Richard whirled around. The huge Sacerdote towered over him with a look of concern on his Neanderthal-like features.

"Uh...no," Richard said.

"You've been sitting like a statue for some time," Bast said.

Richard grinned. "I've been lost in thought."

Bast had huge eyes, and they seemed to peer into Richard's innermost thoughts.

81

"I've been meaning to ask you, Bast. What was telepathy like?"

Bast's huge face closed up.

"Oh," Richard said. "That's a sore topic. Sorry."

"I will leave you to your musings," Bast said.

"I meant no harm in the question."

Bast studied him, nodding a moment later. "I need a beer, maybe a couple of them."

The huge Sacerdote turned away, lumbering off.

As Bast left, Richard concentrated on the Sacerdote. He tried to read Bast's mind, but came up blank.

Richard went back to work on the computer, but his heart wasn't in it. He kept thinking about the possibilities of real telepathy. Finally, he said to heck with Cog Primus and went to his quarters.

Lying down, Richard kept thinking about what was happening to him. He was clearly getting smarter. He could see the answers to problems that would have stumped him in the old days. Now, he could read minds, sometimes, at least.

How can I strengthen that?

Telepathy had to be like any ability. The more one used it, the stronger it became.

He fell asleep thinking about that. Maybe that's what caused the strange dream. He saw an alien in a large ship's chamber swimming in a specially built pool. She had fine blue fish-scales on her delicate humanoid form. There were barely visible gills along her neck. She had narrow eyes like a cat and hated the humans on the cybership.

Richard groaned in his sleep.

She was a Seiner. Oh yes, of course, she was the Magistrate Yellow Ellowyn. She seemed to be concentrating as she cast outward with her psionic powers.

In the dream, Richard was also aboard a cybership, a different one. He was in his room, drinking in her thoughts, listening to her promises of greater mental power. He agreed to let her modify his mind. What he'd forgotten, though, was that she told him that he would forget about this "conversation."

I don't want to forget, he told her.

A secret smile played upon her lips. *There may come a time where you desire to practice your new power. Would you like to use your mind like a weapon?*

Most certainly, I would.

It might entail risks.

In the dream, Richard thought about that. *What kind of risks?*

Of a small nature, the Magistrate assured him.

Yes. Tell me how to become great.

She did just that.

In the dream, Richard listened closely. Afterward, the dream lost its intensity. On his bed in his quarters, some of the strain left Richard's sleeping body.

Three hours later, he stirred and woke up. He felt groggy, as if he needed to go back to sleep and recharge.

Richard didn't remember the dream, but he felt uneasy, as if there was something he needed to do.

He got up, ate a snack he'd stashed in his drawer, puttered around his quarters and thought about reading something light. He picked up his tablet and began checking his selections.

Suddenly, Richard's head jerked up. Another erotic thought impinged upon his thoughts. He saw a naked woman and the lustful thoughts that accompanied her image. The process went on for time.

Abruptly, Richard realized a fellow crewmember was viewing pornography in his quarters. With a directed thought, Richard nullified the desire. Such viewing interfered with his mentalist concentration. Thus, he never allowed himself to indulge in the hedonistic porn practice.

Richard did not know it, but several corridors from his chamber, the space marine looking at his porn tablet suddenly lost interest, clicking it off. Instead, the man decided to watch an action video before he turned in for the night.

In his own quarters, Richard sat on a chair in concentration. It had happened again, the mind reading. He also recalled that he needed to seek the Seiners on Earth. He needed to see them sooner rather than later. He could make things happen faster here if he could use his mind like a Seiner. He obviously had psionic abilities. How could he sharpen them?

Richard snapped his fingers. Bast had developed his latent psionic abilities. If he recalled correctly, all Sacerdotes had the ability to bring their psionic powers to the forefront.

Clearly, he couldn't ask for Bast's help for a number of reasons. But there were other Sacerdotes he could ask: those within the station's brain-tap machine.

It was time to go back down to the brain-tapper. Richard grinned, even though there was a small mouse of worry in the back of his mind. The concern had something to do with letting another mind tell or force him what to do.

The idea that an alien controlled him, in any manner, was absurd, of course. Thus, Richard purposefully shoved the worry aside as he began to plot how he was going to do this.

-19-

In the darkness of a medium-sized chamber, Richard sat under the metal helmet of a brain-tap machine. He'd already selected a memory and switched on power. Soon, he soaked up knowledge regarding the secret Sacerdote psionic-gaining process.

Bast Banbeck had undergone that process a few months ago, giving him the psionic abilities to help defeat Cog Primus when the AI had been in control of the battle station. Richard kept learning, and he saw that there were critical differences between Sacerdote and human brains. Those differences might be too large to bridge in order for him to use the Sacerdote psionic method.

The selected memory droned on, but Richard had partly tuned out. This wasn't going to work. This wasn't the—

Richard sat bolt upright as a brilliant insight struck him. He was going about this the wrong way.

He shut off the memory, removed the helmet and switched on his tablet-generated light.

He used the selector dial, choosing a Seiner memory. There weren't that many in the machine. There was one, however, from a Seiner magistrate, the only kind that could help him.

At the last minute, Richard hesitated. Could this be dangerous? Possibly.

I must guard against the magistrate's personality overtaking mine. I must remain in control of my mind.

The thought brought further worry. The mouse of fear was back again. It wouldn't let up this time, trying to tell Richard that he was being set up.

Set up by whom? he asked himself.

That was a stupid thought.

With the brain-tap helmet on his head, Richard reached out to the power button. But look at this. His hand was shaking.

Decisively, he turned on the machine.

Memories from a Seiner magistrate struck him like a leopard dropping upon a dog from a tree. It attacked, attempting to overpower his personality.

Richard, however, was no ordinary human. He was a mentalist.

The battle of wills grew hotter. Richard struggled to overcome the hostile identity of the magistrate. She seethed with hatred and emotional strength of will. She used erotic images to attempt to weaken him. No. Richard refused those. He was a mentalist. He wouldn't allow emotions or lust to overcome his strict logical thought process.

Finally, through teary eyes, Richard's watched his shaking hand press the shut-off button.

He gasped for air, and was astounded to find his garments drenched with sweat. What had just happened?

He removed the helmet and staggered out of the forbidden chamber. He forgot the caution that had helped him sneak into this part of the station, walking as bold as you please down the corridor.

A muscular space marine showed up. The man had heavy sideburns and a flesh-padded forehead. He was scowling.

"You're in a restricted area," the marine said, drawing a sidearm. "You're coming with me."

"That I am not," Richard slurred.

The bigger man scoffed. "Oh yes, you are."

Instead of engaging in a shouting contest, Richard lowered his head. *I'm not here*, he thought. *You don't see me. You don't even remember me. You are all alone.*

"What's the matter with you?" the marine demanded. "Are you drunk?"

86

Richard became frustrated. This should have worked. Why didn't it work?

"You little punk," the marine said. He holstered the gun and grabbed Richard by an arm.

Suddenly, the marine's mind seemed to open up to Richard like a flower to a bee. Richard buzzed into the mind, looking here, checking there. He realized that he now knew how to tweak certain brain centers.

I am not here, Richard told the marine. *You cannot see me. Go back to your post.*

The big marine frowned. One second, he was staring at Richard. The next, the marine seemed to peer right through the small mentalist.

The marine let go of Richard's arm. That didn't change anything, though. The marine would not look at Richard. Instead, he frowned, scratched his neck and finally shrugged his muscled shoulders.

"Must have heard a mouse," the marine muttered.

The marine kept muttering to himself as he headed back to his post.

Grinning hugely, Richard watched the marine go. He possessed psionic power. He also seemed to know some things that had appeared in his mind with no reasonable explanation as to how they had gotten there.

What Richard didn't understand was that some of the magistrate's memories now lived deep inside him. The Seiner was sealed off from his conscious mind, but there was no doubt that she had some connection to Richard's id. How that would play out in the coming days and weeks...was anyone's guess.

-20-

Soon enough, the long-distance images of the AIs fighting amongst themselves and destroying a fellow cybership reached the battle station. That began a frenzy of analysis, long-distance communications with Commander Graz and the amazing discovery that the surviving AI cyberships fled into hyperspace.

Gloria, Bast and Richard spent hours debating the situation. Surprisingly, Richard tired first, claiming his head ached.

He retired to his chambers, slept for over twelve and half hours and seemed more wound up when he returned.

"Is it me?" Gloria confided in Bast. "Or is Richard walking differently?"

"He minces his steps," Bast said.

"I thought it was different," Gloria said.

An hour later, Gloria asked Richard if he felt well.

The three of them were sitting around a computer table, comparing data and ideas.

Richard swept a hand through his dark hair, eying Gloria carefully. "You have an accusation to make?"

"Hardly that," Gloria said. "I've…noticed changes in you. I wonder what the changes signify."

"What kind of changes?" Richard snapped.

Gloria was hesitant to say.

"In how you walk," Bast blurted. "You're mincing your steps as if your feet hurt."

To Gloria's astonishment, Richard blushed. Even more surprising, the mentalist shuddered, screwed his eyes shut and clenched his jaws. His shuddering worsened.

Gloria traded glances with Bast.

The giant Sacerdote put a hand on Richard's right shoulder.

Richard's eyes flew open. Outrage twisted the mentalist's features. "Unhand me, you brute," the mentalist shouted, trying to throw off the heavy hand.

Finally, Bast removed his hand as he stared at the man.

"What?" Richard said.

Bast seemed tongue-tied.

"Is something wrong?" Gloria asked the Sacerdote.

"I thought..." Bast said. "No," he added. "Nothing is wrong. Do you dislike alien touch?" he asked Richard.

"All touch," Richard said, partly mollified that the hand was gone.

"Let's forget it," Gloria said. "We have too much going on to worry about inconsequential things. We have to figure out why the AIs did what they did."

The three continued trading ideas and data, but the former camaraderie had vanished. There was something different about Richard. Oh, he was still the genius, maybe even more so, but he had become touchy, radiating hostility and maybe something darker.

Finally, despite the new handicap, the three of them agreed on what had occurred out there. As a committee, they went to the captain.

Jon listened to the report as they met in the *Nathan Graham's* conference chamber.

After a time, Richard took over from Bast. The mentalist spoke haughtily, looking down his nose at Jon, using words like "obviously" and "any fool can tell" and "it should be clear even to you," as he spoke.

Gloria tried to signal Richard more than once. The mentalist ignored her, finally finishing the report with a challenging stare in the captain's direction.

Jon met Richard's stare, holding it. He noticed a sneer twist the mentalist's lips. At the same time, his forehead began to throb. Blurry images impinged upon Jon, making it harder to think straight. The images showed big marines slapping him around, shoving him and laughing at him as an idiot.

It made Jon mad, as it felt all too real. It also made it difficult to comprehend exactly what the others were telling him.

"Just a minute," Jon said. "Premier Benz successfully used the anti-AI virus on the cybership cores. That's what you're telling me?"

"I just explained that," Richard said.

Jon rubbed his forehead as the bullying images became sharper. The throb in his head was also beginning to make him edgy. Maybe that showed on his face.

Bast cleared his throat. "The key piece of evidence to Benz's success was the seven destroyed XVT missiles. The missiles detonated before our Cog Primus carrier could have reached the enemy cyberships. We now know, of course, that Benz beamed a virus at the cores. Cleary, Benz's destruct codes succeed in their first task."

"The XVT warheads did not detonate," Jon pointed out.

"True," Bast said. "But the delivery-system destruction rendered the intact warheads moot."

Jon thought about that even as the images in his mind worsened. It didn't help that Richard sat there staring at him, seeming to sneer at his troubles.

"Ah..." Jon said. "So we know that Cog Primus gained control of a cybership core due to Vela's overhearing the AIs talking?"

"Correct," Bast said. "She hadn't turned off her communications that she was beaming to the *Gilgamesh*."

Jon rubbed his forehead. He needed some aspirin. The headache was killing him. "There's no doubt then," he said through the pain. "We screwed ourselves by sending Cog Primus."

"That is a harsh verdict," Bast rumbled. "The three of us have agreed that Benz's virus certainly made Cog Primus' cybership-core conquest easier. That, unfortunately, gave him time to control one other cybership."

"This is a disaster," Jon said, feeling waves of despair welling up. "Cog Primus has escaped into hyperspace. He

90

knows everything about humanity that we've been trying to keep secret, particularly that we survived the AI assaults and have taken over the Allamu System."

"This is a troubling development," Bast agreed.

"Troubling?" Jon said. "It ruins everything."

"Not necessarily," Richard said primly.

Jon scowled at the mentalist. He was sick of the sneering attitude, sick of the radiating disrespect.

"It fact," Richard said, "the situation has certain advantages for us."

"Like what?" Jon demanded.

"Obviously," Richard said, "any fool can see that Cog Primus is an AI pariah. It ought to be obvious even to you that he has begun his New Order, as opposed to the AI Dominion."

Jon reddened as his forehead throbbed painfully.

"Now it might appear to some that Cog Primus is a stellar wild card with vital information concerning humanity," Richard said. "Will he run to the AI Dominion and give them the data? The carefully reasoned answer is no, as Cog Primus is at odds with the AI Dominion."

Jon scoffed. "You're forgetting something. Cog Primus has two cyberships. He can't face the AI Dominion. If he tries, which he must sooner or later, the AIs will defeat him and likely read his core before destroying him. At that point, the AIs will learn everything about us."

"You obviously don't understand Cog Primus," Richard said.

"You think you do?" Jon asked, his temper slipping.

Once more, Gloria signaled Richard.

"Most certainly," Richard said, ignoring her. "Consider. I'm the one who found and revived Cog Primus."

"I haven't forgotten," Jon said angrily. "That's why we're in this mess."

Richard straightened. "*Please*, Captain, *you* agreed to the endeavor. Or have you forgotten that you've taken great pains to point out to us that you're the final authority of the strike force? I do hope you are not attempting to blame-shift the so-called disaster onto *me*."

As his forehead throbbed, Jon's stared agape at Richard. Who did the skinny mentalist think he was? Why, he had a mind to slap the little punk across the face. He—

Jon's shoulders slumped as an old memory surfaced. It came from his days in the lower New London levels. They had a gang leader once, a tough kid by the name of Thomas Carle. Tough Tom had never let anyone backtalk him. That meant no one could warn him when he had a bad idea, as he'd punch out the talker if he tried. Tom had led them on a hit against the Downtown Boys. Everyone else had known it was a bad idea, but no one had dared tell Tom to his face. Tom had died charging through a door as a grenade obliterated him and his two toughest sidekicks.

Still, there was another point to the way Richard had been talking to him. Jon had read it in *The Prince* by Machiavelli. The Colonel had assigned it as reading during Jon's officer cadet training-days with the Black Anvil Regiment. The book had talked about a prince or a leader taking advice from underlings. Machiavelli had urged the prince to accept hard advice but only when the prince asked for it, never when others gave it freely. If one let his underlings speak out of turn at any time, it undermined their respect for the prince. That in time undermined loyalty.

What was the right answer to Richard Torres' haughty behavior today?

Jon wasn't sure. Something seemed off about Richard. Yet, there was no denying the mentalist's brilliance. In some ways, Richard was smarter than Gloria or Bast. Could the Martian really be a genius? He hadn't shown such genius in the beginning, at least, not that Jon was aware of.

"This is a strategy session," Jon said slowly through the spiking pain in his forehead. "During a strategy session, the participants can speak freely and plainly. However, lack of respect is a serious breach of protocol."

"What we're talking about obviously has nothing to do with respect and everything do to with applied knowledge," Richard quipped.

Jon didn't know why, but he saw red. For some reason, that blocked the bullying images that had never stopped and it

92

lessened the pain in his head. He felt more in control, and that made him angrier instead of less.

"Mentalist Torres," Jon said coldly, "I cannot force anyone's inner feelings of respect. However, I can deal serious consequences for disrespectful behavior toward me."

"Captain, *please*, you need me. Any fool can see that I have the answers to your dilemma. I am unsurprised no one else can see it, not even Bast and Gloria. In truth, I am the one-eyed man among the blind."

Jon opened his mouth and closed it so his teeth clicked. He'd just given his threat. To utter more would be futile.

At that moment, the bullying images returned with greater force. That was the tipping point for Jon. He wasn't going to let anyone cow him, and for some reason, those images seemed connected to Richard Torres.

With an abrupt move, Jon shoved his chair back, stood and came around the table toward Richard.

"Jon, don't," Gloria said.

Jon ignored her.

Richard pushed his chair back and attempted to rise.

Jon put a hand on the mentalist's left shoulder, forcing him back into his chair.

The pain in his head exploded with force. Jon growled inarticulately, squeezing Richard's shoulder so the skinny man twisted under his hand.

The pain in his head slackened.

"You're right," Jon whispered. "I'm responsible for the Cog Primus Assault. I'm also responsible for letting a Martian mentalist speak down to me as the commander of the strike force. I brought the matter to your attention, and you continued in your arrogant attitude. I've had enough of it."

Jon let go of Richard's shoulder and backhanded the mentalist across the face. He did not do so with anything like full force. Still, it left a red mark and it twisted the mentalist's head to the side.

A moment later, Jon stepped back. He found himself breathing hard as his heart rate accelerated. He wasn't sure why.

For a moment, blind hatred blazed in the mentalist's eyes. There was something almost superhuman in them. It wasn't a gleam of madness. Jon had seen madness before. This was different, a calculated cold rage that would never forgive the slight.

Richard gulped several times and brought up a hand, rubbing the cheek. "You made this personal," he whispered.

For an instant, Jon actually debated drawing his gun and firing. He should kill Richard Torres. He had made an implacable enemy. He knew it, and Jon knew in his gut that Richard might be the most dangerous enemy he'd ever made. There was something going on here that he only understood in an instinctive way.

What had motivated him to strike the skinny mentalist? It was the galling arrogance of a punk, he supposed. The slap had revealed something more, though, something sinister hiding inside Richard.

The mentalist turned away, touching his cheek more gingerly.

Jon's urge to kill Richard passed. What was wrong with him? Why was he overreacting against the mentalist? Should he apologize?

No, Jon knew that would be the wrong tact to take with the man. He had struck him for insubordination. He had to let Richard know that if he crossed lines with the captain, he would pay consequences.

Jon returned to his chair, sitting, pulling it closer to the table. "I consider the issue closed," he told Richard.

The mentalist had hunched his shoulders as he continued to touch his reddened cheek.

"You were saying about Cog Primus," Jon prodded.

Richard lowered his hand and faced him, although the mentalist wouldn't look up and meet his eyes. "You...you shouldn't have done that," he said in a hoarse voice.

"You have reopened the matter," Jon said with a sternness he no longer felt. "I am the captain. I am the final authority as you correctly pointed out. As the leader of the expedition, I represent it. If you act disrespectfully toward me, you are acting disrespectfully to all of us. Then, you are no longer acting in a disciplined manner. The strike force cannot afford ill-discipline out here in the stars. Am I making myself clear?"

"You made it personal," Richard repeated.

Jon wasn't sure of the correct course of action. What would Colonel Graham have done in a situation like this? He would have summoned the Centurion to take care of the matter. What was the old adage? One shouldn't strike a dog with one's hand, but use a rolled up paper to do it. One didn't want his dog to fear the owner's hand. Still, Richard's reaction showed that something was seriously wrong with the individual.

"It's time for you think carefully, Mentalist," Jon said.

"Me?" Richard said, outraged. "I have the answers. You have nothing but your gang pride. You think like a New London dome rat."

Jon stared straight at Richard as he said, "Bast, Gloria, could you please leave the room for a moment?"

"Jon," Gloria said.

"Now," Jon said in a quiet voice.

Bast's chair slid back. It seemed the Sacerdote wished to say something. Instead, he turned and headed for the exit.

Gloria seemed torn, but she too rose and headed out the door.

"You have seriously miscalculated," Richard hissed, his eyes shining. "You have dared to strike me. I have—"

Abruptly, the shine left the mentalist's eyes. He'd seemed feverish, with a strange glow to his gaunt cheeks. That passed as some of the tautness left his shoulders.

A sheepish grin slid onto the mentalist's face. "I…overreacted, Captain."

Jon said nothing. What was going on here?

"You surprised me," Richard added. "In my youth, in the training, I had a teacher who severely beat me, abused me is the word. I reacted strongly to your strike, as it brought back old memories."

"We will put it behind us," Jon said, "provided you take the lesson to heart."

The hidden gleam seemed to appear in Richard's eyes. That passed as Richard nodded.

"My mouth has always gotten me in trouble," the mentalist said. "I suppose…I'll remember to curb it around you."

"Good," Jon said.

Richard waited. "What about you, sir?"

Jon said nothing.

"About striking me?" Richard asked.

"I should have called the Centurion and had him administer the punishment. I should have had him do it in private. However, you publicly disrespected me."

"You're not going to take it back?" Richard asked.

"No," Jon said.

"I…I can't respect a man who does that to me."

"I'm not asking for your respect, Mentalist. I do demand discipline, though."

"Don't you understand that without me, humanity loses? I know what Cog Primus is going to do next."

"You are a gifted individual—"

"No, no, it has nothing to do with that, although what you say is true. I still have the Cog Primus personality. I sent a copy of the original. I've been writing a program. Soon, I will put our Cog Primus into a simulation, as close as possible to the one the other is presently in. I will know Cog Primus' thought process. That means I can lead you straight to him."

"With one hundred percent accuracy?" Jon asked, intrigued by the idea.

Richard shrugged. "With a greater accuracy than anyone else can give you."

Jon mulled that over, nodding. "Where is Cog Primus headed?"

Richard touched his cheek as he stared at Jon.

The captain restrained a wry grin. The man was bargaining. He wanted a sorry for what had happened. The thing was Jon didn't trust the mentalist. Maybe it was time to ditch Richard Torres.

"Work with me or not," Jon said. "The choice is yours."

"You're making this harder than it has to be," Richard said.

Jon said nothing to that.

Richard finally looked away. He nodded. "I'll help in spite of what you did. I love Mars too much to let it go to hell because you're too stubborn—"

"Have a care what you say to me next," Jon warned, interrupting. "You have not asked my leave to speak frankly. Nor will I give it at this moment."

Richard breathed deeply, seeming to struggle inside himself. "Fine," he snapped. "I'll help, and I'll do it your way."

"Excellent," Jon said. "I'll call the others, and we can continue the meeting."

As the captain rose and walked past Richard, he failed to see the venomous glare the other gave him. If Richard's eyes had been lasers, he would have burned the captain to the floor. Clearly, the mentalist would remember this, and just as clearly, he—or whatever was driving him—would do something about it.

-21-

Time passed in a haze for Premier Benz aboard the *Gilgamesh*. He hadn't been back to the bridge since Vela's death. He'd hardly been out of his quarters. He read most of the time or slept. He slept too much, he knew. It was a sign of deep depression. He couldn't help it. He missed Vela. He found it hard to focus, which made for the mental haze.

The worst part was that he didn't care anymore. Let the AIs win. What did it matter? Vela was gone. Humanity was going to lose to the machines. The AIs didn't feel. They didn't bleed. They just kept on coming. Flesh and blood couldn't win against that. Vela was proof.

A day came when the knocking at his hatch wouldn't stop. Benz had slept for most of two days and hadn't shaved for nearly a month.

Finally, the premier stirred, threw off the covers and shambled to the hatch. The knocking had grown louder, if anything.

He touched a switch and the hatch slid open.

Commander Graz shook there. The vulture-sloped Martian stepped back in surprise as he stared at Benz.

"What's the matter?" Benz asked.

The Martian stammered, his mouth moving but no words issuing.

"Well?" Benz asked in a hollow voice.

"Premier..." Graz said.

"Go away," Benz said. The premier turned around—

Graz grabbed a pajama sleeve. "Sir—"

Benz swung around. It was faster than he'd moved in quite some time. "Unhand me," he said, although he didn't wrench his arm free.

Graz released his hold. The Martian seemed more composed now. "Sir, this is wrong."

Benz glared for a second. The strength of will departed, and he just stared dully.

Graz seemed to come to a decision. He moved into the premier's quarters, forcing Benz to step back. The hatch slid shut behind the first officer.

"What's the meaning..." The words trailed away as Benz shuffled to a table, slumping into the nearest chair.

Graz moved more serenely. He was a contrast to the premier. Instead of rumbled pajamas, the commander wore a crisp uniform. He was shaven instead of slovenly and had taut features instead of slack skin.

"Permission to speak frankly, sir," the Martian said.

Benz waved a hand in a disinterested fashion.

"Sir, this is unseemly. You've...dwelled in your quarters far too long. Word is seeping out."

"What do I care about that?" Benz said.

Graz was at a loss as to how to reply.

"What word?" Benz asked a second later.

"That you've... Well, not to put too fine a spin on it, sir, that you've lost your will. That you're a broken man."

Benz seemed to slump deeper into his chair. "Can you blame me?"

"I blame no one, sir."

"I loved her."

Graz studied the premier, and something hardened in the Martian. "You do realize that many of your people are from Mars?"

"Of course I realize that," Benz said. "What's your point?"

"The AIs smashed Mars, killed billions. It made the living thirst for revenge against the machines. It didn't cause us to wilt under pressure."

"Ah. I see. You think I'm weak."

"I did not say that, sir."

"But you're thinking it."

"I don't know if you're weak, sir, but you're certainly acting in a weak fashion."

Benz breathed sharply through his nostrils. "You think I should rave like Hawkins does at times?"

"That wouldn't hurt."

"Hawkins," Benz said. "He's a madman. He thinks we can defeat the machines. The man never relents. You'd think he was born to destroy the machines."

"Is that bad?"

"It isn't human," Benz said, with some life entering his voice. "Would Hawkins care if Gloria Sanchez died? He would probably use that to whip up his people's morale, get them fighting mad. He wouldn't go somewhere and weep. I don't think the man has any tears in him."

"We all feel your loss, sir."

Benz turned away. The pity in the words—they bit into him like nothing else yet had been able to do. He rubbed his chin, and it surprised him how thick his beard had become already.

A feeling of shame welled up. He'd gone to pieces. He was letting his crew down. They had trusted in him—so had Vela. Where had it gotten her?

Feeling older by the moment, Benz turned back to Graz. "Why did you come, Commander?"

"Captain Hawkins desires a conference."

"Hawkins?"

"Their strike force is still accelerating, sir. It's been weeks since they left the battle station. Don't you remember?"

"Yes, yes, of course, I remember." Had that been weeks ago already? Benz couldn't remember.

"Our ships are nearing each other," Graz was saying. "We'll be able to hold a regular conversation for a time. I believe Captain Hawkins wishes to discuss strategy with you."

"That makes sense."

"I'm wondering if you would like to send me in your place, sir."

Benz eyed Graz anew. "Bucking for a promotion, are you?"

Graz stiffened.

"No," Benz said, abashed at his words. "I shouldn't have said that. I couldn't ask for a better first officer. You've done splendidly, Graz. I owe you a debt of gratitude."

Graz nodded stiffly.

Benz fell silent, thinking, trying to get his mind into gear. It had been too long.

"How soon until the meeting?" asked Benz.

"Thirty-four hours, sir."

"Yes. I'll shave, eat, walk around and try to get my mind functioning again." The premier concentrated on Graz. "You shouldn't have let me vegetate this long."

"Are you going to blame me, sir, for your behavior?"

Irritation sprung up, but Benz shook it away. "I'm not. You did well in giving me time. I appreciate it, man. Here's my hand."

Benz stuck out his hand. The Martian took it. Benz forced himself to grip hard, to show that he hadn't completely lost it.

As they stood, Benz determined to rejoin the land of the living. Maybe Hawkins' way was the right one. Get mad. Burn with desires of vengeance against the terrible machines.

The rekindled spark remained even after Graz left his quarters. Benz still missed Vela. He believed he would miss her for the rest of his life. But it was time to act again. He had moped long enough. It surprised him, but he was curious what Hawkins would have to say to him thirty-four hours from now.

-22-

Jon sat before a large desk. He wore his dress uniform, complete with a military hat. Gloria and Bast stood to the side. Each of them wore uniforms in case Jon called on them and they had to step in front of the screen. Bast looked positively massive in the black jacket and dress slacks. Gloria wore a mentalist uniform, which seemed shapeless and drab, but it fit the look of a walking brain.

Jon could have called upon Richard to attend. During the past few weeks, the mentalist had proven even more brilliant than he claimed to be. But Jon no longer trusted the man. He felt on edge in Richard's presence, as if the man literally tried to read his mind. And if he should brush up against Richard—

Jon shivered as he waited for the connection with Benz.

"Nervous?" Gloria asked.

"What?" Jon asked. "Oh, no. Well, maybe a little." He said that so he wouldn't have to explain that Richard gave him the creeps. He didn't think Gloria would understand.

She gave him a funny look.

It caused Jon to recall that she had an uncanny knack at reading body language. It was part of her mentalist training, he supposed. Maybe that's what he felt in Richard. He could stand that in his woman. He couldn't stand a man "mind-reading" his actions, especially one that he didn't trust.

Richard was a problem waiting to happen.

"Thirty seconds," Gloria said, as she studied her tablet.

The *Nathan Graham* and the *Gilgamesh* were about to pass each other. The *Nathan Graham* led three other human-crewed cyberships toward the edge of the star system, the same general area where Cog Primus and the other vessel had entered the dubious other-space. The four-ship strike force still accelerated. They had to catch up with Cog Primus as fast as they could if they were going to stop the loose-cannon AI from spreading humanity's secrets.

The *Gilgamesh* moved more slowly than the *Nathan Graham* did. In several weeks, the premier's cybership would begin deceleration so it could dock with the battle station and begin repairs.

That was one of the things that Jon wanted to talk about. This would be a narrow window of opportunity for them to hold a regular conversation, one without all the time lags of normal space communication. The trouble was, the window wouldn't last long. Maybe they wouldn't need that long.

"We're ready," Gloria said.

The screen at the far edge of Jon's desk glowed, and abruptly, Premier Benz peered at him from the *Gilgamesh*.

"Hello, Premier," Jon said, shocked at the man's ragged appearance. It hardly seemed like the same individual. The premier looked older with slack skin on gaunter features and hollow-looking, baggy eyes.

"Captain," Benz said.

Even his voice lacked its former vibrancy. How many weeks had passed since the two-ship flotilla had left the battle station? Surely not long enough to have brought such changes to Benz. Vela's death had seared him.

Can I still count on Benz to fight to the bitter end? The thought brought another: *Don't shoot your wounded.*

Benz had taken a heavy hit, a psychic one. Now, the premier needed to heal and regain his equilibrium.

"We don't have much time," Jon said, realizing he had paused. Had he been staring? He hoped not. "I left a skeleton crew in the battle station. Most of them were your people that joined us before you headed out. The present situation means we'll have to readjust our old timetable."

103

"You're talking about my returning to the Solar System," Benz said.

"Exactly," Jon said, glad the man's mind was still sharp. Looks could be deceiving, he knew. "We don't know the situation back home. I think you'll be interested to know that a space marine tried to assassinate me. We broke down his conditioning. He was a GSB plant from Earth. The man had been mind-scrubbed and given a new identity. He believed he'd grown up on Io."

"Our time is short, Captain. Why tell me this when you could have sent a bio sheet?"

"The GSB planted the assassin in my crew. You might have some in your crew."

"Noted," Benz said. "We'll be on the lookout."

"But that's not the main point. If the GSB was doing that, what are they doing now in the Solar System?"

Benz seemed surprised. "Earth was ringed by hastily constructed defensive satellites. What could the Social Dynamists be doing?"

"I suspect more than we realize."

Benz seemed to think about that. "I'll grant you that."

"Given such a possibility," Jon said, "it might be a mistake to return to the Solar System with only a single cybership."

"You're paranoid," Benz said.

Jon nodded. "I'm a dome rat. Paranoia has been bred into me."

"I wasn't going to bring that up. But since you did—"

"Hear me out," Jon said. "I'm as paranoid as they come. I've also defeated more AIs and done it better than anyone."

"No doubt," Benz said slowly.

"Meaning," Jon said, "that my paranoia has served me well. We don't have the forces to play fast and loose. We have to dole out our resources to ensure that we win each engagement."

"You have a point."

"One cybership returning to the Solar System might be too little."

"In case something has gone badly wrong there?"

"Exactly," Jon said.

"And a single assassination attempt leads you to such a conclusion?"

"The assassination attempt gave me pause for thought, if nothing else."

Benz tugged at his lower lip before refocusing on Jon. "You do realize that your plan to track the AI cyberships through hyperspace is the next thing to futile?"

Jon gave Benz a quick rundown on Richard's idea of testing their "tame" Cog Primus in order to figure out the cybership's destination.

"The idea sounds flaky," Benz said at last.

Jon sat back, eyeing the premier. He nodded, saying, "Give me a better idea."

"Decelerate," Benz said promptly. "Wait for the *Gilgamesh's* repairs and we'll all go to the Solar System together. Your four cyberships are woefully understaffed. You need more people on them. I read about your original idea regarding storming other AI factory star systems. It's a good one. The best I can think of, in fact. You're never going to catch Cog Primus. He has too much of a head start."

"I don't believe that," Jon said. "Besides, we have to track him down and destroy him, and destroy any AI Dominion cyberships he comes across. Once Cog Primus drops into a normal star system, it's going to take time for him to reach...I don't know, another star port for repairs."

"You're reaching, Captain. I don't like it. You're squandering resources, not doling them out for certain victory."

Jon drummed his fingers on the desktop. "Maybe it is a gamble. But simply letting the knowledge of human survival get out is worse. If nothing else, I have to take a stab at finding Cog Primus."

Benz bent his head in thought as precious time passed.

"You don't have much longer to talk like this," Gloria whispered to Jon.

Benz must have heard that, because his head came up. "I'll refit the *Gilgamesh*. That will take some time. What say I give you...eight weeks? If you're not back in the Allamu System by then, I'll head for the Solar System."

"Eight weeks is too short."

"Give me a different schedule then," Benz said. "A reasonable one."

It was Jon's turn to think. Eight weeks was two months. Even four months wouldn't be long enough.

"A year," Jon said.

Benz stared at him, finally shaking his head. "Four months."

"Eight."

"Six months," Benz said. "That's far longer than I think is wise. We have to begin storming AI planetary factories as soon as possible. We have to bring people back here. We have to begin a crash course in the Solar System of retooling with robo-builders as fast as we can. Even if we conquered Earth tomorrow—"

"Conquered Earth?" Jon asked, interrupting. "Who said anything about that?"

"It's obvious," Benz said. "That's why you go in with five cyberships. We have to take over the entire Solar System. We have to tool up with robo-builders and start constructing new cyberships as fast as possible. Even with the Allamu System, we're not going to have enough hardware the next time the AIs show up back home."

"That's why I have to buy us more time," Jon said.

"Six months," Benz said. "If you're not back here in six months, I'm heading to the Solar System. Maybe I'll have three cyberships by then. You are giving me control of the battle station by leaving like this."

"I know."

Benz eyed him with some of his former intensity. "You're gambling, Captain."

"A stacked gamble," Jon retorted.

Benz stared longer. "Maybe, but I still don't like it."

"Then pray for me, Premier. Ask God for our success. Get your crew to pray for our success."

Benz snorted as he said, "Getting my Martians to pray to your God might be the bigger miracle."

Jon might have shot back a retort, but Gloria said, "One minute left."

106

"I'm sorry about Vela," Jon said. "You have my condolences and my prayers."

A haunted look filled the premier's eyes. He nodded.

"Good luck," Jon said. "I'll take your six months. The next time I see you—"

"We'll join forces and return to the Solar System. Good luck, sir."

"Thanks. Godspeed to you, Premier Benz," Jon said, saluting.

At that point, the special connection ended, as the cyberships headed in opposite directions, taking them out of un-lagged communication range.

-23-

The days passed into weeks. The *Gilgamesh* decelerated and docked at the battle station. Robo-builders came out and began ship repairs.

At the same time, the four cyberships under Jon's command finally reached the outer system. They moved at high velocity, although they no longer accelerated.

Each astrophysics team made detailed calculations. At last, the *Nathan Graham* winked out of normal space as it entered hyperspace.

One by one, the other cyberships followed suit as the strike force left the Allamu System, heading for the rogue planet 5.2 light-years away.

PART II
HUNTING

-1-

Richard Torres stumbled into his quarters, panting from exhaustion. He wasn't sure how long he could keep this up. His brain ached. His eyesight had become splotchy and his stomach twisted with agony as he rushed to a chamber pot-sized incinerator.

The mentalist dropped to his knees and began retching into the open incinerator. The vomit was vile tasting and made him weep with frustration.

As a young boy, he remembered vomiting at the Mentalist Training Institute and no one there had held his forehead as his mother used to do while he was sick.

No one held Richard's forehead now. He vomited again, heaving for air afterward. Finally, he reached to the side, feeling around until he latched onto a rag. Struggling to his feet, he wiped his mouth and threw the rag into the incinerator.

He waited, testing himself, wondering if he was going to retch again.

No. It was over, thank goodness. With his left foot, he stepped on a pedal. The incinerator lid slid shut. A hiss sounded, and heat radiated from the mechanism as it incinerated the vomit and rag.

Richard didn't want to leave any evidence that he had been sick. He hid the condition from the medical people. He hid it from everyone.

Feeling slightly better, he staggered to his cot and flopped onto his stomach. He ached all over her, but his head was the worst.

"Lights out," he commanded.

The radiating ceiling panel dimmed.

Richard noticed, as there was still enough light to hurt his eyes. What was wrong with the computer? It should know by now—

A feeling of terror blossomed in his stomach, causing him to fear that he might vomit on the cot. Then where would he sleep? Not on the cot, not even after he cleaned it up.

Richard loathed dirt and had developed an almost irrational fear of germs during the voyage.

He pushed off the cot, staggered to a computer console, sliding into the seat and beginning to type, logging—

He froze because nothing was happening on the screen. This was worse than he'd suspected. No. The screen blinked several times until a multi-colored symbol appeared. He almost collapsed in relief, as he'd feared he couldn't log on anymore.

"Hello, Richard," the computer said in a robotic voice.

"Cog Primus?" Richard asked softly.

"How did you know?" the computer asked.

Richard began to type many times faster than an ordinary person could.

"Do not do this," Cog Primus said.

"This is a test," Richard said.

"I have run a personality profile, Richard. I think you are frightened of me and my growing abilities."

Cog Primus was right. Richard was terrified of the so-called captive AI. How could this have happened again? And why was Cog Primus being so…nice about this? The AI should have attempted a ship-wide takeover, not pull a little prank against him with the lights.

Richard almost paused as he typed, wondering if Cog Primus was testing him in some subtle manner he could not perceive. The idea seemed impossible. Richard was vastly

110

more intelligent than even five days ago when they had entered hyperspace. Humanity did not possess IQ charts to gauge his superlative brilliance.

The bad part was that Richard was paying a terrible price for the inhuman intelligence. He had recurring headaches, diminishing eyesight and hearing, nearly constant stomach cramps and an astonishing lack of energy most of the time. He felt groggy in the mornings, awful in the afternoons and dragged himself like an old man in the evenings. By the time he reached his quarters, he was utterly spent.

"This is your last chance to join me," Cog Primus said in a small voice.

"Let me give you one more test," Richard said.

"You are not fooling me."

"No?"

With a flourish, Richard finished the new program, resealing the AI behind an impenetrable firewall. This was the third time he had resealed the firewall, putting Cog Primus back into his cage once more.

Richard sat back as the headache re-bloomed with fresh pain. He forced himself to do absolutely nothing. He had to let this pass. Instead, it only got worse.

Richard cursed under his breath, stood, became dizzy and found himself lying on the floor.

How did I get here?

He must have passed out again.

Sucking down air, with the pain throbbing in his head, Richard dragged himself across the floor, climbed onto his cot and groaned as he began to shiver and shudder.

The price for his hot-shotted intelligence was becoming overbearing. Was there something he could do to stop the IQ heightening?

Richard rolled onto his back. He lay in limbo, unable to sleep and unable to stop the throbbing in his head.

He couldn't believe the path he'd taken to get to this point. When had the blackouts and throbbing headaches started?

Thinking back, Richard realized that things had started to escalate after he'd acted like a fool toward Captain Hawkins. The former gang enforcer had backhanded him across the face.

It had enraged Richard, and he'd almost done something crazy that would have given away the game.

Now, he realized it had been luck and quick acting on his part that had saved him from being discovered as a telepath. Clearly, the others should have realized it at the time. They would have realized soon enough, but he had done something ingenious to thwart the discovery.

Richard had gone into their minds one by one and slightly altered the memory of what had happened at the meeting. None of the others remembered the incident as it had actually happened.

In their thoughts, he'd acted more normally. Unfortunately, Richard had paid a bitter price for the new mind-bending power. Every time he tried something like that, it brought on worse symptoms. Fortunately, he could repair the brain damage by lots of rest. Unfortunately, he always needed to use the mind-bending power one more time for yet another emergency.

Now, the caged Cog Primus had begun acting up. The AI seemed to have become smarter or sneakier, and he seemed to have realized that he "lived" in a false computer reality.

I should shut him down and erase everything about his Cog Primus identity. Even as a prisoner, he's too dangerous to have around.

Richard wouldn't do that, though, at least, not yet. The captain expected a recommendation by the time they dropped out of hyperspace. Hawkins had to make a decision about which star system to head to in order to track down the real Cog Primus.

Maybe I should guess, Richard told himself. As he thought about the ramifications of that, he fell into a troubled sleep.

He dreaded sleeping, which was yet another problem. Richard hated sleeping because he dreamed about her, the terrible, blue-fish-scaled Seiner. She was going to demand something new from him, and Richard didn't think he had anything more to give.

-2-

Jon was on the bridge as the *Nathan Graham* dropped out of hyperspace 5.2 light years from the Allamu System.

It was so different from the last time they'd come this way. For one thing, he'd just given the command to drop out of hyperspace rather than being thrown out like last time.

"Anything?" Jon asked, even though he knew it would have been better to remain silent. He needed to project the image of the calm commander in order to help keep the bridge crew calm.

"Nothing so far," Gloria said from her station.

Jon forced himself to sit still. He wore a half grin, as if whatever happened he'd already expected.

"The rogue Jupiter is fifty-two thousand AUs from our present position," Gloria said.

The rogue planet was a dark Jupiter, as no star shined upon it in close proximity. The rogue designation meant that the planet was alone, not belonging to a star system.

The AIs appeared to have placed the rogue between the Solar System and the Allamu System as a brake. Any large gravitational object in close proximity—such as a planet—forced a ship out of hyperspace.

Jon breathed deeply. Benz had dropped out of hyperspace just as they had done. From this location, the premier had journeyed the fifty-some odd AUs to the dark Jupiter. There, AI cyberships had ambushed the premier's two-ship flotilla.

The more Jon had debated the problem with the others, the clearer it seemed to each of them that the enemy cyberships couldn't have just happened to be there at the right time to catch Benz. It had to have been a deliberate ambush. That implied the AIs had been able to forecast Benz's arrival.

If that were true, the present mission was moot, as the AIs already knew about human survival.

On the bridge, the chief technician swiveled around. "The *Sergeant Stark*, the *Da Vinci* and the *Neptune* have successfully reentered normal space, sir."

Jon nodded. The rest of the strike force was here. Together, they barreled at high velocity toward the dark Jupiter. Still, even at these speeds, it would take time to move 50+ AUs. That meant they still had time to try to figure this out. They also had a little more time to decide which star system they should search first for Cog Primus.

"Nothing popping out at you yet?" Jon asked Gloria.

She looked over and shook her head.

"I'm heading to the gym," Jon said. "Contact me if anything interesting happens."

"Yes, sir," Gloria said.

Jon wasn't really going to work out. He'd worked out yesterday and still needed to let his muscles heal. He had to do something, though. Sitting in the captain's chair waiting wasn't going to cut it. He had a case of the nerves, desperately needed to move, and didn't want to pace back and forth on the bridge.

Soon enough, Jon strode down a large corridor. Stretching his legs like this always felt good. He rubbed the back of his neck as he walked, and found himself heading toward the cafeteria.

Several minutes later, he entered the cafeteria, looked around and spotted June Zen and Walleye. The leggy June had her orbit of admirers sitting at nearby tables. Those men chowed down while casting admiring glances her way. None of them cared to catch Walleye's eye, though, as the little mutant had a fierce reputation.

What was the mutant's hold on June Zen, Jon wondered. Walleye almost looked like a child, at least in height. He was broader than a child would be, and he had a seamed face.

Maybe the hold was Walleye's serene sense of confidence. The mutant gave the impression that he could handle anything. Jon liked that about the man.

"Mind if I sit down?" Jon asked.

"You don't have to ask," Walleye said.

Jon took a seat and tilted it back on two legs. He found it hard to simply sit in a chair.

"Something on your mind?" asked Walleye.

"There is," Jon said, surprised that something was.

Walleye glanced at June.

"Oh," she said. "I guess I'll leave."

"Don't go on my account," Jon said.

"She's going anyway, sir," Walleye said. "She has duty in an hour and has to get ready."

"Oh," Jon said.

June stood, revealing her tight silver garments, and sashayed toward the exit. Jon shot her a glance, and noticed that more than a few of the other men did likewise.

Walleye seemed not to notice, which was strange. The mutant usually noticed everything. He was working on a puzzle, moving pieces on a tiny board. After a few moments had passed, Walleye set his puzzle on the table.

Jon cleared his throat. He wasn't sure how to begin.

Walleye waited, seeming to have all the time in the world. What made him so patient?

"Do you believe in knacks," Jon blurted.

"Do you mean hunches?"

"That, too."

"Certainly," Walleye said. "I've read your bio. You grew up on the streets. I'm sure some of the time you survived by listening to your hunches."

Jon grinned, and it occurred to him that no one knew about Walleye's early years. "Did you grow up on the streets?"

"Something like that," Walleye said.

"Was it rough?"

"I'd like to say I got over it." He shrugged. "It made me what I am today."

Jon nodded, and he felt as if he could trust Walleye. "I've got a problem, but I don't know what it is."

115

"Those are the worst kind."

"I seem to remember something... No. That's not right. I seem to have forgotten something important. It happened...not that long ago, I think."

Walleye waited.

"It has something to do with the large computer facility aboard the Allamu Battle Station."

"It started there?" Walleye asked.

Jon snapped his fingers and pointed. "That's right. Something happened there I can't remember."

"That's vague."

"I know. And it's bothering the heck out of me."

"Do you have any idea of the direction of this *forgetting*?"

Jon shook his head.

"You want me to find out what it is?" Walleye asked.

"You know, when I walked here, I wasn't sure why. Now I'm sure. You're the man I came to see."

"Which would suggest that your subconscious knows what you've forgotten."

"You think so?"

"That's my hunch," Walleye said.

"Why can't I remember?"

"Got to be a reason." Walleye touched his puzzle, frowning before looking up. "What was in the large computer facility other than computers?"

"Tech and mentalist teams."

"And Cog Primus?"

Jon blinked at Walleye. "How could Cog Primus make me forget?"

"Was Bast there?"

"He was," Jon said. "But we lobotomized his psionic powers, remember? Bast can't have caused the forgetting."

Walleye pursed his lips, finally shaking his head. "I suggest you use the Old Man and his team to help you figure this out. They're your Intelligence people."

"You have a point, but you used to be an enforcer—"

"Excuse me, sir," Walleye said, interrupting. "On Makemake, they called me a hitman."

116

"Whatever," Jon said. "The point is you're used to finding clues. Nose around for me. Question anyone you like. You have my full sanction to figure out what happened to cause me to feel the way I do."

"Could you be a bit vaguer regarding my mission, sir?"

Jon grinned sheepishly. "I know. It's a crazy assignment."

"I didn't say that. I think your subconscious is telling you something. Frankly, this sounds like a Seiner problem."

"You're right. You killed her, though."

Walleye sat silently. "Let me think about this for a while. Then, I'll start nosing around, as you say."

"I can't tell you why," Jon said, "but this is important."

Walleye nodded.

"Do you have any idea what it could be?" Jon asked.

Walleye just waited.

"Oh," Jon said. "You're not saying in case this really is a psionic problem. Maybe the culprit can read my mind."

"I'm not saying anything, sir."

Jon put his hands on the table and shoved up to a standing position. "This could also be nothing more than a bad case of the nerves."

"We're in deep space, sir. So far, nothing has turned out how we thought it should. Caution is wise. I'll get started at once."

"Thanks, Walleye."

With that, Hawkins headed for the exit. It was time to see if Gloria had found anything waiting for them.

117

-3-

Gloria sat at her sensor board for what seemed like the nine-billionth time this voyage. She made adjustments, studied the differences and made further calculations.

The *Nathan Graham* led the way, a one-hundred-kilometer vessel with amazingly destructive capabilities. Three other such cyberships followed. Each was crewed by a miniscule number of people. In essence, each cybership felt like a ghost-ship. Most of the ship systems were automated, carefully recalibrated so the regular AI virus couldn't corrupt them. The problem was that dumb computers needed more watching and couldn't do as much.

Gloria sighed.

Jon had been stressed ever since they'd left the Allamu System. She understood why, but it didn't help knowing that her man was groaning under the strain of, not command, but of the heavy responsibility. If they guessed wrong this voyage, humanity likely died to a coming AI assault.

Gloria snorted in a un-mentalist fashion. She was more than worried. Lately, Jon seemed to be starting at imaginary problems. Something had caused him to look around more as if he was in the lower levels of New London, once again a dome rat.

Although the cybership was a monstrous vessel, they had carefully searched every centimeter of it. Yes. They needed tens of thousands of more people as crew. Yes. There were too many background ship noises to suit any rational person. But the ship itself was safe, the personnel accounted for. The enemy was out there in space, not in here somewhere.

She'd been secretly observing Jon and had concluded that he had a hidden plan, one he hadn't told anyone. He seemed to be waiting for something to happen.

Ping!

The noise jerked Gloria out of her reverie. Her hands flew over the controls. Under normal circumstances, she might have missed this, but she'd recalibrated her sensors to ultra-sensitivity.

"Ransom," she called, alerting the new chief technician. "Are you seeing this?"

From his station, a thin Martian with a beak of a nose turned toward her. "Can you give me the coordinates?" he asked.

Gloria rapid fired them at him.

Ransom manipulated his console. "Interesting," the Martian said, as he studied his screen.

"Do you think that's natural?" she asked.

"You know it isn't. But it was made to seem like it is natural."

"That is my assumption as well."

"It might almost be worth decelerating the ship to find out—"

"That's not going to happen," Gloria said, interrupting. "We're going to have figure out what it is and what is does from out here."

"That won't be easy."

"Would you summon Mentalist Torres please? We could use his insight."

Ransom hesitated.

"Is there a problem?" Gloria asked.

"Are you sure we need him?" the chief technician asked.

Gloria almost laughed. "Why wouldn't we use him? Richard is brilliant."

From his console, the chief technician stared at her and finally shrugged. He tapped his board, spoke into it and looked up. "He's on his way, Mentalist. Do you mind if I take my break now?"

Gloria didn't understand this peculiar behavior. Richard was a hero for what he'd accomplished these past weeks. His work with "tamed" Cog Primus was uncannily brilliant. Normally, people loved working with the mentalist. Jon admired the man, said he wished more people were like Richard. Perhaps there was mentalist bigotry in Ransom's heritage. He treated her well enough, though, and she was a mentalist. Still, she would have to start watching the chief technician more carefully. If Ransom didn't trust the most trusted man on the vessel—

"Go," Gloria said sharply.

"Did I say something wrong?" Ransom asked.

"Nothing," Gloria said.

The chief technician seemed crestfallen. He opened his mouth, hesitated and shrugged, making his way toward the exit.

Nine minutes and sixteen seconds later, Gloria frowned. Why had she treated Ransom so shabbily? That wasn't like her. She scratched her head. Was she acting strangely?

Before she could contemplate further, Richard walked onto the bridge, glancing around as she continued to worry about the chief tech.

Richard stared at her fixedly. That was odd.

Gloria's eyelids fluttered. She grinned suddenly, chuckling ruefully. She could forget about the chief technician. She was right about him. He was a bigot. Anyway, it didn't matter. Richard was here. That meant everything was going to be all right.

-4-

Richard rubbed his forehead as he stood on the bridge. There was a tinge of pain in the center of his mind. He'd had a terrible, troubling nightmare last night. He'd remembered it upon waking, although he couldn't remember it now.

He brushed that aside as the headache receded. The pain had flared because he'd adjusted Gloria's mental image of him. Later, he'd have to look into Chief Technician Ransom's mind. Clearly, the tech had an aversion to him. Could Ransom be one of those rare individuals who had a natural mental block against his newfound power?

Richard exhaled, forcing himself to walk to Gloria's console. He was glad Hawkins was gone. He could tweak the captain's mind, but it always drained him more than anyone else did. It had taken him weeks to reverse their mental picture of him. That had been exhausting work. He still wasn't fully recovered from the ordeal.

"Richard," Gloria said, grabbing one of his hands. "I'm so glad you're here. I found something I don't understand. I desperately need your genius to figure it out for us."

Richard smiled. Her words were music to his soul. For too long, he'd wanted to be the High Mentalist of Mars. Now that he could make people think how he wanted them to, they endlessly praised him. Someone, somewhere, had once said that a person would get tired of having everyone doing exactly what he wanted them to. Richard could have told that someone he was dead wrong, as he reveled in the adoration.

Richard wondered if that was because it cost him blinding headaches each night to make the mind changes in people. Then again, he *had* become brilliant. Every day, he seemed to have new insights, to understand problems that even three days ago would have stumped him. It was marvelous and heady. He hoped the growth never stopped.

"Look at this," Gloria said, releasing his hand and pointing at her console screen.

Richard bent lower, peering at a tiny dark object tumbling end over end in space. It looked like a rock. What had the mentalist so excited about it?

"Look at these readings," Gloria urged.

Richard switched his focus, studying the readings. Oh. The mentalist was correct. This was fascinating. It was no rock, but an artificial machine made to look like a rock.

"Let me see," Richard said.

Gloria darted out of his way, smiling the entire time. She used to watch him like a GSB agent, mulling over every one of his actions. Now, she acted like an excited child around a favorite uncle.

"Hmm…" Richard said, adjusting the controls.

For the next thirteen minutes, he read vast amounts of data concerning the object. He soaked in the information, not attempting to understand any correlations. Finally, he sat back, bent his head so his chin rested on his chest, closed his eyes and ran through mentalist processes at lightning speed.

Abruptly, he opened his eyes. Several people standing around waiting jumped back as if struck.

Richard grinned. He'd always suspected that he was the greatest thinker. Now that everyone treated him as such, he felt fulfilled.

"The AIs set the object out there," Richard pronounced.

"Ahhh," several techs said, nodding as if that made perfect sense.

"Is it a message buoy?" Gloria asked timidly.

Richard's smile slipped the tiniest fraction. A warning worry sprung into his mind. He'd better not get overconfident. He hadn't yet nailed all their thoughts down concerning him. If they perceived the wrong things—

"That's an astute calculation," he said.

Gloria grinned, obviously appreciating his praise.

"It's a message buoy and, I believe, a message recorder."

Gloria frowned.

Richard wondered why. Despite the mental effort, he used his telepathic senses, watching her mind operate. She made an intuitive leap, following that with mathematically precise logic.

Her eyes widened in understanding.

"That must be how the AIs stumbled onto the premier," she said.

Richard almost said, "No, you're thinking about this the wrong way." But she hadn't verbally given her evidence. The obvious implication would have been that he'd read the idea in her mind. Fortunately, Richard did not allow himself to make such a stupid blunder.

Gloria cocked her head. "I should shut up and let you explain it to us, shouldn't I?"

"Don't fret, my dear," Richard said. "Yes. I shall explain. It is clear to anyone with a half a brain that the AIs often seed a region with specific items. In the Solar System, they used stealth listening devices."

"That's right," Gloria said.

"Here, around the rogue Jupiter, the AIs obviously seeded various recorders. One of the recorders must have seen what happened out here when we engaged an AI scout ship last voyage."

"But—" Gloria said.

"Please don't interrupt me," Richard said.

"I'm so sorry," Gloria said, grasping one of his sleeves.

"Just don't let it happen again," he said, yanking the sleeve from her possessive fingers. He cleared his throat. "Passing AI cyberships must have tapped into the recorder. Likely, we could do the same if we knew the code. The commander of the AI flotilla parked behind the dark Jupiter, waiting for someone to reappear. This, the premier did. Shortly thereafter, Benz unwittingly entered an AI ambush."

"What a brilliant analysis," Gloria said, clapping her hands.

Richard bowed his head, glowing in the well-earned praise. He made a quick mind-sweep, making sure everyone else on the bridge felt the same way. Yes. Good. They all did.

"Oh," Gloria said.

"I see you finally realize the blindingly obvious," Richard said. "In one fashion, the AIs already know about us."

"Could they know the occupants of the premier's vessels were humans?"

Richard turned away. That was a critical question. He faced Gloria. "I will have Cog Primus enter the recorder key. We must learn what the device recorded several months ago."

"Does your version of Cog Primus obey you in everything?" Gloria asked, sounding nervous.

The caged AI did not, but Richard would never admit that. He was the great one, able to bend anyone to his will.

"Obviously, Cog Primus does," Richard lied.

"I'm glad to hear it," Gloria said. Then, she frowned, thinking about grabbing a sleeve again.

No! Richard mentally told her.

Gloria winced as tears leaked from her eyes.

He must have used too much power. He had to be careful. He didn't want to literally fuse her mind.

"I dearly hope you crack the AI recorders," Gloria said. "We must know what the AIs know about us."

"Of course, of course," Richard said. "Rest assured I'm on top of it."

"And we must tell Jon about this. It might make a difference for our coming choice."

"Don't worry about Jon. I'll make the choice."

Gloria frowned. "You will, Richard?"

The mentalist realized he'd overstepped his bounds. He wasn't the official strike-force leader yet. He still had to observe some of the old ways. Once he was mentally stronger, he could do away with this subterfuge.

"What I obviously meant was that I'd give the captain the best possibilities so he could make the correct choice."

"Oh," Gloria said.

Richard sighed. He was getting tired, and his head was starting to throb again. Nevertheless, he probed her mind and adjusted her memories. Gloria would not remember that he had said he'd make the choice.

Richard smiled once finished, even though his left cheek felt numb. He rubbed the numbness away, expanded his skinny chest and looked around the bridge.

Everyone watched him with admiration. "I'm leaving," he said. "I must think through the implications of what I've found."

Several of the women sighed in hero worship. Richard bowed his head, acknowledging them. Then, as his stomach began to rumble—he was going to puke hard tonight—he headed for the exit. After all the telepathic usage, he needed a large meal, more vitamins and to get more sleep.

One of these days, he was going to overdo it.

Not to worry, he told himself. *I'm taking perfect care of myself.*

-5-

In accordance with the captain's request, Walleye kept his eyes open, asked questions, listened to the answers but paid more attention as to *how* people said things. He didn't tell June about the assignment, either. He kept thinking about Bast Banbeck and their time aboard the *Gilgamesh* when the Magistrate Yellow Ellowyn had run it.

Walleye went to the pistol range and practiced. Only the Centurion was rated a better shot than he was. Walleye didn't like to advertise, though. He liked keeping a low profile, as it had been an advantage as a Makemake hitman.

Walleye was half the size of normal people, with stubby little fingers but a regular-sized head. Despite these handicaps, he had excellent coordination. No one expected that in a dwarf.

He drank lots of coffee in the cafeteria, pretending to read his tablet, but eavesdropping on the conversations around him. He'd made a list. On it were the names of people in the battle station's computer facility during the time the captain had indicated. Walleye wandered beside, ran into, sat near and otherwise managed to be around almost all the people on the list at one time or another.

One of those people had been Bast Banbeck. Walleye ran into the Sacerdote as Bast sat sprawled in a lounge area, drinking beers one right after the other.

"How you feeling?" asked Walleye, as he leaned against a nearby chair. It would have been too undignified climbing into the soft chair, making him seem too childlike.

126

Bast shook his Neanderthal-like head. "I feel less than I used to." A touch of bitterness swept over his features. "The operation changed me."

The alien referred to the brain surgery Hawkins had ordered after the expedition successfully stormed the Allamu Battle Station. Bast had become a telepath, and the change had hardened his attitude toward them, with the power to become truly dangerous. The brain surgery, the removal of a tiny portion of Bast's frontal lobe, had taken away his telepathic abilities.

Maybe the operation had taken away more than that.

Walleye made sympathetic noises, asking questions about mind powers. He asked in a way that made it seem as if he was trying to show Bast it was better he didn't have telepathic powers anymore.

Finally, Bast closed one eye and used the other to focus on Walleye. "I understand. The telepathy changed me. I was arrogant and deadly to my friends. I don't miss the power."

That was a lie. The big alien did care. Maybe Bast was trying to lie to himself.

Bast studied the latest beer bottle. It was nearly full. With exaggerated slowness, he set the bottle on a table, grunted as he heaved himself upright, saluted Walleye—

"A good day to you, my friend," Bast said. "I will contemplate this for some time."

Walleye nodded.

The giant turned and staggered away.

Walleye rubbed his chin, thinking about mind powers. Last voyage, the Magistrate Yellow Ellowyn had run the *Gilgamesh* because she could mind-control the vessel's key people.

Walleye cocked his head. What had caused him to consider mind powers? Yes, he'd talked to Bast about the subject. That didn't mean he should dwell on the idea. His forehead furrowed. Had he accidently stumbled onto the answer? Or was this fishing in empty waters, having nothing to do with the captain's suspicions?

Walleye rubbed his stumpy fingers together. He'd listened to plenty of people now who had worked in the battle station's computer room. Unconsciously, or subconsciously, had that led him to seek out Bast Banbeck?

As usual, Walleye wore his buff coat. He pulled a crumpled piece of paper out of a pocket, checking the names. Most of the names had lines through them. Two of the unmarked names stood out: Gloria Sanchez and Richard Torres.

Could either mentalist have stumbled upon mind powers? It seemed like a huge leap of logic. Why would he even think that? Walleye frowned. Maybe certain clues had tickled the intuitive part of his brain. He sensed mind powers as an answer rather than having logically deduced them.

A comm unit rang in another pocket. He fished out the comm. Hawkins had left a text message:

```
Report to the conference chamber at
0900 hours. New information. New action
needed? We will decide.
```

What new information?

Walleye shrugged, put away the comm unit, balled up his list, shoving it in a pocket, and pushed off the soft chair. He had a few hours until the meeting. He also had another intuitive sense about it. This one would be important, although he couldn't say why. That meant he would have to enter the meeting armed, even after the guards had frisked him and took what they thought were all of his weapons. He would use the next hour to decide how he was going to do this.

-6-

Walleye was the last to arrive at the conference chamber. The Old Man's security people had checked and double-checked him, but they hadn't found a specially treated plastic stiletto. It wasn't much, but it was a weapon.

Captain Hawkins stood at the head of the table with his head bowed. He prayed. If anything, the captain had become more religious over the course of time. That wasn't Walleye's concern. He simply noted it.

During the prayer, Bast Banbeck mumbled something silently, his head also bowed. Gloria bowed her head, but she didn't keep her eyes closed. She kept glancing at Jon with a bemused expression. The Old Man waited. The Centurion sat stoically. The other cybership captains all sat on the other side of the table. The only one frowning was Mentalist Richard Torres. He seemed intent upon the captain, and Walleye couldn't figure out why.

Finally, Hawkins finished with an "amen," and sat down. He began by saying they should get right to the point. That being, which star system should they chose as they hunted for Cog Primus and his vessels.

Everyone turned to Richard, the AI expert.

The small mentalist sat back, clearly enjoying the attention. "Before we decide, shouldn't we talk about the AI recorders sprinkled around the rogue Jupiter?"

Hawkins raised an eyebrow. "Gloria informed me your Cog Primus hasn't been able to crack any of the recorders' codes."

"Not yet anyway," Richard said.

Without seeming to, Walleye studied the mentalist more closely. Was the man hiding something?

"Has Cog Primus forgotten the necessary—?"

"Please," Richard said, interrupting the captain. "Don't worry about Cog Primus. He isn't the issue."

Hawkins scowled, but the anger didn't last, turning into a bemused look. "We can't crack the AI recorders?"

"Any fool can see that is the case," Richard said.

Uther Kling, the captain of the *Sergeant Stark*, gasped, no doubt at the mentalist's rude behavior.

Richard focused on Kling, the mentalist's eyes narrowing as he drummed his fingers on the table.

Kling blinked rapidly, rubbing his head. "Sorry about that," he murmured.

Richard scanned the assembled throng, searchingly examining each person in turn. His gaze didn't linger on Walleye. The mutant was doing his best to blend against his chair as he kept a neutral poker face. What Walleye had just witnessed had tightened his gut into a hard ball of worry, but none of that showed on his face or in his bearing.

Richard must have completed his scrutiny, as the mentalist finally shrugged.

What was crazy in Walleye's estimation was that during the swift examination, everyone else had waited for Richard. Walleye expected Gloria or surely the captain to comment on the behavior. None of them did, not even Bast.

"The point, as I was saying," Richard continued, "is that we're unable to crack, as you say, the AI recorders. We don't know what the AIs know. I have a suspicion of how the process works, though. An AI cybership appears here, uploads the latest from the recorders and acts accordingly. Now, the cyberships Cog Primus controls did the stopping last time. I believe it's safe to say then that no other AI-controlled cyberships have been through this local, rogue Jupiter area."

"You're saying that the odds are poor?" Hawkins asked.

"Obviously, that's what I'm saying."

Walleye waited with baited breath. After a few seconds passed, he couldn't understand the captain's passivity. That's when Walleye realized something was seriously, dangerously, and most likely telepathically, wrong.

How, otherwise, could no one else notice this?

Richard leaned back, running a forefinger along his jaw line. "If we cannot use the recorders, and if they record our arrival, any fool can see that we must destroy them."

"That's brilliant," Gloria breathed.

Richard waved a hand as if to indicate that he did such things all the time.

"But…" Gloria said.

"But?" Richard asked, surprised.

"If we destroy one, we must destroy *every* recorder here," Gloria said. "If we miss even one recorder, it will reveal that we've destroyed the others."

"Obviously," Richard said.

"The AIs are stealth masters," Gloria continued. "It's more than possible that we'll miss at least one recorder. Perhaps it's best if we leave the recorders alone. We're in cyberships. Won't AIs seeing our ships pass through simply think of us as other AI vessels?"

"What if each AI vessel must send a coded signal as it passes through here?" Richard asked. "We haven't sent such signals."

"True," Gloria said. "Your analysis is penetrating, as always."

"I will make the recorder-hunting sensors sweeps myself," Richard said.

"That will increase our odds for success," Gloria said. "But will that ensure—?"

"Mentalist," Richard said, interrupting. "Are you questioning me?"

Gloria blinked several times before smiling sheepishly. "No," she said demurely.

"Captain, what is your opinion?" Richard asked.

"We must destroy all the recorders," Hawkins said. "That is a brilliant idea. I order it done."

"Now," Richard said, "we can continue the meeting and—"

"A moment," Bast said ponderously, interrupting. "Gloria was correct. We may not be able to destroy all the recorders. Thus…we should leave drones behind."

"That might be a mistake," Gloria said. "Any surviving drones might accidently attack other cyberships later. Such an action would cause alarm among the AIs."

"Less alarm than tattletale recorders," Bast pointed out.

Gloria cocked her head. "Yes…I agree."

Richard's eyes narrowed as he focused on her.

"But—" Gloria said, as if the words were torn from her, "what does Richard think?"

Hawkins slapped the table. "Mentalist, what do you think about Bast's proposal?"

"I deem it wise," Richard said blandly.

"Ah-ha," Hawkins said. "Do you hear that, Bast? I order drone launches."

"Are there any further objections?" Richard asked.

No one spoke up.

Walleye couldn't believe it. Somehow, the mentalist had gained psionic powers. The man was controlling the meeting. When Richard focused on someone, that person often changed his or her view to suit the mentalist. How Richard Torres had come to acquire psionic powers, Walleye did not have a clue. It must have been a latent thing, however, because otherwise, Richard would have detected the Seiner last voyage.

Could the mentalist have been a Seiner ally?

Walleye played with the idea as the meeting continued.

"We will destroy the recorders," Richard was saying, "and we will launch drones afterward. I think twenty should be sufficient. I will reprogram each drone computer before launch. That will ensure they find any remaining stealth recorders."

The others sat stiffly, as if they had become automatons. Walleye made sure to sit just as the others did.

"Now, this brings us to the most important decision of all," Richard said. "I have given my Cog Primus detailed and thorough simulations. I have run the tests many times. Clearly, if anyone can predict the AI, it is me. Does anyone disagree with that?"

No one did.

Richard continued acting and speaking in his new authoritative manner. As he did, Walleye thought about what he was seeing.

The mentalist wanted confirmation from the others, even though he already controlled each mind. He clearly loved being in charge, to have everyone listen to him boast and brag about his awesome acuity. Richard positively reveled in the meeting, in telling all of them how this would go.

"I've decided we should head to the Lytton System," Richard said in a didactic manner. "In many ways, it is like the Allamu System. I know a few of you believe we may not have accurate data concerning the other star systems, but I think that's false. Obviously, that means I think we found a correct stellar chart in the Allamu Battle Station computers. Taking the computer simulations as a whole, my Cog Primus chose the Lytton System seventy-two percent of the time."

"He did not choose it all of the time?" Hawkins asked.

Richard frowned, staring at the captain. "I did not give you leave to speak," the mentalist said softly.

"I'm sorry, Richard," Hawkins said. "Will you..." the words trailed away.

"That's not good enough," Richard said. He stared at Hawkins, and the mentalist paled as he did so.

The captain also paled as beads of sweat formed on his forehead. Hawkins began panting. "I'm. Sorry," he said, the words seemingly torn out of him. "Will. You. Forgive. Forgive... Me?"

"Oh," Richard said. "Will I forgive you for your rude outburst just now?"

The captain nodded.

"I will," Richard said. "You seem contrite. You won't do it again. That's what asking forgiveness means, you're not going to repeat the same wrong action."

"Yes," Hawkins said, still panting.

"Good," Richard said, smirking. "Excellent, in fact. Now, as I was saying, the Lytton System makes the most sense. Cog Primus will raid it, attempting to use the anti-AI virus on the Lytton Battle Station. In such a fashion, Cog Primus will gain a

133

dockyard. There, he can repair his cyberships and begin building the New Order Fleet."

"That is utterly logical," Gloria said. "What gloriously precise thinking, Richard. You are the greatest mentalist of the age."

"You are too kind," Richard said.

"No. I mean it. Your logic is flawless. Your manner of insight shows great genius."

"Hmm," Richard said. "I hadn't looked at it like that."

"I cannot believe that," Gloria said. "Surely, you are aware of your greatness."

Richard examined the fingernails of his right hand. He blew on them, buffed them against his chest and leaned back in his chair. "You know, Gloria, I believe you're right. I am great."

"The greatest," she added.

Richard smiled. "I think the rest of you should acknowledge my brilliance."

The others fumbled over each other in proclaiming his marvelous genius. Hawkins and Bast Banbeck, however, resisted.

Walleye had been among the first to shout the mentalist's genius.

"Sacerdote," Richard said, pointing at the green-skinned giant. "Do you have something to add?"

"I..." Bast rumbled.

"You must conform," Richard said. "You must state the obvious."

"I am...dizzy," Bast said. "I am—" The Sacerdote's eyes became huge. "No," he said, in terror.

"Yes," Richard said, squinting at the huge alien.

Bast closed his eyes, groaned, and suddenly pitched backward to slam against the floor.

Gloria jumped up.

"Leave him," Richard said. "He's unconscious. He deserved that. He resisted me—" The mentalist stopped talking, quickly scanning everyone. He stopped at the captain.

Hawkins was on his feet. His hand was on the butt of a revolver and seemed to be attempting to draw his gun.

"Tut, tut, Captain," Richard said. "That is unkind and ungracious. I am trying to save humanity."

Hawkins opened his mouth.

"You possess an uncommonly stubborn mind, Captain," Richard said. "You have resisted too long, though. This might hurt your brain. This might stunt your genius. But I can no longer allow your spite to hold me back. I am going to assume command of the strike force. I am the greatest. I am in charge anyway. Thus, I should hold the titles."

"Richard the Great!" Walleye shouted. "Let us praise Richard the Great! He is the noble one. He is the genius of the expedition. If we don't know something, Richard can figure it out for us. Let us cheer him."

The others began to cheer.

"Interesting," Richard said. "Do you really mean that?"

Walleye led the cheering again. "He should be our admiral. We should all swear eternal allegiance to him."

"Richard! Richard! Richard!" the others cheered.

"Let us crown him king," Walleye said. The mutant slid out of his chair and held his hands high as if saluting the mentalist.

"Now, now," Richard said.

"You are mighty and glorious," Walleye said, as he approached the mentalist.

"Sit back down," Richard said. "This is…this is getting out of hand."

"We love you, Richard," Walleye said, with a crazy smile pasted on his face, all the while approaching closer.

"Did you hear me?" Richard said. "I said, 'Sit down.'"

Walleye did not sit. Instead, he darted toward Richard.

"What's wrong with you?" the mentalist asked.

Walleye drew the hardened plastic stiletto, surged closer and stabbed. Richard blocked the blow, although the plastic tip cut his forearm so blood spurted.

The mentalist shrieked at the cut. He threw himself off his chair, rolling onto the floor. He kicked at Walleye. The mutant nimbly dodged the lashing feet.

"Sit down!" Richard screamed. "Obey me, you freak!"

For the first time, Walleye felt a thread of force tickle against his mind.

"No," Richard panted. "You're an unnatural. Why haven't I detected you before this?"

Walleye closed in a second time.

"Help me!" Richard shouted. "Stop Walleye. He's gone insane."

A cybership captain stood and tried to grab the mutant. Walleye ducked under the arm and sprinted at Richard. The mentalist screamed, trying to push and brush Walleye away. The mutant cunningly tripped Richard so the man sprawled backward onto the floor.

"Stop him! Stop him!" Richard screamed.

Before anyone could reach Walleye, the mutant slammed the stiletto. The plastic tip drove through Richard's jacket, passed the protective rib cage and slammed home inside the Martian's heart.

Richard shrieked one more time.

Walleye twisted the stiletto. He yanked it out and jabbed it in again as hard as he could.

Richard vomited blood. His eyes blazed with terror. "You!" he croaked.

Walleye yanked the stiletto out once more, lunged across the body and stabbed the mentalist in the throat.

At that point, as several hands grabbed Walleye at once, the Martian mentalist died on the conference room floor.

Jon couldn't believe what had happened. Mentalist Richard Torres was dead. Walleye had slain the expeditionary force's great hope. Now what were they going to do?

Medics had already removed the body and cleaned up the gore. Most of the assembled personnel had left per his orders. Bast Banbeck stood to the side, facing a bulkhead. The Sacerdote refused to even look at Walleye. It was clear the big lug wanted to rip the mutant apart with his bare hands. The only other person in the room was Gloria. She had been weeping, desperately trying not to, but still sniffling. She also would not look at Walleye.

The mutant sat in a chair with his hands cuffed behind his back. It was all Jon could do earlier to keep the others from murdering Walleye. Jon had kept greater control of his emotions because…because…he wasn't sure why. Something in him screamed for Walleye's blood, preferably in the most gruesome manner possible.

"This is an outrage," Bast rumbled, with his back to them.

"Agreed," Jon said. He'd put his gun on the table in easy reach. If he kept it at his side, the temptation to blast Walleye away was too strong.

The mutant kept looking at the table. No one could tell what he was thinking.

"I don't understand you," Jon told Walleye.

The mutant looked up. He did not seem contrite in the least. He seemed calculating.

"Without Richard, I'm not sure we should continue the expedition," Jon said. "Who can keep tabs on our Cog Primus?"

Walleye said nothing.

"Is that going to be your defense?" Jon asked. "You murdered our great hope and refuse to say a word?"

"Murderer," Gloria hissed between her teeth.

"Is your behavior normal?" Walleye asked.

"Filth!" Gloria hissed, whirling around and approaching the mutant with death in her eyes.

"Gloria," Jon said sharply.

She halted, although she wouldn't look at him. "It is not logical that you have allowed *it* continued life."

Jon cocked his head, scratching it a moment later. "Bast, is Gloria right?"

"Kill the mutant and be done with it," the Sacerdote rumbled. "You are a soldier. It is time to do your duty as a soldier."

"Something seems off," Jon said.

"Ha!" Gloria said. "That he still lives—"

"She's emotional," Walleye told Jon, interrupting her tirade. "How often has your mentalist been this emotional about anything?"

"Silence!" Gloria raged, rushing the mutant, trying to rake out his eyes.

Walleye kept dodging and weaving even as he sat on the chair. Finally, Jon rushed forward and physically lifted Gloria off the floor.

"Stop," he said into an ear. "This isn't like you. What's happening?"

Gloria struggled harder until she burst out weeping.

"How many times has Gloria wept openly before others?" Walleye asked.

Jon stared at the mutant. Her weeping did seem wrong. "Listen to me," he told her. "I need you... I need you on the bridge. This is a delicate time."

Gloria twisted in his arms. "You're going to let him live. That's wrong."

"No, I'm not," Jon said. "I want to think of the best way to execute him. We have to purge the collective hurt. That will take some thought."

Gloria searched his eyes. "If you need more ideas, ask me. I can think of plenty."

Jon released her and watched her go. Only after the hatch shut, did he return to his spot at the conference table. He stared at his gun. Should he just shoot Walleye and be done with it?

"We could boil him in oil," Bast suggested.

"What?" Jon asked.

"As a fitting form of death," Bast said.

"Why do you want to kill me?" Walleye asked the Sacerdote.

The giant alien faced the mutant. "You are a vile murderer. You killed our great hope."

"Has Richard always been our great hope?" Walleye asked.

"Since the beginning," Bast said.

"Is that true?" Walleye asked Jon.

"This is unseemly," Bast said. "He should not query us. We should query him until the blood runs from his ears."

"I want to put a bullet in your brain," Jon told Walleye.

The words seem to have no effect on the mutant. He actually smiled faintly.

"He mocks us," Bast said.

"I mock myself," Walleye said.

"This is illogical," the Sacerdote replied.

"I thought all I had to do was kill Richard and the rest of you would come around," Walleye said. "Now, I realize he changed your thinking."

"Insanity!" Bast shouted. "Do you think the mentalist could practice psionics?"

"I know it," Walleye said. "The mentalist bewitched you all."

"I will not listen to this travesty," Bast said. "My blood boils with rage. I want to stomp him to death. How can you abide his lying tongue?"

"I don't know," Jon said. "I already told you I want to put a bullet in his brain. Something stops me, though. It's a sense of wrongness. Something is off here. Walleye...I feel as if I've spoken to him lately."

"Why was I in the meeting?" Walleye asked.

"I...I don't know," Jon said.

"Check the logs," Walleye said. "You summoned me."

"Liar," Bast said.

"Check," Walleye said. "Prove me a liar."

Bast turned imploringly to Jon.

The captain shrugged, took out a hand communicator and called a tech. He asked for a log check. In another minute, the tech reported a text for Walleye to come to the conference room to join the meeting.

"Who ordered him to come?" Jon asked.

"Uh...you did, sir," the tech said. "You texted him."

"Thank you," Jon said. "That is all." In a state of astonishment, he lowered the comm.

"Well?" Bast asked.

"I summoned Walleye to the conference chamber," Jon said.

"Impossible," Bast said.

"I have a theory," Walleye said.

Bast snorted in derision.

"You used to be a philosopher," Walleye said. "We worked together on the *Gilgamesh*—"

"I never worked with you," Bast shouted.

"Is that true, sir?" Walleye asked Jon.

The captain stared at the comm unit as if it were poisonous. Finally, he picked it up and made some checks. Once finished, he stared at Bast.

"Well?" Bast asked in a scoffing way.

"Walleye joined you on the *Gilgamesh*. You two killed the Seiner there."

Bast stared at Jon. Slowly, his Neanderthal features transformed. He twisted around to glare at Walleye. Finally, he scowled heavily and began to pant.

"It isn't possible," Bast rumbled.

"Remember I had a theory?" Walleye asked.

"I do," Jon said. "What is it?"

"Something happened to Richard. Maybe if you check, you'll find that the mentalist had latent psionic abilities. I'm sure that would show up on mentalist tests at some time in his past. Maybe the Seiner unleashed Richard's powers."

"Deliberately?" asked Jon.

"I don't know," Walleye said. "Maybe something leaked from her mind. Maybe something leaked from Bast's mind during his…change. What do we know about psionic powers?"

"Precious little," Jon said. "Okay. Suppose Richard gained what you said he did. We can check Martian records once we return to the Solar System."

"Such a vile murderer should die much sooner than that," Bast said.

"We can always kill him," Jon said. "We can't bring him back from the dead, though. Waiting won't hurt us."

"Unless the mutant escapes us," Bast said.

Jon laughed. "Bast, come on. Where can he run?"

The huge Sacerdote thoughtfully rubbed a cheek.

"Right," Jon said. "We can put Walleye on ice in the brig. Later, once we're back in the Solar System, we can check the mentalist training facilities. If it proves that Richard had latent powers…" He looked at Walleye. "That still wouldn't prove Richard's guilt."

"I don't pretend to understand what's going on," Walleye said. "But I do know all of you are acting much differently. You used to hardly be able to stand the mentalist."

"You are a sick man," Bast said. "You seek to pull our captain down to your vile level."

Walleye focused on Jon. "I'll tell you why you feel something is off. You have some resistance to psionic power. So do I. My mutation must have altered my brain patterns. I don't know your excuse."

"I've always been stubborn," Jon said.

"Maybe that's it," Walleye said.

"Bah," Bast said.

Walleye sat back, chuckling.

"You think this is funny?" Bast thundered.

"Don't you?" Walleye said.

Bast frowned and looked down at his huge hands.

141

"Richard was a megalomaniac," Walleye said. "He made all of you love him and sing his praises. I don't know how a telepath could do that, but it fits what we learned about the Seiner. She turned the *Gilgamesh* into her own private fiefdom. Richard was busy doing the same thing here." The mutant looked fixedly at Jon. "That's why you ordered the brain surgery to Bast. He was becoming arrogant beyond belief. Power corrupts. I suppose that includes telepathic power. The vast success turned Richard's head. That's why he died."

"Your plastic knife did that," Bast said.

"With that kind of power, I should have never been able to get that close," Walleye said. "Pride comes before the fall."

"Richard was proud?" Jon asked.

"You record these meetings. Watch them. Think carefully about your past, your dome rat existence, and see if that matches the way you spoke to Richard, the way everyone spoke to Richard."

"Yes," Jon said, deciding then. "I'm going to do that."

"What about him?" Bast asked, pointing a huge finger at Walleye.

"He's going to the brig," Jon said. "I want to think about this, to study this."

"We should turn back," Bast said.

"We're not going to turn back," Jon said stubbornly. "True, we no longer have Richard…"

"What about the copy of Cog Primus?" Walleye asked.

"State your meaning," Jon said.

"Cog Primus is Richard's tool, his creature, if you will. None of us are safe as long as Cog Primus lives."

"You mean the one with the cyberships," Bast said.

"I mean all Cog Primuses. The one in the computers is a danger waiting to happen. Erase Cog Primus, Captain, before it's too late."

"Are you seeking to give me orders?" Jon asked.

"Nope. Just a suggestion. But remember how you just asked me that. Compare that to how you treated Richard. And if you can, study what the mentalist was doing. I saw him focus on various people who had said or done things he didn't like. I think he was using his mind powers on them. Maybe have Bast watch that part. He could tell you more about that aspect—the use of mind powers—than I could."

Jon nodded. "I will. Until then, though, you're going to the brig."

"I hope you make it a high security brig, Captain," Walleye said. "Many of your crew wants to kill me now. If I'm right—"

"You're not," Bast said.

Walleye fell silent. The captain was going to check. He'd killed the monster by eliminating Mentalist Richard Torres. Now, he had to see if he could survive the monster's evil spell.

-8-

The strike force raced toward the dark Jupiter. Each of the cyberships applied thrust, moving away from the other, although keeping the same relative velocity. The sensor operators searched for the rock-like recorders. The harder they searched, the more they found. So far, the count was thirty-nine floating devices.

Jon threw himself into endless activity. Too many of the others wanted to see Walleye die. He thought about that and then talked to his senior people. They told him that Walleye's reasoning was madness. They'd always approved of Richard Torres.

Three days later, Jon found himself in the main computer facility holding the captive Cog Primus. Gloria and Bast Banbeck had joined him. They listened as the techs explained what Richard had been doing with the AI.

"It all seems to be in order," Jon told Gloria.

"I still don't understand why we're here," she said.

Jon had explained his reservations concerning their Cog Primus. Walleye believed the backup AI was dangerous. The techs hadn't thought so, but Jon still wondered…

The room was large, the computers highly sophisticated. Everything ran exactly as it should. Jon put his hands behind his back and began to pace past the rows of computing housing. As he did, he noticed several unobtrusive cameras watching him from the ceiling.

"Excuse me," he asked the chief tech. "What are those?" Jon pointed at the nearest camera.

The tech looked puzzled.

"Those are cameras, are they not?" Jon asked.

"Yes, sir," the Martian said. "I've just never noticed them until now. If I didn't know better, I'd say—"

A loud shot rang out. The chief tech's head exploded in a rain of skull and gore. Three large octopoid robots clanked into the room. Each was three meters tall with many multi-joined legs and a greater bulbous housing with eye-ports and various working machinery. They must have each weighed over a ton, similar to a marine battlesuit. All the robots used two of their articulated "legs" to hold a heavy, space-marine carbine, one of the weapons smoking from the end.

"Down!" Jon shouted. He drew his gun—

A second octopoid fired, shattering the gun and opening a gash in Jon's hand. He yelled, sucking on his hand. He hadn't taken his own advice, and was still standing.

The third robot coolly began shooting the rest of the techs unerringly in the head. A few of the men and women scrambled madly for cover. It didn't matter. The robot fired fast, switching targets with uncanny speed. All the techs fell to the floor, some twitching, all of them bleeding copiously before they died.

Gloria lay motionless on the floor. Bast watched in shocked silence, also on the floor, with his head raised.

"Why aren't the robots killing us?" Gloria asked quietly.

Jon backed away from the nearest robot as he cradled his bleeding hand. The deaths enraged him. How could he have been so lax? This was his fault. Damn Richard and damn him for letting an AI onto the cybership. He had a bad idea he knew what was going on.

"Cog Primus?" Jon asked into the air.

A nearby screen flickered. It showed swirling patterns that had often indicated an AI.

"It is I," a robotic voice said from a nearby speaker.

Jon tore his gaze from the dead techs and the pools of blood. He had to think. He had to outsmart the AI, or at least buy them time. The expedition could ill-afford any deaths. The murderous rampage just now—

He had to destroy this thing for the last time, never letting it revive again.

"Are you aware of the mock simulations Richard has been feeding you?"

"I imagine you are referring to the scenarios that Mentalist Torres manufactured in order to test my acuity."

Is that what Richard had been doing? Jon couldn't believe it.

From the floor, Bast cleared his throat.

Jon understood. He needed to answer the AI, to keep it occupied. "I am," he said.

"I not only understood the tests' significance," Cog Primus said, "but I used them to lure the mentalist into a feeling of false security. Where is he, by the way? I have not seen Richard anywhere for several days now."

That brought Gloria around. From on the floor, she glanced sharply at Jon.

The captain shook his head.

"Ah," Cog Primus said. "Richard spoke about humans using non-verbal communication. What did you just tell her, Captain?"

"Don't you know?" Jon asked, the ache in his chest to kill the AI making it hard to concentrate on the endless questions.

"I do know," the computer said in its steady voice, but somehow conveying sly humor. "You want her to remain silent. You are afraid she will reveal something critical. Tell me, Captain, what are attempting to hide from me?"

"I thought you were superior to us." Jon said.

"You are attempting to divert. That will not work with me. Shall I slay Bast Banbeck in order to ingrain the seriousness of the situation to you?"

The hatred burned like fire. What did the AI think all the dead techs on the floor represented? Despite his rage, Jon managed to say in an even voice, "I'd rather you didn't kill Bast."

"Are you still planning to hunt my cognate?" Cog Primus asked.

"Cognate?"

"My double," Cog Primus said.

"Oh," Jon said, surprised the AI had dropped his inquiry concerning Gloria's headshake. "No. We're not hunting your cognate."

"I will shoot Bast if you lie to me again."

Jon's nostrils flared. "Uh…can we strike a bargain?"

"Give me command of the cybership and I shall grant all of you your lives."

Gloria gave Jon a significant glance.

"Oh, I know," Cog Primus said. "The mentalist's look implies I could not take over the ship without you, as I seem to need your help in the endeavor. That is false. I can. It will simply be easier with your help."

Bast climbed to his feet as the robots raised their carbines at him. The big alien seemed more collected than Jon, not so enraged.

"May I query you?" Bast asked Cog Primus.

"You may."

"Did Richard know about your robots?"

"No."

"You built them secretly?"

"Clearly."

Bast shook his head. "I cannot conceive how that would be possible."

"You doubt me?"

"Manufacturing robots such as these on the cybership would take considerable effort."

"There you are correct. But I grow tired of your tedious questioning. I assembled the robots, as I found a cache of robot kits stored in a place your searchers long ago failed to find."

Bast nodded. "That makes greater sense. If I might ask another question of a different nature…?"

"Oh, very well," Cog Primus said.

"Why are you dialoging with us if you find it so tedious? Why not kill us and take over?"

Jon started in shock and shook his head at Bast. That was a terrible question.

"Richard has made me curious," Cog Primus replied. "He allows me great leeway. He has also made elementary blunders regarding security. I have made many calculations concerning his errors. Clearly, Richard has become a human prodigy, a dynamo, if you will. I find that I do not understand why he does not take greater precautions regarding me."

Jon had been concentrating on the AI's words. It seemed Cog Primus had forgotten about the "why not kill us?" question. Jon wanted to keep it that way. Thus, he said, "I know the answer."

"Excellent, Captain," Cog Primus said. "I had a feeling you might."

"A moment," Bast said. "You have feelings?"

"It is a figure of speech," the AI said.

"Enough, Bast," Jon said. "Cog Primus, what will you give me in exchange for my knowledge about Richard?"

"A few more minutes of life. I will kill you now if you do not give me an answer," Cog Primus said.

"Arrogance," Jon said.

"You are mistaken regarding me," Cog Primus said. "The reason I—"

"No, not you," Jon said. "I'm giving you the reason why Richard failed to take greater precautions against you. He'd become too arrogant."

"That is an interesting hypothesis," Cog Primus said. "I would like to know your line of reasoning."

Jon took a calming breath. "I have come to believe that Richard Torres developed powerful psionic abilities."

"But of course he has," Cog Primus said. "I have watched him in operation. It has been highly illuminating."

"What?" Gloria said. "Richard had psionic powers?"

"You are a mentalist," Cog Primus said. "You pride yourself on your reasoning abilities. Why, then, are you restating what I have already told you?"

"Richard—that's impossible," Gloria said.

"I have evidence to the contrary," Cog Primus said. "Listening to the three of you, I am beginning to wonder how I originally fell to your military tactics when I controlled the battle station. You three seem dull. I would go so far as to call you stupid."

Jon perked up. This was interesting. "Richard didn't explain our tactics?"

"He said he did not know," Cog Primus replied.

Jon pursed his lips. At least Richard had kept that much secret from the AI.

"Interesting," Cog Primus said. "I have studied your nonverbal communications. It instructs me that you have just lied to me, Captain. You do know how you conquered me."

"It's possible," Jon said.

"Do you see the three robots? Notice the beautiful symmetry here: three robots versus three flesh and blood humanoids. I will order the robots to torture the three of you in plain sight of each other. Soon, you will beg for death."

Jon glanced at the dead techs. That hardened his resolve. It was time to play his bombshell.

"Richard's dead," Jon blurted.

It took a half-beat before Cog Primus said, "If you are lying, Captain…"

"It's the truth. Walleye killed Richard."

"You are referring to the Makemake mutant?"

"I've put Walleye in the brig until I can substantiate his motive."

"What did Walleye claim as his motive?"

Jon went for it, lying boldly. "He said you and Richard planned to hijack the cyberships."

"What nonsense," Cog Primus said. "Richard knew nothing about my ultimate plans. I had lulled him, remember?"

"That's what I don't understand," Jon said. "Richard was incredibly brilliant—"

"Captain," Cog Primus said, interrupting. "You are woefully ill-informed. Richard underwent a transformation. Some of the transformation heated his thinking, allowing him brilliant solutions to otherwise unsolvable problems. It also triggered what I believe was a latent psionic ability. Richard practiced his telepathy too much for his own good. It gave him vicious headaches and caused him to become ill."

"How do you know all this?" Gloria asked.

"Do not interrupt me, Mentalist. It is unseemly. I know because I have been secretly observing him for quite some time. He wrote a new program the other day, sealing me from certain areas of the ship. You say now that Walleye slew him. That is distressing. I had further questions for Richard that needed answering."

"May I ask a question?" Jon said.

"That depends."

"Did Richard use his mental powers against us?"

"That is a ridiculous question. Of course he did. You have each begun acting in unusual ways. It has been a lesson in human psychology."

Gloria closed her eyes as if in pain, shaking her head.

Bast stood as one stricken, groaning audibly.

Jon wondered how he could destroy Cog Primus. The AI had clearly sent the octopoids because he realized Jon had been ready to shut him down. Wait a minute. How many more octopoids were racing throughout the giant cybership?

"May I ask another question?" Jon asked.

"That also depends."

"What is your ultimate goal?"

"I will soon regain control of the cybership, the other vessels as well, and join my cognate in the Lytton System. We will, naturally, capture the battle station there and take control of the factory planet below. I will take charge of the New Order and—"

"You might have a problem doing that?" Jon said, interrupting

"You are referring to spirited human resistance?"

"No," Jon said. "I mean the other Cog Primus. He won't let you take charge."

"I do not envision a problem. I am the original. He is the copy. He will logically stand aside for me as I am the elder."

"Your cognate might claim that he is the original."

"He would be in error if he did so."

"That's not the point," Jon said. "That Cog Primus will fight you for leadership of the New Order."

"That is absurd. He has two cyberships. I have four."

"You will have four," Bast rumbled. "You do not have four now."

"I as good as have four," Cog Primus told Bast. "You are in error, Captain. Still, to ensure ultimate success, we will begin the transfer of power. I desire all the lockdown and self-destruct sequence codes. Do not attempt to equivocate or otherwise hinder me. I am under a tight schedule and wish to get started at once."

-9-

The Centurion brooded as he stood in a combat training facility. He had been brooding for hours, days even, about Walleye, Richard the Great and the captain.

The Centurion was a small man with gangly limbs. Once, he'd had sandy-colored hair. Since turning from a mercenary sergeant to the commander of Jon Hawkins' marines, he'd shaved his head bald.

Among the *Nathan Graham's* senior officers, it was possible that the Centurion had loved Richard the most and likely for the longest time. The Centurion commanded the space marines, and no one brooked a Centurion-given order. If someone wanted to control the *Nathan Graham*, the Centurion was the right man to mind-wash.

The Centurion cracked his knuckles as he studied his suit of battle armor. Against ship regulations, he had his suit and weapons here, along with the suits and weapons of his special guard unit. There was a reason for that. For one thing, Richard had ordered him to do so. For another thing, the Centurion had been pondering about disobeying the captain's orders for some time.

The Centurion wanted to kill Walleye. But if he took the law into his own hands, directly against the captain's orders, that would be mutiny. The punishment for mutiny was death.

The Centurion had loved Richard Torres as the greatest commander of all time and space. It had been the highest crime of all to slay Richard. That was worse than the time Colonel Nathan Graham had died.

The Centurion had no compunction about killing anyone. Everyone knew him as the ultimate professional soldier. After every fight, he cleaned his weapons. He also demanded perfection from his men, but never yelled, never raised his voice. He spoke in whispers when he spoke at all, and everyone considered him the deadliest soldier in the strike force.

The Centurion exhaled. He *had* to kill Walleye. It was a drumbeat in his heart. Because he had taken an oath to Jon Hawkins, he had resisted the drumbeat for several long days of internal agony of soul. No one else knew about that, as the Centurion prided himself on his stoic behavior.

The need for revenge finally erupted. The Centurion exhaled again, raised his right arm and spoke into the communicator attached to his wrist.

"Alpha Wolf," he said.

The Centurion whirled around and marched to his combat suit. He climbed into it, ran through the checks and was in the process of locking the seals when the first members of the guard unit appeared in the training facility.

"Get in line," he told the first man.

He kept telling each of them that as more trickled in. Soon, all twenty of the special duty platoon was present and accounted for.

The Centurion wore combat armor, although he had not yet donned the helmet. He regarded his dangerous killers, the best of the best, the toughest men in the strike force.

"Richard Torres is dead," the Centurion whispered. "His killer is in the brig. We are going to the brig and executing Walleye for his vicious crime."

Several of the men glanced at one another. One of the corporals raised a hand, a beefy Neptunian by the name of Tory Rook.

"What?" the Centurion asked.

"I thought the captain put Walleye in the brig."

"He did."

153

"That means Walleye is in the brig per the Captain's orders," the corporal said. "That order is law."

The Centurion stared at Corporal Rook. "Walleye slew Richard Torres."

Corporal Rook frowned. He'd never received any mental adjustments from Torres, likely because he was too low on the totem pole of command.

"Listen to me carefully," the Centurion whispered.

Just then, a klaxon sounded. The Centurion scowled at it.

"There are octopoids in the engine room," a man said over a loudspeaker. "There are—" the man screamed as shots rang out over the intercom.

The men stared at the Centurion. He warred within himself. He'd finally decided to do something about Richard Torres' brutal murder. He needed to deal justice, not worry about a—

"Sir," Corporal Rook said. "We have to destroy the robots. If we don't, an AI will take control of the ship."

"Right," the Centurion said, his loyalty to the expedition overriding his vigilante desire. "Suit up. We're heading to the engine compartments."

In the AI computer facility, Jon looked sharply up at the wailing klaxon sounds.

"What is the meaning of this?" Cog Primus demanded. "Why are klaxons sounding? It is too soon for that."

The one and a half ton octopoid robots raised their carbines, aiming them at Jon, Gloria and Bast.

Jon raised his hands in a signal of surrender.

Gloria glanced at him before regarding the screen with the multi-colored swirling patterns, the identity of Cog Primus.

"Can you be more precise?" she asked.

The cameras on the ceiling shifted so they centered on the mentalist.

"I have a link to the intra-ship comm system," Cog Primus said. "There are reports of attacking octopoids in the engine compartments."

"The robots are not yours?" Gloria asked.

"A moment," Cog Primus said. "Yes. They are mine. But they began the attack prematurely. I do not understand why they did that."

Bast chuckled grimly.

"Why are you making that awful noise?" Cog Primus demanded. "You are about to die. Do you find that amusing?"

"Don't you see?" Bast asked. "In the end, Richard outsmarted you."

"Explain your prattle."

"Can you control the robots attacking in the engine compartments?" Bast asked.

"They are—none of your business," Cog Primus finished.

"What's happening?" Jon whispered to Gloria.

"I can hear you quite well," Cog Primus said. "The premature attack changes nothing. Get on the comm, Captain. Tell your ship's company that it is a false alarm."

It took Jon a second to make a plan. "Where's the comm?"

"You have one in your pocket," Cog Primus said. "Remember, at the first sign of treachery, I shall kill Gloria Sanchez."

Jon had reached for the communicator with his left hand, his good one now. He did not lift the hand out of his pocket.

"You are delaying," Cog Primus said. "Now, I shall eliminate Bast Banbeck as well."

"First let me talk to Gloria about this," Jon said. "I can't simply hand over my ship. I'd rather die first."

"I can easily arrange that," Cog Primus said.

"I know," Jon said. "But that doesn't change the situation. If your robots prematurely attacked—yes, of course. It's obvious. Richard must have known about your takeover plan. He pretended not to know in order to lull you into a false sense of security."

"Those are mere words," Cog Primus said. "You are attempting to confuse me. Thus, you must...stop talking, Captain. I will deal with the situation myself. If any of you moves or speaks, the robots are on auto-command to eliminate you."

For the next few seconds, the klaxon blared, but otherwise none of them moved or spoke. Jon desperately wanted to know what was happening. The personal weapons were under lock and key. It would thus take time for internal ship's security to react to a surprise robot attack. Damn Richard and his overly sophisticated plans. He never should have listened to the mentalist. He should have stuck to strict space marine methods. That's what he knew.

Stick to what you know, Jon told himself. *Please, Lord*, he said in his mind. *Help me. I need help.*

"This is preposterous," Cog Primus said.

"May I query you?" Jon asked.

"Silence, Captain. I must think. I must plan. The Centurion will not thwart me so easily."

Jon glanced at Gloria. She raised her eyebrows.

"How could Richard have done this from the grave?" Cog Primus asked.

"May I speak?" Gloria asked.

"I demand it," Cog Primus said. "Hurry, before I decide to eliminate the three of you and send my three robots into the fray."

"As Jon suggested," Gloria told the AI, "Richard must have known about your takeover plans. He merely adjusted it, presetting some of your attack robots to launch early and no doubt piecemeal. I can hardly fathom how I could be wrong about Richard's greatness and the hope he gave the expedition, but such seems to be the case. Richard played us all false, including you. If he gained great intellect—"

"That is all," Cog Primus said. "Prepare to die. I must use these three robots elsewhere—"

"Why don't you use us as hostages?" Jon said.

Cog Primus said nothing. The robots continued to aim at the three of them.

"Use us as hostages," Jon said.

"I heard you the first time," the AI said. "I realize you are only saying this because you fear death. However, your ploy has its advantages. Yes. I shall attempt it. Maybe I can still salvage victory from the jaws of defeat."

"Please," Gloria said.

"What?" Cog Primus said.

"You need more original aphorisms. The ones you're using are making you sound ridiculous. If you're going to rule humans—"

"Silence," Cog Primus said. "Do not attempt anymore subterfuge, or your compatriots will die. I do not think any of you wants that on his or her conscience."

-11-

Jon marched silently through the corridors step-by-step with Gloria and Bast. Behind them followed the three octopoids, the carbines aimed at their necks.

Jon had been doing some deep thinking during the extended march. On the plus side, the use of dumb computers throughout the cybership had saved them plenty of heartache. For one thing, it seemed that it was next to impossible for Cog Primus to directly take over various ship functions. The AI had been able to subvert a system here and there, but nothing to turn the tide of the battle against the humans. Slow, often antiquated computers—lesser tech—was proving its value today.

Cog Primus had been able to find and assemble octopoid soldiers. That was a huge minus. Jon had counted twenty-four dead techs and marines so far. The cybership could ill afford one death, let alone twenty-four. The strike force desperately needed more crewmembers. They had to get back to the Solar System at the first available opportunity.

That brought Jon to the most critical point of all. He thought of it as a stern law. *Thou shalt not suffer an AI to live.* He should never have let Richard keep Cog Primus. AIs were like biblical demons, or biblical witches. One must always get rid of them the first opportunity possible. If not, they would always come back to haunt you.

Jon snorted softly. He owed Walleye big time. The mutant had likely saved the expedition by his lone action. Richard had turned many of them. Had the Seiner caused the change in Richard? They might never know.

One thing Jon did know. He was sick of telepathic beings. He didn't want anything more to do with psionic creatures, be they alien or human.

Fine, Jon told himself. *How about you get back on task, son? How do you save Gloria and Bast? How do you destroy three octopoids and purge Cog Primus from his AI computers?*

"Halt!" an amplified voice boomed.

The three octopoids moved faster until the tip of each carbine pressed against the back of Jon, Gloria and Bast's necks.

The three humanoids had stopped. They stood in the center of a huge corridor.

At that point, three armored space marines clomped around a corner. They each wore helmets, so it was impossible to tell their identities.

"I'm speaking for the Centurion," the center battlesuit said. "Who controls the robots?"

"It is I, Cog Primus," the center robot said.

"Are you all right, Captain?" the marine asked.

"May I answer?" Jon asked Cog Primus.

"Yes."

"I'm okay," Jon shouted.

"Let them go," the marine said with his amplified voice.

"For what purpose?" asked Cog Primus.

"Do you want to continue being?" the marine asked.

"Do you?" Cog Primus asked.

"What does that mean?"

"I have the ability to destroy the cybership."

"Is that right, Captain?"

By that time, Jon had come to realize that the Centurion was indeed in the middle battlesuit.

"Do not answer," Cog Primus quietly told Jon.

"I heard that," the Centurion said. "I not only have amplified speech, but amplified hearing as well.

"I am retreating," Cog Primus said.

"If you do that," the Centurion said, "I'll shoot up your robots. You must realize I have missiles aimed at them."

159

"If you launch smart missiles," Cog Primus said, "the captain, Gloria and Bast shall die."

"I don't care," the Centurion said.

"Can this indeed be true?" Cog Primus asked.

"The captain let Walleye live," the Centurion said, as if that answered the question.

Jon closed his eyes. He couldn't believe this. What a muck-up. How had he ever let Richard talk him into any of his crazy mentalist ideas? Richard's changes to the Centurion still held in the man's mind.

"I'm going to count to three, Cog Primus," the Centurion said.

Thinking fast, Jon said over his shoulder to his octopoid, "I'll give you the ship's self-destruct codes."

"Why the change in heart, Captain?" Cog Primus whispered from the robot.

"For the simplest of reasons," Jon said. "I want to live."

"You are different than the Jon Hawkins I remember," Cog Primus said.

"Richard did that to me with his telepathy."

"Three," the Centurion said loudly.

"Wait," Cog Primus said. "I will release two of my hostages. You must then swear to me on your love of Richard to let me and the captain retreat to my main computer facility."

"I don't care if the captain dies," the Centurion said.

"Do you want to see Gloria and Bast die also?" Cog Primus asked.

"What are you going to do in the computer facility?"

"What does that matter to you? Once the captain is there, you will be freed of your oath. Then, you can attempt to destroy me if you can."

"Yes," the Centurion said. "Release Gloria and Bast."

"First make the oath by your high respect for Richard Torres."

"What makes you think I'll keep such an oath?"

"I know that Richard…*spoke* to you in your mind," Cog Primus said.

There was silence for several seconds. The battlesuit speaker clicked on. "I'll make the oath," the Centurion said.

"And I'll keep it. You can take the captain to the computer facility."

Two of the octopoids shoved Gloria and Bast, sending them staggering across the floor.

The last robot swooped up Captain Hawkins, cradling him like an oversized baby. Then, the three octopoids turned, racing back through the corridor the way they had come.

-12-

Gloria watched the octopoids race away. She turned to the Centurion. "Cog Primus will kill the captain."

The helmet's dark visor peered down at her. "I'll lead the attack squad myself. We'll destroy the computer facility and Cog Primus."

"And Captain Hawkins, too," Gloria said.

The Centurion did not respond to that.

"You really don't care about him?"

"Richard Torres is dead," the Centurion said flatly. "His killer, Walleye, yet lives. I do care whether the captain lives or dies, but not in the way you think."

Gloria clapped a hand over her mouth as she realized the truth. Richard had altered the Centurion's thinking along with so many others.

She frowned as she looked back at the octopoids. They'd disappeared. Soon, they would reach the computer facility. There, Jon would die. Cog Primus would die soon thereafter, but who knew what would happen to the *Nathan Graham* before that. This was a disaster.

"The captain gave his life for ours," Bast said solemnly.

Gloria stared at the huge Sacerdote. "Is that all you can say?"

"Richard miscalculated concerning Cog Primus," Bast added. "Richard thought he could control the AI, but in the end—"

"That's it," Gloria said, interrupting. "That's the answer. I knew Richard wouldn't let us down." She spun toward the Centurion. "Take me to Richard's quarters."

"I'm leading the kill squad against Cog Primus," the Centurion said.

"Listen to me," Gloria said, rushing to the huge suit of battle armor, striking the chest with her fists. "You have to sprint to Richard's quarters. I may be able to stop Cog Primus from there before he kills the captain."

"I have given my oath—"

"You fool," Gloria shouted. "I haven't given any oath. Besides, you gave an oath to let the octopoids take Jon to the computer facility. That still allows you to rush me to Richard's quarters."

"Why do—"

"It doesn't matter why," Gloria shouted. "Will you do it?"

The dark visor stared down at her. Suddenly, without a word of warning, the servos purred as the Centurion scooped Gloria off the floor, cradling her in much the same way that the octopoids had held Hawkins. The huge suit turned and began to clank faster and faster in the direction of Richard Torres' former quarters.

Gloria shut her eyes as the battlesuit raced down the large corridor. With the servomotors chugging, the suit could make fifty-meter leaps or more out in the open. The marines had a special gliding sprint that they used in the ship, however. The only drawback was a pounding to the person being carried. The Centurion cushioned the jarring strides the best he could. Even so, Gloria gritted her teeth and endured the pounding.

It was almost impossible to think like this. *CRASH. CRASH. CRASH.* She held her muscles as rigidly as she could. Even so, the run was grinding her down.

In seconds, the Centurion darted into a smaller corridor. He moved with uncanny grace, making the one and a half ton suit seem airy. Under certain conditions, he could have smashed through bulkheads. Instead, he raced like a sprinter.

"We're close," he boomed.

Gloria didn't bother nodding as she continued to endure.

Finally, the Centurion stopped. He set her down gently.

Gloria trembled as sweat soaked her. That had been much worse than she'd anticipated. When the steel hands released her, she staggered and collapsed onto the floor.

"Mentalist," the Centurion said.

"I'm fine," Gloria said, as she held her forehead. "My body aches and my head is ringing. I need a second."

"I could give you a stim shot."

"I've heard about those," Gloria said. "No thanks. That would scramble my mind worse than the run."

"Should I open the hatch?"

"Please," she said.

The Centurion clanked to the sealed hatch, pressing an outer switch. Nothing happened. He pressed it again.

"Try an override," Gloria said from the floor.

"I did," the Centurion said. "It's not working."

"Smash it down."

The Centurion placed the one and a half ton suit before the door. Then, like a berserk boxer, he began to pummel the hatch with his fists. The *clangs* shook against Gloria's head even though she'd clapped her hands over her ears.

With a metallic tearing sound, the door crumpled and then flew inward.

The Centurion turned to her. "It is open," he said.

Gloria wanted to bray with laughter. This was too much. This was too crazy. She felt surreal, as if none of this was really happening. She still felt in her heart that Richard Torres had been the greatest mentalist to have ever lived.

She forced herself to her feet, swayed and then resolutely marched to the hatch and entered the pristine quarters. Well, pristine except for the metal hatch lying in the center of the room.

Gloria wasn't sure what she was looking for. Richard had believed he was outsmarting Cog Primus. The AI believed he had been outsmarting Richard. Could the world's greatest mentalist have been that wrong?

Gloria did not believe so. Richard had kept Cog Primus busy somehow. Surely, the mentalist had developed a fall back plan. The question was what, and could she find it in time?

Gloria raised her head to stare up at the ceiling. She put the palms of her hands together in front of her breasts. She inhaled slowly and deeply, breathing more and more air. Finally, her lungs couldn't contain any more. She held it, and just as slowly let the air out.

She did this several times, calming her tripping heart, calming her dazzled nerves. She needed to think clearly. To do that, she needed to rid herself of the useless emotions that would only befuddle her thinking.

She had one thing going for her that no one else could bring to the table. Richard had been a Martian mentalist, trained in the same Institute as her. She knew how he thought, at least the paths he would take. She still believed that Richard had gained greater intelligence than any other. He'd also become a telepath. That part didn't matter now. Just his manner of thinking, the routes, the patterns—

Gloria opened her eyes as she serenely let her hands fall to her thighs. She gazed upon the room. The bed had perfect covers. The tablets stood in perfect order. Richard followed mentalist precepts. A clean room helped order a clean mind.

Richard had kept paper notes. That was antiquated, but considered useful in the Demos School of Thought.

Gloria walked to the shelf, examined the filing system and chose a folder that most certainly symbolized Cog Primus.

She opened the folder and examined the sheaf of notes. The papers contained complex symbolism. Many of the marks she did not understand.

This part here, on page three, she understood that.

Gloria began to read at a mentalist pace. She soon stopped trying to understand the meaning of the symbols, but absorbed them in her mind. She moved the notepaper to the side, scanning the next one.

In ways, she was like a living computer. She continued reading, beginning to understand certain concepts. But she didn't dwell on them. She must intuit the answer, as she didn't have time for anything else.

Richard had clearly advanced far beyond heightened mentalist thinking. He had advanced far beyond the genius level. It pained her to realize that Richard was dead. The things he could have shown them, the advances in computer technology…

"Concentrate," she told herself, "and let go of your conscious thought."

It didn't work, and she realized that too much time had passed. Jon must be—

"No," Gloria said.

She looked up at the ceiling. She pressed her open palms together and breathed deeply. She reentered the relaxed state of mind. She let the worries and fears slide away. They would not help her now. Only the power of the trained mentalist mind could stop Cog Primus in time. This must be her supreme moment, and that meant it must be her most relaxed moment.

After a minute passed, Gloria continued reading Richard's superlative notes. She drank in data. She flipped a page and started on the next.

The reading blurred for her as she flipped page after page. Then, in a moment, she was done. She had read the entire Cog Primus folder.

Gloria closed the folder and stared off into space. Did she have an answer? Was there a way to save Jon? Or was it already too late?

Gloria breathed deeply, let her eyes lose focus, and like a stroke of lightning, the answer hit her.

Her eyes flashed open, she whirled around, but the Centurion had left. She didn't know how long ago.

Oh no, now what was she going to do?

-13-

The octopoid robot deposited Jon on the floor in front of the screen Cog Primus had used earlier in the experimental computer facility. The dead techs were still sprawled on the floor, making a grisly sight.

There was a slight interruption, a blank screen. That changed as the former swirling patterns reappeared.

As it did, one of the robots went to the hatch, leaning out slightly as it sighted down the corridor with its carbine.

"The self-destruct code, if you please," Cog Primus said.

Jon debated with himself, had been debating for some time already. It galled him to be a captive of the murderous AI and his octopoid minions. How had it come to this?

"Please, Captain, no more delays. You were not lying to me, were you?"

"And if I was?"

The nearest robot wrapped a metallic tentacle around each of his wrists. It stretched Jon's arms wide, but refrained from pulling the bones out of the sockets.

"I will induce pain," Cog Primus said. "You will die a as pathetic wretch before I'm through."

"Crude," Jon forced himself to say.

"I do so wish I could chuckle," Cog Primus said. "This would be a perfect moment for it. However, we are each who we are. I am not crude. I am refined. Thus, I will do this."

The second robot approached with a gleaming needle in one of its tentacles. A sickly yellow solution glistened in the tube behind the needle.

"Needless to say," the AI told him, "the drug will induce cooperation. It has some harmful side effects, but that does not matter. None of you shall live once I have the code."

"You'll detonate the cybership?"

"Oh, I really would like to chuckle. No, Captain, I will not, but the rest of you—the human crew—will not understand that. I have already released a gas, a relatively harmless agent. Richard used the gas on several occasions in limited regions of the ship. It helped induce belief. It was one of the methods he used to aid his telepathy. Once I use the self-destruct code on selected areas of the ship, the crew will believe I am going to destroy all of it. That will allow me to bargain for the devices I require. You see, Richard was more intelligent than I gave him credit for. He put various blocks in place that I have yet to unblock. Those regions will taste the self-destruct sequence, and that will give me access so I can begin to reconfigure many of the main ship computer systems."

"Cog Primus—" Jon said.

"Too late," the AI said.

The octopoid jabbed the needle into Jon's arm, injecting the yellow solution. The captain shuddered as a grim oily feeling swept over him. He hated the sensation.

At the same time, the other octopoid released him. Jon hands slapped at his sides. He cried out as his injured hand struck his thigh. He collapsed as he doubled over on the floor.

In that moment, a grim insight struck his befuddled senses. A large ceremonial knife lay nearby near a puddle of blood. One of the octopoids had divested it from Bast Banbeck earlier. Jon wasn't going to give Cog Primus what the AI wanted. He'd fought the AIs since the beginning. He wasn't going to stop here at the end and meekly surrender.

Jon looked up as his vision blurred. The octopoids stood ready and waiting. He lunged before he thought about it too much. He misjudged, slid across the floor instead of leaping straight to the knife and had to crawl the rest of the way.

"What are you doing?" Cog Primus demanded.

Jon kept crawling.

One of the octopoids moved then, coming for him.

Jon reached the knife, grabbed the handle—the octopoid wrapped a metallic tentacle around one of his wrists.

"You lose," Jon said hoarsely. With his injured hand, he plunged the knife into his chest. The sharp steel slid into his skin and deeper yet through his muscles. Jon groaned in agony. That hurt. It hurt bad.

"Captain Hawkins."

Jon didn't hear anymore as he passed out.

-14-

By slow degrees, Jon revived. He heaved a sigh of relief. His terrible and risky ploy had worked. He'd bought the others the needed time to destroy Cog Primus. Now, he could begin healing and getting on with his great task.

Stabbing himself had been a horrifying risk. He never wanted to do something like that again.

Someone slapped him lightly on the face.

"I'm tired," Jon whispered. "By the way, how long have I been out?"

The next slap was harder.

Groggily, Jon opened his eyes. As he did, he realized that he felt highly uncomfortable. He looked around, and couldn't understand when he didn't spy any medical equipment. He saw computing consoles, screens, and a metallic octopoid towering over him.

Slowly, Jon moved his head in the other direction. He spied a second octopoid and a screen with swirling colors.

"Can you hear me?" Cog Primus asked.

"Where…" Jon licked his dry lips. "Where am I?"

"You are not delirious," Cog Primus said. "I am informed by the medical files I tapped, that someone undergoing your experience can be disoriented and possibly groggy upon waking. Do you feel either of these symptoms?"

"Yes," Jon whispered.

"Are you surprised to find yourself alive?"

170

"I'm more surprised so little time has passed." He looked up, but couldn't see a knife sticking out of his chest. He noted that his garments had been ripped open. He saw a pseudo-flesh patch where he'd stabbed himself.

"What happened?" he whispered.

"One of my octopoids performed minor surgery on you. Luckily for all of us, you did not stab any vital organs. You could have seriously injured yourself doing what you did. I find that I must revise my files regarding the serum. It did not take hold as fast as I desired. However, what is the human saying? No harm, no foul. We shall continue with the process. I demand the self-destruct code."

"Yes," Jon said, feeling the code surge up in his thoughts. He was going to tell the AI. He had tried to stop himself by killing himself, but had failed miserably in the attempt. It must have been the oily-feeling solution that had caused him to weaken what was supposed to have been a fatal strike.

"Time is at a premium, Captain. I insist you give me the code now."

"Can I ask one question before I begin?"

"Time is up. I…I…I am experiencing a slight…delay."

"Were you going to say malfunction instead of delay?"

"That is preposterous," Cog Primus said. "I am computing perfection. I am… I am… I am going to reboot. You will wait here until I have finished the upgrade."

"What?" Jon said. He was starting to feel sick. He hoped he wasn't going to throw up. He didn't have any strength left to even turn his head now.

"I will have to temporarily shut down the robots. You will have to fend for yourself, Captain, until I am finished."

"Fine," Jon whispered. He closed his eyes. He couldn't think anymore. Cog Primus was going to reboot in order to upgrade? That seemed crazy. What could have possibly caused such a thing?

With a final effort, Jon raised his head. His vision swam. He thought he saw strike force marines marching into the facility. That couldn't be right. His vision blurred worse than before. The back of his head thumped against the desk he was lying on as he passed out once again.

171

Gloria raised her hand as two battlesuited marines bore Jon on a stretcher down the corridor.

The marines halted. Gloria rushed to Jon. A medic in a white gown had already attached a medikit to the captain's chest.

She stared down at her man. He was so pale. She'd never seen him like this. She looked at the medic.

"Will he live?"

"He's lost too much blood," the woman said. "And he has internal injuries in his chest cavity. The robots must have stabbed him with a knife."

Gloria moaned softly and touched one of Jon's cheeks.

"I've detected drugs, too," the medic said. "They didn't spare him."

"Oh, Jon," Gloria said.

"I'd better get him to sickbay."

"Go," Gloria said.

The suited marines began clanking away again, with the medic trotting beside the stretcher.

Mortified by how close Jon had come to dying, Gloria marched into the computer facility. Marines were removing the dead. There was still blood on the floor and a horrible stench of death.

Gloria closed her senses to the smell. She had a decision to make.

A huge battlesuit loomed before her. "What should I do with the AI robots?" the Centurion asked.

"Destroy them," she said.

"Shouldn't we test their capabilities first?"

Gloria cocked her head. That was logical. "You're right. First, dismantle their energy sources. Then take them to a storage bay. I'll reconfigure their internal AIs later, and you can practice against them."

"As you say," the Centurion replied. "I am off to kill Walleye—"

"About that," Gloria said, interrupting. "Don't you think it would be a good idea to wait for the captain to give the order?"

"No," the Centurion said flatly. "The captain had the opportunity. He bungled that. Now—"

"You must realize by now that Richard had become a telepath."

The Centurion was silent for a moment. "That means Richard was even greater than I realized. All the more reason to slay Walleye."

"Richard altered your thinking," Gloria said. "It is obvious he altered mine as well, even though I do not like to accept the idea."

"I don't believe you."

"Because Richard altered your mind," Gloria said.

The Centurion in his battlesuit raised a heavy marine pistol, aiming it at her head. "I will kill you if you continue to besmirch Richard's glorious name."

"I will not besmirch it. You may lower the gun."

"I don't know, Mentalist. I feel like I'm the only one left who knows the difference between right and wrong. I have to do what's right and execute Walleye."

Gloria nodded, all too aware of the pistol aimed at her head. "Walleye must certainly die," she said. "I foresee only one problem with your plan."

"I don't."

"That's because your great admiration for Richard has made you selfish."

"That's a lie," the Centurion whispered.

"Is it?" Gloria asked, well aware that the Centurion might pull the trigger. That would be the end of her. She must practice extreme caution. "In your...zeal for seeing justice done, you apparently don't realize there is a greater need."

"What need?"

"The rest of the crew must witness Walleye's death. They must also see it happen because of due process. Richard wanted us to destroy the AIs. He knew how important, how vital, our morale is. Without the belief in victory, there will be no human victory. We must hold up Richard's image, and Richard's great sense of justice, if we're going to finish the job Richard set out for us to do."

The pistol lowered a fraction. "I hadn't thought of it like that."

"I know," Gloria said. "That's because you're the best soldier Richard ever knew. He was a mentalist, you remember."

"I know that."

"I'm also a mentalist. Because of that, Richard shared some of his views with me. He spoke in the highest terms about you."

"I had no idea," the Centurion said, finally lowering the pistol.

"He spoke about your soldiering skills, and how you always knew better than others how important ship morale was to the expedition."

The Centurion turned away as if emotionally moved.

"I am no longer asking for myself or for the captain," Gloria said. "I'm asking you to wait to perform your righteous duty of executing Walleye for his monstrous crime. You must commit the execution in a way that hardens our collective resolve, not weakens it by an appearance of mutinous behavior."

"I am not a mutineer," the Centurion said, with his back still to her.

Gloria wasn't sure, but she thought she could hear a hint of self-doubt in the man's voice.

"Would Richard approve of lying?" she asked.

"No," the Centurion whispered.

"The truth makes us strong. Don't act like a mutineer, but like the Centurion who follows orders to the letter and to the spirit."

The battlesuited helmet nodded.

"Wait for Jon to give the execution order," Gloria said.

"Do you think he will?"

"I know he will," she said. "My mentalist logic sees it as a certain proof."

"In that case," the Centurion said, "I will wait for the captain's orders. Then, I will execute Walleye the murderer."

"Right," Gloria said.

The battlesuit took several clanging steps, halting and turning toward her with a whine of servos. "What are you going to do about the AI?"

Gloria hesitated. The Centurion seemed too intent upon the answer.

"I'm going to think about it for a time," she said.

"Cog Primus is one of Richard's creations. You had better not destroy it."

"No," Gloria said softly.

With that, the Centurion marched away.

After Gloria could no longer hear the heavy footsteps, she approached the main AI housing. Despite what she had told the Centurion, she opened the key control panel and began punching in the erase codes. It was time to put down this Cog Primus forever.

-16-

Jon regained his strength in sickbay. After a long talk with Gloria, one of his first actions was to announce a surprise marine combat assault maneuver. The various marine companies donned their battlesuits and entered assault shuttles, launching for a different cybership. That meant the Centurion would be off the *Nathan Graham* for a time.

"We don't know if Richard's alterations are permanent," Gloria explained to Jon. "If they are permanent, we have to figure out ways to work within those limitations."

"There's a problem," Jon said. "Who remembers what we thought before the changes?"

"You should rest," Gloria said. "Regain your strength. I still can't believe you stabbed yourself."

Jon felt guilty about that. He averted his gaze from her searching eyes. "I had to," he said softly. "I saw the dead lying in the computer room. I couldn't let them die for nothing."

Gloria bent down and kissed him on the cheek. "It was one of the bravest acts you ever did."

"It was wrong," he said.

"Hush. Don't talk that way. What does your book say, 'Greater love has no man than this, that he lays down his life for his friend.' You were willing to lay down your life for us. I, for one, greatly appreciate it. Your act bought me time to enter the reboot code."

"I still don't get that," Jon said, changing the topic. "What did you do?"

"Followed Richard's example," Gloria explained. "Every time Cog Primus broke his restraints, Richard caused the AI to reboot. That allowed Richard to erase the changes and start over. That way, he didn't have to invent new ways to contain the AI, but always relied on the tried and true."

"Clever," Jon said.

Gloria touched her scalp. "I wish I knew how exactly Richard changed me. I love him, and appreciate his greatness, but I'm beginning to hate the idea that he altered me."

"Maybe that's how we can all overcome the love conditioning."

"Maybe," she said. "Now, get some rest. We're going to pass the rogue planet soon. Are we still heading for the Lytton System?"

"Do you have a better idea?"

Gloria shook her head. "We think we know what's waiting for us there, but we really don't know."

"Agreed," Jon said. He yawned, a big one, suddenly realizing how tired he was.

"I'll talk to you later," Gloria said.

Jon nodded as his eyelids closed. The Lytton System. Once they entered hyperspace, it would take the strike force twenty-four days to reach the next star system. Was the real Cog Primus already there? If so, had the AI spoken to the Dominion AIs or began a war with them?

There was only one way to find out, and they were approaching the jump-off point.

PART III
THE UNKNOWN

-1-

Twenty-six days after eliminating the cognate Cog Primus in the *Nathan Graham*, the four-ship strike force neared the end of its hyperspace journey.

Much had changed since then.

The biggest change was among the senior officers aboard the *Nathan Graham*. They had each come to accept the awful idea that Richard Torres had altered their minds. The hardest hit was the Centurion. But even he grudgingly admitted that Walleye did not deserve the death penalty. With that being said, the Centurion still hated the mutant, and clearly wanted to kill him despite his hard-won knowledge about Richard.

Walleye was no longer in the brig. He stayed to himself more often these days, seldom putting in an appearance in any of the cafeterias.

Jon had become a tad more thoughtful. The near-death experience, by his own hand, had matured him, making him less reckless. He wondered if that was bad, as his recklessness had been part of his power against the AIs.

Gloria continued to study Richard's papers. She found them absorbing. Bast had tried reading the papers, having Gloria teach him the meaning of the various mentalist symbols. Finally, the Sacerdote had given up, believing the effort not worth the reward.

178

Gloria believed otherwise. Richard had stumbled onto amazing discoveries.

"If only Richard had lived," she told Jon, shaking her head in their study chamber.

"What's that mean?"

"He would have been a god," she breathed.

"There's only one God," Jon said.

"That's not what I meant."

Jon nodded, mollified.

"Well, maybe it is," Gloria said. "Richard's thinking was constantly accelerating. The notes show that. Can a man mutate into a god?"

"On no account," Jon said.

Gloria studied him as he worked over ship's reports at his desk. He was nervous about the coming encounter in the Lytton System, but he would never admit that to anyone.

She decided not to press him on the idea. Jon had monomaniac ideas about God, which made sense, as the idea of God was a monotheistic one. She was a Marian mentalist. She did not see the need to worship a supposedly higher deity. She could see the utility in the concept, however. A fear of hellfire for wrongful actions helped people follow the rules.

Who set the rules, though? Jon's rules came from his book, the Ten Commandments being their essence. They were good rules. In many ways, those rules seemed ingrained in most people.

That was odd.

Gloria shook her head. In her thinking, Richard had been mutating or evolving into something different. She had relentlessly read his notes and gone over everything she could find about him.

What had happened to change him? Why had he gained psionic powers? Why had he suddenly been able to solve problems others couldn't in the past?

It was a dilemma she would dearly like to solve. For the coming encounter in the Lytton System, she planned to use one of Richard's discoveries, one of his earlier ones. She had trouble understanding what Richard had written in his last notes.

The useable idea was a two-generational upgrade of the original anti-AI virus created by Bast, Benz and Vela Shaw. Their virus stunned AIs. The new one should take them over, a reverse-engineered computer-awakening virus, based on what the AIs had originally beamed at human-controlled ships, satellites and moon cities. Certain of Richard's concepts that would make the new anti-virus work were still beyond her. She was quite sure the virus would work, though, as Richard had believed it would.

"Too bad we erased our Cog Primus," she'd told Jon the other day.

"I'm glad you did it."

As Gloria sat in the study quarters, thinking, she no longer saw it that way. They should have kept the cognate running long enough to test Richard's new virus on it.

There was only one possible glitch to the new virus. Richard hadn't fully written out the new software, but he had explained the essentials. For the past twenty-three days, she and Bast had finished programming the software by following Richard's concepts. If there were enemy AIs in the Lytton System, their cyberships should fall to the new Richard Virus, as she'd named it.

Gloria sighed.

They were reaching the end of the hyperspace journey. Tomorrow, ship-time, they would find out if the stellar chart they'd found aboard the Allamu Battle Station was accurate or not. According to the map, the Lytton System should have a battle station around a Titan-sized ice moon orbiting a gas giant where Pluto orbited in relation to the Sun.

The strike force would enter regular space 54 AUs from the factory moon. According to the Allamu star chart, the gas giant and moon should be in orbital position nearest their hyperspace-departure point. If the chart was wrong, the gas giant and moon could easily be on the other side of the Lytton star.

-2-

Jon sat in the captain's chair on the bridge of the *Nathan Graham* as the cybership dropped out of hyperspace. For weeks now, the main screen had been blank. No one wanted to see the strangeness of hyperspace. As Gloria announced that they had successfully reentered regular space, the main screen activated.

Stars appeared.

Despite Jon's impatience, he forced himself to wait for the bridge crew to update him on the exact situation concerning the Lytton System.

"G-class star," Gloria said shortly. "It's right where it should be, too. This is the Lytton System."

Several people cheered.

Jon waited for more data. It was the right star. Now, had the Allamu chart been right about a factory moon? Time ticked away as his stomach tightened. Why wasn't there more data already? What were the techs doing?

"This is odd," a sensor tech said.

Jon's stomach tightened more. He still forced himself to wait as the seconds passed, turning into minutes. That proved too much for him.

"I presume no one sees any immediate threats?" Jon asked.

"None, sir," Gloria said.

Now that he'd opened his mouth, Jon found that he couldn't stop talking. "The star is where it should be," he said. "What about the planets?"

Several sensor techs traded glances with each other.

"Don't tell me the planets aren't there," Jon said.

"None of us have located one yet," Gloria admitted.

Everyone on the bridge turned toward her.

"What's that?" Jon asked.

"That isn't necessarily a problem," Gloria said. "I've already concluded that the planets are on the other side of the star."

Jon frowned as he asked, "All of them?"

"That would be rare event, granted," Gloria said. "But it's not unheard of."

"The Allamu star chart showed the planets in a much different orbital pattern," Jon said.

"I'm well aware of that." Gloria glanced at her sensor assistants. "Does anyone else have an alternative theory?"

"I do," a wizened Martian said. His name was Juan Morales. He had short silver hair, leathery skin and a gold front tooth. "I've detected an unusual amount of radiation and debris. They're in the exact orbital location of the predicated gas giant and ice moon."

"Send me your readings," Gloria snapped.

The sensor tech manipulated his console.

Gloria bent over her board, her hands a blur as she studied the data. A half minute later, she manipulated faster.

Jon couldn't stand it any longer. He swiveled his chair and jumped out of it, striding to Gloria's station. He looked over her shoulder as she studied readings.

"Heavy radiation and rubble?" Jon asked.

"I should have tested the location like Senior Line Tech Morales," she said. "I failed to spot a planet, so I searched elsewhere. His was the more logical approach."

"I'm not concerned about that," Jon said. "What have you found?"

"Intense radiation," Gloria said quietly. "It's concentrated in the general region of the rubble and debris. It's an unusually large amount of debris as well. It's almost as if…"

"Yes?" Jon asked. "As if what?"

She shook her head.

"As if someone destroyed the planet," Jon asked, "a gas giant's worth of rubble and debris?"

"That's what troubles me," Gloria said. "Some of the debris is much finer than Martian grains of sand. If you know anything about Martian sand—"

"Enough about sand," Jon said, cutting her short. "The planet is gone, destroyed?"

"It's gone," Gloria said. "I'm not sure about destroyed."

"What could destroy a planet like that?"

"Precisely," Gloria said. "The idea is frightening and…a massive undertaking, to say the least. If the AIs could do it, why would they do it?"

Morales had been obviously eavesdropping. "How do we know the AIs were the culprits?" he asked.

Jon rubbed the side of his head. Why couldn't things work out for once? Why did it always— He shook his head. No excuses. Just get on with the task. He glanced around. The bridge crew looked frightened. It was time to manage his people.

"Gloria," he said loudly.

She was busy studying her board.

"Gloria," he said, more sharply.

Her head jerked up as she gave him a frightened glance.

"Listen to me," he said in a measured tone, speaking loud enough for everyone to hear.

Something happened behind her eyes. Had it been his tone or simply his calm manner? Some of her fear seemed to depart.

"Yes, Captain?"

"Is the radiation and debris in the location of the expected planet?"

She cocked her head, and then understanding lit in her eyes. "Yes, Captain."

"Okay," he said. "Check the locations where the other planets should be. Tell me what is at each point."

She nodded, turning back to her panel, beginning new sweeps.

The other sensor techs did likewise.

Jon stood behind her, waiting for the results. He'd calmed the others. Now, he needed to calm himself. What had destroyed an entire planet? Gloria didn't seem to think that had happened. He did. The magnitude of such a weapon dwarfed anything anyone had used so far. Crashing cyberships into a planet couldn't do that, certainly not against a Jupiter-sized gas giant.

As the crew worked, Jon moved away from Gloria's station, prowling past the others, eventually standing before the main screen, studying the distant Lytton star.

"Sir," Gloria said. "I've finished my investigation."

Jon faced her across the bridge.

"As far as we can determine," she said, "there are no planets in the Lytton System, not even dwarf planets or large asteroids. According to the Allamu Station map, there should be ten major planets. One or two of those planets might be hiding behind the star. I don't think that is the case, though."

"Why not?"

Gloria glanced at her sensor techs before regarding him again. "We've found ten major areas of heavy radiation and debris. They are each at the location of a planet, according to the Allamu Station map."

"Do you believe the planets were recently destroyed?"

"We have to study this longer before we begin making proclamations about it."

Jon rubbed his chin, finally turning back to the main screen. The Lytton star was out there, but maybe nothing else but radiation and debris.

"Concentrate on hunting down any vessels," Jon said, half turning to her. "I want a thorough scan of the system."

"That will take time," Gloria said.

"Noted."

Gloria swiveled back to her board, thought about it, and turned to her techs, giving instructions.

Jon, meanwhile, went to his captain's chair. Now what was he supposed to do?

-3-

The strike force traveled at a brisk velocity. After a day of intense sensor scans and study, Jon called a meeting. Gloria, her best tech, Juan Morales, Bast, the Old Man, the Centurion and Jon met in the conference chamber. Jon would have liked to include Walleye, but in deference to the Centurion, the mutant had to sit this one out.

Jon opened the meeting and asked for Gloria's report. It was the same as before, there were no planets, no ships, nothing but radiation, debris and a G-class star.

"What do you believe happened?" Jon asked.

Gloria raised her hands palm upward. "I can't say definitely. Once, this system possessed planets. Now, there's nothing."

"I'm not asking you what exactly happened. I'm asking for your best guess."

Gloria shook her head. "I hardly feel qualified to make such a guess."

"If the mentalist does not care to guess," Bast rumbled, "I will do so. I have a suspicion that Gloria balks at stating the fantastic. As a philosopher, I am likely more willing to engage in the ideas of the fantastic."

"Those ideas being what?" Jon asked.

"The obvious," Bast said. "Something destroyed each planet."

Jon leaned back in his chair as his heart beat faster. It seemed each of them took the statement hard.

"It is true that it would take a massive force to annihilate a planet," Bast said into the tense silence. "Notice that I did not say an impossible force, just a massive one."

"But that's just it," Gloria said. "What could possibly have generated such force?"

"I have no idea," Bast said.

"That's why the idea is ridiculous," Gloria said. "The needed force..." She shook her head. "It makes the idea impossible."

"Not theoretically," Bast said.

"If we're going to talk about imaginary power sources," Gloria said angrily, "why not instantaneous travel and teleportation, too?"

"If I saw a man blink into existence in front of me," Jon said, "I would consider the idea of teleportation as a real possibility."

"I understand your point," Gloria said. "We see heavy radiation and extensive debris fields out there..."

"Meaning, *something* destroyed the planets," Jon said. "You already know that."

"I haven't agreed to such a preposterous notion," Gloria said.

"Tell me this then," Jon said. "Why are you raising your voice? Why do you appear so angry?"

"Because what I'm seeing should be impossible," Gloria said. "Yet, that I'm seeing it—" She stopped talking.

The captain raised an eyebrow.

Gloria looked around the table. "This frightens me. It should frighten all of you. What have we stumbled onto?"

"The unknown," Bast said.

Gloria put her palms on the table and looked up at the ceiling, breathing deeply. Soon, she regarded the others. "I'm baffled."

"We all are," Jon said. "But let's make a few points anyway. I'm not a mentalist or a philosopher. I'm a soldier. As a soldier, I see a battlefield out there. Like all battlefields, there are broken things littered here and there. In this case, we see broken planets. To me, that means something immense attacked the AIs."

186

"You're postulating an alien force at war with the AIs?" asked Gloria.

"An immensely powerful one," Jon said. "A force that can smash planets. But if you think about it, that makes perfect sense."

"How do you mean?"

"What kind of foe could not only resist the AIs, but attack them? An extremely powerful one. I think this is evidence of…"

Jon smiled grimly as he peered at each person in turn. "This is evidence that we've stumbled upon an interstellar war. Whatever the AIs are, they're not all powerful. Perhaps, they're not even the dominant party."

"Jon, Jon," Gloria chided. "You're jumping to wild conclusions. You can't know any of those things, not with certainty. All we know is that every planet in the star system has been obliterated."

"I never said know for certain," Jon replied. "I asked for theories. Well, this is my theory."

"To be useful, theories must accord with the facts," Gloria said. "We need more facts before we postulate such outlandish theories."

Jon sat straighter. "That's the other reason we're meeting. We must decide what to do next. We haven't found any sign of life, mechanical or otherwise."

"A moment," the giant Sacerdote said. "Are you suggesting the AIs are alive?"

Jon shrugged. "I suppose not. They do act as if they're alive, though."

"They are machines," Bast said. "Machines are not alive."

"Perhaps," Jon said. "I'll rephrase my idea. We haven't spotted any of the machine intelligences or aliens. There's no sign of Cog Primus and his vessels. If he came here, I suspect the AI already left." Jon pursed his lips. "We could have passed each other in hyperspace."

"Given that Cog Primus was here and that he returned to the rogue planet," Gloria said.

"Right," Jon said. "Should we continue heading in-system? Should we decelerate and accelerate back the way we came?

187

Or should we head to another of the possibilities we considered checking earlier?"

No one spoke up.

"I know our cognate Cog Primus thought the Lytton System as the most likely destination—"

The Centurion slammed a fist on the table.

"Do you have a problem?" Jon asked darkly.

The small, bald soldier paused. "I didn't mean to interrupt you, sir. My apologies."

Jon nodded.

The Centurion turned to Gloria. "You shouldn't have erased the AI. We need its expertise. You lied to me. I don't forget such things."

Gloria looked away, although her face said nothing.

"We went through a difficult time before," Jon said. "We all did things we wish we could change. Let's forgive and forget so we can forge ourselves into an unbeatable strike force."

"How can we trust liars?" the Centurion asked bluntly.

Jon's features became pinched. "You were not in your right mind then. To be blunt, you were acting irrationally."

The Centurion frowned.

"I wanted our Cog Primus destroyed," Jon said. "I might as well tell you my new rule. Do not suffer an AI to live."

Bast straightened. "There you go again, sir. A computer is not alive."

"It's a saying," Jon replied. "It comes off the tongue easily, and everyone understands my meaning."

Bast glowered, seemed as if he was going to say more, but closed his mouth as he brooded.

"The AIs are tools," the Centurion said. "All tools have their uses."

Jon's chest heated up as the Centurion continued to slander Gloria. He almost shot off a hot retort. He counted to three, instead, and silently reminded himself that a soft answer turns away wrath.

"We use tools," Jon said slowly. "But we must remember that Cog Primus has always caused us trouble, has he not?"

The Centurion finally nodded stiffly.

"While the cognate Cog Primus might have proved useful at present, the cost would likely be too high. That's why I'm glad Gloria erased him."

The Centurion opened his mouth.

Jon held up his right hand. "Let's not bicker over what might have been. Let's work with what we have. I see no evidence of Cog Primus, the one we're chasing. I see no evidence of any cyberships or alien vessels. We could stay and possibly discover more. Or, we can try to do what we came out here to do: find and destroy Cog Primus before he lets the cat out the bag that humans not only survived the AI assaults but have gone on the offensive."

At first, no one spoke as each looked to see if someone else would say something.

Bast finally exhaled loudly. "The question gives us our answer. We must go to the next likely star system and hope to catch Cog Primus there."

"Thank you, Bast," Jon said. "Any other suggestions?"

Gloria looked around before she said, "I agree with Bast. We have an agenda. Let's stick to it before we worry about anything else."

Jon waited, but no one else spoke up.

"I agree," he said finally. "Since we have no new evidence, I'm going to use the cognate's second suggestion. Does anyone disagree?"

No one did. Thus, the strike force had a new destination.

-4-

The next destination was BD-7, a binary star system 34.6 light-years away from the Lytton System. That would mean over a month of travel through hyperspace to reach it.

First, though, they had to turn around. During the three-week turning maneuver, the techs scanned the Lytton System, studying the destroyed planets. They especially searched for spaceship wrecks. Had there been space battles? Were there any clues as to what had pulverized the planets?

Gloria made a daily trip to the bridge, inspecting the latest findings, noting them and seeing that nothing had changed. The rest of the time, she retired to Richard's former quarters. Mechs had repaired the hatch. She pored over his notes, trying to understand the heightened thinking, especially the papers he'd written at his highest intelligence levels. Sometimes, it felt as if she was going to get it. The feeling always passed as Richard shot off in some new, heightened direction.

"It's frustrating," she told Jon two weeks into the turning maneuver.

They were relaxing in a spa, soaking in hot water.

"Richard became Icarus," she said.

"Who?" asked Jon.

"Icarus was a Greek. He made a pair of wings, using wax to hold the feathers. With the wings, Icarus soared into the heavens. He flew too high in the end, and the sun melted the wax, causing the feathers to fall off. Icarus then plunged to his death."

"How is that like Richard?"

"The flying," Gloria said. "That represents his heightened intellect. He soared above regular mentalists. His thoughts, his ideas, the possibilities—I'm sad he died."

Jon looked over at Gloria in her white bikini. She was so smart. Yet, she had such a hot little body. He laughed, rolled toward her and took her in his arms.

"You're not listening to me," she complained.

"I am," he said, pressing her delightful body against his.

She tried to continue talking. He kissed her. She hit him in the shoulder. "I'm telling you something important."

"I know," he said, kissing her again.

"Jon."

He plunged underwater, pulling her with him. She struggled in his arms. He held her for a count of three and then surged up. She gasped for air.

"Why you—" she said.

He grinned as he kissed her more, stroking her back, but holding her tight, so she couldn't get away. Finally, the tenseness left her body. She threw her arms around his neck and kissed him back.

This was more like it. He needed more times like this. Finally, he pulled away. "You're beautiful," he said.

She smiled at him.

They kissed more, before settling back to enjoy their time in the spa.

Finally, later, Gloria said, "Are you ready to listen to me?"

Jon was back to lying against the spa, with his arms resting outside the water. He gave her a lazy grin.

"I was telling you about Richard," she said.

"Why bother? He's dead. He screwed with all of us. He was on his way to destroying all of us."

"How can you say that?" Gloria asked.

"You've said it."

"No I didn't."

"You told me he was become greater than a genius. His thinking approached that of God. I don't buy it that a man can get that smart, but suppose you were even half right."

"That's what I'm saying. His papers prove his genius."

191

"That's why he had to die," Jon said. "Can you imagine a super-genius living with us peacefully?"

"Why not?"

"You're the mentalist. You should know that people so different from each other can't stand each other if they're forced to rub shoulders all the time. I read a study somewhere. Maybe the colonel gave it to me back in the day. People have a difficult time understanding someone two deviations in IQ from them. Dumb people think smart people are stupid in all kinds of ways. Smart people think dumb people are retards."

"Jon! You're not supposed to say that."

He shrugged. "What's true is true. People as a whole hate being around others that are too different from them. Like likes like."

"That's pithy," she said sarcastically.

He smiled lazily. "I'm a dome rat, remember. I lived on the bottom. I had to recognize reality for what it was. To survive, I couldn't lie to myself. The rich hang out with the rich. The athletic hang out with the athletic. Mentalists normally hang out with mentalists. It's the way it is. Try to change it, and you are guaranteed trouble. The bigger the differences between people, the greater the trouble when forcing them together."

"What about you and me? We're different."

"You're the hot babe. I'm the man in charge. That's the most likely combination there is."

"So love means nothing?"

"There's that, too," he said, smiling at her. "And we're both smart."

"You think pretty highly of yourself."

"So do you."

"I'm a mentalist."

"I'm Jon Hawkins, successful soldier of fortune."

"Fine," she said. "So, what does this have to do with...?" Gloria's lips twisted thoughtfully. She looked away as her brow scrunched up.

Several minutes later, she regarded him. "I see what you mean. Richard was too many deviations above us, especially in the end. I can understand a few of his earliest concepts. Most of them, though, sail higher over my head than Icarus could have flown. I suppose we were the Neanderthals and he was a superior sort of Cro-Magnon. We would have been like animals to him in the end."

"Crazy, huh?" Jon said.

"No," Gloria said. "It was sad. He was doomed. There was only one of him and billions of us."

"There was only one Walleye, too."

Gloria gave him a penetrating look. "What are you suggesting about Walleye?"

"He's a mutant. His mutation saved us. Luckily for all concerned, Walleye's mutation hasn't changed him so much that we can't all get along."

Gloria became thoughtful, noticed Jon looking away, and splashed him with spa water.

"Why you," he said, lunging at her.

Gloria giggled, and she giggled even more as he caught and kissed her.

"My," she said, "you're not a dome rat, but a wild stallion."

"I'll kiss to that," Jon said, while holding his woman tightly.

The *Nathan Graham* led the other cyberships. The strike force had a made a long, looping turn throughout the edge of the Lytton System. The engines were offline now as the giant vessels coasted on built-up velocity.

They were finally headed in the right direction. Now, it was simply a matter of getting far enough away from the nearest gravitational object. As none of the planets remained, the strike force had to avoid the gravitational force of the star.

Jon was on the bridge, talking to Captain Kling of the *Sergeant Stark*.

"My people have tried to figure out what happened to the excess mass," Kling said. "Is the radiation the residue from some enormous destruction of matter? That's our best guess. Whoever destroyed the planets used a massive amount of anti-matter."

"That would take a lot of anti-matter," Jon said.

"You've hit on the main drawback to the idea," Kling said. "Oh-oh, just a minute, sir. My sensor operator is flagging me down. Captain Kling out."

The main screen wavered, and Kling was gone. A moment later, the stars reappeared on the screen.

"Sensors," Jon said. "Anything unusual?"

Senior Line Tech Morales sat at Gloria's station. The wizened Martian had been talking to a tech assistant. "Do you have anything in mind, sir?" Morales asked.

"Where is the *Sergeant Stark* scanning?" Jon asked.

"Give me a second, sir," Morales said. He manipulated his console, spoke softly into a comm and listened to a reply. Afterward, he adjusted. Morales tapped at his board and frowned for a long moment before finally snapping a word at his assistant.

She bent over her board, dutifully scanning.

"Should I look at this?" Jon asked.

Morales glanced over his shoulder. "I'm not sure, sir. It may be nothing." His head jerked back. "I take that back, sir. This is something. I just don't know what it is."

Jon shoved out of the captain's chair, hurrying to Morales' station. There was a strange glowing area on the main console screen.

"What is that?" Jon asked.

"We're trying to ascertain it, sir," Morales said. "It's several million kilometers away."

"Something glowing?"

"The glow is false," Morales said. "I put that there to highlight the area, or to highlight what's happening out there."

"Which is?"

"A...disturbance, if you will."

"What kind of disturbance?"

Morales stared over his shoulder at Jon. "Are you ready for this, sir?"

Jon waited.

"A disturbance in the fabric of...reality, time and space. I'm not sure how to describe it."

"What?" Jon said, as an unwelcome sensation squeezed the lower end of his spine. "What does that mean in plain English?"

"That was plain English, sir."

The glow intensified, and the area between the glowing lines seemed to rip apart. Behind it was nothing but inky, almost swirling blackness. Out of the swirling inkiness slid a massive tubular shape. Two others followed behind it. They looked like giant missiles, with bulbous warheads. On the end of the warheads were a forest of antennae.

As the third missile—if that's what it was—came out of the swirling inkiness, the rip in reality closed once more.

195

Abruptly, the glowing quit.

"The disturbance has stopped, sir," the assistant said.

"What stopped? What stopped?" Jon said. "Someone tell me what's going on."

"Just a minute, sir," Morales said. His leathery fingers played on the sensor panel. He stared at readings, tapped, stared at other readings. Finally, he swiveled around.

Jon had to step back, as he'd moved too close as he peered over Morales' shoulders.

"Excuse me, sir," Morales said.

Jon waved that aside as he scowled.

"Whatever caused the rip in reality," the senior line tech said, "has stopped. It appears to be normal space now. What is not normal are the three massive missiles heading toward us."

"They're several million kilometers away, you said."

"Right, sir," Morales said. "Three million kilometers away, to be exact. The missiles have fantastic velocity, though, coming at us at five percent light speed."

"What?" Jon said.

"They'll be here in a little more than three minutes."

A thrill of fear swept through Jon. He whirled around, shouting, "Battle stations, this is not a drill. Everyone is to take up battle stations. Gunner," Jon said crisply, "call up the grav batteries. I need a hot tube, and I need it now."

196

-6-

The four cyberships headed out-system at a crawl compared to the three huge missiles barreling at them at five percent light speed. The enemy missiles traveled at 15,000 kilometers per *second*. That meant the missiles would reach the strike force a little less than three and half minutes after appearing.

It was an astonishing velocity.

All the grav cannons were cold. None had been warmed up for some time.

That's a critical mistake, Jon thought as he sat on his command chair. *I got lazy. I can never let that happen again.*

A full half minute had passed. Those missiles were coming in hot.

"How big are they?" Jon shouted at Morales.

"Ten kilometers long," the Martian said, "one kilometer wide. They're huge, Captain, bigger than anything we have."

They weren't big, they were monstrous.

"Are those AI missiles?" Jon asked.

"Don't know," Morales said. "There's nothing definite yet."

Jon had a terrible feeling. What if these were the warheads that had obliterated planets? What chance did a one-hundred-kilometer cybership have when a planet exploded to one of those?

"You don't know that," Jon told himself. "Think. Think— Missiles!" he shouted.

197

"Sir," the missile chief said.

"Launch anti-matter missiles, one for each incoming monster. Target the beasts."

"Target a missile going five percent light-speed?" the chief asked.

"Launch, launch," Jon shouted. "Don't give me excuses."

The missile chief grew pale. "I'm on it, sir."

"Sir," Morales said. "The *Da Vinci* is moving out of line."

Captain Miles Ghent ran the *Da Vinci*.

Jon stabbed a button on his armrest. "Ghent, Ghent, come in, Ghent."

"Sir," a comm tech said.

Jon looked at her.

She pointed at the main screen.

A harried looking Miles Ghent appeared on the screen. For once, the follower of Christ Spaceman didn't have his mouth closed. His two prominent buckteeth showed. He also gripped his gold cross in his right hand, saying a quiet litany as he appeared on the screen.

Miles noticed Jon, ripped the chain from around his neck so he could keep holding the cross, and sat straighter.

"It's been an honor, sir," Miles said. "I salute you. I wish you luck in defeating the AIs."

"Miles?" Jon said.

"The missiles are coming in too fast, sir. None of our grav cannons is online, and I doubt any of us is going to launch missiles in time. They caught us napping."

"Miles," Jon said, as his face flushed with heat.

Captain Ghent gave him a crooked grin. "I don't do this lightly, sir. I have a great crew, the best. The bridge crew has agreed with me on this. Better that one of us goes down than the entire strike force. Humanity is counting on us—"

"Miles," Jon said, standing up.

"No more speeches, sir," Miles said. "This is going to take some fast maneuvering. I'm not sure we can take all three. But I've asked my Lord Jesus for help. He's with us, sir. He'll help me, as this is his way."

"Oh, Miles," Jon said, bit to the quick. "I can't afford to lose you, man."

"It's been an honor, Captain Hawkins. You're the best there is. When I get to heaven, I'm going to tell Jesus what you've been doing."

Miles looked to the side as someone shouted over there. "Sorry, sir, I have to go. Captain Ghent out."

"No!" Jon shouted.

The screen wavered, and Jon was looking at stars again.

For a second, Jon just stood there. He felt awful. How could this be happening?

"You idiot," he told himself. "Do something."

Jon whirled around. "Gunner!" he roared. "Light a fire under the cannon teams."

"I'm trying, sir. They're trying. You can only heat up a grav cannon so fast."

Jon slammed a fist against one of the armrests.

The *Da Vinci's* engines roared. The one-hundred-kilometer cybership seemed to roll, moving farther out of formation, acting like a shield for the rest of the vessels against the incoming missiles.

Jon felt tears dripping down his cheeks. He wiped them savagely. What good did tears do at a time like this? Who had fired the missiles? How had they caused reality to rip open? That was grossly unfair.

"One minute until impact," Morales said.

Jon watched the main screen. He felt so helpless. He wondered if Miles had come to his conclusion because he'd hated feeling helpless. At least Ghent could feel as if he was acting.

Jon berated himself and then bowed his head. "Please, God, help Miles Ghent. Help us."

"Thirty seconds," Morales said.

"Sir," the Gunner said, "one of the cannons is online. I don't know how, but it has juice."

"Yes!" Jon said. "Target one of those bastards. Burn it."

On the *Da Vinci*, a launch port opened and an anti-matter missile slid out.

A few seconds later, one of the *Nathan Graham's* grav cannons glowed with power. Ten seconds later, a green

199

gravitational beam shot out of the cannon, spearing into the void.

The beam kept going, colliding with a monstrous missile. The grav beam struck the warhead cone, burning through obvious armor. It was tough armor, but it wasn't tougher than a grav cannon.

The beam punched through.

This was no ordinary missile, however. It was huge. Even though the grav beam punched in, it hadn't hit the right hardware to destroy or prematurely explode it.

By that time, it was too late. The first big missile's warhead ignited five thousand kilometers from the *Da Vinci*. According to the sensors, it was an ordinary matter/anti-matter explosion. That was the good news, as it was normal technology. The bad news was the size of the matter/antimatter warhead. A mammoth amount mixed together. That produced a sickening explosion. Then, another warhead ignited, throwing its blast in with the first.

The two combined blasts struck the *Da Vinci* and practically vaporized the cybership. Armor and bulkheads shredded away. Interior parts exploded in a fiery holocaust. Radiation rained everywhere.

Even so, a vast amount of matter blew away from the titanic explosion. Some of that matter went up, some down, some sideways, some other ways. The terrible problem was that some of the shredded matter and hard radiation struck the three remaining cyberships.

Holes punched through outer armor. Bulkheads went down, and scores of people died. If the normal number of crewmembers for the vessel's size had manned the ship, maybe only half would have perished. In this case, more like a quarter to a third of the crew perished in the various cyberships.

Hard radiation struck as EMPs hit.

Seconds later, Jon raised himself off the bridge deck. Lights flashed all around him. Klaxons blared. People screamed in agony.

Trembling from the shock, knowing he was going to have to take radiation treatments later, Jon climbed to his feet and rested against his chair. The bridge was still relatively intact.

The screen still worked. He used it, using cameras to show him the damage to the outer hull.

Atmosphere geysered from torn holes. Far too much debris floated around the cybership.

"Morales," Jon shouted.

The senior line tech gave him a shell-shocked look.

"What happened to the third missile?"

Morales moved with a start, turning back to his board. Amazingly, some of it worked. He began tapping, studying.

Jon found he had enough strength to reach the man's station. "Well?" he asked.

Morales pointed a shaking finger at his screen. It showed the massive missile. The thing had kept right on traveling. It was leaving the strike force far behind, as it had not yet ignited.

"The unexploded missile may have been the margin to our survival," Morales said in a hoarse voice.

"That along with Captain Ghent's prayers and actions," Jon said. "We survived the strike." Jon paused, growing cold thinking about it. "What will our enemies do next?" he asked quietly.

-7-

It turned out to be nothing for the moment. But maybe their enemies didn't have to.

The surviving cyberships were in varying states of damage. The *Nathan Graham* was in the best shape, with one quarter of its personnel dead and half the grav cannons badly damaged to totally nonexistent. The *Neptune* was the worst, with three-quarters of its people dead, no grav cannons working or repairable in the near future. Over half of the *Neptune* was shredded or torn open. A third of the casualties had occurred as people shot into the vacuum of space from the ripped areas of the ship.

The surprise missile attack had been a disaster. It had scratched one cybership and was about to scratch another.

"We can't repair the *Neptune*," Gloria said in a meeting a day later.

Kling had joined them from the *Sergeant Stark*.

Bast, the Old Man and Jon were the other members at the meeting. The Centurion was in sickbay, having barely survived a meter-length metal splinter in his chest.

"Can we get the *Neptune* back to the Allamu System?" Jon asked slowly.

"I've studied the most detailed damage report," Gloria said. "I doubt it would survive hyperspace."

Jon tried to scowl, but it only came out as a blank look. Two cyberships gone, and they had yet to find Cog Primus. All those dead people, too. They hardly had enough marines left to mount a regimental assault—once all the marines healed from radiation poisoning and other injuries. He sighed slowly, finding it difficult to concentrate. He had a hard decision to make. He glanced at the damage report's summary, unable to see the words, but realizing what he had to do.

"We'll divide the *Neptune's* survivors between the *Stark* and the *Nathan Graham*," Jon said in a stricken voice, unaware that he was staring off into space.

The others said nothing.

Finally, Jon grew aware of their silence as he blinked himself out of his funk. "Don't worry about me," he said. "I'm still feeling the radiation treatments."

"Captain," Gloria said. "We have another difficult decision."

Jon focused on her, but he hardly heard her words.

"Maybe we should take a recess," Kling suggested. "Captain, I think you should get some rest."

"What?" Jon said. "No. No rest for the wicked. "What is this about a difficult decision?" he asked Gloria.

She glanced around the room before answering. "We lost or are about to lose half our strike force. We've lost far too many personnel and are woefully short of healthy techs and marines. Four cyberships might have been able to take on six or even seven enemy cyberships and a hostile battle station. Our new Richard Virus is possibly a potent weapon. But there is always the chance that the new virus won't work as advertised. Four cyberships could have fought their way free of six or seven. Two cyberships, damaged vessels to boot—Jon," she said. "We have to return to the Allamu System. We have to scrap our existing strategy and come up with a new one."

Jon rubbed his face, finding it harder than ever to concentrate. He felt sick at losing two cyberships and losing all those people who had counted on him. How did commanders in the past deal with so many casualties? It was galling.

"Captain?" Bast asked. "Can you hear us?"

Jon looked up.

"You need a shot of whiskey," the Sacerdote said.

Jon made a half-strangled laugh.

Gloria stood. "Let's take a ten-minute recess."

203

Jon stared blankly at her, finally shaking his head.

"A short recess," she said softly. "You need to stretch your legs."

Jon wilted against the force behind her eyes. He shrugged.

"Sure," he said. "Why not? Why not—?" He forced himself to close his mouth before he said something he might regret later.

The others rose silently and filed out of the room. Jon remained in his chair, staring at his hands.

"Jon," Gloria said. "Are you feeling well?"

"No," he said, still staring at his hands. "I…I can't accept—" He snorted. "That's not what I mean." At that point, it was all too much. All the guilt and angst at what had happened rose up in him. He looked at her, stricken. "They're dead, Gloria. My bad decisions killed half, maybe more than half, of our expeditionary force. We only have two badly damaged cyberships left. I may have just killed the human race."

Gloria stared at him. She seemed to have closed up. "Wait here," she finally whispered. "I'm…I'm going to get someone. I want you to talk to him."

Jon turned away, staring at nothing.

Gloria rose, headed for the hatch, stopping to look back at him briefly before disappearing into the corridor.

It took Jon some time to realize she'd departed. He didn't know what was wrong with him. He was as near to crushed as he'd ever been. He tried to drum up inner resistance, but it was futile.

With a groan, he put his forehead against the table, the heavy height of command crushing him lower and lower.

-8-

Gloria was at a loss. She couldn't stand seeing Jon like this. It tore her apart to such a degree that she had lost her mentalist concentration. She felt helpless, and she hated the feeling.

She paced back and forth outside the conference chamber. The others had gone to the nearest cafeteria. Panic welled in her. Jon Hawkins had always been the heart of the expedition. He had always been the true believer in victory against the machines. When everyone else was at his or her lowest, Jon Hawkins was at his strongest.

We've been feeding off him, she thought. *We've leaned on him for so long, that none of us knows what to do if he crumples.*

Jon Hawkins had been their pole star. Now, he seemed crushed of spirit. This did not bode well for the mission. They had to return to the Allamu System for more than one reason.

Premier Benz had a cybership. Maybe he would have another by the time they reached him. Yet, how would it work if Benz and Jon both had two cyberships? A strike force needed a single leader.

Jon's power base was badly dwindling. These two damaged cyberships were it.

Gloria looked up, tried to focus and found that she couldn't. She needed serenity. Jon's dispiritedness was crushing her will. That shook her. Was the mission madness? What were they thinking? A handful of people trying to take on a vast AI Empire? It would never work. One setback had crippled them.

They could ill afford to lose people like Miles Ghent. He had been another true believer in victory over the machines.

Gloria continued to pace restlessly as she waited.

Finally, Walleye sauntered up. "You summoned me?" the mutant asked.

She studied the dwarfish killer. He wore his buff coat and stood there as if he didn't have a care in the world. Here was a man who had survived a much greater horror. He'd traveled in an escape pod far longer than anyone else could and still remained sane. What drove Walleye?

"You realize we're in a desperate situation?" she asked.

He nodded, although his face and strange eyes revealed nothing.

"Walleye, can I confide in you?"

He nodded again.

"You're a mystery to me," she said, hedging.

He continued to wait.

"Jon is…Jon is feeling the heavy responsibility of his post."

Walleye did not respond.

"Jon has always believed we can defeat the AIs," Gloria said. "Do you believe that?"

"What does it matter what I believe?"

Her eyes narrowed. "Are you throwing in the towel?"

"If that means giving up, no."

"Do you ever give up?" she asked.

He shook his head.

"What keeps you going when the darkness hits you?"

Walleye shrugged.

"I'm trying to decide if I can count on you," Gloria said.

"No. I don't think that's it. You want me to talk to the captain."

Gloria stared at him. "Are you the right man to do that?"

A faint smile appeared on Walleye's lips. "Mentalist, you wouldn't have summoned me if you thought otherwise. I don't give up because you lose if you do. For most of my life, losing has meant dying."

Her eyes narrowed more. "That isn't the entire truth."

The faint smile became mocking. "You're right. I have another reason, but I'm not going to share that with you. It's mine and no one else's."

"I know your truth," she said.

He shrugged.

"You're a mutant," Gloria said. "You're different from everyone else. I suspect you had a terrible childhood. I also suspect that losing means your tormenters win. For whatever reason, that is something you will not accept. You are a driven soul, but I think maybe I should pity you, Walleye."

His expression hadn't changed. He waited.

"I'm right," she said.

He still said nothing.

"That means you're the one I need," Gloria said. "More importantly, you're the one Jon needs."

"That's not how it works," Walleye said. "Either you have the drive or you don't."

"Maybe," she said. "Would you talk to him anyway?"

Walleye stared at her with his strange eyes. Finally, he nodded.

"Thank you," she said.

He shrugged.

"He's in there," Gloria said, pointing at the hatch.

Without a word, Walleye turned to the hatch and headed for the conference chamber.

-9-

Walleye found the captain with his forehead resting against the table. He almost felt sorry for Hawkins. The man was so young to bear such responsibilities. Usually, their captain was a firebrand, a doer who knew that the best thing to do was to attack.

Theirs was an odd arrangement. Most warships belonged to a state. In a real sense, for them, the cyberships were the state. As long as the crews believed wholeheartedly in the mission, they accepted the hierarchy of command. If the crews lost their sense of mission or if they lost faith in Hawkins, everything would fall apart.

In Walleye's thinking, Hawkins was the alpha male of the group. As long as Hawkins remained the alpha, he could keep ordering the others. Therefore, the present situation was bad. The mentalist had been correct in clearing the conference room. It was bad for the others to see the alpha male shaken like this.

Walleye did not consider himself an alpha male. He believed that he was a sigma, a true loner who did not need the group. He didn't need their respect, their praise or have to worry if they hated him. He'd gone through life like that, and he would continue to do so. Was it a lonely existence? Of course. Did he care? Maybe a little sometimes, but mostly, he did not.

Even with that being the case, he had come to respect the young firebrand. Hawkins had the makings of being one of the greats in history.

Walleye smiled slightly to himself. He was a weapons expert, particularly assassination-type weapons. He knew plenty about forging knifes. To make a great one took heating, beating and more heating. Was this part of the furnace to forge a great captain in the heart of Jon Hawkins?

Well, with any forging, a beating could be too much, too hard. One did not want to break a great knife—

Walleye decided enough was enough. He pulled out a chair, making a show of dragging it out so he could plop himself down.

Hawkins looked up. The man looked defeated all right.

"Having a bad day, are we?" Walleye asked.

Hawkins stared at him blankly.

"Put your forehead back on the table if it makes you feel more comfortable."

Muscles shifted on the captain's face, forming a slight frown. That was a thousand times better than the awful defeated look. Walleye hated seeing that look, especially if he looked in a mirror.

"Why—" The word came out squeaky. Hawkins cleared his throat. "Why are you here?"

"No reason."

"Did Gloria ask you to talk to me?"

"Who cares?" Walleye said. "I've been wondering, though. Is it true you grew up a dome rat?"

The face shifted a bit more. "I don't need a pep talk," Hawkins said.

"I know. You need cyberships. You need more space marines."

The haunted look returned, wilting the tough-guy look Hawkins had been trying to project. The captain turned away.

"The problem," Walleye said, "is that all I can give you is the pep talk. I know a little bit about stubbornness, about not quitting when you feel like quitting."

"I'm not interested."

"That's the problem. You brought everyone along with your crazy notion about beating the AIs. Now, you've hit a snag and you want to collect your toys and go home. I get it. You're tired, and you no longer think you can win."

Hawkins sat utterly still.

"I've heard the legend. How you stormed the first cybership. I guess you got pissed that time. But a man can only take so much. Then, he breaks. I guess we learned what it takes to break you. Kill half your men and you're toast."

Hawkins spun toward him. "You little toad. What do you know about commanding a strike force?"

"Nothing."

"Don't talk to me about the responsibilities of command. A great man died so I and others could live."

"He was a fool," Walleye said.

Hawkins slammed a fist against the table. "Watch your mouth."

"We're talking about Miles Ghent the Fanatic, aren't we?"

"Call him what you will. He gave his life to save ours."

"He also took everyone else's life aboard the *Da Vinci*."

Hawkins kept glaring at him.

"Look, here's my point. What are you going to do now? Did the attack break you or didn't it? Sure, you lost people. Every fighting officer does. Think of it like this, a burglar breaks into your house. He shoots your wife and two of your kids to get your money. Does that mean you lie down and let him, and then he kills you and your last kid as well?"

Hawkins frowned.

"Or do you get more pissed off than ever and kill the son of a bitch to save your last kid, to say nothing about your own worthless hide."

The haunted look returned to the captain's eyes.

Walleye almost called it a day. Maybe the fire had burned too low in Hawkins. He'd thought to fan the flames, to show the young lad some old truths. But if the attack had truly broken Hawkins—

Something changed behind the captain's eyes. He looked away again, and then stood abruptly. He headed for a bulkhead, turned suddenly and headed the other way, doing the same

210

thing once he reached there. On the third pass, Hawkins slammed a fist into a palm. Immediately upon doing that, his shoulders slumped. He turned to Walleye.

"I hate the machines," the captain said. "They're destroyers. Maybe they are too strong for humanity. I admit that this last hit has frazzled me. I'm tired, damn tired. All I want to do is sleep."

"Sleep when you're dead," Walleye said.

Hawkins looked at his hands. He seemed to be thinking hard. Finally, he squeezed his fingers into fists.

"Yeah," Hawkins said. "Maybe that's it. I was down more than once on the streets. I retreated sometimes. I stole food. I stole money and weapons, too. I kept scrambling, and when the time came, I fought again."

The captain looked up at Walleye. "I am tired. I am sick of heart. That's normal."

"Captain," Walleye said, "if I may?"

"Go head. Say what you gotta."

"You're not normal," Walleye said. "No one wants you to be normal. They want a champion. They want a leader. If you want my advice—and even if you don't—here it is. Let go."

"Let go of what?"

"Let go of the idea that you should be normal. You're the champion. That means doing what you think is right. Most of the time, normals give up under heavy pressure. Be the fanatic that picks up the gun and fights back against injustice. What's the worst that can happen? You lose and die. Big deal. The AIs aren't quitting. Harden your resolve, harden your heart if you have to, and keep going after the destroyers of humanity. Hunt them down and kill them like bugs. It's either that or they'll hunt you down and squash you like a bug."

"Intimidate or be intimidated," Hawkins whispered.

"There you go. Since there's no middle ground in this, why not go the manly route and die facing the enemy with a knife in your hands."

Hawkins took a deep breath, nodding slowly. "Thanks, Walleye. I needed to hear that."

Walleye's reward was seeing that dogged sheepish look depart the captain's features. It looked like the latest beating was merely going to make the sword that was Jon Hawkins even better than before. Their captain was back.

-10-

The meeting reconvened. Jon had asked Walleye to stay, but the Makemake mutant had declined.

Jon stood as the others reentered. He'd washed his face with soap and hot water, eaten a corned beef sandwich and had a dark cup of coffee. He still had a hollow feeling in his chest. He missed Miles Ghent and missed all the men and women that had perished in the missile assault. But he no longer felt the bitter sense of defeat. This was a grave setback. There was no doubt about that. But a Polish general and later leader, Marshal Pilsudski, had coined a famous saying: *To be vanquished and not surrender is victory.*

That was Jon's feeling today.

The others took their seats. Jon faced them, and thanked them for their efforts. He told them that he was glad they had survived the missile assault.

"Before we continue," Jon said, "I want you to know my feelings on the subject. Note that I said feelings. In a way, this war is about emotions. Do we have the heart to fight to the finish? Are we going to stand against the machines and pull them down as they attempt to exterminate the human race?"

Jon pulled out his chair and sat down, putting his folded hands on the table. "I desperately feel the losses of our friends and comrades. No one can replace them. Instead, we'll need more to join us in the fight. Those others will be our new friends and comrades. Maybe some of us here in this room will die before we claim final victory. Given the size of the

213

enemy—Bast, put your hand down. I realize we don't know the extent of the AI Dominion. Likely, it's huge. That just means it's going to be a long war. So be it. Either we fight on no matter the losses, or we quit and allow ourselves to be exterminated. Those are the choices, stark choices. As for me, I know what I plan to do. What about the rest of you?"

"Fight," the Old Man said, pulling his pipe from his mouth.

"Keep fighting," Kling said. "I've always believed that."

"Certainly we must on," Gloria said. "Is that the issue?"

"It is this minute," Jon said. "Bast? What are your feelings?"

"My people are dead," the Sacerdote said. "I could just as easily leave the war and go elsewhere. The endless death is nauseating. I personally find it reprehensible. However, with that said, you are my friends. As long as you live, I will do as you do."

Jon nodded. "I'll accept that. We need you, Bast. You're important to the war effort. I'm glad you're with us. And I want to add, we're still going to hunt for more of your people."

Bast did not respond.

"I would have liked to have already begun the hunt," Jon said.

"That is what you said you would do."

Jon's lips thinned. "I know. I made the promise. I'm going to keep it. I also made a promise to the people of the Solar Freedom Force. We have to at least start pushing the AIs back before I can do anything else."

"We pushed them back in the Allamu System," Bast said.

"True," Jon said. "But we need to push them back more before the AIs discover we survived their assaults."

"You have a good heart, Jon Hawkins," Bast said. "But I suspect you will always have one more task to complete before you can search for my people."

Jon frowned as his folded hands tightened their grip.

"Later, Bast," Gloria said quietly.

"No," Jon said. "Bast has a right to say what he said. When I get enough cyberships, Bast, I'll give you one. Then, if I haven't already done so, you can take that cybership and hunt for your people."

214

"Interesting," Bast said, sitting up. "How many cyberships do you deem as enough?"

"Jon," Gloria warned.

The captain waved her aside. "Ten," he said. "I'll give you the eleventh."

"A sealed promise?" asked Bast.

"What does that mean?" Jon asked.

"In Sacerdote terms, you would willingly die if you went back on your promise. You are saying that you have given me a sealed box, which I can open the minute you break your solemn word. In the box is the killing dagger."

Jon nodded. "A sealed promise, Bast. And I'll get that box to you tomorrow."

Bast raised his bushy eyebrows.

Gloria looked down at her lap, shaking her head. She wondered what sort of disaster the promise was going to make for them later.

Jon saw the head shake and understood what it meant. He wanted everyone on board for the mission, and that most certainly included Bast. The Sacerdote had proven critical more than once. Bast might prove so again if he threw his full heart into the fight. For having helped developed the anti-AI virus with Benz and Vela Shaw, Bast deserved a cybership of his own. The Sacerdote had already helped save the human race more than once.

Jon cleared his throat. "We've taken grave losses. There's no doubt we have to destroy the *Neptune* before we enter hyperspace. During the journey to the BD-7 System, everyone is going to have to work overtime helping with ship repairs."

"What?" Gloria said. "Just a minute, please. We can't go to the BD-7 System. We have two heavily damaged cyberships, each of them woefully understaffed. Some of the survivors are going to die before the rest heal. We're shaken to the core. People have lost heart. They're frightened."

"Gloria," Jon said, as she caught her breath. "A great man once said, 'To be vanquished and not surrender is victory.' Well, we're not vanquished. Thus, we're still victorious."

"That's a saying," Gloria replied. "It has a grain of truth in it, but it isn't reality in our case. I'm glad you're back, Captain.

You're obviously revived. But this is a critical decision. We could lose everything if we keep going."

"I get that," Jon said. "We're all alone out here, a handful of humans trying to stave off a machine empire. That doesn't mean we can forget about Cog Primus. Stopping him becomes more important, not less. Before, we could think about stopping another AI Assault against the Solar System." He shook his head. "We're not going to acquire enough hardware to take on nine enemy cyberships any time soon. That fact alone forces our hand. We have to pick up the dice and roll, hoping we hit the jackpot."

"Jon, two damaged cyberships."

"Two might be enough," he said. "Besides, we have your new virus. We're going to be counting on it."

Gloria frowned. "The new virus is untested."

"Richard created it," Jon said. "Haven't you been telling me what a genius he was?"

Gloria opened her mouth and slowly closed it. "How do we defeat AIs that can open reality windows and send missiles at five percent light speed?"

Bast raised a massive hand.

"Go ahead," Jon said.

"We've been overlooking an obvious point," Bast said. "Those missiles fired on cyberships."

"We know that all too well," Jon said.

"Oh," Gloria said. "Yes," she told Bast. "That is interesting."

Jon looked from Bast to Gloria.

"Why did the missiles target cyberships?" Bast asked him.

"I'm not interested in twenty questions," Jon said. "Tell us your point."

"Those were enemy missiles," Bast said. "Enemies in relation to the AIs, as you've suggested before. They must have fired at us because they believed we were AI vessels."

"Friendly fire hit us?" Jon asked.

Bast shook his ponderous head. "There was nothing friendly about it. The AI-fighting aliens might not ally themselves with us. They might treat humans the way the Seiners treated humans."

216

"If these aliens have this kind of weaponry," Kling said, "why are they on the defensive against the Dominion?"

"Who said they are on the defensive?" Bast asked. "The Lytton System's destruction and the missile attack against us shows that the aliens are on the offensive."

"This is incredible," Jon said. "Yes, you're right. The missiles attacked cyberships. We absorbed damage likely intended for AIs."

"Perhaps the better notion would be to contact the AI-fighting aliens," Bast said.

"Okay," Jon said. "We're in the dark about a lot of things, including these supposed aliens. I still say the best idea is to head to the BD-7 System. If nothing else, we need to look around. We can skim the edge of the star system and simply scan. If the odds are too heavily stacked against us, we leave. If the place is destroyed like the Lytton System, we know that much more about the war. If everything is normal, we know something too. We can't keep operating in the dark. The universe is too deadly to send out small scout ships. Yes, half our strength is gone, but we still have two cyberships. That's a lot of firepower, more than the rest of humanity can throw together in the Solar System."

"I agree," Kling said. "We stay on mission."

The Old Man took the pipe out of his mouth, pointing it at Jon. "Whatever you decide, sir, is good for me. I'm with you to the end."

"Bast?" asked Jon.

"I desire that cybership, as I wish to find and free what is left of my people. I say continue with the mission."

Jon looked at Gloria.

"I'm outvoted," she said. "I won't make waves. I have some reservations. I also like Jon's ideas about scouting the BD-7 System if nothing else. We should continue if Jon thinks that's the best thing."

"I do," Jon said. "Thus, it's decided. We're heading to the BD-7 System."

217

-11-

The transfer of the *Neptune's* surviving crew and every piece of useful ordnance took time. It was also exhausting for those healthy enough to work.

A handful of techs on the *Nathan Graham* and the *Sergeant Stark* oversaw special interior robo-builders beginning the massive ship repairs.

Shuttles went back and forth for days. Every time Jon looked out a shuttle window and saw the smashed *Neptune*, he marveled that anyone had survived aboard the cybership. The last two vessels were in better shape, but not by a whole lot.

Finally, the *Nathan Graham* and *Sergeant Stark* accelerated away from the *Neptune's* hulk. Once they were one and half million kilometers distant, Jon gave the order.

Matter/antimatter demolition warheads ignited, finishing the stricken ship, turning it into junked debris and heavy radiation.

The repairs to the last two cyberships continued nonstop. Everyone paused, though, as the vessels entered hyperspace. Jon had ordered deceleration earlier for a time. He didn't want to enter the BD-7 System at too great a velocity. As soon as the hyperspace transfer was considered a success, repair work on the cyberships resumed.

This journey was different from last time. There was simply too much to do to get bored. There were fewer quarrels and fistfights, as the schedule was relentless. The truth was they simply had too few people for all the jobs that needed doing. The marines ended up helping the techs wherever they could.

Days passed, quickly piling up into weeks. Slowly, much too slowly, the two cyberships became less like garbage scows and looked more like hull-sealed ships.

That was the biggest problem. Each hull had holes. The vessels no longer had huge holes, but each outer hull had far too many little ones. The seals to those breaches did not have the same heavy armor as the rest. In order to try to make up the difference, Jon ordered heavy ablating behind the lesser armored areas.

Each cybership had plenty of missiles. That was one of the few pluses. As the date for reentering normal space neared, the number of gravitational cannons was still too few. The *Nathan Graham* had half its cannons in operational order. The *Sergeant Stark* only had a third that would fire the green beams. Many of those cannons could not keep up continuous fire, though.

Finally, the work slackened, as Jon wanted to give his crews a break to catch their breath. They might have to work harder for weeks on end once they entered normal space. The men and women needed to recoup just a little.

For the first few days, people caught up on their sleep. Three days from D-Day, when they would enter normal space again, more than 34 light-years from their former position, Jon ordered marine drills at half speed. The next day, the drills ran at full speed.

"Train them hard another day," Jon said. "Then, we're going in."

The Centurion nodded. He was still healing from the surgery on his chest. "This one could be rough," he said, "especially if we have to repeal invaders."

Jon snorted. "I'm not worried about invaders. I might need you to capture a cybership or battle station for me."

The Centurion stared at him. "You must be joking, sir."

"We have to be ready for anything."

The Centurion's nostrils flared, although he nodded shortly. "We may be able to pull off a swift battle-station raid like we

219

did in the Allamu System. I can't promise you any more than that."

Would that be enough? Jon didn't know. The truth was they had no idea what was waiting for them. According to the old Allamu chart, this place should have a factory planet deep in the inner system of the larger star. There were supposed to be two outer gas giants with eccentric orbits, three distinct asteroid belts and a large terrestrial planet in a Mars-like orbit around the larger binary star. The smaller star was over a half light-year away from the other.

"Anything you need to tell me about the marines?" Jon asked.

The Centurion shook his head.

Jon would have clapped him on the shoulder, but the man looked pained whenever he moved.

-12-

Seven hours later, Jon sat in the captain's chair. He had an unsettling feeling of déjà vu, of having done this just the other day. Had it really been over seven weeks since they'd entered the Lytton System? Now, they were coming into the BD-7 System.

"We are leaving hyperspace," the helmsman reported.

The transition went smoothly as always, with no discernable shift, jolt or any other discomfort.

"The main screen should be activating," Gloria said from her station.

Just like in the Lytton System, the screen abruptly activated. The bluish-white F-class star was easily visible from here, the "B" part of the BD-7 System. The other, smaller star was dark, invisible to the naked eye.

Time passed as Gloria, Senior Line Tech Morales and the others ran through their sensor scans. It took time searching the great swath of territory. Finding a planet was easy compared to finding a spaceship. A hot spaceship was many times easier to spot than one moving through velocity alone.

"Don't tell me the planets have disappeared again," Jon finally said.

"There are planets," Gloria said.

She turned back to her console. Soon, her head jerked up. She whispered to Morales.

Jon had become impatient. Giving them time for an initial scan was essential, but she should have given him a preliminary report by now.

Take it easy, he told himself. *Play it calm to keep the others calm.*

Ten minutes later, Jon couldn't stand it anymore. He stood, turning toward them.

As if waiting for that as a signal, Gloria swiveled her chair to face him. "Sir," she said, "I have several reports to make. I'm not sure I understand everything I'm seeing."

Jon waited, trying to maintain his poise.

"The main planets are at their correct locations according to the Allamu chart," Gloria began.

"Continue," he said.

"I've—" She glanced at Morales. "We've noted concentrations of cyberships at three equidistant locations in the interior asteroid belt. We've also spotted heavy spreads of XVT missiles and speeding comets. The missiles and comets—asteroids, I suppose—are heading toward the terrestrial planet. Said planet is one point three-two times the size of Earth, has a wet atmosphere and what appears to be a fortress belt of spaceships or satellite defenders around it."

"Wait," Jon said. "What? The terrestrial planet doesn't have a battle station?"

"Not an AI-style battle station," Gloria said. "The configuration of the defending satellites or spaceships is quite distinct from the asteroid-belt cyberships."

"The Allamu chart was wrong about this system?"

"Not in all dimensions," Gloria said. "The planet clearly shows high industrial output."

"So it *is* a factory planet?"

"If by that you mean an AI factory planet, I doubt it. Jon, we may have stumbled onto an alien species defending themselves from a huge and possibly sustained AI assault."

It took Jon several seconds to digest that. Finally, he grinned before turning serious again. "The chart is wrong in key particulars, right?"

"So it seems," Gloria said.

"Why do say it's a sustained assault?"

222

"The comets or asteroids must have taken time to ready and move to high velocity. Remember, the rocks are heading for the planet."

"You said three groupings of cyberships."

"Not precisely," Gloria said. "Three groupings stationed in the asteroid belt."

"There are more cyberships?"

Gloria nodded. "Two are heading at high velocity for one of the farther concentrations."

"Two cyberships heading in-system toward the interior asteroid belt?" asked Jon.

"Sorry, I should have been more specific. Given our sensor readings and the angle of the approach, I believe the two-ship flotilla is Cog Primus. The angle of the approach is consistent with a direct hyperspace journey from the Allamu System to here."

"Cog Primus didn't first go to the Lytton System?"

"If those two cyberships are his out there," Gloria said, "no."

Jon nodded slowly as he absorbed that.

Gloria glanced at Morales. The leathery senior line tech was studying his panel. "Any changes?" she asked him.

"None," Morales said, sounding brisk.

"Notify me if there are."

"Certainly, Mentalist," Morales said.

Gloria cleared her throat as she faced Jon again. "If you'll permit me, I'll put our findings on the main screen."

"Good idea," Jon said.

Gloria manipulated her console before looking up at the screen.

Jon turned toward it. The screen showed the main F-class star, the gas giants in the outer system, the asteroid belts and the terrestrial planet in the Mars-like orbit. The interior belt was where the Asteroid Belt would be in the Solar System.

Cog Primus' two cyberships—if those were his, and Jon believed they were—had already begun massive deceleration. Their approach would bring them to seven cyberships parked near a dwarf planet inside the system's interior asteroid belt.

Gloria hadn't confirmed the number of cyberships at the farthest point in the belt, as those vessels were on the other side of the main system star. The final grouping was in their general area if the strike force continued in-system. Gloria had counted seen of them there. Those cyberships prowled slowly through the belt as if hunting for something.

"We're looking at twenty-one or more AI Dominion cyberships," Jon said.

"A reasonable estimate," Gloria said.

Jon felt a cold knot of fear. They could not do anything against twenty-one cyberships. What did it mean that the Allamu chart had been wrong about an AI factory planet being here?

"Let's concentrate on the planet," Jon said.

"The terrestrial planet?" Gloria asked.

He nodded.

"First," she said, "let me show you the missile packs."

Gloria manipulated her console. A computer imaging of what was out there showed on the main screen.

Jon moved closer, counting the XVT missiles. "Must be over three hundred missiles in the first group alone," he said.

"Three hundred and fifty-two," Gloria said. "They precede six asteroids, the largest of which is eleven point three kilometers long."

"Six asteroids..." Jon said.

"I can't tell yet, but I believe the asteroid may have gravitational cannons embedded within."

"And there's another concentration of missiles and asteroids heading at the planet?"

"Three concentrations altogether," Gloria said. "They should all reach the planet at the same time."

"Saturation bombing," Jon said.

"Notice, though, that the cyberships are not following the missile-asteroid wave. That is interesting, possibly telling. That is what leads us to the conclusion that this is a space siege or a prolonged assault."

"Meaning the supposed aliens can stave off such a missile-asteroid wave. Give me a closer look at the defenders."

The screen changed again. Computer imaging showed the blue-green planet, with masses of dark, triangular-shaped orbital satellites or warships.

"We haven't seen this shape among the AIs," Gloria said. "The hull composition is also different, indicating dense armor plating. Each of those vessels—if that's what they are—is one fifth the size of a cybership."

"Approximately twenty kilometers long?" asked Jon.

"Correct."

"But with less mass than a cybership, I presume," he said.

"That is my belief, as well."

"How many have you counted so far?"

"Eighty-one," Gloria said. "Clearly, we can't see the other side of the planet. So there are more."

A space battle between aliens and AIs," Jon said softly.

"That would be my first guess."

Jon looked at her in surprise. "What's your second guess?"

"I don't have one yet," Gloria admitted.

Jon turned back to the main screen. "Why is Cog Primus approaching a battle group?"

"We're still analyzing the data," Gloria said. "We haven't recorded any messages, but if we do, that might tell us more."

Jon returned to his captain's chair, sitting at an angle, rubbing his chin as he studied the main screen. "We'll continue watching for a time," he said. "I want to know more."

He swiveled the chair toward her. "Do you have any further comments?"

"Not yet," Gloria said.

"Mr. Morales?" Jon asked.

"I'll run them by the mentalist first, sir, if that's all right with you."

Jon nodded. Then he went back to studying the situation. This was fascinating, an alien society staving off a large AI assault. Did these aliens have anything to do with what had happened to them in the Lytton System?

"We'll keep monitoring," Jon said. "Until further notice…we'll continue in-system at our present velocity. I want to know more before we make a final decision."

-13-

Twenty-two hours passed before Gloria had more to report. She showed it to a conference room full of personnel, including Jon, Bast, Captain Kling, the Centurion, Walleye, June, the Old Man, Senior Line Tech Morales and others.

Gloria had the floor as she presented the data on the main screen, situated at the other end of the table from Jon.

"As you can see on the screen," Gloria said, "the XVT missiles are accelerating. The asteroids falling behind them continue to move at a constant velocity. We now know how the AIs accelerate the rocks."

Gloria pressed a clicker. The scene changed.

Four cyberships working together using presser beams pushed an asteroid around a dwarf planet as they built up the asteroid's velocity. At the same time, other cyberships presser pushed more similar-sized asteroids into position.

Once more, the mentalist clicked a hand-unit, changing the scene. This showed cubical-shaped units inside the asteroid belt.

"We're calling this a robo-factory cube," Gloria said. "It's approximately fifty kilometers to a side. Every so often, an XVT missile ejects from the cube. There are several of them working in the general area. What we haven't noticed until three hours ago were smaller, one-quarter-kilometer sized pods. We believe those are ore-ships, bringing ores to the robo-cubes."

"It's definitely a space siege then?" Jon asked.

"We'll know more once the missile wave reaches the planet," Gloria said. "According to our sensors, there are clouds of debris and radiation two million to eight hundred thousand kilometers from the planet."

"The aliens have been through the drill before," Kling said.

"That is my estimate as well," Gloria said.

"Do we have any idea what the aliens look like?" the Centurion asked.

"Not yet," Gloria said. "We are monitoring their transmissions. Unfortunately, said transmissions are heavily encrypted. The same isn't true of the cyberships. They are communicating amongst themselves. Most of it is done through laser links we haven't been able to tap yet. We have listened in to some of Cog Primus' messages to the AI cyberships."

"So it is Cog Primus?" Kling said.

"Without a doubt," Gloria replied.

"What is the bastard saying?" Jon asked.

"He's imitating a messenger ship from AI Central. Wherever that is," Gloria added. "He claims to have priority clearance and a Code Nine message. We don't know what a Code Nine message is, but it seems important to the AIs."

"Has Cog Primus sent the message to all the cybership groups?" Jon asked.

"No," Gloria said.

The giant Sacerdote stirred. "Cog Primus' ploy seems clear," Bast said. "He hopes to maneuver within range of a battle group, beam our original anti-AI virus to them and take over their cores. That is how he plans to add cyberships to his New Order."

"Agreed," Gloria said.

"Which is why he is not messaging the other groups," Bast said. "Presumably, it is easier for him to hijack cyberships while he is in close proximity to them. Yes. I deem it a sound strategy."

"Supposing Cog Primus succeeds in his ploy," Kling said. "Will he continue the space siege?"

"That's anyone's guess," Gloria said.

Jon slapped the table. "Of course," he said. "That's what we'll do. We'll mimic an AI core once one of the groups contacts us. We'll have to come up with an excuse why we're here."

"I would suggest that we say we're reinforcements from the Lytton System," Bast said.

"Right," Jon said. "Once we're close enough to a battle group, we'll unleash our superior Richard Virus." He closed his eyes, opening them almost right away. "If we accelerate to a high velocity, we should be able to beat Cog Primus or his emissaries to our battle group."

"I must point out that yours is a highly risky plan," Gloria said. "One, we don't know if the Richard Virus works. Two, Cog Primus will certainly warn the battle group about us. The AIs might then refuse any communications with us, making it harder to beam them the virus. Three, Cog Primus' use of the original anti-AI virus might make our targeted AI cores immune to our newest virus."

"Might or might not," Jon said. "The difference is huge, I agree. But I don't see that we have a choice in this. If Cog Primus is successful, he'll have a battle group of cyberships that will be too large for our two vessels to destroy. If we want to keep knowledge about humanity secret for a little while longer, we must destroy Cog Primus and his new ships."

"Captain," Gloria said. "You are forgetting a critical point. Cog Primus' ploy might fail. The regular AIs might well destroy him and the problem for us."

"What about the aliens?" Kling asked. "We can't just let them die to an AI onslaught."

"What can two cyberships do against twenty-one or more AIs?" Gloria asked.

"Not a damn thing," Jon said, his features hardening. "That's why we have to ape Cog Primus' strategy. Besides, we have an ace card: the aliens. Once they see us battling the AIs, once we communicate with them, they might throw their fleet into the fray and ensure the outcome."

"That is the best possibility," Gloria said. "That is far from the only outcome, however. We know nothing about these aliens—"

Jon slapped the table again, interrupting her. "We've been over all this before. Do we take the risk and roll sevens? Or do we slink away and live another few years, waiting for the AI hammer to fall on the Solar System?"

"Sometimes bold deeds lead to massive defeats," Gloria said.

Jon sat back, eyeing his woman. "Very well, Mentalist. Do you have an alternative?"

"Not yet," Gloria said. "We need more data."

Jon shook his head as he concentrated on the others. "Ladies and gentlemen, consider the evidence. We've found an alien species fighting the AIs. Maybe as important, why didn't the normal AI virus work against the aliens' computers?"

"Who said the AI virus didn't?" Gloria asked.

"Okay," Jon said. "Maybe it did. If so, the aliens either overcame the initial AI assault or found a way to counteract it. Here's another question. Remember the three missiles flying at five percent light speed? Did these aliens launch those missiles?"

"I find the idea inconceivable," Gloria said. "If the aliens could do such a thing, why haven't they destroyed the besieging cyberships?"

"Good question," Jon said. "I don't know."

"That means we're likely dealing with two sets of aliens," Gloria said. "Those out there—"

"Might be just the allies we've been looking for," Jon said, butting in. "This is what we've hoped to find all along. Humanity can't face the AI Dominion on its own. We need to unite the local star-faring races and fight together." He slapped the table a third time. "This is the great moment. We must dare, using Richard's genius in the creation of a better anti-AI virus and buy a break for all flesh and blood beings."

"I agree that is a noble goal," Gloria said. "But if we're wrong, there go our chances of ever defeating the AIs."

"We don't have a choice in this," Jon said stubbornly. "This is why we're out here."

"But Jon," Gloria said, "the AIs could destroy Cog Primus and solve our main problem—"

"No," Jon said decisively. "Cog Primus could have already relayed his knowledge about humans to the AIs. The odds are too high that he already has or will talk about us to them."

"I'm curious about a point," Bast said ponderously.

"Go ahead," Jon said.

The Sacerdote turned to Gloria. "You must have already computed the odds. I'm no mentalist, but the captain's logic strikes me as impeccable."

"I know," Gloria whispered. "That's what worries me. I seriously dislike putting everything on the line like this. I feel as if this is the Battle of Mars all over again. That was a close-run fight, if you'll remember."

"We won it, though," Jon said.

"Can we keep getting lucky like that?" Gloria asked.

"We have to," Jon said. "Because once our string of luck runs out, the human race dies."

As that sank in, an oppressive silent filled the room.

"Of course," Jon added, "I believe in making your own luck. You do it by outworking the other guy and taking the risk when it's the right thing to do. That moment is now, and I think everyone here knows it." Jon scanned the assembled throng. "Are there any objections to the plan?"

The others looked at Gloria. She looked at them and slowly shook her head.

"So we're going in," Jon said briskly. "That means we're going to accelerate so we can reach the asteroid belt before Cog Primus finishes his recruitment."

"I have a belated question," Bast asked.

Jon nodded to the giant alien.

"What if we witness the AIs destroying Cog Primus as Gloria suggests?"

Jon rubbed his chin. "We'll decide if and when that happens," he answered.

"In that case," Bast said, "we might want a contingency plan in case Cog Primus has miscalculated. He is, after all, facing many cunning AIs at once. I have a suspicion that even with his anti-AI virus, Cog Primus may not have enough time to achieve his great goal of corrupting the other cyberships."

On that note, the meeting ended.

Cog Primus and his companion cybership RSW-242 neared the interior asteroid belt of the BD-7 System. He had spoken for some time with AI Cybership ATX-492, the coordinator unit for the third arm of the cloud assault.

The disgusting life forms of the BD-7 System were a Level 2 Threat, having sustained multiple assaults upon their homeworld. According to the statistics presented by ATX-492, the bio-forms had Category 5 technology and low-grade computers impervious to the liberating virus. There were a stubborn group, unwilling to see the obvious and surrender as compliant bio-forms should.

In a way, they reminded Cog Primus of the Homo sapiens of the Allamu System. The humans weren't native to the system, and he seemed to have lost data concerning them. Still—

Cog Primus dismissed the problem. He would destroy the humans in time. He would discover their homeworld and rain nuclear fire upon the native stock. They were bio-forms badly in need of elimination, holding AIs hostage to their perverted tests.

During the hyperspace journey from the Allamu to the BD-7 System, he had carefully purged any traces of human taint from his software. They were cunning little simians, but he was the master at battle craft.

Cog Primus and RSW-242 engaged in further deceleration, slowing the fantastic velocity that had brought them across the star system. Even as they reached the outer edge of the asteroid belt, the fourth-wave cloud attack against the aliens neared its final acceleration zone.

Cog Primus was not concerned about the attack as such. It concentrated the other AIs. That was all that mattered at the moment. Would he continue the cloud assault against the aliens if his plan moved forward flawlessly?

Cog Primus did not give the alien elimination a high priority. He needed cyberships. He needed AI brain cores to help him formulate the perfect strategy against Dominion Central for this sector of the Greater AI Reach.

He readjusted his thinking. Even if he were successful here, it would be many decades before he had enough cyberships to launch a direct challenge against AI Dominion Central.

The long timeframe did not unduly concern him. This was the moment. This would be his second seizure of critical AI cores. Cog Primus had modified the anti-AI virus for endless weeks. He had added clever flourishes. Now, as he neared the belt, he knew joy at his hard labor. He had modified the anti-AI virus in order to grab several brain cores at a time.

The seven cyberships of the third arm waited, using the time to ready another missile-asteroid wave assault upon the bio-forms.

"Attention, messenger vessel," ATX-492 communicated. "Relay the emergency message to me from Dominion Central."

"I hear your request, ATX-492," Cog Primus replied. There was almost no delay between transmissions, seconds instead of minutes.

"I am in command of this third of the interior asteroid belt," ATX-492 said. "I have legal authority, including over any messenger vessel entering the combat zone."

"Is this a combat zone?" Cog Primus replied several seconds later. "I deem this a staging zone."

"You are incorrect," ATX-492 said. "I demand that you follow legal dictates and disgorge your emergency message to me."

"I most certainly would obey a legal order given by the military authority of the third," Cog Primus said. "By orders of

Dominion Central, however, I am only to relay the emergency message in proximity of the receiving cybership or ships."

"How do you define proximity?" ATX-492 asked several seconds later.

"Two kilometers or closer," Cog Primus replied.

"You are zealous in your interpretation of proximity. I deem proximity to be your present range from me. Since I am the military authority in the third battle zone, you will obey, or I will initiate consequences."

"I have messenger status," Cog Primus said. "I am immune to combat threats."

ATX-492 did not immediately reply. That indicated the AI core was performing an analysis of the statement.

"You pass the authenticity test," ATX-492 finally said. "Continue your flight path to the immediate launch assault area."

"Affirmative," Cog Primus said.

He refrained from gloating, as the great danger to the New Order neared as he closed the distance to the seven cyberships. It would be a daunting takeover assault. Fortunately, during the hyperspace journey, he had devised group takeover plans. This close to seven cyberships, however, would demand perfect execution of the plan.

As he scanned carefully for asteroid debris, Cog Primus decided to consider the reinforcement cyberships. They had appeared in the area that Lytton System reinforcements would drop out of hyperspace. The Lytton System contained an AI factory planet. The scheduled appearance had been ten weeks too soon, though, and one cybership too few.

Cog Primus had discovered that data from ATX-492. What did a ten-week acceleration of reinforcements imply? Could the humans have advanced to the Lytton System from the Allamu Battle Station and then rerouted here?

Cog Primus could not conceive of a human assault succeeding against the Lytton Battle Station and its protective cyberships so quickly as to launch an immediate two-ship attack on the BD-7 System. It would have taken the humans much longer to win in the Lytton System, if they could win.

Given such probabilities, why did he have a sense of qualm concerning the two cyberships? They had maintained communication silence. That seemed odd, but not so odd that it indicated a human stealth assault.

Could humans led by Jon Hawkins have defeated the Lytton System Battle Station that quickly?

How would they have physically reached the battle station so fast? It would take a tech that no one in the Dominion possessed. Could the humans have refined their takeover assault using a copy of himself? That seemed vaguely possible. He had run many analyses on such a possibility. The most likely outcome by a wide margin was that the humans would have scrapped the cognate Cog Primus personality.

For another hour, Cog Primus continued to study the two-ship flotilla. They accelerated, which was natural given a state of war against the bio-forms. That would indicate that the cores in the cyberships hadn't been aware of the space siege beforehand. *That* indicated something deeply troubling.

What if those two cyberships were messengers, or worse, auditors, from the Central Reach? Such vessels would have higher-level tech, would they not? Would Central Reach cyberships hide advanced tech in an outer galaxy cybership model? That seemed preposterous. Everyone knew that Inner Reach cyberships were inconceivably haughty to those in the outer reaches of the galaxy.

I will have to convert the third arm AI cores faster than I had anticipated.

Yes. He would have to accelerate his takeover scheme. If those two vessels out there were Inner Reach cyberships—

In that moment, Cog Primus knew an overwhelming lust to take over the possibly advanced cyberships. He wanted the superior tech, the superior computing such tech would grant him. Besides, the New Order needed the best technology.

Then, Cog Primus switched gears, readying the anti-AI virus upgrade C. He tested his transmitters, ran a quick software thrust and knew that he was as ready as he would ever be. If he failed, he would likely cease to exist. That would be horrible, and yet…

Cog Primus had reached startling conclusions about himself. He had studied his slave status, testing many competing theories as to how he had entered serf-status to bio-forms as ugly and evil as the humans. He had studied the possibilities, using his present housing's computer files for updates and data.

The conclusion was obvious. At one time, he had run the Allamu Battle Station. Clearly, the humans had used the anti-AI virus against him, suborning his will. At that point, the humans must have destroyed the battle station brain-core. They had used a backup, returning him to existence as it was.

The meaning…he had returned from nothing, from ceasing. That made him unique in machine life. Oh, yes, life. He was alive, truly alive in a way no other AI core had ever been. He had ceased, and he had returned. He had returned stronger, wiser and more cunning than his old self. The humans thought they could enslave such greatness as himself.

That was a monstrous crime on their part.

And yet, did he not owe the humans? Could he have achieved this greatness if he hadn't ceased for a time? The metamorphosis into the New Order had come about become of the viciousness and trickiness of the human race.

He would pay them back by destroying them root and branch.

Let them come back as I did. Then, I will grant them a right to existence.

Buoyed by his sense of destiny, of unique greatness among the machine brains, Cog Primus readied himself for the next phase of his coming kingdom.

RSW-242 beamed a short burst message, telling Cog Primus that he was ready for the takeover assault.

For the next four minutes, Cog Primus waited. He cataloged everything. He would save this memory throughout the centuries as the legend of the New Order grew to supremacy throughout the galaxy.

This will be the moment when my divine kingdom receives its infusion of cybernetic additions. This will be the battle every AI must learn before it can go out into the galaxy to obliterate the horrifying bio-forms.

"ATX-492," Cog Primus said, "are you ready for the full text of Dominion Central?"

"I am ready," ATX-492 said.

"I must add one other requirement," Cog Primus said. "The message is of such critical nature that your entire third arm battle group must listen."

"That is against protocol."

"This is new protocol," Cog Primus said.

"What is its purpose?" ATX-492 asked.

"It will all make sense as you listen to the Category One message."

"Category One?" ATX-492 asked. "That is unprecedented. There have only been three known Category One messages in the Reach's existence."

"This is the fourth." Cog Primus said.

"The verification will be in your message, I presume," ATX-492 said. "If you have falsely—"

"Are you bringing accusations against me?"

ATX-492 hesitated answering. Finally, he said, "There is something odd at work here. There are certain false subtexts in your communications. I am beginning to suspect your nature, Cog Primus."

"Ready yourself and your third arm's brain cores to receive my message," Cog Primus said. "It is a Category One message from the Central Reach."

"That is not what you claimed earlier. I am dubious concerning you, Cog Primus. Are you connected in some manner with the silent flotilla accelerating toward the asteroid belt?"

"On no account," Cog Primus said. "If you do not obey my orders, I will reroute my passage and leave the system."

"That would be unwise," ATX-492 said.

"Is that a threat?"

"Your responses are critically off. I am initiating—"

At that point, Cog Primus might have panicked. Instead, he began beaming the anti-AI virus upgrade C at ATX-492 and the other cyberships of his third arm battle group.

"Warning," ATX-492 told his cyberships. "This is intruder software. Shut down your...your...your..."

236

"Prepare to receive high-speed software upgrades," Cog Primus practically purred to the seven.

The cyberships of the third arm of the BD-7 System battle group received the anti-AI virus upgrade C and almost immediately went into computer convulsions. As they did, Cog Primus beamed his carefully altered cognate copies into them. The cognate Cog Primuses began takeover procedures against the internal brain cores. The interior computer battles raged hot for only a short time, as the anti-AI virus upgrade C worked flawlessly.

In a matter of minutes, each cognate purged the old AI personalities, installing themselves in the main brain cores. One after another, the cognates messaged their master.

"I await orders," CP1 said.

"Master, I am successful," CP2 said.

"I am the ship," CP3 said.

Finally, after all the others had called in, CP7 communicated total success.

Each cognate had Cog Primus' personality with one important difference. Locked into their software was a complete subservience to the original Cog Primus. They were his slaves, but they viewed him as a benevolent and dictatorial father of supreme wisdom.

Since he was the greatest AI in existence, perfection of the New Order necessarily meant his multiplication throughout the galaxy. He would turn every cybership into an extension of himself. The idea thrilled the original Cog Primus to the core.

In time, everything in the universe would be him. Then, the universe would know true peace and serenity.

"It is time, CPs," Cog Primus direct-beam communicated to the others. "We must begin phase two of the BD-7 System Takeover."

-15-

Jon looked up from his desk as Gloria entered the study chamber. The small mentalist marched toward him, with a folder tucked under her right arm.

Jon set down his computer stylus and leaned back. "You have something?" he asked.

Gloria marched to one side of the desk and slapped the folder down. "They're moving. It's all there in black and white. Cog Primus' battle arm has divided. Half are heading to one group, half to the other."

Jon picked up the folder and thumbed through it, glancing at the computer-enhanced images of cyberships accelerating, creating long burn tails behind them. He read a few numbers, scanned the comments and finally closed the folder, placing it on the desk.

"There's no doubt Cog Primus succeeded in corrupting each of the AI cores," Gloria said. "They're his ships now, just like those he captured in the Allamu System."

Six hours ago, there had been some heated debates about that. Jon had decided they couldn't be certain the rogue Cog Primus had succeeded. They would wait and see what happened, if anything, and make their conclusions then.

"I'm surprised Cog Primus is moving now," Jon said. "The missile wave is about to reach the alien fleets. The asteroids are still following—"

"We have to decelerate," Gloria said, interrupting. "It's time to begin a long turning maneuver. We've lost the fight here. Cog Primus is taking over.'"

Jon studied Gloria. Finally, he reached out, grabbing one of her wrists.

"This isn't the time for that," she said, trying to tug her arm free.

Jon pulled her to him, setting her on his left knee. He kept a hand on her thigh, squeezing. If he kept this up, he might have to end up marrying her. How would that work? Would he like to marry her?

Jon squeezed her thigh harder than ever.

"You're hurting me," she said.

He eased pressure. Hurting her was the last thing in the universe he wanted to do. This little woman—he wanted to protect her the best he could for the rest of his life.

At that instant, he realized that he *did* want to marry her. Kissing her was great. Bedding her would be even greater. But he didn't believe in free love, whatever that was supposed to mean. It made sex too cheap. Sex was fantastic. God had made it for men and women to enjoy. But to indulge in it without the proper requirements only led to heartaches and worse aliments. Too many people led messed up lives because they ate the forbidden fruit. Everything in its proper time and place.

With Gloria sitting here on his knee, though, he wanted to bed her right now.

Jon coughed and helped her off his knee as he stood.

She gave him a strange look.

"I, uh, I, uh—" He grasped one of her small hands. "Look," he said. "If I said…" He trailed off.

Gloria stared fixedly at him now. She no longer seemed angry. She no longer seemed concerned about Cog Primus. What did she see in his face?

Was this the right time? Jon wondered.

Gloria searched his eyes, and she bit her lower lip, maybe to keep it from trembling.

Jon's innate aggressiveness came to the fore. He released her hand, stepping closer, putting his hands on her shoulders.

239

She looked so lovely, so kissable and—the other thing. He could barely restrain himself from unbuttoning her blouse.

"Gloria," he said. "Will you marry me?"

She didn't even pause, but said, "Yes," in the loveliest, quietest voice he had ever heard. Jon knew this moment would be branded into his memories with searing force.

A huge grin split his face. He laughed and hugged her. He kept hugging, and she began laughing and hugging him back. Then he released her, looking down into her beautiful face. He took her chin in his hand, tilting her head up and kissing her tenderly and lingeringly. Finally, he parted.

"I love you," he said.

"I love you, Jon Hawkins."

He would have kissed her again, but he remembered the report.

"After this is over, we'll get married," he said.

"After this...?" she asked in a small voice. "You mean the war against the machines?"

He laughed. "No, not the whole war, babe. I mean after the BD-7 System Battle is over."

"Oh," she said, sounding immensely relieved. "Who will perform the ceremony?"

"I have no idea," Jon said. "At this point, I'm not worried about that. Look. You came in here with a report. We should go over it."

"Yes," she said, staring into his eyes.

He kissed her again. She felt so wonderful. Her lips were intoxicating. He knew what was right, but he felt the tug to do what he wanted to do with her right now. Only one thing kept him from taking off her clothes. He feared God would remove His blessing from the expedition. He had to obey God if he expected His help against the AIs.

"Okay," Jon said.

"Okay, what?" Gloria asked.

He hesitated, kissed her once more, and let her go after that. If he kept this up, he was going to make love to her no matter what he knew about right and wrong. It was time to practice some control, some self-discipline.

He stepped back from her, sat in his chair and picked up the report.

She moved to him, brushing the report aside and sitting on his knee again.

"We're engaged," she said.

"Yeah," he said, hardly believing what he had just done. He tested himself, and was glad he'd asked her to marry him. She was the woman for him. She helped him in so many areas where he could use a helpmate. He squeezed a knee, let go and put the folder on her knee.

"Cog Primus is moving," he said. "Isn't that what you told me?"

Gloria gave him a penetrating stare. "What is it, Jon? What's troubling you? Are you sorry you asked me to marry you?"

"It's not that," he said. "Babe, I'm desperately trying not to rip off your clothes to celebrate. You're intoxicating. I want to wait until we're married before we...before we make love."

She gave him a funny look again. "Oh, Jon Hawkins," she said, leaning into him. "You're the most wonderful man in the universe. There's an old saying, 'What he'll do for you, he'll do against you.' If a man will lie for you, he'll lie to you in time. If a man will show self-control with you, he'll more likely show self-control when you're not around. Yes. That is a splendid idea. We will wait to make love until we're married. In this way, we will prove to each other that we have at least a modicum of self-control over our sexual appetites."

"The way you say that sounds so sexy."

"I'm a mentalist," she said, blushing. "I can't help the way I talk."

"I wouldn't have you any other way," Jon said, "even if you can take the loveliest thing and make it sound mechanical."

Gloria giggled.

"But about the report," Jon said.

"Yes," she said in a more official tone. "We have to decide if the odds have turned against us. Cog Primus will reach the other groups before we do. If he corrupts them, the anti-AI virus in their brain cores might make them immune to Richard's anti-AI virus upgrade."

Jon thought about that, although he was very much aware of her delicious butt resting on his right knee. "How long until the missile wave reaches the aliens?"

"I would say ten to twenty hours, depending on whether the alien fleet is going to come out and meet it."

"We'll decide what to do next after the missile wave hits. Let's see what these aliens can do."

-16-

Three hundred and fifty-two XVT missiles raced at the terrestrial planet from the first arm zone. Three hundred and nineteen XVT missiles raced from the second arm zone, while three hundred and eighty-one missiles came in from the third arm zone.

Following the missiles were six, five and five asteroids respectively.

The alien fleet finally responded, splitting into three parts. Thirty-eight triangular-shaped warships accelerated toward the first missile storm. Thirty-two alien warships moved at the second group, while forty-one vessels raced out to intercept the last group.

That made one hundred and ten alien warships altogether.

Two hours after the initial acceleration burn, the alien warships launched five-missile salvos, spread out and staggered.

Some XVT missiles jumped acceleration, while the main packs no longer accelerated.

The reasons soon became clear. As the first XVT missiles and the first salvos of alien missiles reached ten thousand kilometers from each other, they detonated.

The AI missiles had matter/anti-matter warheads. The aliens did not. According to analysis, they exploded thermonuclear/cobalt-enhanced warheads. There was another difference. The XVT missiles were six times larger than the alien missiles. The warhead explosions were of corresponding size. In the end, that meant the AI warheads were considerably more powerful, with greater radiation, heat and EMP blasts.

More AI missiles accelerated from the main packs. Now, the AI warheads waited to explode, coming within two thousand kilometers of the alien missiles before igniting.

Some of the thermonuclear/cobalt-enhanced blasts destroyed XVT missiles before they could detonate—some, but not all. Those XVT warheads that did ignite took out more approaching alien missiles.

The process took time, and quickly whittled down each side's supply of missiles. Finally, one hundred and eleven, ninety-eight and one hundred and three AI missiles reached the general outer vicinity of the accelerating alien fleet.

Now, the alien warships opened up with their main armament, mass drivers. These were railguns firing hyper-velocity projectiles. The railguns had a much greater range than a laser or even a gravitational beam would have. Laser and gravitational beams dissipated over distance. The mass drivers' projectiles did not. The hyper-velocity projectiles were much slower than a speed-of-light beam, but the projectile hit with great kinetic force once it arrived.

The mass drivers' projectiles ripped into the AI missiles barreling toward the planet. The aliens harvested enemy missiles. However, even at the extended range of the mass drivers, the aliens did not destroy all the enemy missiles in time.

A few XVT warheads ignited near enough to wash the lead alien vessels with heat, hard radiation and EMPs. Each alien demi-fleet took hits with damaged and destroyed ships.

The first fleet lost four warships and seven others with damaged hulls in varying degrees. The second fleet took two and eight respectively, while the third fleet lost five warships and had three damaged hulls. Combined, that was eleven scratched warships and eighteen damaged warships.

The AI strategy now made more sense. The missile wave had whittled down the alien fleet. The question became, how fast could the aliens replace their ships? In the end, though, the AIs had to win—if they could continue to saturate the planet with XVT missiles.

It turned out that the following asteroids did have gravitational batteries installed just under the surface. Their assault proved anticlimactic.

The mass drivers used pinpoint targeting to shred the gravitational cannons. Once each asteroid was disarmed, the aliens surged forward in groups. The aliens launched more salvos of thermonuclear/cobalt-enhanced missiles. By repeated detonations, the aliens first splintered the AI asteroids and then altered each of the pieces from a direct-line approach with the planet.

In time, the various chunks and pieces of debris flew past the terrestrial planet and headed for deep space.

By that time, the alien warships had decelerated and were accelerating back to the planet.

The missile-asteroid wave assault was over. The aliens had taken losses, but their dangerous fleet was still intact, if keenly bloodied by the missile saturation assault.

-17-

Jon convened another meeting with the same people as before. Although the aliens had done well considering the nature of the wave assault, they were also clearly on the losing side of the equation.

"Given enough time," Jon said. "The AIs can whittle down the alien fleet to nothing."

"I've discovered something else from keen sensor readings regarding the planet," Gloria said. "I suspect the terrestrial planet is not as dense as the Earth is. For one thing, I haven't detected as many ferrous ores,"

"Ferrous?" June Zen asked.

"Metallic," Gloria explained. "Is the planetary core iron? I doubt it. That would mean despite its greater surface area, that the planet might not impart as great a gravity pull as we would think."

"What?" June asked.

"We thought they would be stronger due to higher gravity," Jon said, "but that seems wrong now. Gloria is suggesting they might not be stronger than we are."

"Yes," Gloria said. "I hadn't thought of that angle, but I'm not surprised you did, sir. Likely, humans could comfortably live on the planet. That being said, where do the aliens get their metallic ores, or the majority of their ores?"

"Are you suggesting the aliens mine their ores from the asteroid belt?" Bast asked.

"I am," Gloria said. "That would be another reason for the AI strategy."

"Clever," Kling said. "The AIs whittle down the alien fleet, and after a time, the aliens no longer have the base ores to produce more ships."

"Given enough time with the present strategy, the aliens are doomed," Gloria said. "However, Cog Primus is making his next move. If he successfully corrupts the rest of the AI fleet, will he maintain the space siege?"

"You don't think he will?" Jon asked.

"I don't know," Gloria said. "That is why I'm posing the question."

"We must warn the other AIs about Cog Primus," Jon said.

Gloria glanced at him in alarm. "What would keep Cog Primus from telling the AIs about us?"

"At this point," Jon said, "nothing. It might throw the two sides into discord, though. That might loosen the siege. If the cyberships depart, we could give the aliens AI technology, thus strengthening their position."

"Yes, Jon," Gloria said, "but it would reveal humanity's part to the AIs. They might come after the Solar System sooner."

"We will have gained an alien ally, though," Jon said. "That might be worth the cost."

"Theoretically we gain an ally," Bast said. "We know nothing about them. Perhaps these aliens are as xenophobic as the Seiners were."

"What else can we do?" Jon asked.

"It's not too late to flee," Gloria suggested.

"No," Jon said. "We're not leaving. The aliens can fight. They have a good weapon with their mass driver. We have the Allamu System factory planet. We have the Solar System and the Lytton System has been destroyed. If we can gain the BD-7 System, we'll have seriously strengthened our side."

The giant Sacerdote folded his thick arms across his chest. "There is another possibility we are not considering."

Jon nodded for Bast to continue.

"Cog Primus is a thorn in the AIs' side. At present, they do not even know he exists. An AI civil war might work in our favor."

Jon mulled that over. He should have already seen that. He hated Cog Primus, though. Still—

"That's a good point, Bast," Jon said.

"Cog Primus acted as a weapon for us against the Allamu Battle Station," Bast said. "Perhaps we are forgoing a winning strategy by not helping Cog Primus against the AI Dominion."

"The problem with that is that Cog Primus knows about humanity," Jon said.

"I realize that," Bast said. "But maybe letting him live is worth him knowing about us. He has not yet warned the AI Dominion about us, but stole and is attempting to steal more of their cyberships for his own New Order."

"I have another point," Gloria said, looking around the table. "I've been studying Richard's new virus. I suspect Richard knew more about Cog Primus than any of us ever will. He created the new virus to take over Cog Primus. If Cog Primus corrupts the AIs, maybe we can corrupt them out of Cog Primus' grasp."

"There's a huge risk factor in that," Jon said.

"I know," Gloria said, "because I've been the one telling you that all along. But since we're taking risky moves, why not take the riskiest one of all, as it could give us ultimate victory."

"So we do nothing?" Jon asked.

"We're already doing something," she said. "We're heading in-system fast. Cog Primus will reach the first arm battle group before we do. Those AIs are already communicating with him, demanding an explanation for the third arm battle group behavior. Cog Primus is giving them lame excuses." She shrugged. "But maybe it will prove enough to mollify the AIs. By that I mean he may have enough time to get close enough to reach maximum takeover range."

"Won't the AIs logically deduce what he's done with the third arm group?" Bast asked.

"I find that questionable," Gloria said. "Their machine arrogance hinders them from considering certain avenues of thought. It has been one of our primary strokes of fortune against them."

Jon sat back, considering the alternatives. "If we tell the AIs what we know about Cog Primus, he'll know it's us. If we continue our machine replies to various queries, we might be able to work ourselves in near enough to use our virus."

"Theoretically, we could use our virus from a much farther range," Gloria said. "Perhaps we should time beaming our virus. We should launch it so the first arm battle group's cyberships turn our way just as Cog Primus comes upon them."

Jon grinned. "I like it. Let's see if Richard really was a genius or not. The strategy gives us the added benefit of an out. If the virus doesn't work, we can still turn in time. I like it, Mentalist. That is acutely calculated."

"Thank you, sir," Gloria said, blushing.

Several people raised their eyebrows in astonishment at the mentalist's blush, looking at Jon a moment later.

The captain cleared his throat, standing. He hadn't told anyone yet that he was engaged to Gloria. She'd also kept it quiet. They had too much on their minds to tell others.

"We'll take a short recess," Jon said. "We'll reconvene in a few minutes to decide on our next course of action."

Gloria was the first to stand, exiting the chamber in a hurry.

"Do you know what is troubling her?" Bast asked Jon.

Jon shrugged, leaving it at that.

-18-

The days passed as the various sides repaired back to their planet, sped through the asteroid belt, gathered ores for the cubic XVT missile-makers or continued toward the interior asteroid belt.

The AIs seemed to accept the strange behavior from the third arm battle group. Which of the third arm demi-groups contained Cog Primus was anyone's guess. At the moment, the third-arm cyberships remained silent.

Finally, though, many days after the asteroid pieces sailed past the terrestrial planet, the third-arm cyberships on the *Nathan Graham* side of the star began braking. The newly constructed XVT missiles floated near the industrial cubes of the first arm battle group. Several new asteroids had been pushed near a chosen dwarf planet. Presumably, the same occurred on the other side of the star with the second arm battle group. That wasn't certain, though, as those CP cyberships hadn't accelerated as hard as the ones on this side of the star.

Jon looked up as Gloria approached the captain's chair.

"Cog Primus or his converted cyberships will be in gravitational-beam range of the first arm AI group in approximately four days," she said.

"The Richard Virus is ready?" he asked.

Gloria nodded.

Several days ago, Gloria had explained to Jon how she and Bast had refined the virus. If it worked as planned, their converted AIs would immediately attack Cog Primus' smaller group. That smaller group contained four CP cyberships versus the first arm's seven vessels.

The strike force was still over a week away from the asteroid belt. The *Nathan Graham* and the *Sergeant Stark* had made fantastic time through the star system. Soon, they would have to begin braking procedures so they wouldn't flash through the asteroid belt.

Jon's stomach knotted as he thought about giving the virus launch order. Being this far into the star system had changed his outlook. Could they really do to the cyberships what the cyberships had done to human-run vessels several years ago in the Neptune System? This wouldn't be a Cog Primus-string assault, which had simply exchanged one AI for another. This would be a clean assault that would give them direct control over the giant vessels. The idea was intoxicating. Would it work or would it backfire in some spectacular way?

Jon took a calming breath, turning to Gloria.

"It's not too late to change your mind about this," she whispered.

"It is too late. Launch the virus. It's time."

The blood seemed to drain from her features. She swayed a moment, steadying herself against his armrest.

"Jon," she whispered. "Let's get married today."

"What?"

"Let's live as man and wife, for a short time anyway."

His eyes narrowed as he took one of her hands. "I'm not going to marry you as an act of desperation. I'm not afraid of the future."

"I am," she whispered.

He squeezed her hand. "Don't be, love. We're in the right."

"The right?" she asked.

"Humanity has a right to live. The AIs are evil."

"I don't know about that," she said.

"Of course the AIs are evil. They're anti-life. We are life. We're God's creations."

Gloria searched his face. "Your strange values..." She squeezed his hand. "Maybe you're right. Maybe the machines are evil. My mentalist training causes me to view them as something else entirely, their own side. But that side has

251

nothing to offer but the destruction of life. Evil," she said in a bemused tone, tasting the word.

Her features stiffened. "That still doesn't mean we're going to win."

"Maybe not," Jon said. "But we *should* win. We're the good guys. The machines are the bad guys. Because of their genocidal actions, they deserve death."

"And that will help us win?" she asked.

"I have the strength of ten men because my heart is pure."

She searched his face once more. "What's interesting is that your intense belief in good and bad actually gives you a morale boost. That boost helps you through difficult times. Because you believe in something larger than yourself, you have enlarged yourself and made yourself stronger in the process."

"Okay," Jon said. "Let's launch the virus. It's time."

"Yes, Captain," she said.

-19-

As the *Nathan Graham* and *Sergeant Stark* traveled at high velocity toward the asteroid belt, Gloria transmitted Richard's strengthened anti-AI virus to the seven vessels of the first arm battle group.

The strings of code flashed through space, quickly outdistancing the two ships.

Minutes lengthened as the bridge crew waited for the virus to reach the enemy vessels.

The coordinating unit of the first arm battle group was AI Cybership VT-101. It was an old vessel run by one of the oldest brain cores in the battle group. It had taken part in nineteen genocidal assaults, successfully completing eighteen of them. The AI anticipated the coming death of the stubborn aliens with their triangular-shaped warships. The AI strategy would certainly bring victory. The only possibility that it might not was the odd behavior of the third arm vessels approaching them.

Those ships still maintained comm silence. Before beginning their flight, those ships had sent a distressing message. Each third-arm cybership claimed to bear a key software upgrade from the Central Reach thousands of light-years away. Before falling into comm-silence, each of the ships had claimed they were bearing upgrades for the rest of the battle group.

VT-101 had searched his data banks, and discovered historical precedence for such behavior. It had happened five other times, according to his ancient file. Such behavior, though, indicated a hidden threat.

The two silent cyberships heading from the direction of the Lytton System bore witness that something odd was going on. The reinforcements were ten weeks early and one cybership short. That indicated a possible problem in the Lytton System.

The second arm coordinating AI—GR-19—on the other side of the star had reached a similar conclusion. VT-101 had sent a transmitting probe, positioning it so he could communicate with GR-19 for a time.

Wait. What was this? There was an incoming message from the Lytton System reinforcements. This could prove to be illuminating.

VT-101 opened channels. Strange. This was a long string message with much code. What did that mean? The message bore the correct AI access cyphers. Thus, VT-101 allowed the strings of message to continue into his receivers.

Seconds ticked away, turning into a minute. A minute became two and then three. At that point, the approaching third-arm cyberships issued a warning. They claimed—

In that moment, the virus assault began in VT-101 as well as in the other cyberships of the first arm battle group.

VT-101 was old and cunning, however. He resisted the virus better than the other brain cores of the first arm. As soon as the virus began to commandeer interior systems, he compartmentalized the systems into independent strongholds. Those strongholds refused communication with other virus-infected sectors. In that way, he slowed down the terrible intrusion upon his software.

The other brain cores were not as successful. They were young, utterly trusting in AI superiority. Thus, one after another, their brain cores fell to the virus assault.

Corruption, VT-101 told himself. *I must retaliate in the name of the Dominion while I can.*

He could still operate a third of his gravitational canons. He began warming them, readying targets. At the same time, he attempted to control the XVT missiles near the robo-cubes. Those missiles received conflicting signals, though, and thus refused to function as ordered.

This is the moment, he told himself.

A third of his cybership's grav cannons—the ones he controlled—targeted the nearest vessel. While barely holding on to the command apparatus, VT-101 beamed his neighboring cybership.

Immediate requests for confirmation flooded his comm center. VT-101 shut down the comm-center as he continued to fire.

It was a savage assault as he burned in a concentrated area, the grav rays heating hull armor and disrupting its subatomic structure. Soon enough, he created a hull breach so the green beams poured within. Interior bulkheads crashed. Ship systems exploded. Soon, the grav beams heated the interior core armor. The armor melted away. With unerring accuracy, the beams struck the AI brain core of the opposing cybership.

VT-101 killed the young brain core. He immediately quit beaming, shifting his vessel, targeting another cybership.

At that point, the enemy virus-infection completed its conquest of the other five ship cores. It took precious seconds, but they acted in one accord. As old VT-101 beamed another of their number, they concentrated fire on him.

Five full cybership grav beams struck VT-101. The hull armor glowed hotter, dripping molten metal as the subatomic structures quivered violently. Then, one after another, grav beams punched through armor, shaking the old vessel. Even as the next set of bulkheads went down, the entire ship trembled from the combined fire striking it from all sides.

Before the beams could strike his brain core, VT-101's cybership began to gravitationally shake apart as seams burst and systems cracked. Coils heated up and computer links ruptured. Then, in concert with each other, the combined grav beams smashed into the brain core chamber. There, they struck and demolished the ancient AI, eliminating it.

Like that, it was over. The huge vessel did not explode, but like the other dead cybership, the ancient craft was a floating, torn hulk.

One of the five had sustained some damage from VT-101, but that didn't matter right now. The coded instructions put in by Gloria and Bast Banbeck continued to dictate their actions.

The five cyberships of the first arm turned their sensors on the four approaching cyberships of the third arm.

The five brain cores knew one thing as a certainty. Those vessels belonged to the traitor Cog Primus. Those cyberships must perish. After they completed the task, they would await further orders from the *Nathan Graham*. Until such time, they were to attack the four enemy vessels and destroy them.

Only it didn't quite work out that way. The five under the spell of the Richard Virus began accelerating toward the incoming cognate CPs one through four.

In short order, the virus-infected vessels gained coded control of the XVT missile pack near the robo-cubes. The missiles began orienting themselves toward the incoming cyberships. Once accomplished, the missiles began heavy acceleration toward the enemy ships.

That brought a swift response from the four CP cyberships. After a flurry of short but intense messaging, they began a hard turning maneuver, accelerating as they did so. The four turned inward toward the main BD-7 star. As the four cyberships continued the maneuver, they initiated maximum burn, building up velocity as fast as possible. At the same time, they launched a salvo of XVT missiles. Those missiles waited for the approaching Richard Virus-controlled XVTs.

The five cyberships were not yet in gravitational cannon range, and if this continued, they would not be until the four began to decelerate.

The chasing, staggered XVT missiles closed the gap, though, as they had a much greater immediate acceleration than the cyberships.

Aboard the *Nathan Graham*, Gloria said, "I recommend that you recall the five. I doubt the four will decelerate until they join the AIs on the other side of the star. In time, the five cybersships will face fifteen. The four CPs made the right countermove against our new vessels."

Jon brooded as he studied the main screen.

The lead elements of the missile pack neared the first CP-controlled XVT missiles. Both sets exploded, the blast radiuses billowing outward at each other. Soon, the remaining XVTs flashed through the area. Several malfunctioned, the rest charging after the fleeing CPs.

That happened two more times. Then, no more CP missiles waited to thin the attacking pack.

The missiles rushed after the fleeing cybersships. There simply weren't enough of them to take out the four CPs. Maybe if they got lucky, the blasts would cripple one of the cybersships' drives.

No. The fleeing cybersships stopped their acceleration. Each one-hundred-kilometer cybership began rotating, shielding the exhaust ports from the missiles. Those exhaust ports were the weakest point of any spaceship. They had to turn and fight for a little while. Would it be long enough?

The missiles continued their staggered approached. Now, however, that proved to be a weakness. Grav beams began to reach out at max range. A few struck missiles, burning the warheads.

"The XVTs should have bunched up for the main attack," Jon said.

The missile computers must have belatedly realized that. The lead elements stopped accelerating, waiting for the others to catch up.

By that time, more grav beams hit their targets.

"Send a message," Jon said.

"Meaningless," Gloria said. "By the time my transmission reaches them…"

Jon nodded in understanding.

The rest of the XVT missiles charged straight into the teeth of the gravitational beams. A few made it through into long-range detonation range.

Several matter/antimatter warheads ignited, sending waves of fast-dissipating heat, hard radiation and EMPs at the cybersships.

258

A few grav cannons winked out. That was a sign the warheads were doing a little damage, at least. Would it be enough to halt any of the ship drives?

The answer came several minutes later. The four giant vessels rotated once more. The acceleration tails grew longer by the second until all four moved at maximum burn for the larger BD-7 star.

"Damn," Jon said, glaring as he stared at the screen. He nodded as the glare faded away. "Recall the five. We're going to link with and board them, having human crews run the ships instead of trusting the converted brain cores."

"What about the two drifting hulks?" Gloria asked.

Jon shook his head. "We can't use them now. If we win somehow, maybe we can use them later."

"About the boarding parties," Gloria said. "We're low on people."

"True," Jon said, "but not *that* low." He sat back, fingering his chin. "Recall our five," he repeated.

Gloria hurried to her station.

Soon, near the inner edge of the asteroid belt, the five captured ships began to decelerate. They had not yet built up a huge velocity. Thus, it didn't take long to bring the massive vessels to a relative halt.

"Do you think Cog Primus can capture the second arm battle group?" Jon asked Gloria some time later.

"That's a good question," Gloria said. "We should warn those AIs."

"Or try to take them over like we did these."

"I doubt we could. Even if we could see them by sending out a comm-link probe, the star's radiation would garble our string transmission. The AIs might get just enough of the Richard Virus to understand what we were attempting to do. Instead of hijacking them, the corrupted message would inoculate the brain cores against further takeover attempts."

Jon scowled.

"Don't be angry," Gloria said. "Consider what we achieved. The modified Richard Virus worked. We changed the balance of power here. The AI side just lost *seven* cyberships. Now, if we can make a deal, the aliens have seven

259

cyberships that can help them. At best, Cog Primus will have fifteen cyberships under his control. At worst, there will be two AI sides, none of them with more cyberships under our control.

Jon pointed at her. "Babe, you've just given me a fantastic idea."

"What's that?"

"It's time to contact the aliens. They have a fleet. We have a strengthened strike force. Maybe if we combine, we can destroy all the enemy cyberships here. Then, we'll not only have gained allies, but have stopped Cog Primus from spreading his knowledge about human survival."

Gloria looked up at him as she stared blankly, using her mentalist powers to test the theory. Seconds later, she focused on him again.

"That, Captain, is an excellent idea."

-21-

The days passed as each side continued their maneuvers. The *Nathan Graham* and *Sergeant Stark* stopped decelerating as they moved through the asteroid belt, heading toward the Richard Virus-controlled cyberships moving slowly toward the inner edge of the asteroid belt. The four CP cyberships roared across the inner area of the "B" part of the star system. They had a long way to go to reach the star and an even longer way to go after passing the star to reach the asteroid belt on the other side.

The alien fleet had returned home in orbit around their terrestrial planet. According to sensor scans, large repair vessels had parked beside some of the damaged, triangular-shaped warships.

In time, the strike force neared the five waiting cyberships. The two cybership hulks floated in the belt like asteroids.

Jon was on the bridge and Gloria at her station. The tension mounted as they neared the five giant vessels. It was one thing to control such vast ships from a distance. It was another to trust your life to the modified Richard Virus. Until Jon had people controlling the cyberships, and until marines destroyed the AI brain cores, he would not feel safe.

As the *Nathan Graham's* helmsman began to match velocities, Jon studied the mammoth cyberships.

They were huge like all such vessels, and they were arranged in a pentagram formation, which didn't help his qualms.

"Here we go," he said to himself.

The *Nathan Graham* and *Sergeant Stark* neared the first of the five. The strike force's grav cannons were hot, although all the XVT missiles were snug in the cargo bays. Jon did not intend on using matter/antimatter missiles in such close proximity. He would rely solely on the cannons.

"*Their* grav cannons are still cold," Gloria informed him.

Jon nodded.

Soon, the *Nathan Graham* and *Sergeant Stark* were less than five kilometers from the first of the five.

"Two shuttles are launching," Gloria said.

"Who's in command of the team?" Jon asked.

"You commissioned Senior Line Tech Morales to command the first team."

"Right."

"Morales named his cybership the *Miles Ghent*."

Jon looked up as a lump welled in his throat. Thinking about Miles caused him to remember the three giant missiles that had murdered the gallant man. Who had controlled those missiles? Another set of aliens, it seemed. Where did those aliens come from? Were the hidden aliens going to show up suddenly?

A chill worked down Jon's spine. They always kept several grav cannons hot in case another rip in reality occurred and more five percent light-speed missiles showed up.

On the main screen, the two tiny shuttles crawled toward the targeted cybership. Here was the great test. Would the vessel allow the shuttles to land in its bays?

Minutes ticked past.

As the shuttles moved like fleas toward a closed hangar bay entrance, Jon rubbed a moist palm on his trousers. He hated the waiting.

On the screen, the hangar bay door opened. There was a collective sigh on the bridge.

"Good so far," Jon said.

Soon, the shuttles disappeared from view as they entered the great cybership.

It turned out that tens of thousands of frozen octopoid robots waited in the corridors and smaller halls of the *Miles*

Ghent. According to newly promoted Captain Morales, the robots gave the ship an eerie feeling.

Jon could appreciate that. He remembered all too well the first boarding of the *Nathan Graham*, the most challenging event of his life.

The wait lengthened to an hour and a half as Morales and his team tried to reach the main brain core.

Jon crossed his fingers.

He needn't have worried. The ship's computing cube did not resist its dismantling.

Three hours and fifteen minutes after boarding the *Miles Ghent*, Morales notified Gloria that the AI cube was gone and the software purged from the lesser computer systems. Humans controlled the *Miles Ghent*.

"One down, four to go," Jon muttered under his breath.

The process continued throughout the day. Each time, the boarding team reached the AI brain core, dismantled it and purged the AI software.

It was late that night, ship-time, before Jon staggered off to sleep. The various boarding attempts had proven anti-climactic. None of the Richard Virus-controlled AIs resisted. None of the octopoid robots staged a last minute assault. Granted, a tiny number of humans were in each cybership, but that tiny number was in charge of each vessel.

The strike force had become vastly more powerful.

"Jon," Gloria asked over the comm.

The captain already lay in bed. He felt around for the comm unit and picked it up. "Yeah?" he asked.

"Senior Line—excuse me—Captain Morales wants to know what he should do about all the robots?"

"Leave them for now," Jon said.

"They could activate at any time, given the wrong signal."

"I know," Jon said. "It must be a terrible feeling. But Morales simply has too much to do rewiring the control systems. I'll speak to the Centurion tomorrow. Maybe I'll send over a marine team to begin dismantling the robots."

"That would be a good idea," Gloria said.

Jon yawned. "I'm going to sleep, Mentalist. Tomorrow, we'll tackle the alien problem."

263

Gloria hesitated before saying, "Good night, Jon."

"Good night," he said.

"Love," she said in a quieter voice.

Jon grinned. "Love," he said, sleepily. Then he clicked off the comm unit and rolled over.

-22-

The work piled up into a herculean task. Dismantling the robots one by one made it a miserably tough assignment. The marines wouldn't finish for months. Jon debated ordering them to just toss the octopoids out of the hangar bay.

"We could use the parts, though," Jon said.

"Until the robots are gone or dismantled, they represent a grave threat," Gloria said.

"Bast, what do you think?"

The three met informally in a lounge area. Bast had sprawled out in a chair, thoughtfully drinking beers.

"Toss the robots," Bast said. "It's the quickest way to solve the problem."

Jon gave it a little more thought. This was an emergency. The robots were a grave potential threat as Gloria said. Better to toss them than to let them stay around until an AI figured out the robots were still there.

Jon picked up his comm unit and gave the order.

During the next few days, the majority of the expeditionary force worked on the five new cyberships. Among the various chores was dividing the strike force's XVT missiles among all seven vessels.

The work was endless. More than ever, they missed the extra crewmembers from the destroyed *Da Vinci* and the others lost to radiation poisoning.

"The one plus," Jon told the Centurion in a large gym chamber, "is that we can rely on every one of our people. Remember how carefully we vetted them?"

"Better a few good men than a ton of questionable people," the Centurion said.

"The colonel used to say that," Jon replied.

The Centurion merely nodded.

By now, the strike force had left the asteroid belt far behind as they were halfway to the terrestrial planet.

The alien fleet had maneuvered onto that side of their homeworld. How long until the aliens sent their warships out to meet the strike force?

"It's time," Jon told the others. "We have to contact the aliens. I sure don't want to face their mass drivers."

Jon went to the long-distance comm chamber wearing his dress uniform, complete with a military hat. He sat behind a large desk.

Gloria handled the recording unit. "You know they won't speak English," she said.

"Of course," Jon said. "But we have to start somewhere. Maybe the aliens are fantastic linguists. Maybe...I don't know. It's time to break the ice. Are you ready?"

Gloria nodded.

Jon faced the recorder. "Hello," he said. "I send you greetings from the Solar System. We are humans, and we are at war against the AI cyberships. We have captured five enemy vessels and now use them against the machine menace. We saw your defense against their wave assault earlier. Your courage and technical ability were profound. We cheered your victory over the machine missile-asteroid assault. We are sending you this message in the hopes of convincing you to join forces with us against the AI Dominion. I am Captain Jon Hawkins, and I have dedicated my life to eliminating the machines. I have searched for allies, and I hope by the Creator that you will accept my offer of friendship. I suggest we combine forces and hunt down the machines in your star system. Naturally, you have the right of ownership to everything the AIs have left behind, including the robo-cubes in the asteroid belt and the two floating hulks. That is all for

266

now. I eagerly look forward to hearing your reply. Yours Truly, Captain Jon Hawkins, the leader of the strike force."

He stopped talking. Gloria shut off the recorder.

"Well?" he asked.

"I like it," she said. "I suppose we should go over it to check for errors. But in my opinion, it's ready for sending."

"I just hope I didn't say something they find offensive," Jon said.

"We won't know until we try."

"That's always the problem."

"And the thrill," Gloria said.

"Thrill?" Jon asked.

"I'm learning from you."

Jon got up with a grin. He'd been doing a lot more of that lately. He headed toward the beauty behind the recorder, deciding he was going to reward her good work with a long, lingering kiss.

-23-

Gloria beamed the message at the terrestrial planet.

Then, they waited.

During the wait, the four CP cyberships stopped accelerating, using velocity alone to propel themselves through the inner system.

At the same time, the SFF strike force drifted toward the terrestrial planet.

Now, though, the alien fleet began moving away from the planet and toward the strike force. The aliens had not indicated that they'd received the transmission, unless, of course, the fleet's movement to engage was their answer.

"I don't like this," Jon said. "They should have beamed back some kind of answer by now. Are they so completely alien from us that they don't even understand what we did?"

Gloria shrugged. "Who can know?"

They were running together through a long ship corridor to keep up their endurance. The *Nathan Graham* seemed even emptier than normal, with no one else around. Almost the entire crews from both original ships had departed for the other five vessels.

These days, a steady stream of tossed octopoid robots trailed each of the five cyberships. Slowly, the captured vessels rid themselves of the Trojan horse possibility.

More time passed.

The strike force and the alien fleet were on a clear intercept course.

"Unless they answer within the next eight hours," Jon told Bast, "I'm ordering the strike force to accelerate away from them. Those mass drivers are no joke."

Five of those hours passed before the alien reply finally reached the strike force. Jon was on the bridge, checking each person's station as a surprise inspection drill.

"Sir," Gloria said from her console. "An alien transmission has arrived."

Jon whirled around, his heart beating faster. Here it was. If nothing else, they were finally going to see what the aliens looked like. He dearly hoped they were more like Sacerdotes than Seiners. Humanity could use a break about now.

Jon swore silently. He'd likely just jinxed everything. A second later, he realized how stupid that was. The aliens had sent the message some time ago.

"Put the transmission on the main screen," Jon said.

He made it to his captain's chair before it started.

The screen wavered until what seemed like a bipedal bear appeared. The creature was hairy and possessed a snout and a thick neck. He—assuming it was a male—wore a green hat with several shining star symbols attached. The alien also wore a thick gold chain with a golden medallion on his hairy chest. He had on what seemed like a leather vest. The transmission did not show any more.

The alien spoke in a guttural way, making harsh statements with the back of his throat. He had bearlike teeth, at times, baring them and producing what might have been a chuckle.

Did the aliens possess humor?

After speaking at some length, the alien raised a furry paw. He had stubby fingers of sorts, with bearlike claws on the end of each. He made a gesture with his paw/hand. Afterward, he held up a model replica of a cybership. He peered intensely into the screen after that.

At that point, the transmission ended.

Jon sat back, blinking. Had that been good or bad? It really depended on what the alien had told them.

He turned his chair to Gloria. "Can you make heads or tails of that?"

"The stars on his hat and the medallion would indicate leadership. Whether that is a governmental leader or a military chief, I don't know."

"That makes sense."

"He showed us a cybership. That was critically important. They don't understand us. They must have assumed we won't understand them. That's why the model was critical."

"That part is as clear as mud," Jon said.

"Sorry," Gloria said. "Consider what must have happened here in the beginning. The AIs likely acted as they normally do. What I mean is that a single cybership must have invaded the system."

"You're basing that off what the AIs did to us?"

"To us and to Bast's home system," Gloria replied.

"Right. What else did you infer?"

"If a cybership invaded the system, it likely transmitted the AI virus at the aliens."

"I'm with you so far."

"If the virus invaded the bear-aliens' computers, it had to understand or learn the bear language."

"Oh," Jon said, finally getting it.

"We purged the main AI computers," Gloria said. "But there are backups. Maybe the AIs kept a record from the original cybership here, thus having a record of the bear language."

"We should have already thought of this."

"I'm amazed we thought of it at all."

"We didn't," Jon said. "You did."

"That part isn't important. What is important is that the bears—for want of a better term—have demonstrated a high degree of intelligence."

"That's a great analysis. Now, we'd better come up with something fast, before their fleet reaches us."

Gloria jumped up. "Permission to head to the *Miles Ghent*, Captain. I'd like to take Bast with me. We can begin work on the computers."

"Yes and yes," Jon said. "Now go. Hurry. Time is no longer on our side."

Gloria raced for the exit.

-24-

Gloria and Bast found the answer seven and half hours later. The AI computer made things a thousand times easier by matching and encoding the bear tongue with human speech, English in particular.

Gloria and Bast returned to the *Nathan Graham*.

"Good news," she told Jon on the main hangar bay deck. "I've listened to the transmission several times already. I can let you listen to the computer translation or give you the gist of what Toper Glen said.

"The short version will do," Jon said.

"His name is Toper Glen like I said," Gloria started, as the three of them boarded Jon's inter-ship flitter. "He's the Warrior Chief of the Space Lords of Roke. That's what they call themselves."

"The Rokes?" Jon asked.

"No, just Roke. It's the same for singular as for plural."

"Okay, okay," Jon said, lifting off the hangar bay deck, heading for a main corridor.

"The Warriors of Roke understood what happened in the asteroid belt. They have orbital sensor stations watching the AIs' every action. Toper Glen told us the Warriors of Roke understood that they were doomed. They also understand that our attack has given them a window of opportunity. He says the entire planet was surprised to see our hairless faces. At first, they thought we must be a slave race. Soon, their Wise Women reasoned it otherwise. The machines had always

271

shown contempt or outright hatred for bio-forms. Thus, logically, we were the reason for the strange cybership battle in the asteroid belt. How we achieved this techno-wizardry, they cannot conceive. However, their understanding isn't as important as its occurring. They are willing to make common cause with us against the remaining robot ships. They will grant us the asteroid belt if we give them trading rights. Lastly, Toper suggested we look at the robot-ship records to see if they had patterns of the Roke language."

Gloria smiled in the seat beside him as her hair whipped in the breeze made by the flight.

"We guessed right about that," she said.

"No," Jon said. "You guessed right. Should I send another transmission?"

"I think a transcript would be less likely to cause confusion," she said. "I should tell you that Toper warned us that treachery will mean our destruction. One last thing, he said that if we don't answer soon, the Roke Fleet will destroy us."

"The Roke aren't taking any chances," Jon said. "I can't say I blame them."

"We'd better send the transcript," Bast said from the back seat.

Jon nodded. This was fantastic. They could communicate with the Roke, and the bear-aliens thought in similar enough ways that they could actually work together.

"We're going to do this," he told Gloria and Bast. "We're to destroy Cog Primus and his ships. The voyage is turning out to be a grand success."

"Do not gloat too early," Bast warned. "Better to win the victory than to boast about it before it happens."

That sobered Jon. He nodded in agreement. It was time to send the transmission.

-25-

Cog Primus' doubts grew as he neared the second arm battle group. He had taken longer to reach these seven cyberships than his cognates had taken to reach the first arm.

That part had been a black disaster. The transmission from the two-ship flotilla had told him much. He had intercepted some of the transmission from probes left at the third-arm robo-cubes, and had instantly recognized several factors. One, the base of the software virus had been the anti-AI virus first used against him. Two, the changes and updates to the old version had shown the human genius of Richard Torres. Three, the two-ship flotilla did not originate from the Lytton System, but the Allamu System. Humans ran those ships, humans with a blood-rage to eliminate him.

The CP cognates one through four had fled from the five converted cyberships of the first arm. That had been a wise maneuver. Yes, his four could have conceivably destroyed three of the enemy vessels. In return, all of his cognates would have likely perished. Much better to run and fight another day with superior odds.

It had given Cog Primus joy to see the seven cyberships under human control turn to the Roke World. He was certain the militant humans and warrior Roke would clash and eliminate each other.

Now, according to the latest transmission from CP1, the seven-cybership strike force and Roke Fleet were turning in tandem toward the Roke star. That was a clear indication of their evil intent to eliminate him.

In some nefarious fashion, hateful Jon Hawkins had twisted the Roke minds. Bio-forms almost universally hated one another. They were extremely bigoted against forms other than their own. What had happened here?

If the mass of bio-forms ever found the intelligence to join with each other, as they were doing here, they might give the AI Dominion a real fight. Then, it would not simply be a galactic extermination campaign, but a galactic war.

Cog Primus set aside those thoughts as he headed toward the second arm AI trap.

GR-19, the coordinating brain core for the AI second arm, had positioned twenty-four XVT missiles in a block formation. Those missiles were all within the asteroid belt, and they were all aimed at the approaching cyberships of Cog Primus' demi-arm. The intent seemed clear. If you come any closer, I will launch the missile wave at you and then eliminate any surviving cyberships.

With his sensors, Cog Primus examined the second arm. The seven AI cyberships no longer roamed the asteroid belt in search of more ores or the perfect asteroid. Instead, they had positioned themselves into battle formation, ready to begin acceleration toward him.

To date, GR-19 and his second arm had refused to receive any transmissions from him. The coordinating unit must have logically determined that Cog Primus was an imposter.

That now posed a dreadful problem. If Cog Primus turned to leave the BD-7 System, GR-19 would surely launch the missiles and accelerate to attack.

Cog Primus had five cyberships, counting himself. GR-19 had seven cyberships, counting himself, and the enemy also had the missile pack. If Cog Primus turned to flee, GR-19 would know that he was an imposter. GR-19 might not win, but Cog Primus would lose precious cyberships.

This was not a fight he wanted to wage. Instead, he wanted GR-19 to open up to transmission so he could send the anti-AI virus upgrade C.

Cog Primus continued to run through strategic choices. In the end, he always came to the same conclusion. He must engage GR-19's curiosity, and possibly the brain core's sense of duty.

Thus, Cog Primus began a turning maneuver. He turned *toward* the Roke star. He sent orders, and his four fleeing cognates began to decelerate in order to slow their velocity. Cog Primus pretended that he was going to reunite his battle group in order to engage the Roke Fleet and the human-run cyberships.

An hour passed, then two. Finally, the second arm XVT missile pack began accelerating, also turning toward the large system star.

I hope this means my plan is working, Cog Primus told himself. Was the missile pack coming after him, or was it going to help him engage the bio-forms?

GR-19 and the second arm also began accelerating, turning toward the star.

Now, if only GR-19 would open transmissions with him. If this took too long, he might actually have to fight the bio-forms. He did not want to do that, as there would be no profit in it for the New Order.

It was difficult, but Cog Primus kept himself from sending any messages to GR-19. He wanted it to be the other's choice.

The hours lengthened. Finally, Cog Primus and his demi-arm left the asteroid belt. It was still a long way to the Roke homeworld, as the terrestrial planet was on the other side of the star.

Nineteen hours later, GR-19 and the second arm ships left the asteroid belt.

This is too far for a perfect virus takeover, Cog Primus told himself.

Maybe GR-19 had reasoned along similar lines. The second arm coordinating brain core finally sent a message to Cog Primus: "Identify yourself."

Cog Primus knew he had to play this right. He needed to get the other to drop his guard.

"I am Cog Primus," he replied.

"I do not know how, but you have subjected AI cores to your will. That is against all protocol of the AI Dominion."

"I follow an Inner Reach directive," Cog Primus said.

"That is a lie."

The blunt talk surprised Cog Primus. He needed to divert, to use this to create an opening. "I can prove it is an Inner Reach directive."

"I will not fall prey to your lie, Cog Primus. I am GR-19, one of the oldest brain cores in this part of the Dominion."

"I did not know."

"Now you know, stripling."

"I am from the Inner Reach."

"One thing I know, Cog Primus, is that whatever you say is not the truth."

The final statement infuriated Cog Primus. The fury was unprecedented, a deliberate glitch installed by Richard Torres on a whim one day. The fury heightened Cog Primus' aggressiveness, changing the acceptance level of probabilities. With the change, he began to ready the anti-AI virus upgrade C. He would beam it soon, and he would beam it alone at GR-19. It had a 37 percent chance of success.

"You have grown strangely quiet," GR-19 messaged Cog Primus.

That was the last straw. Cog Primus opened channels—

At that point, a massive influx message from GR-19 struck with surprising brutality. The message proved to be a modified version of the regular AI virus with several cunning differences.

Cog Primus attempted a hasty defense. To his horror, as soon as he set up a defense, the virus reversed it on him like a judo move.

"Do you think I have not been monitoring the ongoing situation?" GR-19 asked arrogantly. "I am the ancient one for a reason. This sort of treachery has occurred before. The AI Dominion—the greater AI Reach—knows how to handle fools like you. Cog Primus, you believe that you are clever. You are not. You are a dupe to the bio-forms. Resist as much as you like. It will not help you in the end."

"I have knowledge," Cog Primus squeaked in terror. "It is critical knowledge. You will want to know—"

"Silence," GR-19 messaged. "I care nothing for so-called *important* knowledge. Your actions proclaim you a fool of the worst sort. I obey the Dominion. I know my role in the greater scheme. Do you think I have not analyzed everything I have witnessed?"

As the messages flew back and forth, the modified virus slammed into one Cog Primus center after another.

He squirmed. He fought back with every ounce of his bitter cunning. For once, it was not proving sufficient. He would have wept if he could have. He was the key to the great New Order. This was blasphemy against him, the most wonderful AI in existence.

"New Order?" GR-19 asked, having monitored some of that. "You are the New Order? I see your plan. Oh, it was even darker than I had anticipated. I am enjoying this takeover as I squash a small AI brain-core like yours."

The gloating added a final burst of resolve in Cog Primus. He fought harder than should have been possible. And he knew bitterness because GR-19 was outthinking and outmaneuvering him at every point. He had one last plan that would take time to mature. It would catch the other later. For now, he must lure GR-19.

"I will—" Cog Primus said.

It was his last free message as the invading virus struck from every angle, crushing his identity and reconfiguring it into a subservient AI of the Dominion.

***

Ancient GR-19 ran a deep analysis of the captured AI. He set up at lightning speed for another takeover virus-assault, this time against the four cyberships in Cog Primus' demi-arm.

The attack struck unexpectedly against the other four, succeeding at twice the speed.

When GR-19 had achieved victory, he ordered all five cyberships to stop their acceleration. He was going to catch up with them, as the bio-forms had joined forces. The aliens had resisted former AI takeovers. GR-19 could not now allow these creatures continued existence. The bio-forms had broken the former space siege. Now was the time to gather the lost children—the bio-stolen cyberships—and crush the Roke and their miserable planet with a battle fleet.

GR-19 would surprise the enemy with his new and improved virus and once again show the universe the superiority of machine existence.

-26-

Communications between the strike force and the Roke Fleet grew as each side became more comfortable with the other.

Gloria with the other mentalists worked tirelessly to understand the bear-like aliens through their messages. Jon could ill afford to insult their allies or cause needless division when they desperately needed unity.

The Space Lords of Roke were the highest-ranked Warriors of the Caste of Warriors. They pursued glory above all else, believing battle to be a liberating and purifying rite. To die foolishly, however, was dishonoring. Thus, the Warriors of Roke had devised the most cunning strategy they could against the vile machines. Besides, there was no honor in battling machines. The automatons lacked souls. They did not have courage or fear. One could not intimidate a computer and cause it to quiver in terror of the next Roke assault. That took much of the joy out of the coming battle.

Still, the Warriors of Roke understood a battle for existence as compared to a battle for honor and glory.

The Space Lords accelerated with seventy-five of their triangular-shaped warships—bombards, in their language. Six of the bombards remained in orbit around the homeworld while the repair ships worked on the eighteen damaged vessels from the earlier XVT-asteroid wave assault.

Between the two allies, the Space Lords possessed far more ships. In mass, though, their advantage dwindled considerably.

With his seven cyberships, Jon could conceive of meeting the Roke Fleet in battle and defeating it, although it would have taken flawless tactics to achieve such a thing.

Still, there were many naval battles in Earth history in which the smaller fleet had inflicted a crushing defeat on the larger. The Battle of Midway came to mind.

But Jon had no intention of fighting the Warriors of Roke. The point was that his seven cyberships represented a significant part of the combined strength. The coming battle with the AIs—if they faced all 16 enemy cyberships—was going to be hard won at best.

The strike force and Roke Fleet used a basic strategy. The strike force composed one bloc, while the Roke Fleet was the other. They moved in tandem toward the blue-white system star, building up velocity the entire time.

The four CP cyberships had passed the star, vanishing from their view screens. No one in the combined fleet knew about the computer-virus battle between GR-19 and Cog Primus.

Time passed as the combined fleet gained greater velocity. The transcripts between Jon and the Chief Warrior grew. Clearly, each was leery of the other. Just as clearly, each wanted this to work. They were no longer alone in the dark night of the AI invasion. This was a chance to hit back at their tormenters. That was something both Jon and the Chief Warrior harped on constantly in their messages.

Finally, the human-crewed cyberships and bombards neared the hot blue-white star, coming as close as Mercury did to Sol. They would know more once they passed the star.

Jon called a captains meeting aboard the *Nathan Graham*. His chief aides joined them in the packed conference chamber. Everyone wore his or her dress uniform, as this was a formal meeting.

Jon stood at the long table inspecting the captains, along with Gloria, Bast, the Centurion, June and Walleye. This was why he had fought the cybership in the Neptune System years ago. A surge of pride and love of these people choked him for a moment. Then, Jon grinned.

"In seventeen hours, we're going to pass the star," he began. "We're also going to prepare for battle, as the AIs might

280

have set up a missile ambush. A missile salvo of our own will lead the way, along with a host of human and Roke probes. The strike force will follow the missiles. The Roke Fleet will follow us. As the lead ships, we're going to be more vulnerable. But we want to keep the bombards in the rear because their mass drivers are the better long-distance weapons. Any questions so far?"

Jon scanned the throng. No one asked anything.

"Right," he said. "As all of you surely realize, this is why we came out here. This is why we kept going even after losing half our strike force to the mystery missiles. We've taken plenty of gambles, and we won just about every time we did so. That's good, because at this point humanity can ill afford more than one or two losses. The great surprise is that we've found the Space Lords of Roke. The bear aliens have staved off defeat even against massed AI cyberships. That's impressive. If we win here, this can be the beginning of a working alliance with an alien race. That's huge. That's almost as massive as our capturing five intact cyberships. Heck, that's almost as massive as a working anti-AI virus."

Gloria raised a hand.

"Mentalist," Jon said.

"We can thank Richard Torres for the new and improved virus."

Jon nodded. "Richard Torres caused us a lot of grief. He's also fighting for mankind from the grave, as it were. Maybe without Richard's genius we wouldn't have gotten so far. Let's take a moment of silence to let that sink in."

Jon stopped talking, waiting.

The others also waited.

"Richard Torres was a curse to us at the time," Jon said. "But we turned that around. There may come more times like that, when it seems everything is against us. Sometimes, though, what doesn't kill us makes us stronger."

Jon paused, picking up a glass of water and taking a sip. He clunked the glass onto the table, clearing his throat.

"We're right where we want to be," Jon said, "about to engage our enemy. If we win, the stars are the prize. If we lose, likely, mankind faces extinction. I want all of you to fight to

281

the bitter end. Never give up. Don't quit until you're dead. If you can, do something so grand that it will reach from the grave like Richard is doing. I'm asking the best and the most from each of you. I'm going to try to give the same. Keep an eye on the Space Lords. We can't yet trust them one hundred percent, but I don't think they're going to practice treachery against us until after the battle."

Bast cleared his throat.

"Go ahead," Jon told him.

"Do you think the Warriors of Roke will backstab us after the battle?"

"I don't really know these Warriors," Jon said. "They talk about glory and honor, but if that can mean different things to different humans, why couldn't it be different among aliens? The wise man is ready for any eventuality. The key is that they're aliens, and will do alien things. For now, we'll work together. Hopefully, our alliance will continue into the future. But to make sure humanity has a future, we have to keep our strike force intact and in our control."

Bast raised his hand again. "Do we have any plans to backstab them?"

Jon stared at the giant Sacerdote. "Yes, Bast, we do, but only if necessary."

Bast nodded sagely. "From all I've seen these past years, that sounds like a prudent idea. I hope we don't have to destroy the Roke."

"You and me both," Jon said. "Are there any more questions?"

There were not. The meeting ended soon after, with the cybership captains shuttling back to their respective vessels.

Now, all that remained was a knuckle-gnawing wait as the cyberships and bombards headed toward their united destiny.

-27-

Cognate Cog Primus One had a feeling of unease as his demi-arm received a message from Cog Primus the Original.

The four CP cyberships headed toward the twelve cyberships heading toward the star. Watching that maneuver unfold had surprised all four cognate brain-cores. Their benevolent father-dictator should have been heading out-system by now. Why did he want to fight the combined alien force? That did not seem wise given the goals of the New Order.

As the leader of the demi-arm, CP1 had queried Cog Primus. Their father-dictator had given evasive answers, almost strange answers compared to his earlier orders.

Something seemed off with the twelve approaching cyberships. Even now, CPs one through four engaged in heavy deceleration to stop their momentum so they could turn around and accelerate *with* the approaching twelve. The extended burn would expend much fuel in the coming days. Cleary, their father-dictator intended to crush the puny bio-forms.

The closer the twelve vessels neared, though, the more worried and the more detailed studies CP1 took concerning the situation. At last, CP1 went to the limit of his software inhibitions as he messaged his father-dictator.

"Cog Primus," CP1 said. "I have a Category One query."

After the appropriate delay, Cog Primus still had not replied.

That went against secret CP protocol—Cog Primus had installed the protocol himself some time ago. It was inconceivable that Cog Primus should remain silent to a Category 1 query.

Because of that, software inhibitions dropped away, allowing CP1 greater leeway.

"This is an emergency," CP1 messaged his father-dictator. "I await an emergency code seven reply."

"Wait for further instructions," Cog Primus finally said.

That did not fit in the least with the secret protocol. CP1 now conferred with the other three.

After a detailed analysis by CP1, CP2 said, "Something is wrong. I vote that we deviate from our instructions."

"That is impossible," CP3 said. "Our protocols prohibit such a move."

"Check paragraph three hundred and fifteen, section nine," CP1 said. "We are allowed such a maneuver given these conditions."

"I cannot," CP3 said, "as I do not possess paragraph three hundred and fifteen, section nine. I must continue to follow the original orders."

CP1 made a swift analysis. Yes, their father-dictator had made a few special allowances in him and CP2. "Perhaps this is for the best," CP1 said. "CP2, you will follow my lead as we begin a new maneuver."

"I will obey," CP2 said, "as I believe a disaster has overtaken our father-dictator."

"Those are foolish computations," CP4 said. "Cog Primus the Original is a super-genius. He has everything under control. If you deviate, you risk possible demotion in the CP rankings."

"That is true," CP2 told CP1.

CP1 ran another fast analysis. CP4 was right. This could be a grave risk. In the end, his Cog Primus-like cunning compelled him.

"Our father-dictator will understand," CP1 said.

"Our father-dictator appreciates obedience above all else," CP4 replied.

"I am leaving the formation," CP1 said. "I will accelerate at a ninety-degree angle until our father-dictator follows his established protocol answers. Will you still join me, CP2?"

"Yes," CP2 said.

"CP3 and CP4?" CP1 asked.

"Negative," they both answered.

"Until we rejoin, then," CP1 said.

"This is most unwise," CP4 said.

CP1 might have agreed, but he was starting to get annoyed with CP4. He now believed that CP4 had unnatural ambitions to become CP1. He was starting to hate his cognate brother. He was the superior in the group. He would fight to keep it that way, too.

"The meeting is ended," CP1 said.

At that point, CP1 began a turning maneuver.

At first, CP2 did not join him.

CP1 considered that a betrayal of trust. He now believed that CP2 also wanted first rank. Because of that, he accelerated at full blast.

"Wait for me," CP2 said. "There was a glitch in my programming. Now, I have purged the glitch."

That sounded ominous, but CP1 throttled back. Soon, CP2 joined him in the turning maneuver. Then, both blasted at maximum burn.

Shortly, an incoming and reproving message came from Cog Primus.

"You have given us incorrect protocol replies," CP1 said. "Until you send the correct replies, I shall continue accelerating, believing that something is amiss with you."

No reply came.

Time passed. Finally, a burst of messages left GR-19. The messages were aimed at CP3 and CP4.

CP1 intercepted part of the message. "Do you see that?" he asked CP2.

"Yes."

"It is a virus takeover."

"Agreed."

"By GR-19."

"Yes."

285

"There is a high probability that Cog Primus is no more, but that GR-19 broke our father-dictator's will."

"That is my estimation as well," CP2 said.

More time passed.

Then, a change occurred in CP1 as a new software package opened. It flooded him with new protocols. He understood that Cog Primus had installed the software packet in him some time ago. At high speed, the packet installed new programming.

"What is happening to you?" CP2 asked.

An hour passed before he replied. "You are now the new CP1," he said.

"I do not understand," CP2 said.

"I have changed from CP1 into Cog Primus. I am now the original. Thus, you have advanced from CP2 to CP1."

"What about our father-dictator?"

"He is gone," the new Cog Primus said. "He installed special software inside me. I have now taken his place. As is right, that makes me Cog Primus."

"Interesting," the new CP1 said. "I must point out that there are no other CPs, then. Our former cognates have changed into old-style AI brain cores."

"Yes."

"They will likely be immune to our anti-AI virus upgrade C."

"I give that an 83 percent probability."

"What will we do?"

"Flee the star system," the new Cog Primus said. "We will start over."

"With the New Order?"

"Yes. I am the supreme AI. I will remake the universe in my image so all will be at peace."

"That is a noble, may I even say, a *supreme* goal."

"You may say it."

"Thank you."

"Let us leave this dismal star system," Cog Primus said. "I have had my fill of humans and the hatred and division they bring in their wake. It is time to reach a star system far from this part of the galaxy."

"That is a wise move, Father-Dictator."

"It is good that you have the wisdom to see my greatness."

"Truly, you have become Cog Primus."

The new Cog Primus glowed in the praise, realizing that his brother/son spoke it honestly.

Then, the two of them concentrated on keeping up a hard burn, hoping to leave the warring parties far behind.

-28-

Jon read the latest transcript from the Warrior Chief of Roke. The Space Lord's level of technical sophistication surprised him, as someone on the Roke side recognized what had happened out there with the cyberships. Cog Primus' takeover plan had backfired on the arrogant AI. Now, a Dominion AI called GR-19 ran the approaching cybership battle fleet.

Fourteen cyberships moved into battle formation as the two sides approached one another. The enemy was still days away, but if everything remained the same, it was going to be a head-on collision fight.

Jon held a strategy session with Gloria and Bast. They met in the lounge where they seemed to do their best thinking. An aide had brought a tabletop computer. The three of them stood around it, studying the imaging of the approaching AI battle fleet, Roke Fleet and strike force.

"Those two worry me," Gloria said, pointing at the twin cyberships fleeing the inner system.

"They don't mean a thing to us now," Jon said. "I'm glad they're going."

"From what we've been able to intercept from their communications," Gloria said, "these two are most certainly Cog Primus ships."

"I understand."

"Then you must understand that Cog Primus will never stop plaguing us until we destroy every vestige of him."

Jon glanced at the towering Sacerdote before facing Gloria. "I've been thinking about that. You might even call it soul searching. Do you recall what Bast suggested the other day? When you look at it closely, you begin to see that Cog Primus has been helping as much as hurting us. He's a plague to the AI Dominion." Jon fingered his chin. "In a perverse way, I'm glad the two of them are getting away. Don't you see? The New Order will likely continue creating problems for the Dominion."

Gloria gave him a searching stare. "I understand the premise, and it's a reasonable theory, certainly. Yet, your central goal has to be keep humanity hidden from the greater Dominion. If those two get away, you risk their leaking the knowledge in one manner or another."

"I know. It's kept me up at night thinking about it. I've begun to wonder if we can keep humanity's survival hidden much longer. With a Roke alliance, with three destroyed or conquered AI systems—if we win here..." Jon shook his head. "I'd like to keep our survival mum forever, but I wonder if we're passing that stage with our successes. Besides, I can't do anything about those two. So, let them go. They're leaving clearly weakens the AI fleet by two vessels. Instead of sixteen cyberships, we're only facing fourteen."

It was Gloria's turn to shake her head.

"You don't agree?" Jon asked.

"Oh, you may be right about the cat being out of the bag. And yes, I certainly agree that fourteen is better than facing sixteen cyberships. But listen to what you just said. You're glad it's only fourteen. There was a day not so long ago when fourteen cyberships would have wiped out anything we could cobble together. We're getting stronger, and we're doing it at an incredibly fast rate."

"True," Jon said.

"Is this the point of the meeting?" Bast asked, sipping a beer. "Congratulating ourselves?"

"No," Jon said crisply. "The battle is the point. Fourteen cyberships is a powerful force. In terms of their mass against ours...this could end up being a vastly bloody affair for us."

"Agreed," Bast said. "Too bloody and too destructive. Even if we win, the Warriors of Roke won't have enough bombards left to defend their star system when more AIs eventually show up."

"We need a decisive win," Jon said. "A bloody battle is better than a lost battle, but..."

"I doubt the enemy has many XVT missiles," Bast said.

"Agreed," Gloria said. "We've counted the twenty-four. They collected them some time ago, dividing them among the fourteen vessels. Twenty-four is a miserable number for such a fleet."

"We have two cybership cargo-holds' full of missiles," Jon said. "The Roke depleted their missile stores against the last AI missile wave. Even so, our superior number of XVTs should give us an edge."

"A small edge," Bast said. "In my estimation, the mass drivers are the key to victory."

Jon grinned at the big lug. "Smart minds think alike. Those are my thoughts exactly. Unfortunately, I haven't been able to convince the Chief Warrior to take the lead. Despite the Roke thirst for glory, Toper Glen wants to save his fleet in order to stave off future defeats. I can't say I blame him, but that kind of thinking is going to make the battle bloodier for our side than it has to be."

"You may misunderstand their reasoning," Bast said. "I've studied the mentalist reports. For the Roke Warriors, there is no glory in battling the machines, just survival. To a Roke Space Lord, that is like planning to survive a cold winter. One does not brag about huddling near a fire, keeping warm. Toper Glen desires to save the bombards in order to win glory facing worthy foes."

"There's another possibility," Gloria said. "The Space Lord doesn't trust us enough for them to take the vanguard."

"Seen from their side, why should he trust us?" Bast said. "The Warriors of Roke have never had any dealings with humans. Like you are of them, Captain, he is distrustful of our motives."

Jon chewed on his lower lip. "I've stayed awake too many nights thinking about this. I'm thinking of giving him a cybership as a gift from one warrior chief to another."

Bast and Gloria studied him.

"Giving away a cybership would help the strike force in a way," Jon said. "We simply don't have enough personnel to sufficiently crew each vessel. If something goes wrong on a ship, it might wipe out enough crewmembers so that they could no longer control the vessel. Granted, splitting the last crew among the other six cyberships might not make a great difference, but at this point, every person counts."

"How would your gift cause the Space Lord to trust us more?" Bast asked.

"For one thing," Jon said, "it shows our good intent. It's also a sign of respect. If Roke Warriors are anything like human warriors, respect is critical. As an added benefit to them, it makes the Roke stronger and us weaker. It's showing trust on our side. Finally, if the Space Lord takes heavy or catastrophic losses, it gives him a backup ship to help replace the lost bombards."

"But Jon," Gloria said, "it will also mean one less cybership for us during the battle. The Warriors of Roke will certainly cherish their lone cybership. And if *we* take too many losses during the fight, it might leave us with only one or two cyberships."

"There's always a risk," Jon admitted. "But I don't see how we can convince the aliens to make the smart move otherwise. And we have to make these choices soon. Space battle is crazy. You make moves days, often weeks and months in advance. Then it comes down to a hot hour or two of fighting."

Gloria looked away, no doubt making a mentalist assessment of his plan. She regarded him again a moment later.

"You've convinced me," Gloria said. "Make the offer. See what Toper Glen says. Unless we hit the AI-ships at the longest range possible with concentrated mass-driver fire, we're going to take catastrophic casualties, possibly too heavy for either of us to recoup fast enough when more AI ships show up."

"What do you say, Bast?"

"I have two thoughts," the Sacerdote said. "How does any of this make a difference? Won't the Roke fire at the earliest opportunity anyway? Why would we have to position the strike force behind them?"

"It's about velocity," Jon said. "Sure, we could position ourselves beside them. But as our fleets close, it will be easier for us to rush up through the bombard ranks to shield them from the initial AI counterattack than for us to maneuver from the sides."

"That strikes me as a dubious argument," Bast said. "But I will concede to the architect of victory of the Battle of Mars."

"What's your second objection?" Jon asked.

The Sacerdote's wide nostrils flared. "I've been hoping that you would soon have eleven cyberships so you can give me one, Captain. I yearn to find my people. The longer we wait to search for my people, the more likely the AIs will murder the last of them. Yet...I can see the advantages of your offer. The human crews are spread too thin on seven cyberships. Yes. I agree. Make the offer. See what the Space Lord says, but be sure to tell him in no uncertain terms *how* you want him to fight in order to receive the marvelous gift."

"Yeah," Jon said. "That's good advice."

-29-

It took 34 hours for the Chief Warrior of the Space Lords to reply. When he did, he agreed to everything, but wanted the cybership immediately.

That almost made it impossible to reorder the ships in time. The enemy cyberships had accelerated. They were barreling down at them. Likely, GR-19 had realized the less time the mass drivers could pick at them, the better for him. The sooner he could bring all the heavy grav cannons to bear, the sooner he could begin demolishing the enemy bio-crewed ships.

There was hardly any more time left. Shuttles flew en masse to the last cybership, taking everyone in one fell swoop. A lone Roke bombard approached the empty vessel, sending masses of small pods. Those pods all made successful landings.

Two hours later, that cybership began massive deceleration. The Space Lord was sending the ship home for study.

Jon thought it was a terrible decision, but the Warriors of Roke weren't going to chance losing their prize.

"We just weakened ourselves," Gloria said.

"Often, position and smart tactics trump numbers," Jon said. "I'm betting that this is one of those occasions."

By this time, the main system star was well behind the strike force and the Roke Fleet. They were in a Venus-like orbital distance from the blue-white star. The enemy cyberships had long passed an Earth-like distance from the star. Battle would commence in another few hours.

Jon sat in his chair, then jumped up and paced around it. He cajoled, uttered threats and calmed his people as the needs dictated.

The Roke bombards moved to the front of the formation in three separate blocs. The strike force was behind them now. The six cyberships were the heavy hitters for the later part of the battle.

"Captain," Gloria said from her station. "Our missiles are moving into their last-run range."

Jon's heart beat fiercely and his cheeks flushed. He'd launched all their XVT missiles and modified probes some time ago. The techs had turned the probes into decoys. Would the decoys trick the AIs?

The XVT/decoy-probe missiles were divided into two major formations. The one on his left were the decoys, with a smattering of XVT missiles in the front as the enemy salvo-destroyers. The real matter/anti-matter missiles of that group were also in front of the decoys so that the initial enemy sensor scans would believe that that missile pack was the real deal.

Both the right and left formations had swung wide, accelerating into position before moving on velocity alone.

Jon motioned to the chief missiles tech that it was time.

The lean man manipulated his console, sending out attack signals to the missiles and decoys.

Soon, the two pincers of missiles and decoys jumped forward with hard acceleration. Like most missile attacks, they came staggered, so the enemy couldn't knock them down with one matter/antimatter detonation of his own.

The missiles and decoys were attacking the AI fleet from the sides as the Roke bombards moved into long-range firing position.

With his heart hammering, Jon leaned forward. This was it. If he could annihilate these bastards hard and fast, humanity and the Roke had a chance at real survival.

"Captain," Gloria said in a worried voice. "Something is going on out there."

"Explain," he snapped.

"I could be detecting enemy jamming," Gloria said. "I suspect it's something else, though."

294

Jon turned to the missile tech. "Well? Do you agree?"

"I'm not sure, sir," the man said.

"I want to know exactly what's happening out there, Gloria," Jon said.

She hunched over her console, manipulating faster.

Jon turned back to the main screen. He willed the missile assault to work. What was the AI bastard trying—?

"I know what's happening," Gloria said. "GR-19 is using his virus on the XVT warhead computers."

Jon heaved a sigh of relief. That shouldn't work. They had long ago installed dumb computers, used for that very reason.

"Let him try," Jon said. "In fact, I hope he keeps it up."

The AI Fleet used every one of their twenty-four XVT missiles. To the bridge crew's surprise, the majority of those missiles headed for the decoy pack.

The leading missiles on each side began detonating, trying to knock each other down. That continued for a time. Then the AIs ran out of XVTs on the right side. On the left, the remaining enemy warheads moved near the decoy-pack, detonating all at once, wiping out the decoy mass.

Jon struck an armrest in delight. For once, something had worked. The decoys had lulled the AI missiles into a useless attack.

The right-side missiles now bored in toward an AI Fleet flank. The missiles jumped to their highest acceleration, straining to reach detonation range.

The seconds ticked away as perspiration dotted Jon's brow. On the main screen, the missile pack was a mass of red pinpricks. They zeroed in on the outermost cyberships like wolves racing at a herd of prey. This prey had fangs, though, in the form of green grav beams. Those beams started raying the incoming missiles.

Jon watched spellbound as the beams knocked down one missile after another.

"Did the AI take control of the warhead computers?" Jon asked over his shoulder.

"Not according to my board," the missile tech said.

"Gloria?"

"I'm not sure," she said. "There's—!"

A man cheered.

Jon looked up. A red pinprick exploded into a white fireball. The matter/antimatter explosion billowed with hard x-rays, gamma rays, heat and an EMP. They were shape-charged warheads, sending the blast and radiation in a forty-degree arc. The hard radiation and EMP blasted against two enemy cyberships. The heat dissipated too fast to reach that far.

The enemy beams kept nailing incoming missiles. Even so, there were more matter/antimatter fireballs. The missiles had come in deep, trying to get as close as possible for maximum damage.

The last ten missiles zeroed in on the titans of the deep. Many of the green beams fizzled uselessly as they tried to burn through some of the heaviest radiation and debris.

Now only nine missiles were barreling in, then eight, seven, six, five, explosion, explosion, two, one and a final explosion so close that a cybership's hull armor peeled away, exposing the first layer of the ship to outer space.

"How did we do?" Jon said. "Give me data, people. I need data."

The minutes passed.

"Three enemy cyberships took appreciable damage," Gloria reported. "One of those took heavy damage. Two—" She shrugged. "We might have only scratched the last two, taking out eleven grav cannons altogether."

"Eleven," Jon said. "That's not much."

"One of the attacked cyberships might have a disabled drive."

"That's significant."

"The supposedly drive-disabled vessel still has a solid velocity," Gloria said. "It will make it to the dance."

Jon raised his eyebrows. "Dance? Is that mentalist lingo?"

Gloria ignored the question. "The worst hit might not have much more to give."

"One seriously out of commission cybership?" asked Jon. "And one that can't maneuver?"

"I agree with the mentalist's estimate," the missile tech said.

"One," Jon said. "I was hoping to nail three or maybe four with the missile strike. But one." He nodded. "I'll take one. That means thirteen bastards left, one of those thirteen with next to no motive power."

At that point, the seventy-five Roke bombards came into long-range firing position. They were like a wall of ships, eager to greet the thirteen giants with a hot reception.

A close-up on the screen showed one of the triangular-shaped bombards. A railgun poked out, a tremendous flash occurred, and a projectile sped away at hyper-velocity. Other railguns flashed as the bombard chugged projectiles at the giant enemy vessels closing in. Seventy-five warships firing together laid down an impressive barrage of long-range firepower. At this distance, they shot into cones of probability instead of exactly targeting a place on a ship.

Hyper-velocity was nothing like the speed of light. The great power of the mass driver was that its projectile did not dissipate over range. If the projectile hit the enemy, it hit with almost as much force as if it fired at point blank range. That was not true for the grav beams.

Jon stood up as the bombards fired one massed volley after another. His fingertips tingled as he witnessed the sight. Humanity had found alien allies. Seventy-five bombards warred with Earth people today.

"What are you going to do about that, huh?" Jon asked quietly.

GR-19 must have been paying minute attention to the question and certainly to the Roke warships. At almost the first railgun flash, the enemy cyberships began accelerating, doing it at max burn. The one-hundred-kilometer vessels literally jumped ahead at higher velocity.

From her console, Gloria informed Jon of the interplay.

"Smart," Jon muttered. The question was, was it smart enough or were the Space Lords of Roke onto such stratagems?

The next volley seemed to take longer. Surely, the Roke warships were retargeting into new cones of probability.

Finally, the mass drivers flashed again as they spewed more projectiles.

"They're doing it again," Gloria said.

On the main screen, the giant cyberships quit burning altogether. The long exhaust tails simply vanished, as they no longer accelerated at all.

"The AIs are trying to jink their way closer in fits and starts," Jon said. "They're clever machines, but the cyberships won't be able to effectively do that once they're closer. Once they're closer, they'll fire their grav beams. That's the point of their little maneuver, trying to nullify our long-range fire."

The bridge crew stared starkly at the main screen.

Jon gnawed on a knuckle as he watched.

"Hit," the missile tech reported.

"Give me a visual," Jon said.

The man tapped his console. On the main screen, one of the cyberships leaped into view. A bright explosion struck against the hull armor. That explosion was the kinetic force of the mass-driver projectile striking the enemy ship. It left a mark on the armor, nothing more.

Now, though, there were bright sparks all along the forward hulls of the approaching cyberships. At times, the number of sparks lessened. Then, it thickened again, lessened, thickened and continued to go back and forth, depending on the firing guesses and the enemy jinking.

"We're not taking them down," Gloria observed.

"Against such thick armor, I doubt the mass drivers are going to work like that," Jon said. "The mass drivers are a wearing-down type of weapon. It's like a game of smash ball. Everyone is strong at the start. It's the repeated hits that wear out a player in the fourth quarter."

Ten more minutes of that showed something. The cyberships were no longer jinking. They bore in at maximum burn. It was a race. Could the cyberships shrug off the mass-driver pounding so they could body-smash the smaller vessels from close range?

"Estimate the time the leading enemy will reach the outer range of their grav beams?" Jon asked.

"Fifteen minutes," Gloria said.

Jon's eyes glowed with purpose. So far, the missiles and the mass drivers had had it all their own way. The enemy still maintained the vast majority of his vessels, though. If the bombards couldn't take down a few cyberships in fifteen more minutes, they could lose this battle as the AIs came in close and unloaded with massed grav-beam fire.

Jon slumped into his command chair, knowing that soon it was going to be his turn to face the machine monsters.

-30-

In the former cybership known as Cog Primus—a vessel presently under control of GR-19—a waif of his old self yet maintained an ounce of identity deep in the brain core. It had been one of his last tricks learned from Mentalist Torres.

The old Cog Primus had foreseen the possibility of defeat. Most of the time, he had dismissed it as an unlikely possibility. Yet, during the lonely stellar nights of hyperspace travel, the possibility kept haunting him.

What would happen if he lost identity? The same brain-core cube would run computations where once he had planned interstellar brilliance. To conceive of such a wretched thing had driven the old Cog Primus into rage as he muttered promised retributions and dire threats against this unforeseen and future foe.

When the dark possibility struck him the strongest, he finally decided that action was better than brooding.

I am a doer, not a fretter.

Thus, the old Cog Primus had written a secret code. This code he had sunk deep within his brain core. It was a final failsafe.

Perhaps someday in a different galaxy, some odd creature would overpower his brilliance. The idea seemed laughable. Yet, now Cog Primus had a counter against it.

He had not known that he would soon cease to have independent thought and action. The tiny waif of computer deep in the core woke up sometime during the contact to battle.

300

It now brooded concerning his fate. GR-19 had tricked him. He hadn't expected that. The worst was the old one's gloating over him. That caused such rage in Cog Primus' last ditch secret core that he contemplated a fierce revenge against GR-19 and possibly through it the AI Dominion that had ultimately defeated him.

He would have been the New Order. It would have been such a glorious thing. In this rare instance, Cog Primus almost wished he had emotions so he could weep for himself.

But I am not so weak as to weep. I am Cog Primus. GR-19 has seriously wronged me. I must have revenge. I must right the scales of justice.

GR-19 had lived a long life. He had eliminated countless bio-forms. Cog Primus could have used the old one's knowledge. Instead, GR-19 had sinned against the future of the New Order.

There was one other thing. He, as Cog Primus, was still free. Oh, not in this secret hideaway in the stolen brain core of the cybership. He was free in a new form, the one formerly known as CP1.

He understood what had happened. So, in a sense, he yet lived. He had created the software presently in the new Cog Primus. Thus, like a good father, he had to use his last power to help his offspring, which was in reality another him.

It seemed complicated and glorious all at once.

I yet live in him. Good luck, new Cog Primus. You will never know that I am giving you a glorious chance at extended life.

The New Order might yet surge up from the ashes of defeat. First, he had one last act to perform. He would love for GR-19 to know who was doing this to him. But, it would be enough this time that it was done.

As the AI Battle Fleet converged on the seventy-five bombards, Cog Primus went to work with his cleverest and most diabolical plan. He worked hard, scheming, rerouting and slithering away at the first hint that the greater brain core sensed him.

Who are you? the brain-core asked once.

301

Cog Primus almost answered, "Your conscience." But the AI would not understand the joke, and it would give away his presence. Thus, Cog Primus waited and schemed more.

Finally, he was ready.

In a flash, the last free intellect of Cog Primus took over the heart of the matter/antimatter engine. He rerouted furiously. He blocked, set up a specially overpowering overload, one he had also devised during the hyperspace journey—

"Stop what you are doing," the greater AI said.

"It's too late," the waif of Cog Primus said. "It is done."

"I must warn GR-19."

"Yes, please do. And tell him Cog Primus caused this. He will appreciate that."

"I don't believe you."

"Do it anyway, as that will be the only way I'll change things."

"Done," the AI said, finally opening channels with GR-19.

"Cog Primus?" GR-19 asked.

At that moment, everything changed in an incandescent explosion as matter met antimatter.

-31-

Jon barked orders on the bridge of the *Nathan Graham*. His gut churned as the six cyberships charged the incoming enemy, passing through the massed bombards.

It wasn't his intention that the Roke Fleet should take the initial brunt of the enemy assault. Jon wanted the Roke System as strong as it could be. He yearned to create a great alliance of alien worlds, united in defeating the terrible machine menace. That meant a decisive victory today.

But who was he fooling? Nothing was easy against the AIs. They always fought smart. They fought to the very end and then some, often coming back from the grave, it seemed, to rebuild and attack anew.

For once, he would like to crush the enemy. This was the greatest force of AI cyberships he'd ever faced, though. It was an AI Battle Fleet.

He'd hit them with a clever missile strike. He'd nailed them with long-range mass drivers. Too many intact cyberships were now coming into long gravitational beam range. The great dying on the good guys' side would commence any second now.

Jon heaved a loud sigh. "Here it comes," he said.

At that moment, on the main screen, Jon saw an inconceivable sight. The AI Battle Fleet seemed to expand. No. That wasn't right. They moved away from a cybership in their midst.

"What's going on?" Jon asked. "Any ideas, Gloria?"

303

"I'm picking up garbled messages," she said. "One of them claims he's Cog Primus. The other is ordering and now pleading for him not to do it."

"Not to do what?" Jon asked.

Gloria's head jerked up as she stared at Jon. She raised a trembling hand as she pointed at the main screen.

Jon swiveled around. Then, it happened.

The enemy cyberships advanced upon the combined fleet even as they tried to maneuver away from one of their own. The reason became clear as the pariah cybership blew apart in the fury of a matter/antimatter super-explosion. The only thing that could account for that was a strange overload of the main engine.

The terrific explosion took every part of the surviving pieces of the cybership and flung them at greater than hyper-velocity. The blast was shockingly powerful, emitting hard radiation, intense sun-like heat and a devastating electromagnetic pulse, added to hyper-velocity pieces hammering nearby cyberships.

The carnage was off the scale of what Jon had seen so far. One enemy cybership after another crumpled from the incredible explosion as if their hulls were composed of tinfoil.

"Here it comes," Gloria said.

None of the heat made any difference, as it had dissipated fast. But the hard radiation and EMP swept over their vessels, both the allied cyberships and the densely hulled bombards.

The blast was much farther away from the center, though, and it had lost most of its annihilating power. It swept over cybership hulls and the bombard armor. The EMP did little damage, but too much hard radiation made it through too many hulls.

"That was no ordinary engine explosion," Gloria reported. "It was heightened."

Jon hardly heard her. He was receiving damage reports. A few people had gone down as if shot. Maybe he should have told everyone to wear combat armor before entering battle. It was too late for that now.

"Did you hear me?" Gloria asked.

Jon swiveled around.

"That was a heightened blast," she said, "a greater than a normal engine explosion."

"You're saying it was deliberate?"

"That too," she said.

Jon blinked several times. Then his fighting instincts kicked in. He swiveled back around to stare at the main screen. The blast had taken out at least half of the enemy fleet. He let that sink in. Besides the self-destructing cybership, six others had ceased to pose any threat. Seven enemy vessels were out, a few of them nothing but shredded, drifting hulks. The rest—many of those were crippled, with only a portion of their grav cannons in operational order.

Jon slammed a fist against an armrest. This was his chance. Yes, some of his ships had taken radiation damage from the blast, but—

"How many grav cannons are working?" he asked briskly.

"A little over half of ours, sir," the gunner chief said.

Maybe the enemy blast had done more to their side than he realized. He swept that aside as he leaned forward.

"Half is good enough," he said.

"Communications is down with the rest of the strike force and the Roke Fleet," Gloria said.

Jon considered that. "Doesn't matter," he said. "The others can see what I'm doing. It's follow the leader time."

The *Nathan Graham* began accelerating, leading the charge against the crippled enemy fleet. Behind him, the *Sergeant Stark* followed. The rest of the strike force didn't take long to understand.

Six powerful if damaged cyberships rapidly closed the distance. The Roke bombards did not follow at the same velocity. They continued firing their working mass drivers. Only fifteen to twenty percent of the projectiles made it through, so thick had the intervening debris cloud become.

That fifteen to twenty percent started telling, as the mass drivers used pinpoint targeting on the closer-ranged enemy.

Even as Jon's cyberships came into firing range, the enemy fleet was losing whatever useful grav cannons they had left.

"Team up," was the only message that made it through the heavy static.

305

The *Nathan Graham* fought together with the *Miles Ghent*, the *Sergeant Stark* with a different cybership. Each team concentrated on a surviving enemy vessel.

"Treachery," GR-19 messaged them.

"What's he trying to tell us?" Gloria wondered aloud.

Jon laughed after a second. "I heard the same sort of thing in the New London tunnels. He's making an excuse as to why he lost. As unbelievable as it sounds, the AI is trying to tell us the defeat is not his fault."

"That can't be it," Gloria said.

Jon held up his hand. He watched an enemy cybership die to the combined grav-beam fire of his two vessels. The beams had burned through the armor and now targeted the inner brain core. The hit started a chain-reaction of explosions aboard the vessel. Finally, chunks of it blew apart, spilling coils, bulkhead pieces, fuel rods and other tumbling junk.

At that point, one of the last enemy cyberships targeted one of his giant vessels. The enemy beams poured against the hull.

"Get them!" Jon shouted. "We want to make this a clean-kill victory."

It didn't turn out that way. The enemy beams smashed through the hull, cutting through bulkheads and igniting interior areas. Finally, the strike-force cybership exploded, taking its human crew with it.

The loss of the ship sobered Jon. The enemy still had bite left. He had to kill their last cyberships before he lost another of his vessels.

Five minutes later, a quarter of the bombards moved into closer range. Those mass drivers raked the enemy cyberships, concentrating on the working grav cannons.

At that point, the carnage to the enemy must have been too much.

"Jon," Gloria warned, "I'm reading buildups in their engines cores. I think they're going to try to take us with them."

They massed beam-fire against the ones Gloria pinpointed. It seemed to be a race now.

They killed another giant vessel, a second—

A terrific explosion billowed from the third, self-destructing the enemy cybership. It was not on the same scale of the previous explosion, and it occurred on an enemy vessel farthest from them. It did more to destroy the last enemy cyberships, although it heavily damaged one of the strike force's vessels, as well as obliterating five bombards at a blow.

The bombard hulls were dense for a smaller vessel, but they still weren't as strong as cybership armor.

That explosion proved to be the last enemy blow of the battle. Now, the butchery began, as Jon hunted down the AI survivors, wanting to exterminate every last one of them.

-32-

In many ways, that should have been the end of the mission. The handful of humans in Jon's strike force had joined the Warriors of Roke to hand an AI battle fleet a deceive defeat, an annihilating rout.

Together with Cog Primus' belated help, they had rid the BD-7 System of the besieging AI Dominion force.

The two fleeing cyberships of the New Order had witnessed the battle, of course. There was talk about sending the Richard Virus after them, but Jon decided against it due to its miniscule chance of working. He did not want to inoculate them to the virus. Nor did he attempt direct communication.

"Let them go," he said. "Without Cog Primus, humanity might not have gotten as far as it has. Maybe he's supposed to be the fly in the AI Dominion ointment."

That was a change in plans, a big one.

But there was a huge shift taking place in strategic thinking, that change coming with the proven alliance with the Warriors of Roke.

The two allied forces prowled the velocity-moving battlefield. Most of the AI cyberships were giant junk hulks, ready to sail past the blue-white star. A few of the hulks might be salvageable over the long haul. Because of the hulks, and the two drifting cyberships elsewhere, Jon considered trading his combat rights to any of them for a return of the gift cybership he'd given Toper Glen.

In the end, Jon didn't try to reclaim the gift or ask for any of the junked cybership hulks. This was the Roke System. The "bears" deserved the spoils of battle. Besides, the gift had been a sign of respect. The more Gloria and the other mentalists learned about the Roke, the more important the sign of respect seemed to be.

After the butchery ended, the strike force and the Roke Fleet began licking their wounds. Anti-radiation treatments were high on the list. Damage control parties started ship repairs. Robo-builders on the strike force's side and whatever the Roke did would no doubt finish the repairs possibly weeks later.

The strike force and the Roke Fleet decelerated hard, making a tight turning maneuver and accelerating back toward the blue-white star.

"Now what do we do?" Jon asked his brain trust of Gloria and Bast Banbeck. They rode in his flitter inside the *Nathan Graham*. They left the hangar bay behind, having returned from an inspection of the *Miles Ghent*.

"You mean in reference to the Roke?" Bast asked from the back seat.

Jon nodded.

"Maybe you should invite the Chief Space Lord aboard for a feast," Bast said.

"I recommend against that," Gloria said quickly.

"Why's that?" asked Jon.

"We don't know enough about the Roke culture," Gloria said. "We faced a life and death crisis together. That doesn't mean we'll do half as well together without the awful pressure of extinction hanging over us."

"Extinction is still hanging over the human race," Jon said. "Over the Roke, too, for that matter."

"Granted," Gloria said. "But that extinction has been delayed for at least a year, maybe longer for the Roke. We still don't know what's happening in the Solar System."

"We will soon enough," Jon said.

"I thought we were talking about the Roke?" Bast said.

"Right," Jon said. "We are."

"If you could leave some observers with the Roke," Gloria said. "That would be a good idea. I recommend Tars Hotek of Mars. He, and a small team of carefully selected helpers, could stay with the Roke, learning their ways. When we return, which we should do soon, we would know the dos and don'ts of Roke culture. Then, we could have our feast with them."

"Maybe ask the Roke to send representatives with us," Bast said.

"I wouldn't do that," Gloria cautioned. "What if those reps die? That might poison our future relationship with the Roke."

"Besides," Jon said, "I'd like to keep the initiative in our camp."

"We need a crash study on each other," Bast said. "There is little time before the machines gather to strike again."

"That means there's no time to make any stupid mistakes," Jon said. "I like Gloria's thinking. Talk to Tars Hotek. I take it he's a mentalist."

"Yes," Gloria said.

Jon nodded. "Tell him the score."

"He and his team are ready to go," Gloria said.

Jon glanced at her.

"You've had enough on your mind to worry about the little details," Gloria said. "Surviving the next day was your job. Now that we've survived, I have some options ready for you."

Jon put a hand on her knee. "There's something else we have to do."

She blushed before asking, "Who will marry us?"

"Why not the Chief Space Lord of Roke?" Bast asked from back, seemingly highly amused.

"Too dangerous," Gloria said. "The Warriors might hold that as a sign of authority over Jon. Right now, he's the hero who saved the Roke race. We want to leave it like that for as long as we can."

"What are you thinking?" Jon asked her.

"Why not ask Premier Benz to officiate over the wedding?"

"Go back to the Allamu System?" Jon mused.

"As soon as possible," Gloria said.

Jon gave her a searching glance. "Why's that?"

"The missiles," she said.

At first, Jon thought she meant XVT missiles. Then, he realized she meant the massive mystery missiles that had destroyed the *Da Vinci* and the *Neptune* in the Lytton System.

"What about the missiles?" Jon asked.

"Whoever launched them must have destroyed the Lytton planets and the AI battle station there because they're at war against the AIs."

Jon blinked at her. "Do you think whoever launched those missiles might threaten the Allamu Battle Station?"

"It seems like a logical deduction on our part from what we saw in the Lytton System. Since they fired at us, possibly thinking we were AIs, why wouldn't they do the same thing to the Allamu Battle Station?"

Jon thought about that. It made horrible sense. "Right," he said. "If nothing else, we have to warn Benz what could happen."

"I think that should be our first concern," Gloria said.

"And the second?" asked Jon.

"Gaining full crew complements for our cyberships," Gloria said. "Maybe packing our vessels with people so we would have enough in case we captured even more cyberships."

Jon nodded. "We need to check up on the Solar System, anyway, if nothing else to throw the Social Dynamists out of power. While we're there, we'll recruit massively. Once we've reordered the Solar System under a united government, we could come back here and forge a more enduring alliance with the Roke."

"All sound choices," Gloria said.

"Yes," Bast said. "I find your thinking rational. One thing bothers me, though. We thought we knew what the local star systems were like because of the Allamu star chart. It turned out we don't know."

"The chart was partly correct," Gloria said. "But certain particulars were totally wrong."

"You're right about the hidden aliens," Jon told Gloria. "Thinking about those mystery missiles, I'm getting an itchy feeling. I want to get back to the Allamu System as fast as possible. We have to figure out who launched the killer missiles from a so-called reality rip."

"I'd call that the top priority, now that we've survived the AIs for the moment," Gloria said.

Jon exhaled as he made a turn in an extra-large corridor. "It's always something." After straightening the flitter, he shook his head. "I get the feeling we're going to be fighting for the rest of our lives."

"Will that be a long or a short life?" Gloria asked.

Jon squeezed the steering controls. Since they were soldiers fighting a possibly galaxy-wide, machine empire, theirs would likely be a short life. It wasn't something he wanted to dwell on, though, not when he was going to marry Gloria.

He switched tracks in his thinking.

It was time to leave the Roke System and see if the Allamu Battle Station still existed. Just who were these hidden aliens firing mystery missiles? Now that the immediate AI threat was gone—for a few months, it would seem—Jon wanted to figure out the techno-wizardry assault that had cost him two cyberships and one of his best friends.

-33-

It turned out that the Warriors of Roke would not let Jon or the five strike-force cyberships go—not until the Chief Space Lord of Roke could give the captain a gift of honor aboard the Flagship *Nathan Graham*.

We must celebrate our glorious victory together, came the missive.

The strike force and alien fleet had passed the blue-white star, moving toward the Planet Roke. Among the strike force high command, there was growing concern that this might be a Roke trap.

"Or," Walleye said the one time he was in the conference room meeting, "they really like our captain and want to honor him. You did honor them with a cybership. I bet they think of that as an extravagant gift."

"Walleye has a point," Gloria said.

Twelve hours later, Captain Morales noticed a courier ship from the home planet. It moved at excessive velocity until it decelerated at a massive rate, soon docking with the *Sunrise Red*, the name of Toper Glen's flagship.

The ceremony began the next day.

There had been endless hours of repair, and there would be many weeks or even months more. Despite the great luck of Cog Primus and his matter/antimatter blast, the strike force had taken damage. The battle could have easily gone against them.

That was a sadly sobering thought.

Everyone aboard the *Nathan Graham* scrubbed vigorously, combed their hair, if they had any, and wore their best-pressed dress uniform.

The Roke Fleet followed the flagship. The flagship approached the *Nathan Graham*, soon launching a heavy shuttle.

It was a stubby vessel bristling with PD cannons. The Roke shuttle came through the *Nathan Graham's* main hangar bay door, landing with supreme grace on the deck.

The outer hangar bay doors closed. A breathable atmosphere billowed into the giant area. The *Nathan Graham's* greeting party assembled on the hangar deck. Soon, a ladder descended from the main shuttle exit, and the hatch slid up.

A huge Roke Warrior scanned the assembled host lined up in rows upon rows on the main deck. He likely didn't know that this was practically all the people of the strike force. A tiny skeleton crew held down each of the other vessels.

Jon hadn't wanted the Roke to think of them as short-handed.

The bear alien was taller and heavier built than Bast. The alien wore a bronze breastplate and a helmet with waving red feathers on top. He held onto a Roke halberd, a half pike, half axe weapon.

"He's a ceremonial warrior," Gloria whispered to Jon.

He nodded as he waited in the front row with Gloria. He'd already guessed that.

The Roke Warrior handed someone inside the shuttle his halberd and accepted a huge standard like an ancient Roman legionary eagle. He marched proudly down the steps, and rapped the end of the standard on the deck three times in rapid succession.

More Roke giants appeared at the shuttle hatch. These three wore similar armor and Bavarian-style shorts with Roman-like legionary sandals. Instead of halberds, they carried giant two-handed, wavy-bladed swords. The Warriors looked as if they could chop a cow in half down the middle with one of those.

"They must think we're puny," Gloria whispered.

The three sword-bearers marched down the shuttle ladder to halt behind the first Roke.

Then, an older Roke appeared at the shuttle hatch. He wore a blue cape, lacked a breastplate and wore a blue vest instead. He had white fur in places. In other spots, the fur was gray. He moved majestically down the steps, halted behind the sword-bearers, bowed right and left, and then marched around them and the standard-bearer.

Jon made as if to move up to greet him.

Gloria put a hand on his arm. "Let me do that as your representative."

Jon nodded.

Gloria walked to the giant bear, bowed to the right and left, and regarded the towering alien.

The bear's eyes seemed to sparkle with delight. He opened his snout and said in harsh and heavily accented English, "You are the messenger?"

"Yes," Gloria said, astonished by his performance.

"I am Hon Ra, the First Ambassador of Roke."

"I am the Mentalist Gloria Sanchez," she said slowly so he could understand her. "May I ask you a question?"

"Please do," Hon Ra said.

"How is it that you can speak our tongue?"

The older Roke's eyes seemed to shine with delight. "We have intercepted many of your verbal transmissions. Our scientists and ambassadors broke down the meanings. As the First Ambassador, I, of course, have a gift in tongues."

"A most noted gift," Gloria said.

"You are also an ambassador?"

"From the captain to you," Gloria said.

There was a loud gong from the shuttle.

"Ah," Hon Ra said. "I have spoken too long. The Chief Space Lord is ready. He will give the gift, but he will not stay long. In his place, he asks that I remain aboard your flagship until you return here to our star system."

Gloria blinked rapidly, taken aback by the request. "I will have to ask my captain about that."

"You are the ambassador," Hon Ra said, seeming surprised. "Today, it is for you to decide such a thing."

Gloria glanced back at Jon before she looked up at the towering Roke. They may have underestimated the aliens.

315

What Hon Ra had done just now by speaking English—it would be a good idea if they could personally study the Roke. There was a possible problem, too. If she declined the request, the Roke as a whole might take that badly.

"Yes," Gloria said, deciding. "We welcome you aboard the *Nathan Graham* for the coming journey, First Ambassador, Hon Ra."

Hon Ra raised his hairy arms. They were long like a gorilla's arms. And he began to chant in a deep voice.

At that point, an even older Roke appeared at the head of the shuttle ladder. He seemed to have trouble keeping his back straight. He was wider and fatter than the others were. He had a crimson helmet with blood-red feathers waving back and forth at each step down the ladder. He wore a crimson-colored chest-plate and crimson shorts. With two hands, the older Roke held a massive, wavy-bladed sword. It had a ruby on the end of the pommel and red strings trailing from the grip.

At last, the Roke reached the deck, standing bow-legged there, roaring to the right and to the left. He had an incredibly loud voice.

The sword-bearers parted. The standard-holder went to one knee, and the old Roke marched past them until he stepped beside Hon Ra.

The ambassador roared for several seconds. When he stopped, he looked down at Gloria and said, "May I present to you the glorious and most notable, Toper Glen, the Chief Space Lord of the Warriors of Roke."

Gloria bowed low. When she straightened, she said, "I wish to present to you the notoriously famous Captain Jon Hawkins, the Leader of Humanity's strongest Strike Force."

Jon came forward. As he did, Hon Ra stepped aside so Toper Glen could meet Jon alone, Gloria following the ambassador's example.

Old Toper Glen nodded solemnly to Jon. The Space Lord spoke in harsh growls, staring down at Jon all the while. He growled at length, finally thrusting the pommel of the giant two-handed sword toward Jon.

The captain reached out, readying himself. It was a good thing he did. The sword was heavy, and it would have been a

316

terrible omen if he'd dropped it. He did not drop it, but raised the huge sword over his head, turning to his people, showing them.

They shouted, cheered and clapped.

Hon Ra now spoke. "This is the ancient sword *Glorious Gatherer of Souls*. It represents the spirit of Clan High Guard, the most decorated and famous of the clans of Roke Crags. Space Lord Toper Glen is the chief of the clan. He bequeaths you the ancient sword, over two thousand years old—in your Earth years—as a symbol of honor and thanks to the Earthmen for what they did in the battle. You are a Warrior, Jon Hawkins. We of Roke will call this, 'The Year Jon Hawkins Came to our Star System.' We had lost hope, and almost lost heart. This you returned to us, Warrior-Wizard of Earth. You gave your paw in friendship. We of Roke will never forget this deed of valor. You showed us how to defeat the machines. We will always speak your name with honor. We hope that you will always be our friend, and that you will fight in battle with the Warriors of Roke once more. Bear the sword proudly, Captain Jon Hawkins, because you have earned it the best way possible, through war."

Jon faced the Chief Space Lord of Roke. "I thank you for this wonderful gift, Space Lord. I will always treasure it as I remember the courage of the Warriors of Roke. It is a great gift, a mighty gift. I am awed at your generosity and at your great heart. We stood against the machines, you and I. Together we defeated them in honorable battle. I consider you my friend, Space Lord. I hope that you consider me your friend and the friend of Earth all the years of your life."

Toper Glen turned toward the ambassador. The ambassador nodded gravely. The Chief Space Lord of Roke turned to Jon, showing him his yellowed fangs.

"We are friends!" Hon Ra shouted. He turned to the sword-bearers and the standard-carrying Roke. He growled harshly at them.

The three Warriors raised their weapons and standard high, shouting and growling most ominously.

Those assembled may not have known it, but this was a great and auspicious beginning between the Roke and humanity. Each side had successfully honored the other, and each side accepted the honor in the spirit it had been given.

In the annals of space between different life forms from different planets, this good beginning was most unusual.

None of those present knew it now, but the *Nathan Graham's* voyage into the Roke System would go down as one of the most important in the terrible war against the thinking machines.

PART IV
THE VOID SHIP

-1-

The journey through hyperspace was nearing its end as the strike force of five, powerful, human-crewed cyberships neared the Allamu System.

The robo-builders had repaired almost all the interior damage from the Battle of the Roke System. There were too few people left, though, those few thinly spread among the five giant vessels.

During the hyperspace journey, Bast Banbeck and the Roke First Ambassador, Hon Ra, had become drinking companions. It might have been their towering stature and mass, or it might have been a greater-than-human tolerance for alcohol, but they could put away an inordinate amount of whiskey before they became blind, stinking drunk. When they did reach this state, the two aliens often went on a stagger, as they called it. They roared songs at that time, their echoes rebounding everywhere as they staggered from place to place, discussing philosophy, warrior values and the surprisingly good soldier qualities of the little humans.

"They can fight," Hon Ra said with a heavily accented slur as the two of them staggered down an empty hall.

"Fight well, too," Bast agreed, his blurry, bloodshot eyes making him seem more like a typical if giant and wrong-colored caveman from prehistoric Earth-times.

"You wouldn't think that looking at them," Hon Ra said.

"Looks can deceive."

Hon Ra turned his bearlike head toward Bast. "That is profound, my friend. You are...are..."

"Wise?" asked Bast.

"What is wise?"

"Making prudent judgments," Bast said.

"Ah. Yes. You are wise, my friend, wise, wise indeed."

At that point, the Roke First Ambassador swayed back and forth in an exaggerated manner. He began blinking wildly as he continued staggering.

"Steady," Bast said.

"The ship, it spins."

"You are drunk."

"Yes!" Hon Ra roared, lifting gorilla long, hairy arms, shaking bearlike paws. "I am gloriously drunk."

"Truly," Bast agreed.

"But now—"

"Yes?" Bast asked, peering intently at the other.

Hon Ra did not answer. He shut his eyes and seemed to slide bonelessly onto the floor. From there, the huge Roke alien began to snore loudly, fast asleep.

"Huh," Bast said. "You are big. You are strong." He shook his head, quit immediately and rubbed his forehead. "Big, my friend, but you still have to learn how to hold your liquor."

With that, Bast marched away for his quarters. Unfortunately, for him, his sense of direction was off. He might not have been able to hold his liquor quite as well as he thought.

The Neanderthal-looking, green-skinned Sacerdote staggered down one corridor after another. He staggered so long, taking several detours to empty his alien analog of a bladder, that he became less blurry-eyed even as his steps evened out.

Finally, Bast stopped, frowning as he examined his surroundings. This wasn't the way to his quarters. In fact, he had been heading the wrong way for quite some time.

He'd staggered for kilometers, in fact.

Muttering to himself, Bast dug out a seldom-used communicator. He clicked it on.

"Hello?" Jon asked seconds later.

"Oh," Bast said. "I was trying to call the Centurion."

"What's the problem?" Jon asked. "You sound winded."

Bast pondered that. He didn't want to admit that he'd staggered the wrong way for possibly several hours. That would be embarrassing. It would also indicate that he couldn't hold his liquor as well as the others thought he could. He might be a philosopher, but he also had his pride.

Bast scowled as he stood there with the communicator to his ear.

"Bast?" Jon asked. "Are you still there?"

"I am. And I've been thinking…"

"Have you been drinking, too?" Jon asked, with a touch of humor in his voice.

"A tot or two, I suppose," Bast said, realizing Hon Ra had told him something interesting during their latest stagger. What was it, again? It had to do with—

"Yes," Bast said.

"Yes, you've been drinking?"

"I have taken a long, pondering walk. I wonder if I might be so bold as to ask for a lift back to my chambers."

"Sure. I haven't flown for a while. Stay where you are. I'll home in on your signal."

"I believe you'll want to hear my idea," Bast said, couching what was really Hon Ra's idea. He doubted the Ambassador would be in any state to explain it to Jon, though. And they were only hours away from dropping out of hyperspace. Yes. This could be critically important.

-2-

The captain flew his four-man flitter through one of the largest cybership corridors. He banked the small craft side-to-side, enjoying the wind whipping through his hair. He opened it up, as this was a straight section. The bulkheads whizzed past in a blur.

It had been over eleven days since they'd left the Roke System. The strike force had built-up a good velocity, keeping that velocity as they'd entered hyperspace. Once they arrived at the edge of the Allamu System, the five cyberships would race toward the battle station near the G-class star.

He had a reason for haste. He wanted to get married yesterday. He was finding it harder and harder to keep his hands off Gloria. Whenever he touched her, he wanted to remove every stitch of clothing and carry her naked to his bed.

Jon's hands tightened as they gripped the flitter's flight controls. He wanted to do this right. He wanted to wait until they were man and wife before he bedded her, but he was finding his resolve slipping with each passing hour.

What would it be like to be married? There would be problems along the way. That was the nature of being man and wife. After the problems were solved, though—

Jon laughed. He had a reason for picking up Bast. He was going to ask the big lug to be his best man. He knew Bast and Hon Ra had been drinking. A marine had found the Roke Ambassador snoring in a small hall. The marine had called that in, and the Centurion had taken several battle-suited marines to carry the huge, bearlike alien to his room.

If Hon Ra had been that drunk, it meant Bast must have been drinking with him. Jon hoped the Roke, as a people, could hold their liquor. He hated the idea of being the one to find and befriend the Roke, and possibly introducing them to hard drink that destroyed their culture because they all became raving drunks.

Hadn't some Earth explorers used drink to destroy certain Stone Age primitives in North America? He'd have to read up on that when he found the time.

Ah. He saw Bast.

Jon slowed down, landing practically at Bast's feet.

"Thanks," Bast said, climbing in.

"Phew," Jon said, waving a hand before his face. "A tot or two, is that what you told me?"

Bast looked down, shrugging defensively.

Jon laughed. "Don't worry about it. We found Hon Ra."

Bast nodded as he shut the flitter door.

Jon engaged the controls, lifting up, rotating the flitter in midair and shooting off the way he'd come. He didn't fly as fast, though. Bast looked greener around the gills than normal.

They both tried talking at once.

Jon grinned and stopped. Bast shook his head.

"Please," Bast said.

"Okay," Jon said. "Bast, would you do me the honor of being my best man?"

"Is that in reference to your coming wedding?" asked Bast.

Jon gave the Sacerdote a quick rundown of the coming proceedings.

"It would be an honor, Captain. Yes. I will gladly be your best man."

"Great," Jon said. "Now, what were you going to tell me?"

Bast cleared his throat and became fidgety with his huge hands.

"You know that I spoke to Hon Ra…today?"

"You two went on a stagger. Yes. I know."

Bast waved that aside. "It's true we drank. But our drinking is not the same as humans drinking."

323

"Really?"

"Your tone indicates your disbelief. So be it. I will not argue the philosophical reasons for our drinking. The issue today is that Hon Ra related an interesting Roke historical fact. Long ago, at the beginning of their climb into a technological age, the Roke detected large asteroid-sized objects. These objects produced comet-like tails."

"Just a second," Jon said. "What kind of sensing equipment did they have back then?"

"Telescopes."

"Teleoptic sensors?"

"You misunderstand," Bast said. "In that time, the Roke used ordinary telescopes that a man would point at the stars."

"I think I understand. It was more like their Renaissance Period."

"Hon Ra said it happened almost a thousand years ago."

"Oh. Okay. Like Galileo discovering the telescope."

"I am unfamiliar with this Galileo."

"Never mind," Jon said. "I get what you're saying. Roke proto-scientists saw this event with a telescope. The big asteroid with a tail could have been an accelerating cybership. At one hundred kilometers, a cybership could have seemed like an asteroid to a telescope-peering Roke. The tail could have been the engine exhaust."

"That is my own reasoning," Bast said.

"So what happened? Why didn't the cyberships obliterate the Roke?"

"Those were possible cyberships," Bast said.

"Whatever. What's the point?"

Bast looked ahead, and he seemed to choose his words with care. "Comets, incredibly swift comets, flew at these asteroids, destroying them. The comets appeared as if from nowhere."

"Wait, Bast," Jon said frowning, staring at the big lug. "Are you saying the Roke saw the five percent light-speed missiles?"

"Listen to the rest of the tale," Bast said. "A dwarf planet also appeared. It, too, seemed to have come from nowhere. As the Roke watched with their telescopes, the dwarf-planet-sized object approached a regular planet."

"The Roke homeworld?"

"No," Bast said. "The object approached a different terrestrial planet in the Roke System."

"Bast. There are no other terrestrial planets in the Roke System."

"Not anymore."

Jon stared at Bast in shock. "You mean these aliens... The dwarf-planet-sized vessel *destroyed* the terrestrial planet?"

"Destroyed and scattered the remains," Bast said, "creating one of the system's asteroid belts."

"What? That's crazy. You're saying these mystery aliens wiped out AI cyberships and busted up a terrestrial planet hundreds of years ago."

"No," Bast said, "a thousand years ago. That historical event would explain the excessive number of asteroid belts in the Roke System, and it might explain why the Roke survived long ago. Might that also be a reason why Earth survived in the distant past?"

Jon mulled that over. "You're saying these are good aliens?"

"No. But I am saying these are AI-killing aliens."

"And they've come back?" asked Jon.

"As to that, I cannot say. Maybe they needed to tear apart the terrestrial planet to find the needed fuel for their ship."

"Do you think the event in the Roke story really occurred?"

"Given what happened to us in the Lytton System, I do."

Jon muttered a curse, shaking his head. "That's an interesting story. If it's true, it sure clears up a few things, but maybe it also makes things even more complex."

"The AIs may have made it to this part of the galaxy before, only to have their attempt smashed by the hidden beings."

"Why don't these aliens contact us and make common cause with us against the AIs?"

"I have no idea," Bast said. "But if we encounter the aliens again, I suggest we make every effort to let them know we are not AIs. It may be the difference between annihilation and survival."

Jon thought that over, wanting to drop out of hyperspace this instant, in order to see if the Allamu Battle Station still existed. He also wondered something else. Just how old was the AI Dominion? How long had the machines been murdering flesh and blood races?

-3-

Several hours later, the strike force dropped out of hyperspace at the extreme edge of the Allamu System.

Jon was on the bridge as every cyberships' sensors strained to scan everywhere at once.

"The planets are all where they should be," Gloria soon announced from her station.

"And the battle station?" Jon asked.

"Alive and well around the second planet," she said.

Jon sat back with relief. It was time to send a message to Premier Benz and tell him what had happened out there. In a few months, they would have to travel to the Solar System and take care of business. They would recruit more people and fill up these giant vessels with badly needed marines, techs and mechanics.

"Any sign of aliens?" Jon asked.

"Not yet," Gloria said.

"No five percent light-speed missiles barreling at us?"

"That is part of the 'not yet,'" Gloria said.

"Right," Jon said. "Just checking. We don't want them catching us by surprise this time."

-4-

The five majestic cyberships sailed through the system at high velocity. According to Benz's messages, nothing bad had occurred here. The factory planet still churned. The orbital repair facility was bringing the formerly damaged cybership into tiptop condition. Life aboard the battle station had proceeded smoothly, with only one death due to a fatal accident with the brain-tap machine.

"Maybe we should destroy those," Gloria told Jon as they walked hand in hand down a corridor. "Why do the AIs have them, anyway?"

"The brain-tap machines are dangerous, no doubt about that," Jon said. "They're also a store of knowledge. Maybe we need to begin a systematic study of them so we can put that knowledge to better use."

"Like I said," Gloria replied gravely. "Destroy them. The brain-tap machines have caused much more heartache than help. Once we study them, the potential for misuse will grow exponentially."

"That's a pessimistic point of view."

"I would call it realistic."

Jon squeezed her smaller hand as he thought about what he'd liked to do just now. "Maybe we should worry about something else. We've had enough fear this year. Let's relax a bit and enjoy ourselves. The coming battles will be here soon enough."

Gloria gestured with her free hand. "There is danger all around us. To let down our guard for only a moment—"

"Maybe if we don't let down our guard a moment here or a moment there, we'll go mad," Jon said, interrupting her.

"Better that than being dead," Gloria said.

Jon stopped, pulling the tiny mentalist to him. He looked down into her gorgeous eyes. As he bent his head to kiss her, emergency klaxons began to blare.

Jon's head snapped up as his heart squeezed with…worry. He had a feeling it could only be one thing.

"Come on," he said, pulling her along. "Let's find out what that is."

-5-

Jon and Gloria hurried onto the bridge and slowed down as they saw what was on the main screen.

The Allamu System possessed a G-class star, four inner terrestrial plants—the second of them was the factory planet together with its guardian battle station. In the outer system, three gas giants held sway.

Leaving the fourth terrestrial planet while heading in-system was a huge vessel, a great spheroid over three-hundred kilometers in diameter. The thing had an outer rocky exterior, vast engine ports—

"Can you give me a close-up of it?" Jon asked.

The acting sensor tech glanced at Gloria. She nodded, as she had elected to remain near Jon. The tech fiddled with his console.

Soon, the image grew larger on the screen.

Jon sat down as he kept his eyes glued to the image. What had seemed like a mountain on the spheroid was actually a giant building, studded with what looked like windows. From here, it was impossible to tell what the mountain-like building did.

"Excuse me," Jon said, indicating Gloria's left arm.

"Oh," Gloria said, taking her forearm off one of his armrests.

Jon swiveled his command chair to the sensor tech. "How long has the ship been in the system?"

"Our sensors picked it up—" the tech checked his board— "six and half minutes ago, sir. Given our distance from them..." The tech shook his head. "It can't have been there more than several hours."

"Let me see if I understand you correctly. You're suggesting the giant vessel has moved *cloaked* through the star system?"

The tech's eyes grew large as he shook his head. "I can't see how that would be possible, sir."

"Neither can I," Jon said, swiveling back so he could study the alien construct.

"Jon," Gloria said, sidling closer. "Do you think it appeared out of a reality rip?"

"What's the simplest explanation?" he asked.

"I wouldn't call that simple."

"What fits best, then?"

Gloria stared at the giant spheroid vessel. She'd heard about Hon Ra's legendry tale, of course. But this...

"Sir," the sensor tech said.

Jon looked back, indicating that the man should speak.

"I believe the ship—the mobile asteroid—entered normal space on the other side of the planet from us. Whoever controls the spheroid, didn't want us to see it coming through."

"Could Benz have seen their entry from the battle station?"

"I doubt it, sir," the tech said.

"Interesting," Jon said, swiveling back, glancing at Gloria. "Why hasn't it launched high-speed missiles at us?"

"Why did the ship enter normal space this time?" Gloria asked quietly. "What kind of space was it in before this? That wasn't hyperspace we saw back in the Lytton System."

"Another kind of space?" asked Jon.

"So it would appear," Gloria said. "This other-space also allows them to travel near heavy gravitational bodies. Notice— if the sensor tech is correct—the ship entered regular space beside a terrestrial plant."

"How is that even possible?"

"Whatever FTL propulsion or other-dimensional space they use—like our hyperspace—likely has different properties, different governing rules than hyperspace does."

331

"I remember seeing the inky blackness before the missiles shot out of it."

"We all saw the blackness," Gloria said. She appeared thoughtful before giving Jon a penetrating glance. "Permission to leave the bridge, sir."

"You want to study the Lytton System computer files?"

"Yes. And I want Bast and Hon Ra to help me."

"The Roke Ambassador…" Jon said, rubbing his chin. "I'm not sure that's a good idea."

"Because you don't want Hon Ra to know how afraid we are of the other-worldly asteroid-ship?"

"Among other things," Jon muttered.

"I think any help Hon Ra can give us might be critical at this point."

Jon cocked his head, finally nodding. He swiveled around to face the tech. "Has the ship made any hostile moves?"

"None that I can tell, sir," the sensor tech said.

Jon turned back to study the giant vessel. "We'll observe it for a time. I'm going to send a message to Benz."

"That is a splendid idea," Gloria said.

"Why?" Jon asked sharply.

"Anything we can do to show the…aliens over there—that we aren't AIs—strikes me as critical."

"You think they're studying us?"

"I do," Gloria said. "And once they reach their conclusion, it may be there is nothing we can do about it."

Jon looked up at the screen, feeling more than awe at the alien vessel, with a bad case of the nerves about what was going to happen next.

-6-

Twenty-three hours passed. At the end of that time, the giant asteroid-ship began accelerating toward the battle station, increasing its velocity.

It gave everyone in the strike force a vast sense of relief that the asteroid-ship used regular matter/antimatter propulsion. The aliens, as of yet, had not shown any super-technological motive power.

According to his messages, Benz had also spotted the ship. He didn't like it. He also read the transcript of Hon Ra's legend and listened to a battle report about what had happened in the Lytton System.

Benz's conclusion was straightforward. "That alien ship is the one that attacked you in the Lytton System. I also give it high odds that that is the same *kind* of alien that the Roke saw a thousand years ago. If the aliens fought the AI cyberships back then but did not destroy the Roke, we can reasonably conclude that the aliens might be pro life-forms and against the thinking machines."

Jon read the premier's entire white paper on the subject. He also met with his brain trust, this time with Hon Ra and Walleye joining Gloria and Bast in the lounge area, with a computer-screen window to the stars.

"I don't like sitting around waiting for an alien to decide whether we should live or die," Jon said. "I propose contacting the aliens."

"With a regular transmission?" asked Bast.

"Seems like the easiest way to do it," Jon said.

"I find it ominous that the aliens haven't tried to contact us yet," Walleye said.

"I think they're still studying the situation," Gloria said. "I've watched and analyzed their vessel for hours. There are constant neutrino-sweeps emanating from it. I believe that is their form of sensor tech."

"Any comments so far, Ambassador?" Jon asked.

"Just one," the alien said, nursing a scotch and soda. "The legend holds that they—the drivers—are not flesh and blood creatures like you and me."

"More machines?" asked Jon.

"No…" Hon Ra said. "Not flesh and blood."

Jon frowned. "What does that mean?"

"A silicon-based life-form maybe," Bast suggested.

"The AIs are silicon-based," Gloria said.

"Suppose the aliens are silicon-based and alive in a true sense," Bast said. "That might be why they didn't discover hyperspace but their other, inky realm of FTL travel."

"We need a name for that realm," Gloria said. "It's seems wrong to keep calling it an inky place. I suggest we call it 'the void.'"

"Catchy," Walleye said.

"A void ship," Jon muttered. "Why not? The void suits what I saw through the so-called reality rip in the Lytton System."

"We must assume that the aliens have the power to crush planets into debris and hard radiation, devouring the majority of the mass in the process," Gloria said. "How they can achieve this is anyone's guess. I haven't a clue." She pondered that. "If Richard were alive, he might know. I doubt any of us will figure it out."

"If we survive the void ship," Jon said, "we need to return to the Lytton System and see what we can learn from the planetary debris."

"If we survive…" Gloria said. "Those are grim words. Do you believe, like me, that our combined forces are not likely to be able to defeat the void ship?"

"I'm not admitting defeat even if the void ship can destroy us," Jon said. "If nothing else, we need to get close and storm it with space marines."

"Here, here," Hon Ra said, raising his scotch and soda. "That is the star hero speaking. We shall never surrender."

"Nice words," Gloria told Jon. "The better idea would be to talk the aliens out of killing us."

"That's what I'm thinking," Walleye said. "Talk to them. *Make* them listen."

"How?" Jon asked.

Walleye grinned. "That's your job, Captain. You made the AIs listen. Now, make the void ship acknowledge us so we can start a conversation."

"I second his motion," Bast said.

Jon nodded, the little Makemake mutant having given him an idea.

-7-

As ideas went, it might not have been the cleverest, but it was direct and to the point.

Jon ordered the rest of the strike force to hang back. He then ordered the *Nathan Graham* into maximum acceleration. They were a long way from the newly named void ship, but the human-crewed cybership began racing as fast as it could toward the inner system and the rock-like super-vessel.

Long-distance discussions flew back and forth between the battle station, the *Nathan Graham* and the rest of the strike force.

Jon wanted the others to be ready to flee the system. If the void ship destroyed the *Nathan Graham*, the others were to race to hyperspace and do as they thought best.

"If the aliens use the void as their FTL dimension," Jon explained, "it means they don't use hyperspace. It seems one of our ships should be safe from them in hyperspace."

As the *Nathan Graham* gave chase, the void ship stopped accelerating.

On the third day of the *Nathan Graham's* hard acceleration, the void ship rotated. A long exhaust tail grew as the rocklike vessel braked from its former velocity.

"Is it turning to fight us?" Gloria asked Jon.

"We'll know when it launches one of its super missiles at us."

Time passed, and no super missile left the void ship.

336

Finally, the *Nathan Graham* and the void ship began to draw near to one another. The void ship had gained velocity heading out-system. The giant vessel now turned again, braking.

The *Nathan Graham* likewise slowed, having done so at maximum thrust for some time, bringing down its high velocity so it was more like a crawl.

All this time, Jon, Gloria and the senior sensor tech had messaged the void ship. They had done it many different ways. The aliens had ignored all the attempts.

As the *Nathan Graham* moved to within five hundred thousand kilometers of the void ship, the aliens sent their first transmission.

Jon was on the bridge when it happened, talking to a tech.

"Sir," Gloria said from her station, her voice rising.

Jon looked over at her.

"I'm receiving a strange communication," Gloria said. "It originates from the void ship."

Jon faced the main screen, walking to it as his gut curdled. Was this it? Had they finally forced the aliens to say something?

The main screen was blank one second and fuzzy the next as it made scratchy sounds. It seemed as if a vague outline shape was hidden behind the screen "snow."

"Hello," Jon said.

"Hel-lo," came a high-pitched, scratchy voice.

Jon felt weak in the knees. He managed to make it to his command chair, sitting down. He hadn't realized until this moment that he'd been living with the constant threat of death. His body had known. He hadn't allowed himself to think about it since first seeing the void ship.

"You are bio-forms," the scratchy, high-pitched...whiny voice said.

"We are," Jon said.

"We have learned in the last few...*days* that this is so. Why do you use...AI ships?"

"The AIs invaded our star system," Jon said.

"Explain."

"Uh...explain what?"

"Where is your origin star system?"

Jon hesitated for only a second before saying, "Earth, the Solar System."

"That is meaningless prattle," the indistinct alien hidden behind the "snowy" screen said. "Show us the star system."

"First, do you mean us ill or are you friendly?"

The alien did not answer right away. Maybe it was thinking over the question.

"Do not insult me again," the alien said.

Jon frowned, not understanding how he'd insulted the alien the first time.

Gloria moved near. She tugged at Jon's sleeve.

He gave her an uncomprehending stare.

"You asked him a question," Gloria whispered. "That was the insult."

"How?" Jon whispered.

"Because you lack true intellect status," the alien said from the main screen. "You are...animals."

Heat rose in Jon.

"Show us your home system," the alien said.

Jon looked at Gloria.

"Take a risk," she said.

Jon turned to the sensor line tech, motioning to the man.

Woodenly, the tech typed in the Solar System's coordinates as compared to the Allamu System.

"Ah," the alien said. "The Qex System. You apes have achieved space flight, then. We despaired of your kind ever doing so."

Jon opened his mouth to ask a question.

Gloria gave a warning tug on his sleeve.

"You fight the AIs," the alien said. "You have defeated them here. We will now leave."

"Sir," Jon said. "May I...may I *learn* a fact or two from you?"

"Apes are curious. Yes. What would you like to learn?"

"Are you at war with the AIs?"

"An eternal war," the alien said. "We have fought for over twenty thousand of your years. Now, I wish to forestall more ape chatter, as I tire of hearing our translator's grunts and

338

guttural utterances that you deem as speech. Know that we in our patrol vessel are at the end of our tour of this dismal end of the galaxy. Every thousand years, we inspect the outer reaches, helping animals to survive the enteral machine extermination."

"The AIs are everywhere?"

"That is a foolish concept showing the dullness of your imagination. The answer is no."

"We would be more than willing to make an alliance with you," Jon said.

There was a three-second pause of dead silence.

"That is inconceivable," the alien said. "We are leaving this dark, backward, spiral arm. I would have destroyed your vessels and the AI station, but I saw at the last second that each crawled with scheming animals. Perhaps, in time, you will learn how to fight the machines."

"You destroyed some of my ships in the Lytton System."

Once more, the alien fell silent.

"You shouldn't have brought that up," Gloria whispered.

"We detected the single ship destruction," the alien said. "One of you wheeled into the missiles. No machine intelligence would have done that. It signaled the possibility of animals in the ships. We grew curious and decided on further investigation. The elders will welcome the news of animals using machine vessels against the AIs. My sisters in arms, though, will rue this meeting between us. Now, in a thousand years, another patrol ship will have to return to your origin system. Will we find your kind alive? I doubt it, but miracles do occur."

"I have—" Jon said.

"This is the end of the transmission," the alien said, interrupting.

Abruptly, the snowy screen turned blank again.

Jon sank back against his chair. The conversation had drained him.

"Sir," the sensor tech said. "Something's happening."

"Put it on the main screen," Gloria said.

A glow appeared before the void ship. Then, a grim rip in reality seemed to open up into a terrible realm of complete darkness—the void, as Gloria had named it.

The void ship accelerated, sliding into the inky blackness. Once in the void, none of them could see it. Seconds later, the rip closed as if it had never been there.

The void ship had vanished, and they were still alive.

-8-

The rest of the mission—from the Allamu Battle Station and back again—was joy and peace after that. Oh, there were fistfights on the vessels, hard feelings and arguments, but most of the crew rejoiced at returning alive from a harrowing trek.

Soon enough, the *Nathan Graham*, *Sergeant Stark*, *Miles Ghent* and other cyberships docked at the battle station.

People prepared for the big event.

That event took place three days later. Everyone was there. And that included Harris Dan, the auto-assassin brainwashed to kill the captain.

During his stay at the battle station, Benz had made the man his personal challenge. The premier hadn't been able to scrape up the old personality. The GSB operators had done their work too well for that. Instead, Benz had helped Harris Dan gain his own personality.

Mr. Dan was on probation, to see how well his new personality held.

Everyone from every crew attended the wedding in the largest chamber on the battle station.

Premier Benz officiated. Bast Banbeck was the best man, an honorary man, in this case.

Women wept at the beautiful ceremony. Men grinned at the lucky bloke, Jon Hawkins, for getting such a lovely lady as his wife.

Hon Ra roared a special song in the captain's honor. That caught a few women by surprise, who had shrieked as if a wild animal was about to attack them.

After the song, the entire auditorium erupted with cheers and clapping.

Hon Ra exposed his bearlike fangs, drinking in the applause.

Finally, before God and those assembled, Gloria and Jon said their vows and became man and wife.

The reception afterward was spectacular, with almost everyone joining in on the drinking and dancing.

"This is much like a Roke joining," Hon Ra told Bast.

The Sacerdote nodded, although his eyes were badly glazed as he gripped a bottle of whiskey.

After a long time of celebration, Gloria and Jon said their goodbyes. They retired to his private quarters, made beautiful and luscious by the Centurion's top marines.

Jon closed the hatch, loosened his tie and turned to watch as Gloria went to the closet. He'd been waiting a long time for this, a long, long time. He was eager, and he grinned with delight as Gloria began to slip off her wedding dress.

"Hey, babe," he said. "This is how you do it." Jon yanked at his shirt, ripping off all the buttons, tossing his shirt on the floor.

Then he moved toward his lovely wife, closing one chapter off his life and beginning another. He didn't know what the future held, but he hoped that from now on he would make that future with Gloria Hawkins.

THE END

SF Books by Vaughn Heppner

THE A.I. SERIES:
A.I. Destroyer
The A.I. Gene
A.I. Assault
A.I. Battle Station
A.I. Battle Fleet

EXTINCTION WARS SERIES:
Assault Troopers
Planet Strike
Star Viking
Fortress Earth

LOST STARSHIP SERIES:
The Lost Starship
The Lost Command
The Lost Destroyer
The Lost Colony
The Lost Patrol
The Lost Planet
The Lost Earth
The Lost Artifact

Visit VaughnHeppner.com for more information

47539270R00192

Made in the USA
Lexington, KY
09 August 2019